THE ILLEGAL

Also by Lawrence Hill

Fiction

The Book of Negroes

Any Known Blood

Some Great Thing

Non-Fiction

Blood: The Stuff of Life

Dear Sir, I Intend to Burn Your Book: An Anatomy of a Book Burning

The Deserter's Tale: The Story of an Ordinary Soldier Who Walked Away from the War in Iraq (with Joshua Key)

Black Berry, Sweet Juice: On Being Black and White in Canada

Women of Vision: The Story of the Canadian Negro Women's Association

Trials and Triumphs: The Story of African-Canadians

Television

The Book of Negroes mini-series (with Clement Virgo)

Film

Seeking Salvation: A History of the Black Church in Canada

THE
ILLEGAL

— A NOVEL —

LAWRENCE HILL

HarperCollins Publishers Ltd

Published by HarperCollins Publishers Ltd

First edition

HarperCollins books may be purchased for educational, business,
or sales promotional use through our Special Markets Department.

HarperCollins Publishers Ltd
2 Bloor Street East, 20th Floor
Toronto, Ontario, Canada
M4W 1A8

www.harpercollins.ca

Canadian Cataloguing in Publication information is available upon request.

ISBN 978-1-55468-383-3 (hardcover)
ISBN 978-1-44344-879-6 (signed edition)

Printed and bound in the United States of America
RRD   10   9   8   7   6   5   4   3   2   1

For Miranda—
always full of love, understanding and inspiration.
This one is for you.

Freedom State & Zantoroland
in the **Ortiz Sea**

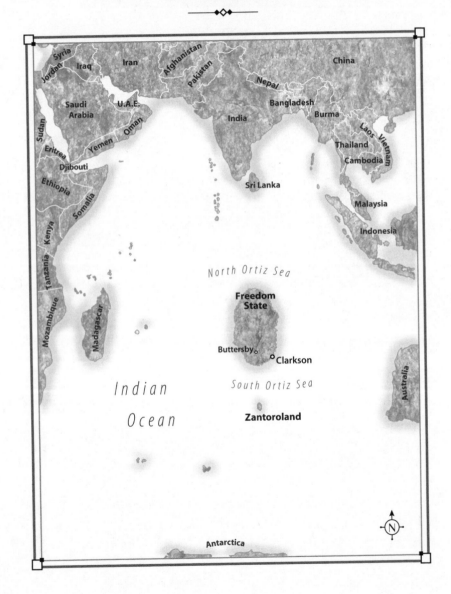

Freedom State, 2018

GO HOME."

The words came from the runner on Keita's left. White, and surely from Freedom State. Limp brown hair, flopping as he ran. Arms too high. Choppy gait. Running was the smoothest dance in the world. Keita had been trained to picture his own legs like wheels. He had learned to strike with his feet soundlessly, transfer weight through the balls of his feet, roll off the toes and spend more time flying than earthbound. Anybody could run, but few with grace. This competitor ran as if his tires weren't inflated. Keita didn't say a word. Didn't acknowledge that he spoke or understood English. He just kept running.

The runner on his shoulder said it again. "Go. Fucking. Home."

A rude man. He deserved to suffer. Keita bumped up the pace. Sooner or later, the obnoxious fellow would start to hurt. The name of the game was to inflict more pain than he felt. So Keita—a stranger in a strange land whose only transgression was to exist in a place where his presence was illegal—would use speed to break this man.

Keita had studied a map of the Buttersby Marathon. It was an out-and-back route: 21.1 kilometres east along the Chelting Escarpment, a 180-degree turn, and 21.1 kilometres right back to the finish line. A few kilometres after the halfway turn, they would climb back up the marathon's one and only hill. It would curve, steepen and keep rising for two kilometres. Challenging, for sure. But what were two kilometres uphill at sea level in Freedom State compared to the Red Hills of Zantoroland at altitude?

They ran along a winding road bordered by the tallest pine trees Keita had ever seen. A hundred years ago, somebody must have set out to create the most peaceful tree-lined road in the world. On each side of him, as high as he could see, trees defined the bends in the road. They had grown so big and thick that they created their own microclimate; it was a warm day, but it felt five degrees cooler in their prodigious shade. Running this race was like swimming in a lake back home in Zantoroland and suddenly hitting a pocket of cool water.

Here along the marathon route, massive, branchless trunks reached many storeys into the air and exploded into a riot of needles and cones. Keita inhaled the smell of pine. Odd, to find such welcoming trees in this hostile land. Perhaps if he were free, he could appreciate all of this beauty. To Keita, the treetops looked like glorious afros of the sort he had seen in photos of African Americans in the 1970s. Way up above, the afros wove together. They made Keita think of people in church pews inclining their heads to pray. Keita imagined two of the treetop heads to be his own mother and father.

Driving just ahead of them were three police motorcycles. One carried a race official, who sat facing backwards to keep his eye on the leading marathoners. Keita tried to put the police officers out of his mind. They would never suspect him. Not in a race. Not under their noses.

The motorcade rounded a corner, and the instant it slipped out of sight, the fellow to Keita's left threw a low punch. Keita saw the blow coming and stepped to the right, but it glanced off his umbilical hernia. The hernia, now the size of a golf ball, throbbed. Could the other runner tell it was there, under Keita's shirt? The runners rounded the corner, and the motorcycles came into sight again. It wouldn't be enough to beat his aggressor; Keita wanted to make him suffer. But the aggressive runner remained close.

"Gonna mess you up," the man said.

Keita drifted to the far side of the road. The runner stayed with him. Keita swerved back. The name-caller stuck to him.

A string of orange cones marked the halfway point. The runners rounded the turn and began to run back in the direction from which they had come. Keita glanced at the large digital clock, which showed 1:05:11. He would have to pick up his pace slightly. The second half of the race would be harder because of the hill, but there was extra prize money if the winner came in at under 2:10. Keita wanted to finish under the bonus time but didn't want to run faster than necessary. He had to save his legs for the next race.

Keita's adversary tucked in behind him, and a third runner trailed by a step. Another white guy from Freedom State. Two hundred metres back in the direction of the finish line, they blew past the fourth- and fifth-place runners. Six hundred metres farther along, they encountered another trickle of outbound runners.

Keita glanced down. The hernia embarrassed him. When the television news in Freedom State wanted to show hungry kids in Zantoroland, they zoomed in on a child with a hernia. A swollen belly. And meagre hair, faintly reddish from malnutrition. Perhaps it was to blame for Keita's recent bouts of thirst. The hernia was small, but in the weeks since he had gone into hiding in Freedom State, staying in black market guest houses that took in undocumented people at dusk and booted them out at dawn, he had often experienced an unquenchable thirst.

Today, however, he had gulped down cups of electrolyte drink at each water station, and so far he felt strong. Today, he hoped his body would not betray him.

Keita had to make enough money to get the hernia fixed. Leaving aside money to keep himself fed, clothed and well hidden, he would need thousands for the surgery. If he won another few races, he would check out a private clinic. But first, he had to win *this* race.

The jerk remained one stride back.

"Right on your ass, sonny boy," he said. "Go run in your own fucking country." He poked Keita's shoulder. "Roger Bannister," he sneered, referring to the name on Keita's bib. "Not on your life. That's a white man's name."

Keita glanced back at his nemesis. A snarling face, snot in the nose, mouth hanging open and a race bib that said *Billy Deeds*.

"What you looking at?" Deeds asked him.

Keita kept running. Deeds would expect a race up the hill, so the best strategy was to cause him pain before they got there. A kilometre before the hill, Keita kicked up the pace and put on a burst for a hundred metres. Deeds and the third runner stayed with him.

"Is that all you got?" Deeds said, but Keita heard the strain in his voice.

Keita coasted for two hundred metres, then attacked again for fifteen seconds. He glanced over. Deeds was starting to slap the ground with his feet.

"Gonna kick your ass, nigger," Deeds panted.

"Billy, shut up with that." It was the third runner. Another white guy.

Keita glanced at his bib. Last name was Smart.

"Sorry, buddy," Smart said. "He's just messing with you."

"Stay out of this," Deeds said.

At the base of the hill, they passed the twenty-four-kilometre mark. Smart dropped back a few metres. Deeds was still on Keita's tail but breathing hard. Keita picked up the pace once more, drilling down just under 3:00 per kilometre. They were passing a river of runners, and some held out their hands to congratulate him. Keita high-fived one or two, just to pretend that he was feeling no pain.

As the grade of the slope increased, Keita employed the trick that he had been taught while training in the Red Hills. *Want to shatter your opponent's confidence? Just when he starts to hurt, you sing.*

PART ONE

Zantoroland, 2004–2018

I T HADN'T RAINED IN WEEKS. A FINE LAYER OF RED DUST had settled in the doorway, on the windowsills, under the pews and on the pulpit. Keita Ali was not supposed to be sweeping while wearing his shoes. He had asked for months before his parents relented and bought the Meb Supremes. The training shoes had cost eighty dollars. Keita had promised to lengthen their lifespan by walking barefoot except while training. But he was so in love with his Meb Supremes that today he had left the house with them hidden in his knapsack as he walked along the red clay road leading away from the family's summer cabin in the mountains.

It was not until he reached the Faloo Zion Baptist Church and unlocked the door that he slipped on the shoes, laced them up with double knots and began sweeping and dusting.

The shoes felt as light as slippers, as snug as socks. They had the perfect tread for sure-footed running in the Red Hills, here at two thousand metres altitude. He was only ten years old and not supposed to run more than three times a week, four kilometres at a time. "You are young and must save your legs," Keita's father had told him. Keita had feigned compliance. His father was a smart man, but he'd never been a runner. Nobody would be the wiser if Keita snuck in a few extra, longer runs to take full advantage of training at altitude.

Spending two hours on Saturday morning volunteering in the church, pushing a broom and cleaning under Deacon Andrews' desk, would normally have bored Keita, but it thrilled him to feel the new shoes hug his feet. Sometimes, after he said good night to his parents, he put on the Meb Supremes and wore them to bed, imagining his Olympic victory in twelve, sixteen or twenty years. Once he had taken the fantasy to its conclusion—crowds cheering and the president giving Keita the gold medal and the bonus that would make him a rich man—he would take off the shoes and put them away, so that his mother wouldn't catch him in the morning. Then he would fall asleep listening to the sound of his father typing in the next room.

Keita's father, Hassane Moustafa Ali, had a silly nickname— Yoyo—but he was a serious man: always working, always writing. Yoyo kept two manual Olivetti typewriters, with paper and spare ribbons handy, as well as battery-powered lanterns so he could keep writing at all times, day and night. The authorities in Zantoroland cut the electricity every night at ten o'clock, and it didn't come back on until seven in the morning. And then there were also blackouts. Yoyo kept a supply of candles and stuck to his typewriters. He paid Keita's older sister, Charity, to edit his copy and retype it on the computer. And he paid Keita to check all the connections for the home network, to keep them free of dust and double-check that Yoyo's stories for newspapers around the world had been sent out properly by email.

Keita settled down every night to the sound of his father's fingers hammering. He would listen for the ding at the end of each line and then Yoyo slamming the carriage return lever. Ding, slam, hammer-hammer-hammer. Ding, slam, hammer-hammer-hammer. Keita sometimes imagined what his father was thinking. *This one is for the* New York Times. *Two more like it, and I can pay for a new roof. This one is for the* Toronto Star. *So I can buy tickets for Keita and me to go watch the Zantoroland National Track and Field Championships next month.* Keita longed to attend the races with his father. They would watch Mohamed Paloma defend his 5,000-metre title. As Paloma rounded the final turn on the final lap, he would be right on the shoulders of his competitors and preparing to outsprint them to the finish line. *Kick it, kick it, kick it, baby,* he and his father would shout for Paloma, as their national hero set a new world record.

Yoyo kept confidential story notes and drafts hidden in a row of teapots on a kitchen shelf. Pieces for the *New York Times* were folded and rolled into the red teapot. The green teapot held stories for the *Guardian.* Potentially incendiary stories went in the yellow teapot. As he returned to imagining what his father was writing, Keita wondered whether a person could be punished for having thoughts, or only for committing those thoughts to paper.

"Papa, what's incendiary?" Keita had asked one day.

Charity had cut in: "Are you aware that if you open the dictionary, you can locate any word in twenty seconds? Amazing, isn't it?"

"Papa," Keita had repeated, and his father had explained.

As Keita swept the red-orange dust, he wondered if the stains on his shoes would reveal that he had been wearing them while working in the church. No, they wouldn't—running on the roads would cause the same discoloration. As the dust flew up in puffs around his heels, Keita imagined the world's fastest marathoner racing over a kilometre-long bed of Zantoroland dust. With each footfall, a ball of fire would erupt from his heels. *Incendiary.* One day, the licks of fire would scorch the path Keita ran, all alone and way ahead of his competitors, toward the Olympic Stadium. His parents and sister would fly in to watch him win the race that would change their lives forever.

Outside, a car horn blew repeatedly. Mad, unabashed honking. Keita set his broom down. It was just past eleven.

From the church door, he saw a pickup truck with men standing in the back. From his father, Keita had learned of the situations where strange men were best avoided: coming out of bars, roaming the streets in mobs and looting during blackouts. Unless they were workers en route to diamond mines or banana plantations, men standing in the back of pickup trucks were also not to be trusted.

The truck travelled slowly along the road, still a good distance away. Keita estimated that he had thirty seconds, maybe a minute. He started the stopwatch function of his running watch. He closed the doors and turned off the lights so they would think the church was shut and empty. Keita peered through a window. The truck was now idling at the foot of the lane, forty metres from the church door. The men were shouting. It was hard to make out the words. Political slogans? Keita kneeled low to stay out of sight. He heard the truck tires turn on the road. The shouting gradually diminished in volume. Keita looked out the window to see the truck pulling out of sight. One minute, five seconds.

Keita timed everything. He knew how long it took him to jog once around the 400-metre track: two minutes, fifteen seconds. He knew how long it took him to race the same distance flat-out: fifty-nine seconds. Keita knew how long it took to help Charity do dishes: on average, eight minutes. How long it took to sweep the floor. How long to walk to school. Run to school. Eat a peanut butter and jelly sandwich. Keita even knew how long it took to lace up both running shoes. Cleaning the church did not take long: thirty-five minutes, if he worked quickly. He resumed sweeping.

The church doors were flung open. In came Deacon Andrews and ten choristers. Charity was among them. Keita did not hate his sister, but she was eleven years old and teeming with bossiness, and he didn't want to be one single bit like her: head of her debating team, top of the class in all subjects.

Keita ran up to the deacon. "Men just drove by in a truck! Shouting."

"Threats?" the deacon asked.

"I couldn't hear, exactly."

Deacon Andrews put one hand on Keita's shoulder. "Hooligans," the deacon said, "cannot interfere with the will of God." But he promised to keep the rehearsal short, just to be safe.

★ ★ ★

KEITA STOOD BY THE WALL TO LISTEN TO THE CHOIR REHEARSE "Rock My Soul (In the Bosom of Abraham)." Keita didn't know the choristers that well. He had met Mrs. Rowe, Mrs. Pollock, Miss Shinozaki and Miss Dixon. He didn't know their first names and had never seen the inside of their homes, but when they opened their mouths to sing, Keita felt as if he had known and loved them forever.

Keita listened for a while and then walked out to the porch that wrapped around the front and sides of the church. Wind had deposited the red dust everywhere, so he swept vigorously for a few minutes. He did not mind the task. Soon he could return home to a pancake lunch. He looked up and past the two parked cars that had brought the choristers, down the church lane and along the dirt road as far as the rolling hills allowed him to see. There, a kilometre down the road, cresting one hill before descending the slope after it, flew a pack of twenty runners.

Keita shouted into the church, "Marathoners!"

The hymns stopped abruptly and the choristers hurried out to join him on the porch. Mrs. Pollock put her hand on Keita's shoulder and gave it a little squeeze. "One day, you'll run with them."

Keita heard Charity compliment Mrs. Pollock on her new blue dress. His sister would say anything to get ahead. She was as thin as he was but several inches taller. She stood like a schoolmaster, hair pulled into a bun, lips taut, chin up, hand on hip. Little Miss Perfect. Even on the newspaper route that the siblings shared, Charity delivered every paper on time and pounded on doors to collect payment. Keita, on the other hand, bribed his friends to help, promising his mother's cookies and tea. He avoided walking door to door to collect payment, knowing that Charity would pick up the slack.

From a distance, the pack of runners resembled a cloud of dust in the wind. "Look, Charity," Keita whispered. "Look at them coming. Look how fast they go."

Keita felt a surge of pride. His country produced the fastest marathoners in the world. Zantorolanders had swept first, second and third place last year, two oceans away in the Boston Marathon. If you won Olympic gold for Zantoroland, every citizen would know your name. The president would give you a free house and a hundred thousand dollars. Later, you could have a coaching job for life. You would be world famous, like the Eritrean American marathoner Meb Keflezighi.

The runners were bunched tightly together. They all wore the same gear: running shoes, white socks, white running shorts stained with the red dust, and the blue-and-red singlets reserved for the top twenty runners in the national marathon squad. The runners spilled along the road like blood out of veins, passing over yet another hill. Brown arms swung in loose unison and legs churned smoothly, feet nearly soundless on the dirt road, apart from the crunching of pebbles. When they were within earshot, Deacon Andrews led the choristers into song with another verse from "Rock My Soul."

As the runners drew near, they sang right back:

So high, you can't get over it
So low, you can't get under it
So wide, you can't get around it
You gotta go through the door.

The runners sang well and in tune, all twenty of them, raising their hands in salute as they flew past the church. None of them seemed to be suffering. Perhaps it was early in the run. Keita followed every bending knee, every foot touching down only to resume flight. And then, in an instant, the runners rounded a curve in the road and disappeared.

The choristers went back inside and rehearsed five more songs, and then Deacon Andrews told them to drive straight home. Just to be safe, in case the troublemakers came by again.

Charity took Keita's wrist. "Come home," she said.

Keita pulled his arm free. "I'll stay and help the deacon."

"Dad and Mom would want you to come home now."

"Dad and Mom said I had to come here to clean. To work for my shoes."

She touched his wrist again, gently this time. She didn't usually touch him like that. She gave him a little smile. When she wasn't trying to rule the world, Charity was a good sister.

"Brother," she said. "Come with me."

"I'll be safe. In these shoes, I'm uncatchable."

"I'll tell Mom and Dad to expect you in an hour. Don't make them wait or worry." Charity left with the choristers.

Keita ran his cloth along the varnished pews. The deacon picked up another cloth, and joined him.

"What is your father up to these days?"

"Writing," Keita said. "What else?"

"He's the only man who is trying to tell the world about the Faloo people. We used to be looked up to in this country. Politicians, business leaders, shopkeepers. But now we're in danger. Your father is a great man. Courageous. Some might say too courageous."

Keita nodded politely, but he wasn't sure what that meant. How could a person be *too* courageous? He stepped out to shake his dusting cloth on the porch, and saw them coming. Ten men, carrying big sticks and cricket bats. Not the same men who had been in the truck. Different men. Swaying a bit on the road. Were they dancing? No. They were drunk.

Keita shouted for the deacon, who rushed to the porch. "You must leave," he said. "Now."

He turned and locked the doors. Then he took a cellphone from his pocket. Keita heard a woman answer.

"Martha," the deacon said, "get the constable to come out to the church. Troublemakers are on the way. Love you."

The deacon picked up his Bible. Keita stood with him. It didn't feel right to leave him alone. A line of sweat ran down the side of the deacon's forehead. The men were just a hundred metres away now, and Keita could hear them shouting like football hooligans. What did they want? Every second word from their mouths was a curse.

13

Keita could run! He was the quickest boy in his school over every race, from 100 to 1,500 metres. He could run, and they would never catch him. But what about Deacon Andrews?

"Fucking Faloos and their fucking church," one of the men called out. "Let's burn this shithole down!"

"Keita, I will teach these young men the language of God," said the deacon. "You get running."

Keita ran across the yard to the road, but stopped about fifty metres away. The deacon had walked out to meet the men. Keita didn't understand why these men hated Faloos. Keita's mother was a Faloo, but his father was a Bamileke, from Cameroon in Africa. Yoyo had written for a newspaper in France about the growing unpopularity of Faloos as shopkeepers and business people. Keita wished that he were 100 percent Bamileke, like his father. He wished that he, too, had come from Africa—a continent thousands of kilometres to the west of Zantoroland. Maybe then these men wouldn't hate him.

The men with sticks surrounded Deacon Andrews, who held the Bible closed in his hand and quoted from Exodus. The deacon towered above the men, but they attacked him like a pack of hyenas: from the front, from the sides and from behind. They knocked the Bible out of his hands. Keita watched it somersault through the air and land in a ditch. Deacon Andrews flung off the first man as if he were a small dog. He flung off the second. Then the men drew knives, and one of them shoved a blade deep into the deacon's belly. Keita heard a wailing, furious cry—the likes of which he had never imagined a grown man could make.

"You are not men," the deacon cried out. "You have no souls."

Moments ago, the deacon had stood strong like a tree, but now he lay like uncoiled rope in a pool of blood.

One of the men turned toward Keita. "Get the kid!" he shouted.

A man with a cricket bat turned toward Keita, who set off running, checking over his shoulder to take a measure of his pursuer's speed. The man was quick, and now he threw down the cricket bat to run harder. Keita set out at 400-metre speed, sure that after a hundred metres, the pursuer would give up. But the man must have been a runner in his youth. At two hundred metres he was closing the gap. Keita tried to suppress his rising sense of panic and focus on running as fast as he could manage at a pace he could sustain over a distance.

Keita was ascending a steep hill when the pursuer gave up and headed back toward the church. At the top of the hill, bent over and gasping for air, he turned and saw the men bashing in the church windows and throwing burning sticks inside.

Within minutes, the Faloo Zion Baptist Church erupted in flames. Laughing and shouting, the men ran off in the direction they'd come from, shaking their sticks above their heads. Keita waited until he was sure they were not coming back. Then he ran back to the deacon and dropped to his knees. But Deacon Andrews was not breathing. Blood pooled under his head. He was motionless, an arm splayed out on the red earth.

Keita wished that the deacon were just pretending. He wanted the deacon to get up and fetch his Bible. It didn't seem possible that a person could be so big and strong one moment, and lifeless the next.

"Deacon Andrews?" The deacon didn't stir. "Deacon Andrews," Keita said, louder. Still no response.

Keita knew what his parents would tell him: *Run, Keita. Just run.*

So he got up and ran, focusing on his breathing, just as he had been coached. *Inhale deeply, fill the diaphragm, exhale. Control the air. Keep the oxygen moving through your blood. Breathe. Run.*

CHAPTER TWO

O N THE LAST PERFECT DAWN OF HIS CHILDHOOD, with the sun rising out of the Ortiz Sea and casting a soft light over Yagwa, the capital of Zantoroland, Keita awoke in his family's home. He was twelve years old and training every day to become a champion runner.

Keita rose from his bed, pulled on his shirt, shorts, socks and shoes, and slipped out of the bedroom that he shared with his sister. Apart from the bathroom, the house had only one other room, which shared three functions: there was a small study in the corner where his father wrote, a bed for his parents curtained in another corner, and a space with a fridge, stove, table and couch where the family gathered. "Liquidity," as his father called it, was a bit short, and the family had been required to give up their summer home in the Red Hills, but they still had more than most residents of Yagwa: the windows of their home weren't broken, the roof held, the door locked and they had an air-conditioning unit that worked when the electricity was on. Keita passed through the front room and out the door.

It was a clear sunny day. To the south of the city and beyond the flatlands with their orange and lemon orchards, Keita could see the mountains in the distance.

Keita had studied maps, and he knew that Zantoroland—only one hundred kilometres long and eighty wide—was but a speck in the Ortiz Sea in the Indian Ocean. Africa to the west and Australia to the east were far too distant to be seen, but Keita knew they were there. Looking down Blossom Street, Keita could see the port and the waters of the Ortiz Sea. There were fifteen hundred kilometres of open water stretching north to the nation of Freedom State. Like all schoolchildren, Keita knew that Freedom State had enslaved Zantorolanders for some two centuries but, after abolishing slavery, had deported most black people back to Zantoroland. Ever since that time, adventurous Zantorolanders had braved the Ortiz Sea in fishing boats, taking their lives into their hands as they tried to slip back into Freedom State, one of the richest nations in the world.

Keita passed through the Faloo district, where all the houses were similar—purple, pink, green or blue two-room matchboxes with gardens and briskly swept stone steps out front, and outhouses and family burial grounds out back—and jogged down the gentle slope of Blossom Street into the heart of town. *Slow and easy*, his father always told him. *Not every run should cause pain. Some should just be to celebrate your working limbs, breathing lungs and beating heart.*

The street levelled out, and the pavement came to an end at the edge of the more heavily populated district where the Kano people lived in mud-brick houses with corrugated tin roofs. The roads were narrow, muddy and potholed in that neighbourhood, not safe for running.

"We don't have much," Yoyo had said a hundred times, "but for those who are truly poor, running symbolizes privilege."

Keita would reply, "But I don't have money. You never let me have any!"

And Yoyo would say, "Your shoes would fit perfectly on someone else's feet."

To avoid taunting the shoeless and to stay on the smoother pavement, Keita skirted the Kano district and ran to the heart of Yagwa, which held two banks, a library, a cinema, three restaurants, the Pâtisserie Chez Proust and all the shops kept by the Faloo business people around the four sides of President's Square. In the middle of the square was the Fountain of Independence, surrounded by the outdoor stalls of the market vendors who sold meat, bread, cheese and produce every day but Sunday. It was still early—5:15 a.m.—and the vendors were busy hauling goods on flatbed wagons to their stalls.

A group of six men walked by the fountain, each limping and leaning on a red cane. They looked broken, beaten, with shreds of clothing, torn sandals and bleeding sores on their feet.

One of the men startled Keita by calling out to him. "Boy, give me a dollar."

Keita stopped running. "I'm sorry, I have no money."

"Then give me your shoes. You're only a child. You don't need them."

Keita's mouth fell open.

"Leave him alone," another man said. "He's the journalist's son."

"Whose son?" the first man asked.

"Yoyo Ali, the journalist."

"Well, in that case, son, go with God, and tell your father that the returnees send their best."

Keita's father, who because he was a journalist knew everything, had spoken about these men before, and sometimes he stopped to give them coins. "Returnees," Yoyo had said, "are good men who have been broken." Keita waved nervously and resumed running, heading down to the President's Promenade. He ran on the imported white marble, admiring to his right the South Ortiz Sea, and to his left, to the south above and beyond the town, the Red Hills crowned with pink clouds. At the far end of the Promenade, he came to the Olympic Stadium. His country would never host the Games, but nevertheless, it named its best track as if it had. Keita had hoped that his father would take him to a track meet that very day, but Yoyo was to fly overseas to Cameroon to research a story for the *New York Times*. He would be leaving the house at noon but had promised to take the family out for a treat that morning.

Keita turned west to run along the north edge of downtown and up the sloping streets leading back to the Faloo residential district.

At home, he showered and changed. After they all ate their oatmeal, Yoyo took them to Chez Proust. Keita and Charity were each allowed a hot chocolate and one madeleine. Keita took his madeleine *à l'orange*. Charity ordered hers *au citron*, which, she said, was *beaucoup plus sophistiqué*.

"Stop being such a snob," Keita said, "you're not French. The French only ran this country for thirty years, and that was ages ago."

Charity countered, "If you want to be a famous journalist, you have to know how to be at least a wee bit *sophistiqué* and how to order your madeleine *au citron*. And stop dunking. That is so disgusting."

Charity asked her mother if she could taste the Drambuie displayed behind the barista.

"No," Lena said. "For one thing, it's seven in the morning. For another, Drambuie is expensive. And for a third, you're still a child."

"I'm thirteen. I'm pretty much an adult."

"You are far from an adult," Lena said, "but I'll review the names of the liqueurs for you." Lena asked Patrick the barista, a family friend, to place some bottles on the counter. "Repeat after me," she told Charity. "Drambuie is made from whisky and honey, and it hails from Scotland."

Charity repeated what her mother had said.

"Grand Marnier and Cointreau both have an orange flavour and come from France . . . Amaretto is from Italy and made from almonds or apricots . . . Kahlua is made from coffee beans and comes from Mexico . . . Limoncello, a lemon liqueur, comes from southern Italy."

Charity repeated all the details.

"Your future husband will appreciate such worldliness," Lena said.

"I don't want a husband," Charity said. "I just want to be a journalist and see the world."

Lena laughed. "Then go see the world, my darling girl. Bet every day on your own abilities, and you'll be able to do anything you want."

Keita hated conversations that led back to his sister's brains, so he asked his father to explain once again how the madeleines from Zantoroland had become world famous.

Yoyo said the madeleine was Zantoroland's only claim to fame, aside from marathoners. The Germans, the French and the British had all taken turns colonizing Zantoroland and populating it with African slaves, and although France had ruled the country only briefly, it had left an indelible mark with its madeleine. The student, Yoyo said, eventually surpassed the professor.

"You can go to the best pâtisserie in Paris," Yoyo said, "and you will not find a madeleine that competes with the ones made here. To make a great madeleine," he said, "you begin with a scallop-shell baking pan. Then, you take the best flour and combine it with butter, vanilla, sugar and eggs. The real trick is to get just the right amount of lemon zest. In France, they just serve the madeleine straight up, like a plain doughnut. No imagination. But here in Zantoroland, we create a little glaze with the zest of an orange or a lemon. This makes the Zantoroland madeleine one of the wonders of the world. And that, my son," Yoyo said, smiling playfully, "is why Zantoroland will one day outstrip France as an economic power."

Charity snorted. "We'll never outstrip anybody."

"What's 'outstrip'?" Keita asked.

"Outperform," Charity said.

"May I have another madeleine?" Keita asked.

"No," Yoyo said, "but you can finish mine."

It was a long walk home from the café. Keita could have run it in eight minutes or walked it in twenty, but it took their mother an hour. Keita had brought a water bottle along, because he knew his mother always needed it—even when she was seated and still—but it didn't help much. She never seemed to be able to get enough to drink. Lena puffed as she walked. Even though she kept herself trim, she walked up the sloping street like an old woman, stopping repeatedly to bend over and catch her breath.

At home, she gulped down several cups of water and took a nap.

Yoyo sat by their bed for an hour, holding her hand and reading. Then he packed, grabbed his shoulder bag, kissed his wife and children, and left the house.

Work often took Yoyo from his family, and Keita hated it when his father went away. It was easier to leave, Keita reasoned, than to stay behind. He waved as his father walked down the road. Then he went to the calendar and marked the day his father would return.

HOURS AFTER THE DEPARTURE, WHEN KEITA IMAGINED THAT his father was high in the air and flying northwest across the Indian Ocean, neighbours shouted in through the window, telling him to turn on the TV. Jenkins Randall—commander-in-chief of the army, and member of the Kano ethnic majority—had staged a coup d'état in Zantoroland. A thousand troops had left the National Barracks, shot the guards posted outside the Presidential Palace and stormed the residence. The president—a duly elected Faloo named Porter Goodson, who had formed a government three years earlier—was hauled from the closet in which he was found hiding, marched onto the lawns of the palace and ordered to confess to crimes against the state. President Goodson refused, and ordered the troops to arrest General Randall. But they remained in place, waiting for the order from their military leader.

General Randall and his troops ordered all the pedestrians they could find to enter through the gates and gather on the presidential lawns to form a suitable audience. Once a thousand people were found to watch, General Randall paid his foe the ultimate insult: he forced him at gunpoint to remove all his clothes. Then the troops opened fire. The president's bloody body was dumped into the Fountain of Independence in the main square.

Randall took control of the television and radio stations and announced that he was naming himself President for Life, declaring that the Kano people were the rightful majority in Zantoroland and would no longer submit to the Faloo minority. In the city, rampaging began.

Masked men attacked Faloo shopkeepers, breaking bones, warning them to close their businesses and stealing whatever they could carry: suits, ties, coffeepots, radios, lamps, laptops. Faloo people barricaded themselves in their homes behind locked doors.

After looting the business district, the marauders moved uptown. Word spread like a grassfire in Keita's district. Lena ordered her children to come inside and stay away from the windows. They turned their lights off. Keita, Charity and their mother could hear shouting and the sound of glass breaking. Then the pounding began at their door.

"Don't answer," Keita said.

"We have to," his mother said. "If we don't answer, they'll just break down the door. But if I open, I'm still in control."

Lena opened the door. "Hooligans," she shouted. "What would your mothers say?"

Three men pushed her aside and came into the house. The leader was tall and gaunt and—like the others—had a white pillow-case over his head, with holes cut for his eyes and mouth. "Where is your husband?" he said.

The leader's voice seemed familiar to Keita.

Lena said her husband was out of the country. The leader said no man would leave his family alone, and that just went to show how cowardly the Faloos were.

"My husband isn't even a Faloo," she said. "He's an immigrant from Cameroon. He's a Bamileke. *I'm* a Faloo!" she shouted in their faces. "Do I look cowardly to you?"

The intruders paced in the small space. One of them overturned chairs. Keita watched as one man lifted a water jug from the table and hurled it across the room. Then the mirror shattered. Keita wrapped his arms around himself. Charity got the broom and began sweeping up the shards.

"Enough with the broom," the leader said.

She kept sweeping.

"I said enough with the broom!"

"I know your voice," Charity said. "From the market. The eggplant stand."

"Charity, shush," Lena said.

Charity lunged for the leader's hood, dislodging it. The man shoved Charity hard to the floor and reset his mask. But she got right back up, still holding the broom. The man yanked the broom from Charity's hands and knocked her down again. Keita dove into the man's midriff, pummelling and biting. He too was pushed to the floor, where he landed on his sister.

"Do you want to die?" the leader said.

"If you want to kill us, shut up and do it!" Lena shouted.

"I know you," Charity said. "David. David. That's it. David. From the eggplant stand. Your sister goes to my school."

The man used the broom to knock all the bowls, plates, glasses and silverware off the table. Then he dropped the broom, signalled to his two followers and left the house.

Lena locked the door and looked to Keita and Charity. "You must never—" But she didn't finish her sentence. She clutched her chest, gasped and lowered herself to the floor.

"Mom!" Keita shouted.

Charity tipped her mother's chin back and breathed into her mouth. Keita opened the door, checked to make sure that the thugs had disappeared, and ran from house to house until he found a neighbour who was willing to bring a car around. Keita and Charity helped lift their motionless mother into the vehicle, but there was no pulse, no breath. They inched through the littered streets, holding Lena's hands as they approached the hospital. But they knew she was already dead. Keita took his sister's hand, but he could not cry.

BUSINESS PEOPLE FLED THE COUNTRY, TAKING THEIR MONEY with them, until General Randall temporarily blocked Internet access, closed the banks and shut down the airport. Randall brought out his troops, put a halt to the attacks and the looting, and promised to enforce peace and civility, as long as the Faloo people were pre-pared to respect him as Zantoroland's President for Life.

Yoyo missed the funeral. Two weeks later, he was finally able to fly back home. Shuffling with tiny steps and barely able to lift his head, Yoyo looked as if he had aged twenty years. He was unable to grieve in front of the children. He became silent and thought-ful. He moved as little as possible, like a reptile that has eaten too much. In the household, Yoyo remained formal and almost word-less. He would not laugh, smile or cry, but he told Charity and Keita to be strong.

Keita did not feel strong. When he walked, his veins seemed filled with sludge. His breathing was as shallow as a barely dug grave. He should have attacked the leader with a cricket bat or hurled a vase at his head and spared his mother the confrontation. But he had done nothing.

When Keita opened his mouth, his words sounded like they came from a stranger. He didn't speak with Charity about his sadness or hers, but he often sat beside her on the couch when neighbours and friends brought roasted chickens and plantains and fresh man-goes to the house. On the couch, Keita absorbed the warmth from his sister's shoulders, listened to her breath and parroted her inhal-ations and exhalations. She sat rigid and perfectly straight, just as her mother had done, and she had nothing to say either, but Keita felt he knew her thoughts and her sadness as they breathed together, in and out, in and out, on the same waves of isolation and shock.

Keita longed to sit beside his father on the couch, but Yoyo spent hours a day at his desk on the other side of the living room, pound-ing furiously as he rolled page after page into the typewriter.

"What are you writing?" Keita asked one day.

"He's writing about the coup," Charity said. "It could be his last income for a while."

Yoyo tried for days to get a telephone line. He kept writing and revising, and when he finally got a phone line, he called the *New York Times* and dictated his story, word by word.

* * *

Yoyo called Charity and Keita into his study. "Children, forgive me. I've been distant. It is only because I miss your mother so much."

Yoyo hugged Keita against his left side and Charity to his right. "Let's sing together."

In Keita's household, tears were never allowed with conversation. Only in song could they hug each other fiercely and let their grief flow.

They stood close and sang "I Stood on the River of Jordan," the way Keita had learned it in church, years earlier, from Deacon Andrews. Finally, Yoyo's tears cascaded. Charity started bawling. Singing made Keita finally feel the real meaning of his loss. Singing made his mother's death seem both inconceivable and insurmountable, and for the first time, Keita felt a thousand shards of sadness massing under his skin and threatening to cut their way free.

I stood on da ribber ob Jerdon
To see dat ship come sailin' ober.
I stood on da ribber ob Jerdon
To see dat ship sail by.

O don't you weep
When you see dat ship come sailin' ober.
Shout! Glory Hallelujah!
When you see dat ship sail by.

That night, Keita worried that the troops might come for his father. Who would care for them? Would Keita and Charity be raised by sympathetic neighbours? Faloos, but not people who knew them intimately?

Keita fell asleep to the clacking of typewriter keys. It sounded like rain. It sounded like voices merging. Was it true what they said in church, about his mother's soul ascending to the heavens, where she would be forever peaceful and joyous among the angels? Keita could not stop thinking about his mother's body, inert on the living room floor, and he found himself not believing in the heavens.

When his father did not know where to put his pain, he wrote. Charity studied. Keita went running. Up the path that rose for two kilometres, ascending mercilessly up the mountainside. The climb was so difficult that the locals had given it a name: the Struggle. On days when he could not stop thinking about his mother, Keita would run up the hill, and at the top he would jog back down. Up and down he would run, three, four or even five times, gasping and bawling and gasping and bawling, until he felt dry and empty and ready to lie down and sleep again.

CHAPTER THREE

Y OYO OFTEN LEFT THE HOUSE AT NIGHT AND DID
his interviews away from home, but Keita could not
remember a time when his father was not grinding coffee beans in the mornings. He would talk to his espresso
maker, spooning coffee into it and patting it down with the back of
his spoon until he was ready to screw on the lid and heat the contraption. He had a name for his espresso maker: Wolverton. *Come on,
Wolverton, tell me a story today. What you got in there for me?* Yoyo used a
battery-powered grinder so as not to be hampered by blackouts. He
took his coffee black, which Keita—who needed milk and sugar to
make his palatable—could not fathom.

Yoyo would sip his coffee on the porch while reading one of
the dozen newspapers and magazines to which he subscribed. They
arrived two weeks late in Zantoroland, but never mind—Yoyo
devoured them anyway. Yoyo was frugal beyond belief—he would
rejuvenate stale peanuts by re-salting them, sliding them onto a
greased cookie sheet and broiling them in the oven—but newspaper
and magazine subscriptions were his only indulgence.

Yoyo sat in his rocking chair on the porch and greeted the
schoolchildren passing in their uniforms and backpacks. The children were all barefoot, with shoes zipped into their bags. For greater
longevity, shoes were worn only in the schoolyard.

One day in April of 2009, however, Keita smelled no coffee.
Yoyo was not in the kitchen or on the porch. Charity had already

left the house, but that was typical. She clung to her routines. Each night before she went to bed, she assembled her lunch (one Granny Smith apple, a handful of almonds and ham-and-cheese on rye with mayonnaise, but never mustard), folded her school clothes and piled them on a chair, cleaned her shoes and put them at the door (Keita knew that the surest way to drive her crazy was to hide her shoes), and reviewed her schedule of classes, violin lessons and school newspaper meetings. She met a tutor early most mornings to keep her marks as close as possible to 100 percent. But on this day, she had left for an overnight field trip to a museum on the far side of Zantoroland.

Keita, at fifteen, trained daily with a track club but barely kept any study schedule. What was the point of hitting the books when he had no possibility of matching his sister's success? When his father or his sister inquired about his marks, Keita said that he would happily skip being an overanxious, overachieving A-plus student and opt instead to be a cool B student, a runner dreaming of the glory—and cars—that would accompany his Olympic victory.

Keita slipped on his knapsack and tied his shoelaces. At an easy clip, it would only take him eight minutes to run to school. But it was 8:45 a.m. now and time to get going.

"Papa," he called.

No answer.

Keita was writing a note to his father, teasingly scolding him for being absent at breakfast, when someone knocked on his door. Three times. Politely, but firmly. In Zantoroland, three knocks meant official business. Keita opened the door. He looked down. It was a young boy, around ten years old. Years ago, when his homeland had been different, it might have been a neighbour child come to visit his father. But in recent years, the president had been known to use young messengers. Keita stepped back in alarm.

"Sir," the boy said. "Message about your father. You must report to the Ministry of Citizenship immediately."

"What has happened to him?"

The boy shifted from his left foot to his right. "Don't know, sir."

"Who is detaining him?"

"Don't know, sir, but you must bring a flatbed wagon." The boy turned and ran.

Keita did not have a flatbed wagon. In Yagwa, wagons were pulled by the labourers who hauled oranges, chickens and okra to market. How important could a wagon be? Better that he go straight to help his father. Keita flew out the door and began running.

The Ministry of Citizenship was housed with other government offices in a three-storey pink building on the bay at the south end of the President's Promenade. After the coup d'état three years earlier, Keita had been warned to not approach the building—which was also known as the Pink Palace—or to walk within a block of it. Faloos and dissidents were sometimes snatched off the street near there, never to be seen again. No sane person approached the building unless they had good reason to do so.

ARMED SOLDIERS STOOD GUARD AT THE ENTRANCE TO THE building. Keita informed them that he had been summoned to meet his father.

One of the soldiers nodded.

Keita ran up six steps and into the building. Ahead of him was an office. Not a soul was inside.

"Dad!" he shouted.

No answer. No one was visible in the building. Keita heard nothing but his own voice echoing off the marble floors and the walls adorned with portraits of President Randall.

Keita tried to open doors on the first floor. The first three were locked. It was cold in the building, and he shivered as he remembered his father's words: *It's not truly a Ministry of Citizenship. It's a Ministry of Detention, Abuse and Worse.* The fourth office door that Keita tried was unlocked, so he opened it and entered a square, windowless room with an unoccupied desk and seats all along the walls, like an empty medical clinic. On the walls were more portraits of the president. Keita walked slowly around the room and noticed another door. He was reaching for the handle when the door opened and a man came through. Keita jumped back.

The man was short and thin with a military brush cut, inscrutable black eyes, a nose the size of a plum and what appeared to be a permanent sneer on his face. He wore a black suit and a black tie.

"Hello," Keita said, "I am—"

"We know who you are. Where is the wagon?"

"I came for my father."

"Not ready to leave," the man said.

"May I see him?"

"You were instructed to bring a wagon. Are you deaf, or are you dense?"

"I don't have a wagon, but I wish to see my father." Keita wondered if it was safe to argue. What would Charity do? His sister, he knew, would not take no for an answer.

"Wait here," the man said.

"May I ask—?" Keita began, but the man raised his palm, turned and passed through the door, which closed behind him.

Keita waited a moment. He tried the door. Locked. He pounded on it, but there was no answer.

Keita had no book to read, no material to study. He waited. And waited. And waited. In his hurry to leave the house, he had forgotten to put on his watch. There was a clock on the wall, but the hour and minute hands were fixed at noon. It seemed to Keita that an hour or two passed, but nobody came to see him.

Then, from the other side of the locked door, he heard a voice. "Nooo," it wailed. It sounded at first like a child, loud and insistent, but then it didn't sound like a child at all. Keita waited for the sound again, listening carefully. When it came again, he knew.

Keita stood up and pounded on the door. No answer.

"I don't know!" his father cried out, just beyond the locked door.

"Dad!" Keita pounded on the door.

Now his father's voice came from farther away. Keita shouted again. "Dad!"

The door swung open and the short man stood before him. Keita tried to see into the room, but the man blocked the way.

"You are a poor listener," he said. "No wagon, and not patiently waiting either. Well, if you must, come in. Be quiet, or you will make matters worse."

"I want to see my father."

"That will have to wait."

The man stood to the side and Keita stepped into the room. Then he felt a blunt, hard blow that left him dizzy. The man had punched him. Keita raised his hand to stop the blood from his nose.

"It will get worse than that if you show any more insolence," the man said.

"What is happening to my father?" Keita said.

"You are how old?"

"Fifteen. What is going on?"

"Fifteen is too young for questions. But let me tell you something." The man looked straight into Keita's eyes.

Keita thought of his sister, strong and bossy, and all the passion that his father had channelled into a thousand newspaper articles. He stood firmly and stared right into the man's eyes.

"Your father is not a good man. He is neither law-abiding nor respectful."

Keita was quite sure that the only lawbreakers in this building were the short man and his cronies, and he wanted to say so. He did not want to cause his father more pain, but he could imagine his sister pushing harder.

"There is no need to hurt my father. Tomorrow, you will have to live with the things you have done to him. Let him go. I will take him now."

"You could have seen him two hours ago, if you had done what I said."

"What is it with the wagon?"

"Disrespectful question!"

"I don't have a wagon!"

"You can find a wagon if you put your mind to it. Bring it to the front door, where the soldiers wait, and then come back here and knock on the door."

His father's voice again: "I work alone, and I don't know!"

"Dad!" Keita shouted.

All that came back was a long, slow moan.

Keita wondered if he could overpower the man, or run past him to find his father. But there would be other men, and he would not succeed.

"I will be back with a wagon," he said.

He left the building and ran to the market, where he found the woman who had sold mangoes and bananas to Charity and him a hundred times.

"Please, I need to borrow your wagon."

She pointed to the oranges and lemons stacked high on it.

"I promise to bring it back," Keita said.

"I cannot do that, son."

Keita fished a five-dollar bill out of his pocket. It was all he had.

"Son, a wagon costs more than that."

"It's for my father. They are holding him in the Pink Palace."

"Oh my Lord. Why did you not say?"

The woman spread out a tarp on the ground. Keita helped her unload the wagon and set the fruit in a pile.

"Here," the woman said. "Take it and hurry."

It was laborious and frustrating to haul the wagon through the crowded market, and to ask people to step out of the way to let him pass. They took their time, assuming a boy couldn't be in a real hurry.

"Please," Keita said over and over, "it's an emergency. Please let me by."

He made better time once he got on the President's Promenade; then he could run and pull the wagon behind him.

At the Pink Palace, Keita left the wagon at the foot of the steps to the entrance. He ran up past the armed guards and inside, into the office where he had last seen the short man. The door was locked again. He pounded on it. This time, it opened right away.

"Stand aside."

Keita moved to the left. Two large soldiers stepped out of the room, carrying Keita's father. One held Yoyo by the legs and the other under the armpits. His eyes were closed. He didn't turn his head to look at his son.

"Dad!"

"Move out of the way," the short man said.

They lugged Keita's father through the building to the exit. They pushed through the door and down the six steps, then they placed Yoyo on the wagon.

Keita ran to his father's side and felt for a pulse. Yoyo's heart was beating. He was breathing. But his face was bruised. His feet were bare and swollen.

As he pulled the heavy wagon, Keita looked back every few moments to be sure that his father was safe and not falling off. His arms soon ached. His back ached. But his father was alive, and Keita could take him home. This time, people saw the load Keita was carrying and got out of his way. Cars swerved around them. Pedestrians avoided him. But it wasn't until he was back in his own neighbourhood that people offered assistance. Three men helped pull the wagon over the last kilometre, relieving Keita and his exhausted arms. They pulled Yoyo on the creaky flatbed wagon all the way to the Alis' front door and lifted him into the house and to his bed. Then they came back with a car and drove Yoyo to the Yagwa Hospital.

The doctors did not believe the story that Zantoroland's best-known journalist had fallen down the stairs. But they did not ask any questions that might require Keita to say something that might attract trouble, and they did not issue a bill for treating the two broken fingers on each hand, the broken ankle, the other badly bruised ankle, the split lips or the concussed head.

The nurses told Keita to go home, but he would not leave his father's side. Finally, they wheeled in a cot so Keita could sleep there.

Charity returned home the next day and went straight to the hospital. Yoyo had by then regained consciousness, and she put her hand on his shoulder and wept.

"It's all right, children," Yoyo told them. "I'm still here."

The nurses knew he had no wife at home. They fed and bathed him and gave him time to learn to use crutches. After four days, Yoyo could get to the bathroom unassisted. On the fifth day, a neighbour drove him home.

For the next two months, the women on the street took care of Yoyo when Keita and Charity were at school. Hardly a night went by without someone bringing fruit, eggs, a chicken or fried plantain. Yoyo tried typing again, but hardly wrote a thing. He could not use either pinkie, and he said his hands throbbed. After three months, he graduated from wheelchair to walker, and in another two months he was able to walk unassisted with an oak cane that he said had come from his own father. He needed help with household chores, especially those involving bending the knees, so while he napped, Keita cleaned. Cleaning was more than a chore; it was a chance to show his father how much he loved him. The house had never been cleaner.

One Saturday morning, while his father snored, Keita removed all the items stored inside the bungalow's only closet. He hauled out the vacuum cleaner, six boxes of books and two suitcases. And then Keita found a red cane. He jerked his hand back as if he had touched a venomous snake. It was the same government-issue used by crippled men in the streets of Yagwa.

Keita showed the cane to his sister. The two of them sat by their father's bed and waited. Yoyo opened his eyes and said, "Is this a news conference or a palace coup?"

"There's a red cane in the closet," Keita said.

Yoyo forced a smile. "Let's not overreact."

"Why do you have it," Keita asked, "and when did you get it?"

Yoyo said a boy had delivered it to the house a few weeks after he was released from the hospital. "Use this," the boy had said. "It is an order from the authorities."

"I thought the red cane was to mark refugees who had been returned to Zantoroland," Keita said.

"Looks like the authorities have widened the eligibility rules," Yoyo said. "Now, it's a sign of all who oppose the government. But I'm not using their red cane. They know who I am, and so does everybody else. Try not to worry. But there is something else you should know about. You are both old enough now."

Yoyo said the president had a taste for yachts and palaces and was anxious to build up his private coffers. "He wants to be as rich as other despots, but there is no viable income tax base, so he has no money to steal from standard revenues." Therefore, the president had begun to instruct his men to kidnap people—especially dissidents— and issue ransom demands.

Yoyo said they called it The Tax. It usually operated in one of two ways. If they kidnapped you and gave your relatives a day or less to come up with a nearly impossible ransom, they were almost certainly going to kill you anyway. They wanted you because you were a dissident, and the ransom was just a way to terrorize and intimidate your family. But if they kidnapped you and gave your loved ones time—weeks or even months—to pay The Tax, they truly wanted the money and might release you.

"Why would they show any mercy?" Keita said.

"If people are going to pay up, they need to be confident that the government will keep its end of the bargain."

"Why are you telling us this?" Charity said.

"They've taken my passport, but you still have yours. You should leave the country when you finish school."

Keita sat closer to his father and took his hand. As long as his father was alive, Keita was not going anywhere. He would stay in the country, try to establish himself as a nationally ranked marathoner as soon as he was old enough to test himself over that distance, and take care of his father. Charity was the one with the brains. She should be the one to take off first. Keita would get out later, if he could.

ANOTHER YEAR PASSED. THOUGH YOYO NO LONGER WROTE regularly, Keita sometimes heard him slipping out of the house late at night to have hushed conversations with visitors on the street.

One fellow with a foreign accent who appeared to be about sixty years old came around a few times, so Keita asked about him. Yoyo said his name was Mahatma Grafton, and that he was a journalist from Canada and an old friend.

CHARITY FINISHED GRADE 12 WITH A 99 PERCENT AVERAGE. She became the first student in the history of Zantoroland to be flown to the United States for university interviews, and the first to be offered a full scholarship—travel, tuition, residence, books, the works—at an American university. She had several offers but accepted the one from Harvard.

Keita knew Charity's favourite foods, so he made them all for their last family supper: guacamole with lemon, diced tomato and a few hot peppers; chicken stewed with yams and ground peanuts; fried plantains; and for dessert, madeleines with jam and vanilla ice cream. Keita spent hours cooking for his sister and father, while they debated world news, speculated about the future of ethnic tensions in Zantoroland, teased Keita about his onion-dicing technique (he diced and re-diced until the pieces were minute) and sang with him.

Charity asked her father if he would ever consider remarrying.

"I'm too old for that."

"The women on this very street would marry you in a flash," she said. "What about Mrs. Pascall, who brought baked chickens once a week for months after Mom died? Or Mrs. Craig, who kept inviting you to church picnics until she finally gave up?"

"Your mother still keeps me company in my thoughts. Anyway, it's too dangerous for any woman to be seen with me."

"You need to stop writing anything at all," Charity said. "Can't you wait for a regime change? Sooner or later, there will be another coup."

"I'm not doing so much these days," Yoyo said.

"Right," Keita said, "and I'm not training every day on the hills of Zantoroland."

"When I'm away," Charity said, "this is how I want to remember us at home. Keita dicing onions into smithereens, Papa wearing his Paris Bistro smock and me in this big fat chair bossing you around."

Keita wondered when he would see his sister again. He had not realized, until her departure drew near, how much he counted on her presence in the house. His heart was held aloft by only a few pillars. With Charity's departure, one of them was being kicked away. How did you say goodbye to someone who had always been with you? Keita longed to throw his arms around her. She was leaving them behind. How could he and their father go on living without her in a country sliding into such hatred?

Keita wanted his sister to be safe overseas and to succeed at university, but when it was time for her to go, he felt only grief. He put his arm around Charity's shoulders.

"Get in closer," she said, and she gave him a hug, kissed his cheeks and then stood to receive a bear hug from Yoyo.

"I love you so much, Dad," she said. "You taught me to write. You taught me everything—except for all the most useful things, which I learned from Mom," she added with a grin.

Charity had fit her essential belongings into one small knapsack.

"Miss Efficiency," Keita said.

"It's all I need," she said.

"You've got what you need, up there," Keita said. "You did get all the brains in the family."

"That's not true," she said. "Dad has a few brains too."

Keita laughed, which was better than crying, as his sister slung the bag over her shoulder. He walked with Charity down the red dirt road and waited with her until a cab came along and took her away.

CHAPTER FOUR

A NTON HAMM, A MARATHON AGENT BASED IN Freedom State, had contacted Keita many times to offer his services. He came to Zantoroland often to expand the pool of runners whose careers he managed.

On the first occasion, when Keita was nineteen, he had just finished third in the 10,000 metres in the Zantoroland National Junior Championships. There were only two white men in sight that day. One was a representative from Marathoners First, the world's most famous sports agency for African and Zantorolander distance runners, who went after the boys who finished first and second. The other was Hamm.

He didn't approach the top two finishers. He stood no chance with them. Instead he came up to Keita, congratulated him and offered his card.

"Call me if you continue to improve," Hamm said. "I could take you overseas and get you some international racing experience."

The second time was a few years later, after Keita had won a minor marathon, at altitude, in 2:11:45. The fastest runners in Zantoroland had skipped the race because it offered no cash prizes.

"If you can run this fast at altitude," Hamm told him, "you will run faster at sea level. You could turn some heads in Rotterdam or New York."

Hamm was the only person from Freedom State who had won gold in a track and field event at the Olympic Games. In fact, he was a two-time gold medallist, with world records back to back in the 2008 and 2012 Olympics. But the shot putter had received no lucrative sponsorship offers—even though he was white and from one of the world's richest nations. Slender, attractive men and women who ran the 100 metres or the marathon were able to pull in hundreds of thousands of dollars in sponsorships, but who would look twice at a 320-pound shot putter? Also, Anton Hamm was rumoured to have taken steroids, although he was never caught. He was also rumoured to have an anger management issue. After retiring from heaving sixteen-pound balls more than twenty metres in the air, Hamm started eating much less, stopped weightlifting and walked two hours a day until his weight dropped under three hundred pounds. Then, he started running. He declared in an interview with *Track and Field News*—a magazine Keita had read since childhood—that he had always wanted to be a runner and didn't want his heart to implode at the age of thirty. Within a year, he began to build a small business managing the careers of promising distance runners from Africa and Zantoroland.

Hamm was a small fish in the ocean of big-money marathon agents, and specialized in representing talented but second-tier runners from Kenya, Ethiopia and Zantoroland. Now, he wore beautifully tailored suits over his six-foot-five, slimmed-down, 250-pound frame, and he moved through life with class and elegance—at least, when things were going his way. When they were not, he lashed out as fast as a tiger. Or that's what people said.

When Keita was twenty-three and had won a half-marathon in Yagwa, Hamm approached him again. "I could grow your career," Hamm said. "I'm in Zantoroland all the time. Call me up and we'll have lunch."

Keita was worried about his father and did not want to leave Zantoroland, so he thanked Anton Hamm, took his card again and said that he might be in touch later.

Now, Keita was twenty-four and trying to improve his national marathon ranking. His father was only fifty-nine, but he had paid for his career as a journalist, and he hobbled like an old man. He had little appetite and slept poorly, and he continued to slip out at night, refusing to tell Keita what he was working on. Charity called and emailed often from Harvard. She had been gone for six years, and was in the first year of a PhD program in African Studies. Each time she asked if she could come home for a visit, Yoyo insisted that it wasn't safe and that she should stay put.

The Canadian journalist Mahatma Grafton paid another visit to Yagwa, but when he came to the house, Yoyo wasn't home. Keita stepped outside, as his father always did, to speak to the man. Mahatma was a kind, disarming soul who immediately put Keita at ease and made him feel that he was in the company of a trusted friend. Mahatma led Keita down a block, past a woman hawking barbecued fish and calling out to customers.

"Your old man used to do this, in Baltimore," he said. "Cook street meat, for a few dollars."

"I heard about that," Keita said.

Mahatma stood near and lowered his voice. "Tell your old man it is not worth it."

"I've tried, and so has Charity," Keita said.

"Your father is on to a story. I've tried to talk him out of it. It's dangerous. He has sources in the president's office. He says they're legit. He says they're trustworthy. But I think he should leave the country."

"He can't go," Keita said. "His passport was confiscated."

"If he can't leave," Mahatma said, "maybe you can."

One day, Keita was frying eggs and heating beans for dinner, while his father sat in the armchair and read the *New York Times*, when someone pounded on their front door. Friends who knew that Yoyo had few means often brought him produce or cooked meals, but none of them announced themselves like that. Yoyo stashed his newspaper under his chair while Keita answered the door.

Three government officials in suits and ties stood on the porch. The one closest to Keita said, "Stand at attention for His Excellency, President for Life of the Republic of Zantoroland."

A tall man in an African-style robe stepped from behind them.

The white cloth of the robe was the highest quality cotton, bordered with intricate blue stitching. The man wore sandals made of crocodile leather, and his toenails were thick, yellow and crusty.

Lots of people came to the door to pay homage to his father. But it took effort to not stare at the president and show all the hatred that he felt. As far as Keita was concerned, the president was responsible for his mother's death, his father's torture, and the deaths and disappearances of countless others. He was barbaric, often leaving his victims naked and dead in public places. Keita had been taught at home and in school not to hate, only to forgive. But looking at the president now, he felt no forgiveness.

"No woman in the house to greet me?" the president said. He gave a booming laugh. One of his aides murmured that Yoyo was a widower. "Well," the president said, "every father needs a faithful son to cook for him." The president entered and approached the stove. Because of the unreliable electricity, the Ali home had a small two-burner stove hooked up to two propane gas tanks. When one tank ran out, the other could be activated.

"Quaint and lovely, just like the ways of people up in the hills," the president said.

Keita and Yoyo stood at a respectful distance; they knew to be silent unless they were asked a direct question.

"Eggs and beans," the president said.

"Would Your Excellency like some?" Keita said. Speaking out of turn—without explicit invitation from the president—was the only way he knew to convey his contempt.

"I would accept eggs and beans another time," the president said, "but as they are ready now, please go ahead and eat. Yes. Serve your father, son, and yourself. Be at ease."

Keita removed two fried eggs and placed them, with beans, on his father's plate. His father slid into his chair at the table, his look saying, *Do not speak again unless you are asked a direct question.* Keita served himself, brought two mugs of water to the table and sat with his father.

The president's three aides stood silently at the door, each with his left hand hanging down and his right pulling back a suit jacket and resting on a hip, exposing a revolver.

"So, Mr. Ali, renowned journalist of Zantoroland, how are your eggs this evening?"

"They are almost as excellent as you," Yoyo said.

Keita admired his father's answer. One was required to use the term "Your Excellency" in each phrase uttered to Jenkins Randall. This way Yoyo came close, without quite satisfying the president's requirements.

"You must be proud of your son." The president stood behind Keita and rubbed the back of his head.

Keita felt the big palm moving slowly, methodically. The president's square ring scratched his scalp.

"Yes, I am, Your Excellency," Yoyo said. He took in the sight of the president with his son's head in his hands and asked, "To what do we owe the honour of a visit from Your Excellency?"

"A father who is such a famous intellectual, with a son who is ranked—what now, in the national marathon standings?"

"Fifth," Keita said.

The president removed his hand from Keita's head and placed it on his shoulder. "Fifth!"

"That's correct," Keita said.

"Not easy, in a country known for its runners."

Yoyo glared at Keita, who kept his mouth shut this time. Keita didn't want to show any respect where it was not deserved. But neither did he want to do something to cause his father harm.

The president began walking back and forth behind Keita and Yoyo, clapping his hands once each time he paused behind Keita. "Don't you agree that your father will be pleased to have a long and peaceful retirement and to see his son move up in the national rankings?"

"Yes, Your Excellency," Keita said. He remembered what had happened in the last Olympic Games, when not one of the three

Zantorolander marathoners made it onto the medal podium. It had shocked the nation, because on a good day, any one of them could have won the race handily. When they returned to Zantoroland, all three were imprisoned. Two weeks later, when they were released, each used a red cane and walked with a permanent limp.

"And you, Mr. Ali, have had quite the illustrious career. The *New York Times*, the *Atlantic*, the *Guardian*, the *Toronto Star*, *Le Monde* . . ."

"I've slowed down in recent years, Your Excellency."

"Slowing down is a good thing, Mr. Ali. Gives you time to enjoy life. To enjoy your children."

"Most thoroughly, Your Excellency," Yoyo answered.

The president—a tall man with the girth of a boulder—stooped to speak in Yoyo's ear. "Do you follow boxing?"

"A little, Your Excellency."

"Would you agree that it pains the soul to see a boxer come out of retirement and enter the ring again?"

"I never like to see anyone hurt, Your Excellency."

"Precisely my thoughts. The wise boxer knows when to fight and when it is time to quit."

"It's all about balance and what seems right, Your Excellency."

"I have just the proposition for you, Mr. Ali," the president said. "You are the perfect person to write my authorized biography and to place it with publishers around the world."

"I will give that careful thought, Your Excellency," Yoyo said.

"This project could bring great pride to the people of Zantoroland. You would be richly compensated."

"Due consideration, Your Excellency."

The president stood still behind Keita. He let a moment pass. "Consider the comforts of a bigger home, a cook, an endless supply of good food for your family. It is a well-understood fact that journalists nearly take vows of poverty. How could a widower with children resist the miracle of the fishes and the loaves?"

"There are the fishes and the loaves to consider, Your Excellency," Yoyo said. "But there is also the eye of the needle."

The president stood absolutely still. Keita could hear him swallow.

"Well, in my humble role as servant to the people of Zantoroland, I will not endeavour to rush you to your good senses. Enjoy your eggs, Mr. Ali. And, Mr. Ali Junior, I wish you fleet feet and a minimum of cardiovascular suffering. I'm sure that no father wishes to see his son in pain."

The president left with his aides.

Keita and his father sat in silence, staring at their plates. They sat so long without speaking that both of them jumped when the telephone rang across the room on Yoyo's desk.

"Yes," Keita said too loudly into the receiver.

"Keita Ali. Anton Hamm. I'm in your neck of the woods this week and—"

"Not now, sir," Keita said. He hung up the phone and returned to his father.

SHORTLY AFTER THE VISIT FROM THE PRESIDENT AND HIS men, Keita discovered a tiny device under a chair in the family kitchen. He showed it to his father, who explained that it was a bug for recording conversations.

Yoyo led Keita outside and walked with him to a street corner that was noisy with cars, mopeds and pedestrians.

"Aren't you worried?" Keita asked.

"No," Yoyo said. "What's the point of worrying or letting them dictate your frame of mind?"

"Well, I'm worried about you, Father. And I don't want to lose you."

A young girl walked by, balancing a platter of plantains on her head. She was barefoot, and only ten or so, but she kept the platter perfectly balanced as she walked down Blossom Street toward the market.

"We've done pretty well as father and son, haven't we?"

Keita smiled and took his father's hand.

"Remember that, son," Yoyo said. "We've had nearly a quarter of a century together, which is more than most people get to love each other."

Keita thought about how long his parents had loved each other. About sixteen years. It was true that Keita was lucky to have had so many years with his father. But he couldn't bear the thought of being without him. Yoyo must have sensed his thoughts.

A pack of five runners flew by them. Elite runners, out for a training session. They shouted at Keita as they went. Keita smiled and waved back.

"You've done very well too, son," Yoyo said, "but now you must make wiser use of your talent."

"What do you mean, Father?"

"When you were young," Yoyo said, "I wanted you to become an intellectual, like your sister, because I thought that the life of the mind would offer you more than a decade or two of running. But you have taken your own path, and I respect that. So now I must tell you. Use your legs to the best of your ability. Travel, and travel soon. Fly very far, and do not look back." Yoyo Ali then hugged his son and, as they walked home, asked him to sing "I Got a Robe" with him.

> I got a robe, you got a robe
> All God's children got a robe
> When I get to heaven gonna put on my robe
> I'm gonna shout all over God's heaven, heaven, heaven,
> Ev'rybody's talkin' 'bout heaven ain't goin' there heaven, heaven
> I'm gonna shout all over God's heaven.

When they had finished, Yoyo put his arm around his son's shoulder and said, "The time has come. Call the marathon agent."

It was March 2018, and those were the last words of advice that Keita received from his father.

★ ★ ★

THE NEXT MORNING, KEITA ROSE TO FIND HIS FATHER ALREADY out for the day. He set aside yet another note from Hamm. *Would you like to talk? No obligation to do business.* He went for a run and returned to hear the phone ringing. A man's voice said that Keita could save his father's life only if he put twenty thousand U.S. dollars in an envelope and deposited it on the counter by municipal tax wicket number 5 at the town hall before the end of the business day.

Keita had no possibility of raising twenty thousand dollars in hours. His father, if he were still alive, would know it, and so would his father's captors. Still, Keita tried everything. He spent two hours at his father's bank in Yagwa, trying to persuade them to let him have access to his father's funds. Finally, a woman who had difficulty holding back her tears took him into her office and said that even if they could allow Keita to take the money—which they couldn't— his father's accounts had dwindled and there weren't more than a thousand dollars left. Keita had noticed that his father no longer wore new clothes or used their car, which sat dormant outside their house, or ate much beyond a bit of boiled rice or an orange picked from a park tree.

As a nationally ranked marathoner in Zantoroland, Keita had access to free cafeteria meals each day, and he received shoes, shorts and shirts. But he was given no cash and had no savings, and in a country where the average annual income was three thousand dollars, Keita couldn't find a single person to help him come up with the money. He emailed Charity at Harvard but got no response. He tried calling her apartment number but could not get through. A call to her cellphone led straight to voice mail. Keita did reach Charity's landlord in Boston. He had no idea where she was but promised to leave an urgent note on her door. Keita spoke to every one of their neighbours on Blossom Street, but nobody had money to spare.

Keita knew all this was part of the technique used to break the will of the people attached to those who fell victim to The Tax. They were meant to feel that nothing could be done for their loved ones and that nothing would be done for them either, if their turn came.

Keita tried to imagine what his father would say to him now. *Be calm, and be strong, and be sure to take care of yourself. You have a full life ahead of you to live, so do everything you can to have that life and to live it lovingly.*

Keita spent hours at his father's desk with the lamp burning. He read through Yoyo's newspaper and magazine articles, which were stacked in a neat pile. He rummaged through the teapots and extracted his father's notes. *Deportees from Freedom State? All Faloo? Money laundering?* Keita could not figure out exactly what his father had been working on, but he kept reading his words over and over again. He read them aloud, in his father's voice and accent, to comfort himself. He read them as the ransom deadline came and went. Then he carefully put them away.

Keita knew what he had to do next. He rummaged through the closet for a spade, and went out the back door and dug a grave next to his mother's plot. He dug until his hands bled, and he kept digging until he had dug enough.

At dawn, Keita took the blanket from his father's bed, borrowed a wagon from the market and pulled it to the town square, where he found his father lying naked and dead at the Fountain of Independence.

K EITA KNEW EXACTLY WHAT HIS FATHER WOULD SAY. IF Keita stayed in Zantoroland, he would die. He was his father's son, and that in itself would be a death sentence. He had to get out and stay alive and find his sister. Charity was the last person in the world who truly knew and loved him. She was all he had. Keita would rebuild his life with his sister in another land. It didn't really matter where they went, as long as it was far from Zantoroland.

Keita called the hotel where Hamm always stayed, and agreed to meet the agent for lunch. Then he bathed, scrubbed the dirt from his nails, put on his best shoes, pants and shirt, packed essential clothes and running gear into one large and one small knapsack, and locked the door to the family bungalow.

Would the little trouble with Keita's belly catch Hamm's eye? In the last few months, his hernia had been sore and had been expanding. In addition, Keita was experiencing bouts of weakness and dizziness. These affected his running only in the unlucky moments that they coincided with a training run. Keita had taken to wearing longer, slightly baggy shirts and hoped that the hernia would cease to grow. He did not know if Hamm required his protégés to submit to medical exams. He hoped not.

The lobby of the Five Stars International Business Hotel featured a pet monkey for the entertainment of its international business guests, although monkeys were not native to Zantoroland. On a branch of a fake tree in the lobby, the monkey sat leashed, eating a peanut. When Keita walked in the door, a concierge-bouncer the size of a heavyweight boxer bore down on him in three strides.

"Sir!" he said. "Do you have business here?"

Keita leaned on the British accent of his former English tutor. "I am meeting one of your guests. Mr. Anton Hamm. You'll see him inside the café, on the right." Keita pointed.

The concierge turned to look, and in that moment, Keita strode past him.

When Anton Hamm stood in greeting, he towered above Keita and even above the concierge. Hamm's hand felt like the paw of a bear. He shook Keita's hand gently but applied enough pressure for Keita to understand how easily his own fingers could be crushed.

"Coffee?" Hamm said, inviting Keita to take a seat.

Keita sat and glanced at the menu. Everything in U.S. dollars. Coffee cost twelve.

"It's on me," Hamm said.

When the waiter came, Keita asked for café au lait and a madeleine.

"Most of the runners I do business with have never heard of a café au lait," Hamm mused.

"It's good for dunking," Keita said. He pushed away images of his parents, but they kept coming, like waves on a beach.

Hamm ordered the same. When the waiter left, he said, "I should give up coffee myself, but I'm saving that for later."

"Saving it?" Keita repeated. His voice was emanating from another body.

Hamm was talking again, but Keita was having trouble paying attention.

"One day when I'm old," Hamm said, "a doctor will tell me, 'If you want to recover your health, there's something you'll have to give up.' So then I'll be able to offer him coffee. I need to keep something around to give up later."

Hamm had a loud laugh. It made Keita imagine the sound of the overfed Zantoroland cabinet ministers who were known to dine at the Five Stars.

When the café au lait arrived, Keita slid three sugar cubes into his mug. Hamm rocked back slightly in his wooden chair and Keita heard the faint crack of wood. Hamm raised his index finger to summon the waiter and asked for another chair. When it came, Hamm stood and handed the one he had occupied to the waiter.

"This one needs to be fixed," he said, easing his weight onto the replacement.

A mosquito buzzed around Hamm's head, and his right hand shot up near his ear. He squished the insect between his thumb and forefinger.

"Fast hands," Keita said. He played table tennis but had never been able to catch a mosquito like that. His father had taught him table tennis. His father and mother had taught him everything.

Keita kept his hands flat on the table, so the cracks and the blisters wouldn't show.

Hamm looked at Keita and shrugged. "I have little patience for things or people that aggravate me." Hamm grinned. "By-product of throwing the shot."

"Maybe I'll give up running and take up the shot put," Keita said.

"It's all about explosive energy," Hamm said. "That, plus head games. Shot putters mess with each other's heads."

Hamm ordered toast and poached eggs. Keita scanned the menu. If his father had interviewed someone in the hotel restaurant, he would have come home with a story about the most expensive item. Steak frites with Belgian hollandaise, with a side of grilled white asparagus. Forty-eight U.S. dollars. Keita wondered what a meal like that would cost in America.

"I'll take the oatmeal," he said to the waiter. Keita would eat oatmeal another day in another country if he played his cards right.

"Have it with the berries and cashews," Hamm said. "Good for runners and full of natural stimulants."

"Would you also like brûlée?" the waiter asked.

"Brûlée?"

"With a custard and baked brown sugar glaze."

Keita nodded to the waiter. His father was dead and Keita was ordering the most expensive meal of his life.

Had they tortured Yoyo again? Or killed him quickly? Did he ask for anything before he died? Keita imagined his father saying: *I've had a good life, so go ahead and do it quickly.*

Hamm spoke of the times he had seen Keita run lately: in a ten-kilometre race and in a half-marathon. He mentioned Keita's times; he had memorized them.

"You run very well," Hamm said, "but you could use more coaching. If you like, I'll see that you get some advice from one of the running coaches in America."

"Why would American coaches know anything? Their runners never win. They're barely faster than the runners from Canada or from Freedom State."

"Don't knock Freedom State," Hamm said. "They're investing a lot of money to develop a marathon infrastructure. They may see a breakthrough."

"How do I sign up?" Keita said.

Hamm took a thick envelope and passed it over the table. "Inside, you'll find two thousand dollars U.S. The same amount that every runner gets. No exceptions."

"Thank you," Keita said. "But I meant the contract. What are the rules?" Although he was asking questions, Keita would sign any paper necessary to leave the country.

"The contract is straightforward," Hamm said. "Inside Zantoroland, you can race as you see fit. Outside Zantoroland, I own you. I decide when and where you will race. I pay the entry fees and get you there, arrange your room and board while you're overseas, and I bring you back. I also arrange and pay for your passport and visas."

"What is the percentage?"

"Since I absorb all the costs, I take eighty percent of your winnings. You get the remaining twenty percent, in American dollars, at the end of each running tour, once you are back here."

"Seems steep." Keita said it only because he didn't want to appear desperate.

"If you don't want it, we won't waste any more time."

"I have two conditions," Keita said.

Hamm laughed. "You are in no position to impose conditions."

"Then consider them requests."

"Shoot," Hamm said.

"I want to run Boston. This year."

"The Boston Marathon is in a few days. Are you ready?"

"Yes."

"You're cutting it awfully close," Hamm said.

"You've been telling me for years to get in touch. Well, here I am, and ready to go."

"Boston usually leaves an extra spot for me. I'll get you in. What's the second condition?"

"When are you leaving?"

"I'm flying to the United States tonight."

"I propose to travel with you."

"It will cost me extra to get you a flight that fast. You will have to run like hell in America to make this up to me."

"Understood."

Hamm stood for a handshake. Keita risked taking it and was relieved that the agent did not attempt to crush his hand.

As soon as he landed at Boston's Logan International Airport, he began emailing and calling Charity. He left more messages on her voice mail, but still she did not reply. He had imagined that she would greet him with hugs, screams of joy and tears. They would console each other for the death of their father, and Charity would be able to advise Keita about how to apply for asylum in the United States. Perhaps he would be allowed to stay because of his promise as a marathoner. If not, he would have to go into hiding until a solution presented itself.

Keita had imagined that after the tears and the strategic discussion, Charity would feed him and fête him and tell him all about her life at Harvard, that she would feign disdain that he had chosen the path of athletics over a career of the mind but nevertheless be proud of her brother and bring her friends out to cheer for him on race day. For his sister, he wanted to turn in the fastest race of his life.

The phone lines at home were unreliable, but Charity had always kept in touch. Keita tried to remember when she had last called. Finally, he used some of his precious cash to take a taxi to her apartment. The note Keita had dictated days earlier remained tacked to Charity's door. Her landlord said that though her rent was paid, he had not seen her in a few days.

The race organizers had shifted the date of the marathon to early March, because in recent years temperatures had climbed too high on the traditional race date in April. But this was a cold March day. Exposed to the freezing wind for thirty minutes before the starter's pistol fired, Keita did not feel well. During the long wait, other runners kept shoving past him. When the gun finally went off, Keita tried to follow the leaders.

There were so many elite runners pushing and shoving that just fifteen minutes into the race, he was left unfocused and spent. The lead runners from Zantoroland ran in a pack to protect one another from the shoving, but they were moving too fast for Keita. It was the most prestigious marathon in the world, but Keita's thoughts kept turning to his father and his sister. Where was she? To make matters worse, the hernia was throbbing, and Keita experienced a dizzy spell. He had neglected to drink enough water before the race, and then he missed the first water station. His lips were cracking, and he thought obsessively about drinking water.

Within eight kilometres, he felt he was chasing runners he would never catch. He felt energy draining out of him. The pack of lead runners dropped him, and then the chase pack of twenty runners dropped him. After ten kilometres, he slowed to an easy pace. If he had no chance of running a fast time, it was best to save his legs for another race and take this as an easy training run. But even at a pace he could have managed as a teenager at altitude, Keita now felt ill and desperately thirsty. At water station after water station, he drank greedily and spilled water all over himself. His hamstring clamped so tightly that he had to walk up the last part of Heartbreak Hill. Keita struggled to the finish line in 2:35. He finished sixty-fifth and was the slowest of the fifteen Zantorolanders in the race.

That was it. Keita had no chance of staying in America to build his running career. Hamm would send him home. Keita would be made to disappear one night. His life would end before it had truly begun. No career, no family, no lasting creation or crowning achievement, nothing.

Anton Hamm came to see him in the race recovery area, where Keita was downing cup after cup of electrolyte drink. Keita expected that Hamm would be furious, but he was surprised to see the man appearing calm.

"Not to worry," Hamm said, clapping his giant palm on Keita's shoulder. "Everybody has bad races. You just need a little more time, but not in America. You need a lot less competition. You need to be in Freedom State. How busted up are you?"

"I'm okay. I had a bad day, so I took it easy. My legs will be fine."

Hamm said that he would give Keita two weeks in Freedom State to rest and do light workouts before being tested in a fifteen-kilometre race.

THEY FLEW FROM LOGAN AIRPORT ON A NON-STOP, FIFTEEN-hour trip to Freedom State. Keita sat in economy and Anton Hamm in first class, and as they exited the plane together, Hamm repeated his instructions.

"Nod and indicate that you understand, and otherwise, defer to me. I have your passport, your visa, your papers. Everything will be fine."

They passed through three lines of security with armed guards and immigration and customs officials in uniform. The first line was there to inspect his passport, the second to inspect his visa, the third to go through his bags. At each, Anton Hamm explained that Keita Ali was an elite marathoner from Zantoroland, fresh from the Boston Marathon, come to enter races in Freedom State. Hamm said he was Keita's manager and that he would ensure Keita obeyed all of the country's laws, and then return him to his wife and children and his job as the groundskeeper in a tennis club in Zantoroland before the month-long visitor's visa had expired.

Tennis club? Wife and children? All Keita had to do was nod and smile and watch his visa and passport get stamped and then go back into the pocket inside Hamm's business suit. With that, he was allowed into the third-richest nation in the world.

Inside Clarkson International Airport, Hamm bought Keita a meal and a pack of gum and a few magazines, and then they boarded another flight for Metallurgia, three hours to the east.

IN METALLURGIA, THE FOURTH-LARGEST CITY IN FREEDOM State, Anton Hamm put Keita up in a guest house in a training centre for runners. Keita had a clean room with its own toilet and shower. The guest house had a television, daily newspapers from around the world and rows upon rows of books. They fed him, cafeteria-style, as much as he wanted to eat for breakfast, lunch and dinner, and they showed him the starting point for dozens of kilometres of running trails.

Keita did not dare ask any other runners lodged at the training centre how a person from Zantoroland might slip into hiding in Freedom State. But he knew that he would have to flee before his one-month visa expired, and before Hamm chose to send him back to Zantoroland. Even if Keita ran well in Freedom State, his time here was limited. To stay alive, he had only one option: to go into hiding before he was returned home.

One evening, he went into town to watch a movie and afterwards wandered into a bar. With some hesitation, he approached a black man sitting alone and asked how he could get to AfricTown, which he knew was where the Zantorolanders lived.

"Take the bus to Clarkson," the man said in a low voice, "and when you get there, walk south on AfricTown Road and follow the people."

"And where can I find this bus?" Keita asked.

"Three blocks down. Corner of Millard and Hadfield Streets. But be careful in AfricTown."

"Why?"

"Police raid it, looking for Illegals. I wouldn't go there until things settle down."

"What do you mean?" Keita said.

"It's never been safe to be illegal here, but since the government got elected, they've been deporting people as fast as they can. I don't know what you're running from, brother, but be careful of what you are running to."

Keita asked where a person could hide.

"No papers?" the man asked.

"No," Keita said.

The man said that hotels were obliged to call the police when prospective guests arrived without documentation. But some private homes and guest houses took people in—cash only and no questions asked.

"Thanks, brother," Keita said.

"Peace." The stranger shook his hand.

Keita hesitated, but then he could not stop himself from asking, "Could I use your phone? I need to call my sister, urgently, but she's in the United States. I'll pay you for it."

"Help yourself, man. Don't worry about the money."

Keita called his sister, but she was still not answering and now her voice-mail box was full. A knot formed in his stomach. Would he find Charity? Was she alive? Keita handed back the phone, thanked the fellow and walked away. He had to force back his tears. He had no family with him. No friends. Not a soul who cared the least for him. It was an odd feeling to walk the streets of a country knowing that not a single person knew your name or a thing about you—or would notice if you lived or died.

A WEEK BEFORE THE FIFTEEN-KILOMETRE TEST RACE IN Metallurgia, Anton Hamm announced that he was leaving for a business trip out of town but would be back in time to watch. He took Keita's passport, visa and ID with him. All Keita had was his clothes, the snacks that he had been hoarding from the dining room, the money that he had been saving (twenty dollars a day from Hamm for spending money), plus the two-thousand-dollar signing bonus.

Early the next morning, during breakfast, Keita was summoned to the office for a phone call from Hamm. He reassured Hamm that his run the day before had gone well, his legs felt fine and he was ready for the race.

After Keita hung up, he returned to his room and stuffed his clothes, five apples, four pears, three peanut butter sandwiches, two energy bars and a litre of water into his large knapsack. He shoved his small knapsack inside it, too. He put on his running gear and laced up his shoes. Keita hid his cash in a zippered pocket inside his knapsack, but he kept a fifty-dollar bill in each of his pants pockets. Then he slipped out the door and jogged, with the knapsack pulled against his back, twelve kilometres to the Metallurgia transit station. He paid $150 in cash for a one-way ticket, and in the bathroom, he used the toilet, washed and towelled off, applied deodorant, changed into street clothes and brushed his teeth. Feeling and smelling clean and hoping he looked about as unassuming and ordinary as any black man could look in a country known for deporting every Illegal it could catch, Keita Ali boarded an intercity bus that would leave in a matter of minutes. A day-old *Clarkson Post* had been left on the seat he chose in the middle of the bus, and he made a point of looking at the sports pages because that seemed like something an ordinary Freedom Statonian would do. Perhaps the strategy worked. Nobody stopped, interrogated or looked at him. The bus left at the scheduled hour, although it was only half full at the time.

It was the strangest bus ride Keita had ever taken. There were no chickens or goats aboard. There was only one passenger per seat, and no one stood in the aisles or sat among luggage on top of the bus. As a matter of fact, they didn't even *have* luggage on top of the bus. Keita stowed his knapsack in a space above his seat.

Not a single person sang or laughed or danced during the twenty-six-hour trip. Nobody turned on a transistor radio; in fact, no one seemed to carry one. No strangers met, argued about politics, shared a sandwich or discovered that they were distant relatives. Keita looked out the windows anxiously: Would they come up to police stations or army barracks and be halted there? Would roving bands of soldiers board the bus? There were no checkpoints along the highway, and no soldiers entered the bus to find his passport missing and wait for a bribe. Every six hours, the bus stopped at a gas station and passengers were told that they had ten minutes to get out and stretch or buy a snack. Except to relieve himself, guzzle water and refill his bottle, Keita stayed on the bus, slouched low in his seat.

Apart from the absence of human conversation, it was the most comfortable, commodious, odourless and painless bus ride in the history of mankind. At the end of the trip, which terminated at the very hour the bus schedule had predicted, Keita and forty-nine other passengers were discharged from the vehicle. He followed the others, all of whom acted as if they were complete strangers, as if they had never travelled together or eaten side by side or slept under the very same moving roof.

Keita Ali was anonymous, alone and about to go underground in Clarkson, population 4.5 million—the capital and the biggest city of Freedom State. Nobody knew him here. If something happened to him, nobody would think to notify his sister. Nobody would even know where to find her. Keita Ali could not afford to get caught. If he were deported, he would likely be executed. And then Charity would be alone. If any immigration official or police officer approached him, Keita would run for his life.

PART TWO

Freedom State, 2018

VIOLA HILL PASSED THE TWO-KILOMETRE MARKER in her racing chair. She was making good time on the harbourfront boardwalk. At seven o'clock on a Wednesday morning, there were no toddlers dashing out in front of her, no grannies standing in the middle of the path, no oblivious smokers and no dogs off-leash as Viola wheeled at sixteen kilometres an hour. The sun was coming up. To Viola's right, it struck the waters of Ten-Mile Inlet at a low angle, and to her left, it washed the white stones of the government buildings in soft light. Viola would do a U-turn at the commercial harbour and get back home in time to shower, eat and make it to her shift at the paper. Viola liked to arrive early. Always.

Viola had a cellphone strapped to her arm and plugged into her earbuds. Mick Jagger was getting no satisfaction. Damn right. Viola had been trying for two years to get off the sports page, and she couldn't get any satisfaction either.

Viola had nothing against sports. She liked to work out, and she liked the burn in her biceps, triceps and deltoids when she wheeled three mornings a week. Yes, she liked sports, but she wanted to *write* about news. She wanted people to look for her stories and read them, without knowing or caring that she was blagaybulled—black, gay and disabled—and proud of it. "Blagaybulled" was Viola's own word, and she wanted her words to fly without being weighed down by her identity. In sports, she could not escape it. Every team manager, athlete and sports reader knew her. And she knew them. She knew which ones were thinking, *Here comes that bigmouth in the wheelchair.*

She was strong. And fast. Viola easily overtook walkers and joggers on the boardwalk. So it surprised her when a runner came up from behind and shot past her. This was no jogger. This man was flying. Slim, fit and running faster than 3:30 per kilometre but not even looking like he was working. Black. Short, tightly cropped hair. Medium height. He wasn't wearing long, loose, baggy shorts that hung almost all the way to the knees. No sir, this man had proper marathon shorts, slit up the side of the thighs. His hamstrings were as well defined as rope, and his calves bulged like rocks. He lifted off the balls of his feet as he entered his stride and spent more time airborne than on the ground. Viola enjoyed the view of his working backside until he disappeared around a bend, and then she wheeled faster to bring him back into sight. As she rounded the bend, only a kilometre from the end of the boardwalk and the piers by the commercial harbour, where the multicoloured containers were lifted on and off the decks of the huge ships, the runner was coming back her way. At the same time that she saw him—mid-twenties, baby face, clean-shaven—she heard the sirens.

The runner said, "I'd turn back, if I were you."

"Why?" she asked.

"Mob, up ahead." And then he was gone.

Viola kept wheeling onward. If there was a mob, that's where she would head—and quicker than before. She tilted forward into a racing position and pumped harder with her arms, catching the wheels with her gloved hands and pushing down to accelerate. What were the sirens for, and where was this mob? There. Where the boardwalk ended, up ahead. Five police cruisers, two paddy wagons and a handful of Freedom State Immigration Enforcement vehicles were parked helter-skelter in a lot. There was a boat at the wharf. About ten metres long. Chipped paint. The *Voyager*. Rough shape. But the boat wasn't as shabby as the small crowd of black people on deck. One by one, they were being led stumbling over a gangplank and onto the pier, where they were handcuffed by a police officer and led to the paddy wagon.

Viola wheeled up to the pier. "Excuse me," she called up to an immigration enforcement official. "Excuse me. What's going on here?"

He ignored her.

"Hey, buddy, what's going on?" she said.

"Beat it," he said.

Viola removed the phone from the strap on her shoulder and began filming. All those leaving the boat were black. Mostly men. All thin.

The immigration official turned to face her directly. "I said beat it."

"I'm with the *Telegram*," she said.

"And I'm Barack Obama," he said. The man was as white as paste.

She wheeled past him, right up to the police paddy wagon into which the refugees were being shoved. She saw five men and a woman in there and took a picture with her cellphone.

A man was led in handcuffs right past her.

"Sir," she said, "I'm with the *Clarkson Evening Telegram*. Who are you, and why are you being arrested?"

He was about twenty-five years old and bleeding from a cut above his eye.

"Did someone hit you?" Viola asked.

The man took a look at the officer leading him, and said, "No, I just bumped my head."

"Where are you from?"

"No talking to media," the police officer said.

"There is no law that says you can't talk to the media," Viola said. She tried again. "Where are you from?"

"Zantoroland," the man said. The officer rushed him into the paddy wagon.

"You, ma'am," Viola said to a woman. She was about twenty, walking with a pronounced limp and carrying a bundle of rags in her arms. "Why is this happening?"

"Three weeks on that boat," the woman said. "No toilet, bad water, food rations. Now I can't wake my baby."

"What's your name?"

"Dolores Williams. Can someone help my baby?"

Viola looked around. "I'll see if I can find someone."

"Bless you! And tell my sister I made it. Loretta Williams, in Yagwa City."

A police constable standing on the far side of the paddy wagon appeared to be telling people what to do. Viola wheeled over to him.

"A woman over there can't wake her baby."

"She'll have to wait."

"But the baby could be dying!" Viola said.

"Not my concern."

"I work for a national news outlet and you are telling me that you don't care if a baby is dying?"

"If you weren't way down in that contraption, I'd smack you and arrest you for disturbing the peace. Beat it, before I get angry."

Viola aimed her phone at him. If he did something stupid, she would catch it on video.

"Viola Hill, reporter with the *Clarkson Evening Telegram*, and I'm simply asking you where you are taking these men and women—and why."

The constable started walking away.

"I'm going to call 911 if you don't go see that baby!"

"Christ almighty," he said. "Where's the damn baby?"

Viola pointed to the mother, and the constable walked her way.

Suddenly, cars began streaming into the parking lot by the wharf. Men and women, all white, mostly over forty, gathered at the pier. There were about a dozen of them, three with placards: "Enough Is Enough," "Send 'Em Back" and "Who Invited Them?"

Viola took photos of the placards. Then she wheeled up to the demonstrators.

"Sir," she said to one, "I'm Viola Hill with the *Clarkson Evening Telegram*. Can you tell me why you are here?"

"Who are you?"

"I just told you who I am. Who are you?"

"We're with SIB."

"SIB?"

"Send Illegals Back."

"Who told you that these people were being arrested?" Viola asked.

"We scan the police radios. Our country is wasting good resources detaining this scum. Should have turned the boat around and sent it back home."

"What is your name?"

"Don."

"Last name?"

"None of your business."

"If you turned this boat around, those people would die."

"Is that our problem? We didn't invite them to Freedom State. Our country is not a house without a door. They can't just keep crashing into it with no passport, no documentation, no legal right to be here."

"Why, exactly, are you so worked up about refugees? A mother who was just arrested is worried about whether her baby is still alive."

"And why are you such a bleeding heart? How do I even know you're a journalist? You don't look like a journalist. Do you have ID? How do I know that you're not a refugee too?"

"Just tell me what your problem is with the refugees. So readers will understand."

"In case you haven't noticed, our country is going down the drain. We're supposed to be a wealthy nation. But we have violence, unemployment, dropping exports and then the whole black market system in AfricTown is draining our economy. It costs thousands of dollars to detain, clothe and feed an Illegal for a year. Take 'em out of prisons and send 'em back to where they came from, and bulldoze AfricTown while you're at it."

There was a break in the parade of people, and Viola saw one man lift his hands up and away from the officer arresting him.

"I will go peacefully," the man said. "But no handcuffs. I'm no criminal!"

Two police officers began beating him with billy clubs. He crumpled to the ground. When they stopped, he offered his wrists.

The protestor named Don yelled, "Are you ready? Not so cocky now, eh?"

"Sir," Viola asked the refugee, "what is your name?"

"Desmond Torrance," he mumbled.

"Why did you make the trip?"

"My days were numbered. I took my chances."

The police constable came to stand in front of her, blocking Viola's view of Torrance.

"Listen, girlfriend," he said sarcastically, "back off."

"I'm a reporter with the—"

"I don't give a shit who you say you are. You're impeding police business."

One of the demonstrators with a placard shouted, "Arrest the bitch. Send 'em all back home."

Viola looked at the constable. "What about the demonstrators? Are you asking *them* to leave?"

"Last warning," the cop said.

Viola turned, retreated ten metres, and spun her chair around once more to face the cop. "Satisfied?"

"I'm warning you to stay out of the way. No communicating with the criminals."

"Criminals?"

"None of them have permission to enter Freedom State. This makes them Illegals, which makes them criminals."

Viola did a head count. Fifty people arrested: thirty men, ten women, eight children and two babies. None of them looked like they had showered, eaten properly or slept in weeks.

The police officer slammed the paddy wagon doors. "Before I lock up, there's room for one more," he said to Viola.

"I'm going, I'm going," she said to the constable. "But what's your name?"

"It's on my badge," he said.

Constable Devlin James.

"Where are these people to be detained?"

"Same place we put any other criminals. The City Jail."

VIOLA SKIPPED A SHOWER AND MADE IT TO THE NEWSROOM in time to write and file the story and to send in the photos she had taken, before beginning her shift for the sports department.

Mike Bolton, the city news editor who had resisted every non-sports story she had pitched, called her to his desk.

"Viola, what's your beat?"

"I assume that is a rhetorical question," she said.

"Did anyone ask you to leave the world of sports and file a story about a routine arrest of no consequence?"

"It was on my own time," Viola said. "And it's not routine."

"We have refugees being arrested—off boats or in AfricTown—every week."

"This story—"

Bolton put up his hand. "Stop. Just stop. Next time you have the grand idea to try your hand at writing news, how about going through me first? I have no room in the paper for this story."

"Bolton, your head is up your ass."

"Keep talking. I could have you disciplined for insubordination."

"You wouldn't know a news story if it yanked the pillow out from under your head."

"I am the city news editor! And you're a—"

"What am I, Bolton? Go on. Say it."

"A sports reporter."

CHAPTER SIX

O H, THIS WAS FUNNY. THIS WAS RICH. VIOLA HILL had been agitating for months to get off the sports page. So she could hardly refuse when Mike Bolton sent her out on an assignment dull enough to induce a coma: the Annual Awards Luncheon for the Best Essays Written by High School Students in Freedom State. Bolton said a major political figure would attend. Maybe even the prime minister. Whoever attended, Bolton said, she should get a quote.

Viola arrived early to get a spot at the front of the Dixon Theatre. Being low down in a wheelchair, she had to be in the heart of the action. The only way to grab someone for a quick interview would be to catch their eye or call loudly. The awards were for essays about science, geography, literature, culture and politics. There were two categories: one for students ages fifteen and under, and the other for students sixteen to eighteen. Three of the ten winners hailed from the same school: the Clarkson Academy for the Gifted. Honestly. Anybody suffering from sleep problems should just throw their meds in the trash bin and come to this ceremony. The prime minister had skipped the event and sent a cabinet minister instead.

When it came time to award the grand prize, Viola stopped yawning. It was for the best essay written by a high school student of any age, on any subject. All other award winners had received a thousand-dollar cheque, but this prize came with a catch. The essay writers had had to supply a paragraph explaining what they needed to further their own academic advancement and outlining a reasonable budget.

Federal Immigration Minister Rocco Calder was called to the stage to announce the winner. He was a tall, buff, blue-eyed, square-jawed, middle-aged white dude who was a recreational runner—Viola respected him for that, if not for his politics. Calder, a fabulously successful used car salesman and newcomer to politics, didn't know a damn thing about immigration. He had been transportation minister but had recently acquired the immigration portfolio in a surprise cabinet shuffle. It had to be the worst job in the world: to preside over a national effort to deport people without documentation. But he had no voice, authority or independence in cabinet. Everybody knew that the prime minister and his advisers ran and controlled immigration policies and practices. The government called undocumented people "Illegals," but Viola refused to use the term. As far as she was concerned, it was fair to accuse somebody of *doing* something illegal but not to say that they *were* illegal. Viola wondered if Calder believed in the "Deport the Illegals" movement that had brought his government to power, or if he was just a lemming.

Calder took the steps to the stage two at a time. Students, teachers, parents and education officials filled the auditorium. Calder told the audience that the prime minister sent his regrets but had asked him to convey his regards, and that he was proud to participate in a ceremony celebrating academic excellence. Yada, yada, yada. He summoned the donor of the funds for the best essay prize. A woman climbed up the stairs. White woman, as old as the hills. Blue-eyed too, and hair turned as white as a cloud. Steady step, and a no-bullshit gaze as she looked over the audience. Calder mentioned her name, but Viola didn't catch it. She checked her program. *Ivernia Beech.*

"Ladies and gentlemen," Calder said. Viola sighed. Loudly. What self-respecting modern woman wanted to be called a lady these days? And gentlemen were a vanishing species. "Ladies and gentlemen," the minister repeated, "the best essay by a high school student in Freedom State in the year 2018 is entitled 'North and South, We Are All Ortizians.' The winner, from the Clarkson Academy for the Gifted, is . . . John Falconer."

There was a small round of applause. The very title of the essay seemed to slap the ruling Family Party in the face. Freedom State was in the North Ortiz Sea, Zantoroland in the South Ortiz Sea. The Family Party had come to power for the first time in the history of Freedom State two years earlier and was implementing policies to draw a firm line between those seas, to stop the ships carrying refugees north and to live up to its election campaign promises to initiate a robust deportation program.

"John, would you come to the stage?"

A boy ran up the stairs in his Clarkson Academy uniform. But his tie was loosened, and he wore running shoes. He looked twelve years old. Didn't look like he even belonged in high school. And there was one other thing. Every other prize winner was white. Virtually every person in the audience, except for Viola, was white. But this kid had curly hair and a coffee and cream complexion, and it was clear to Viola that he had some black in him.

"Congratulations, John," the minister said, shaking the boy's hand.

"Thank you, Minister. Could I get an interview with you?"

People laughed.

"Why sure, boy," the minister said.

"Do you promise?" the boy said.

The minister's mouth fell open, but he recovered and said, "Yes, I do. How old are you?"

"I'm fifteen, but you should know that 'boy' is a condescending way to refer to people of African heritage."

A murmur went through the crowd, but the minister smiled. "Well, I'm sorry, son, I didn't know about your heritage. I'll give you that interview, but today we're here to congratulate you."

Ivernia Beech shook John's hand vigorously. "Fabulous essay," she said, "just fabulous." Turning to the audience, she read from a slip of paper: "'John has written a historical essay about the racial politics of deportation in Freedom State in the nineteenth century. His prize is ten thousand dollars' worth of computer and video-recording equipment, which he has requested so he can make a documentary film about AfricTown.'"

She gave the boy the cheque. They posed for a photo.

"You're helping me go after a dream," John told her.

"Go do it," she said. "And while you're at it, give 'em hell."

"I intend to," he said. He reached to shake her hand, but she gave him a hug instead.

"When you're eighty-five, you don't get to give out many hugs," she said. People in the audience laughed. "And when you reach my age, you don't always get to do something meaningful. But to help a student move forward with his artistic passion means a great deal to me."

Mrs. Beech gave John a slip of paper and told him to call her up. "Can't cook to save my life, but I'll take you out to lunch." She smiled and exited the stage.

"Son, that's an incredible achievement," the minister said. "But will it be safe for a young fellow to be wandering about AfricTown with a video camera?"

"Should be safe enough," John said. "I live there."

While the audience clapped, Viola scribbled as fast as she could. She looked up and hollered as John walked off the stage. Sometimes hollering was the only way for a woman in a wheelchair to get any attention.

"John Falconer. Over here, please."

He approached her obediently.

"Viola Hill, the *Clarkson Evening Telegram*."

He shook her hand. "Sounds like a good job. One day, I'd like to write for the *Telegram*."

"It's not all it's cracked up to be," Viola said. "But never mind that. Did you say you live in AfricTown?"

"Yes."

"Where?"

"Bungalow Hill. Brown shipping container. Yellow stripes. Next to Water Tap 17."

"Whose child are you?"

"You know AfricTown?" John asked.

"Born and raised," Viola said. "But I'm asking the questions."

"How about we each ask questions," John said, "'cause now I'm making this documentary, and I could talk to you."

"How about we respect the fact that I'm on a deadline for a daily newspaper? So whose child are you?"

"My mom is Mary Falconer. My dad disappeared before I was born. Bartholomew Falconer—you know him?"

"Nope. And you are fifteen and in Grade 9 at the Clarkson Academy for the Gifted."

"Yep! You still live in AfricTown? It'd be hard to move about in a wheelchair."

"I got out when I lost the use of my legs."

"Oh," John said. "I'm sorry about that."

"Don't be," Viola said. "If I hadn't had the accident, I probably would have stayed. And maybe I'd be dead now, or strung out on drugs or booze. I have to ask you this. John, are you black?"

"You know how it works. My mom is white. But my dad, he was mixed. Half and half."

"Good enough for me. According to the customs of this country, he was black and so are you. You ever heard of any other black student at the Clarkson Academy for the Gifted?"

"I'm the first."

"What's tuition cost?"

"Fifty thousand dollars a year."

"You on scholarship?"

"Ain't no other way," he said with a smile.

"Can I get a copy of your essay?"

He pulled folded papers from his inside breast pocket. "Here—"

"I'll get this back to you. Gotta run. Give me your cell and email."

Viola wrote them down, wheeled away and got to Calder before he left. She asked how he felt about awarding a prize to a student who had criticized the country's immigration policies.

Calder said, "Today it's not about politics. It's about academic excellence. I respect this boy's intelligence."

Viola's story made the back of the A section. Her first byline off the sports page. She persuaded Bolton to run a short excerpt from John's essay as a sidebar.

NORTH AND SOUTH, WE ARE ALL ORTIZIANS
BY JOHN FALCONER
GRADE 9, CLARKSON ACADEMY FOR THE GIFTED

We brought thousands of people from Zantoroland in chains, enslaved them here in Freedom State and used them to build what is now one of the world's biggest economies. But when slavery was abolished in 1834, we solved the "Negro problem" by deporting those same slaves and their descendants. We sent them back by the shipload into the South Ortiz Sea, paying Zantoroland a twenty-five-pound-sterling resettlement fee for each man, woman or child repatriated.

It was a complex job, so authorities in Freedom State created a racial grading system to determine who could stay and who had to go. If you were defined as full black, half black (mulatto), one-quarter black (quadroon) or even one-eighth black (octoroon), you were packed up and sent to Zantoroland. Even if you'd never seen the country. Even if you were born in Freedom State. But if you were defined as one-sixteenth black (quintoon) or less, then you were allowed to reintegrate into the white race and stay in Freedom State.

Most blacks were indeed forced to leave. Some managed to stay. Others began returning illegally in boats. Although the trans-Ortizian slave trade ended in 1834 and the Grand Repatriation drew to a close some two decades later, Freedom State and Zantoroland continue to be connected. A steady stream of migrants continue to move north, settling in AfricTown on the southern outskirts of our capital city of Clarkson. People refer all the time to AfricTown as a slum, a ghetto, a township. It is none of the above. AfricTown is a community. Some hundred thousand people live there, many of them in fifteen thousand used shipping containers owned and rented out by the unofficial queen of AfricTown, Lula DiStefano. I know. I live there, and Lula is my landlady.

Viola had hoped Bolton would continue to let her write for the news department. But she had only been sent to cover the national essay awards because the education reporter had called in sick that day. He returned to the job twenty-four hours later, and Viola returned to sports.

CHAPTER SEVEN

S TERN. SMUG. YOUNG. WHAT DID THEY KNOW? WELL, it wasn't so much what they knew but what they could do. Three young men from the Office for Independent Living, ready to assess her ability to drive, manage her own money and live alone. She couldn't help but think about how badly dressed they were. But she had to get a grip. Ivernia Beech absolutely had to concentrate.

Interrogator Number One stood to get a glass of water. His dress shirt was wrinkled and dislodged from his pants. What was he? Twenty-six? Young enough to be her great-grandson. He was saying something. This was not a court of law, he was saying, but it could make recommendations about her fitness for independent living. And now he was asking a question. *Concentrate.* Yes, she told him, she was aware of who she was and where she was at the time of the accident. He asked where, for the record, was that? Well, she said, it was directly outside the Lox and Bagel on Aberdeen Road, two blocks north of Ruddings Park. Snidely, foolishly, she added, This is in the city of Clarkson and country of Freedom State. He ignored her and asked, When exactly was the accident? Ivernia wanted to ask why he didn't look it up in his stupid report. But that wouldn't be politic, would it? So she just said that the accident took place yesterday at 9 a.m. He asked where she had been going. To the Lox and Bagel, she said.

Now it was the second interrogator's turn. His shirt too was in need of ironing. What was it with twenty-something bureaucrats these days? Did no one teach them how to dress? Was a country's wealth inversely proportional to the ability of its young men to don a pressed shirt in the morning? He asked about Ivernia's son. Naturally, that got her wondering about the worst possible outcome. No matter that she was white in a country where that mattered, educated and well off. When you were over eighty and caused a car accident, you could lose it all. For starters, they could strip her of her driver's licence. Permanently. They could tell the Office for Independent Living that Ivernia Beech was not fit for single living. This, of course, was exactly what her son, Jimmy, wanted: Termination of her driver's licence. Forced eviction from her home. Power of attorney over her bank accounts. With a son like that, who needed enemies? Terrorists who blew up airplanes had nothing over an underemployed, twice-divorced son with nothing better to do than go after his mother's assets. Any man over fifty who still went by the name of Jimmy was a man not to be trusted. Even if he was her son. Thank God Jimmy wasn't in the room. Ivernia already had her hands full.

Now came the last interrogator's turn.

"May I call you Ivernia?" he asked.

"I am three times your age, and you may call me Mrs. Beech," she said.

"Well enough, Mrs. Beech. Could you tell us one more time, in your own words, what happened yesterday?"

Ivernia drew a long breath. Some twenty years ago, when she was in her sixties and still had relatively nimble fingers, she had taken up the classical guitar. If you played an instrument—something new, something you had never touched before—it was said to prevent your brain from rotting. The guitar instructor introduced her to the music of Fernando Sor and encouraged Ivernia to breathe while she played. She told him she had come to study music, not yoga. She had to abandon the instrument after it gave her tennis elbow. And now, as she ran once more through the events leading up to the accident, she exhaled slowly—just as the guitar teacher had taught her—and replayed in her mind the single moment of kindness and light in an otherwise all-around shitty day.

Ivernia had been driving south on Aberdeen Road. She had already passed Main Street. And Queen Street. Now she was entering the thick of The Village—the attractive section of Clarkson lined with cafés, shops, beauty salons and bookstores. Five blocks ahead were the Parliament Building on the left and the Freedom Building with offices for federal politicians on the right. Beyond them was the giant Ruddings Park, and beyond that the railway tracks, the formal end of the city, and after five kilometres of no man's land, the sudden mushrooming of AfricTown. But Ivernia wasn't going anywhere near that far. The Lox and Bagel was located right here, in the heart of The Village, and all Ivernia had to do was find a parking spot.

She was driving her late husband's 1999 Oldsmobile Intrigue. It was nineteen years old, not a speck of rust. Oversized, like a car fuelled with steroids, but it worked like a charm. Southbound traffic kept Ivernia to twenty kilometres an hour. It was a warm spring day. She had the windows down. Above the sound of traffic, she heard a man singing. Good voice. He had a lilting, foreign accent. And he was singing a country song. She glanced to her left. Nothing. To her right. There he was. A young black man was running as fast as her car. What a joy it must be, Ivernia thought, to move one's body with that ease and speed. Like Ivernia, he was heading south on Aberdeen. She wondered why he was in the road, but then she noticed that pedestrians clogged the sidewalk. He was in his mid-twenties. As thin as a pencil. Strapped to his waistband was an iPod, and from it white wires ran up to the buds in his ears. Clearly, he had no idea how loud he was singing the country hit that had become as familiar as the national anthem.

I been running for you, baby
Running all the time
But you're running for another heart
And the heart you want ain't mine.

Ivernia had turned off the radio a good twenty times in the last year just to avoid hearing another note of that song, but it sounded funny and somehow touching coming from this strange runner. Traffic slowed. He ran by her door. His head was bobbing to the music, and yet his eyes were wide open. He caught her looking at him and smiled. She smiled too, and then she pulled ahead of him as the lane before her opened up. It was odd that a man moving that fast could sing as he ran.

She left him behind as she accelerated. Traffic moved quickly, and Ivernia caught two green lights in a row. There, up ahead just one block, was the Lox and Bagel. Parking on Aberdeen was murder. But just ahead of her, directly in front of the Lox and Bagel, a car pulled out. Ivernia slowed down. A space big enough for her Oldsmobile. No fire hydrant. No reason she couldn't park there. She detested parallel parking, but there was no option. She pulled up beside a Jaguar, put the Olds into reverse and checked the rearview mirror. Lots of pedestrian traffic on the sidewalk, but there was nothing between her and the BMW parked behind her. She backed halfway in, turning the wheel clockwise to ease into the spot and then counterclockwise to straighten it out. She stopped midway to make sure she was fine. The Olds was such a big car. Everything looked okay. And then it happened. She was about to press down on the accelerator, ever so gently, to continue reversing, when a baby cried. Loudly. She had meant to jam her foot on the brake, but instead, she mashed it down on the accelerator. The Olds shot back like a spooked horse, and the next instant, Ivernia felt metal crumple and heard glass shatter. A woman began screaming. Ivernia couldn't see the woman or the baby. Had she hit them? She flipped the gear into drive, pushed on the accelerator pedal again, and charged forward, catching and demolishing the back left end of the Jaguar. She put her car in park and turned off the ignition, then opened the door to more screaming.

Ivernia got out of the car. A woman on the sidewalk stood next to a stroller. The baby was in her arms.

"Did I hit you?" Ivernia asked.

"My car!"

"Are you hurt?" Ivernia asked.

"No, but almost. I was this close," the woman said, holding her thumb and index finger apart, "when you smashed into my car. And here I was with my baby."

"But are you okay?"

"This close!" the woman shouted.

Then the singing runner showed up. "Hello, ma'am," he said to the young mother. "May I help?"

She looked grateful. The runner lifted the stroller back to the far side of the sidewalk. The woman had dropped a bag of groceries. He retrieved cans and bags, bending and straightening until he had stored them all in the stroller. The mother spoke to him reverently. It was hard to believe that such kindness could come from a mouth that moments ago had been so harsh.

"That is so sweet of you," she said.

"No worries." The runner then saw Ivernia. Looked straight at her. "Ma'am, are you all right?"

"Yes, quite." But she wasn't all right at all, and he could see it in her eyes.

"Why don't you sit down?" he said.

There was a bench at the edge of the sidewalk, in front of the Lox and Bagel. He led her to it, resting his fingertips on her shoulder. She tried to remember the last time anyone had touched any part of her body in a kind, solicitous way.

"Everything is going to be okay. Nobody is hurt, right?"

She nodded. He straightened, went to her car door, pulled out her purse and car keys and returned with them.

"Sit here. You will need your things. Are you okay, ma'am? Breathe a little."

Ivernia stared at him with glassy eyes. The earbuds were strung over his shoulder. From them, she detected the tinny sound of country music.

"I heard you singing, back there," she said.

He smiled. "I sing when I train," he said.

Train, she thought. What an interesting verb. It must have been inspired by the noun. *To train*. Meaning, to put oneself in motion, just like a train. She heard a siren. She looked up and saw the police vehicle two blocks away.

He said, "God bless, must run, take care. Don't worry. Everything will be okay."

Once more he touched her shoulder. Ivernia felt the calm spread through her body. Nobody was hurt. What was the worst that could happen?

"Wait," she said. "What is your name?"

He hesitated, smiled once more and said, "Roger Bannister. Goodbye and good luck." He set off running again, southbound on Aberdeen Road in the direction of Ruddings Park.

"Roger Bannister," she mumbled to herself. She knew that name. The British runner. The first one to break the four-minute mile. He did it on May 6, 1954. Sixty-four years ago. She remembered. She was twenty-one years old, and it was the day that she and Ernie married. She wished that she had had time to tell that to the runner.

A hand was on her shoulder, a firm hand.

"Ma'am. Ma'am. Were you involved in the accident? Are you the owner of that Oldsmobile?"

She looked into the eyes of a square-jawed police officer whose expression seemed to say, *You've gone and ruined my perfectly good day.* Perhaps Ivernia should have waited for a lawyer. Or fought the charge. Or sought to plea bargain. She knew all about these things. But she was an old woman, and she had no mind for subtleties, so she just looked at him and said, "It all comes down to one thing, Officer. I screwed up. So can we get on with it?"

It was a day later now, and her licence was temporarily suspended, her car impounded, and she was feeling entirely suffocated in the meeting room of the Office for Independent Living. She was bursting with impatience. She wanted out. Whatever they were going to do to her, she wanted it to be over. So here she was telling her three inquisitors one more time that she realized the gravity of the situation but did not want a lawyer.

"Could we just get this done?" she asked, keeping her hands under the table so the three inquisitors could not see them shaking. When you reached the age of eighty-five, hands were simply not to be trusted. Ivernia tried to calm herself by thinking of the gentle face of the runner. The one who had stopped to help everybody, herself included. The runner was the only person who had said a kind word to her that entire day. She wondered where he was from. Zantoroland? From what Ivernia had read in the papers, the country was a mess. There were reports that the Zantoroland government had been torturing and executing members of its Faloo ethnic minority, so people were fleeing the country. But here in Freedom State, the government led by the Family Party kept deporting refugees back to Zantoroland.

Ivernia hoped the runner was not a refugee, or, if he was, that his life had not been too hard and that he would not be caught and deported like the others. She focused on her breathing and on good thoughts. Fernando Sor . . . the runner singing country music . . . marrying her husband on the same day that Roger Bannister ran the Miracle Mile in 3:59. Ernie had been good to her, from their first day together to their last.

Breathe, Ivernia. Breathe, keep breathing, and just answer their stupid questions.

CHAPTER EIGHT

YOU WERE SUPPOSED TO LIVE WITH A MOTHER OR A father or some sort of caregiver when you were fifteen years old, but John had been on his own for a while. His mother would surely make it back home eventually, when she was healthy, and John would welcome her. He tried to remind himself that his mother and he had been through this ordeal before and had always found their way back together. It would be good to live with her again in the half shipping container that they rented from Lula DiStefano, queen of AfricTown. But for now, at the start of his third term as a Grade 9 student at the Clarkson Academy for the Gifted, John was supervised by Lula but living alone in the container next to Water Tap 17 in the Bungalow Hill district of AfricTown. Some hundred thousand people lived in AfricTown, many of them—like John and his mother—paying rent money to Lula.

John had not seen his mother in two weeks. The last visit had not gone well. She was still in the secured area of the Wintergreen Psychiatric Institute, and she was still speechless and lying in a fetal position. He didn't like having to play the role of parent and ask the nurses questions: were they bathing her enough, changing her clothes, brushing her teeth, and what about that big bed sore on her hip? He especially hadn't enjoyed it when some power-tripping nurse tried to turn the tables and interrogate him about where he was living and who was taking care of him. What is your street address? she asked. There is no street address, he said, it's AfricTown. Who is taking care of you? she said. Lula Brown, he said, lying. Where does she work? She has no job, John said. What is her telephone number? Again he lied: We don't have telephone service. He got out of there before she could consult with her superiors or try to interrogate him further.

The next time, instead of visiting the hospital, John would call and see if his mom was well enough to come to the phone on the psych ward. It was too upsetting to see his mother reverted to infancy. And he had a sudden, great responsibility on his shoulders and could not afford to screw up. He now had the fancy computer and video-recording equipment worth ten thousand dollars. Using his overall 95 percent average and his position as the third-highest-ranked student in all of Grade 9, John had won permission from his headmistress to spend his spring term filming the documentary about AfricTown and the fate of Zantorolanders in Freedom State. He was exempted from all but his Journalism in the Age of Apathy class, provided that he made up the other courses in the summer. He had much work to do, and he couldn't afford to get caught up in a web of well-intentioned questions from nurses in his mom's hospital. Questions like that could lead to nothing but bad results. In John's opinion, well-intentioned adults were inordinately gifted at fucking up the lives of parentless teenagers who were perfectly capable of carrying on by themselves.

Clarkson Academy admitted thirty-five students in Grade 7 and kept them until graduation from Grade 12. Two years earlier, when John had written the entrance exams, he competed against thirteen hundred other students. He placed nineteenth, which was good enough to get in but not good enough for a full scholarship. You had to place in the top ten to get that. They offered him ten thousand dollars, far short of the fifty thousand he needed to attend. He was able to talk them up. Yes, he truly lived in AfricTown, he told them. Yes, he was truly a citizen of Freedom State, and here were his citizenship papers. Born and raised in the country. As was his mother.

Yes, he was in fact the child who had written the entrance exams. They put him through more tests to be sure and then agreed to cover twenty-five thousand of his fees, plus his uniform, plus his books, plus hot meals at school. But he would have to find his own transportation to school, because it was considered unsafe to send a school bus to fetch him in AfricTown. And he would have to find sponsors to cover the remainder of his annual tuition fee.

So John had approached Lula DiStefano, who in addition to being his landlady, happened to own the infamous Bombay Booty brothel and the nightclub known as the Pit.

"Say what?" she said. "You? Puny little child of AfricTown? You telling me that little Mr. Falconer has a brain on fire?"

John said that he could attend the school if he could find the twenty-five thousand a year to pay the rest of his tuition.

"How will you get to school and back?" she asked.

"I'll walk."

"How far is it?"

"Five kilometres, one way."

"You'll wear out a pair of shoes every month."

"I might need some help with that too."

So Lula had provided twenty-five thousand the first year. He finished fourth in his class in Grade 7, and after that he was on full scholarship, but she still had to pay for books, uniforms, shoes and special outings, and she ended up giving him spending money for clothes and food, because his mother didn't make much as a house-cleaner, even when she wasn't in the psych ward.

All of this was very good. Except for the ways that it was very bad. "I own you for life, child" was how Lula put it. She acted like she meant it too.

JOHN AWOKE WITH A START, AND WITH HIS BACK SOAKED IN sweat. He'd been having nightmares again. In his dreams, his mother had been pacing at night and getting into all sorts of trouble while he slept. But as he climbed out of bed, he reassured himself that all was fine: she was still in the hospital, and he was still alone at home.

It was a tiny living space, even when his mother was not there. Their one room, half a shipping container, rented for a hundred dollars a month, though Lula eased up on the payment obligations whenever John's mother was too ill to work. In the room: a four-drawer dresser for all their clothes, two single Murphy beds that folded up against the wall when not occupied, one fold-up kitchen table that doubled as a homework desk, two chairs, a portable stove attached to a butane tank, a large cooler that with ice became a fridge, a transistor radio, several reading lamps with spare light bulbs and spare batteries, and four pots whose purposes were never inter-changeable—a soup pot, a dishes pot, a wash pot and a chamber pot.

John heated up water on his butane stove, washed his hands and face, and then stepped out of the container in his underwear to sniff the morning air—the March day was about twenty degrees Celsius and clear and sunny—and to throw the water into the open ditch that passed behind the water tap, carrying sewage, waste and grey water to what everyone called the Cesspool at the far southern end of AfricTown. The end of the community where nobody wanted to live and only the most desperate did.

After pitching the water, John put on his shorts, T-shirt and runners. His school uniform, tie and dress shoes were in his locker at school. No sense wearing out the clothes on the long walk to the Bombay Booty and then to school, and no sense putting on any fancy clothes that might get him mugged in AfricTown. John's mother liked to cook him porridge, when she was home. Raisins, cinnamon, oatmeal, a touch of cream and sugar on top—she knew how to make it perfectly. But she wasn't home, and he didn't have time to cook and clean, so he went to the Korner Kook, as he did most mornings.

Jerzy Kook Kook had been selling street eats, as he called them, since before John was born. John had once asked him how old he was, and Jerzy said, "Beyond dying." He stood bow-legged at his butane-fired frying pan in his shorts, muscle shirt and sandals, with spatula in hand, taking orders from the five people lined up ahead of John. Jerzy had a box of eggs, three slow-cookers of rice that had been boiled up with onions, red peppers and carrots, and his crate of oranges, which he called Zantoroland Fresh. For fifty cents, John got one fried egg, a big scoop of rice and half a sliced orange. He had to bring his own plate and fork, but that didn't take long to wash.

"What'll it be, Professor?" Jerzy said, when John stood before him.

Jerzy always called him that. It annoyed John, but he had discovered that if he complained about it, the old man would just keep saying it.

"The usual," John said.

"You're too young for the usual. How about lox and cream cheese with, whaddya call it, eggs Benedictine?"

"It's eggs Benedict, and you don't have any of that stuff. Just the usual, please."

"Thank you, Professor, for correcting my English. I charge everybody else a dollar for this meal, but you get the gifted student rate."

"Thanks, Jerzy. I'm in a hurry today. Gotta work before school."

"Stay outta that brothel, once you hit puberty."

"Thanks a lot, Jerzy. I already hit puberty. You need proof?"

"I ain't need no proof of puberty at fucking six o'clock on a Wednesday morning," Jerzy said. "Give me your plate. Your egg is ready. Fried, over, and not quite runny. I make the best damn eggs in AfricTown."

"Jerzy, you make the best damn eggs in the Ortiz Sea. North or south. Hell, let me be the first to say it. You make the best damn eggs in the entire Indian Ocean."

"That's better. Be nice to me, boy, or I'll up your rate."

"I'm always nice to you."

"I'm telling you, don't go wasting your hormones in that brothel. Not a good place for a young buck with a brain, and I'm serious."

"Okay, Jerzy. I hear you. Gotta go."

"Go be bright. Go be the best damn student there is. What was your rank when you finished eighth grade?"

John sighed. "Number three."

"Ain't good enough. Here's what I want from you, if you want to keep up your egg scholarship."

"Egg scholarship?"

"A fifty-cent breakfast that costs everybody else one dollar hard cash is what I mean by an egg scholarship. You want to keep it, you got to be the best damn student in the school. In the country. In the Ortiz Sea, north and south. And in the whole motherfucking Indian Ocean. From the British Indian Ocean Territory all the way south to Antarctica, and from Madagascar to Australia, you gotta be number one."

"I'll see what I can do about that, Jerzy. But now I have to get to work in that brothel."

THE BOMBAY BOOTY HAD RUNNING WATER AND ELECTRIC-ity. Marble floors, rooms with king-sized beds and ensuites. It was the best-known brothel in Freedom State. The Pit next door, where brothel clients went to eat and drink and to watch dance and music shows and bet on snakepit wrestlers, had the finest amenities going. The two buildings were connected, so customers could move discreetly from one to the other. Lula DiStefano owned both businesses, as well as most of the fifteen thousand shipping containers in AfricTown. Of those fifteen thousand homes, only the few hundred nearest to the Bombay Booty had running water and electricity. Some of the others took bootleg electricity, but one or two people died each year trying to hook up wires to siphon electricity from the main line and run it to their homes. The containers shared public taps. There were about a thousand of them, or one for every fifteen shipping containers, with an average of seven people in each container. Some of the containers had windows, but none of them had bathrooms. You could go to the crapping grounds for free. Or you could use one of the concrete bunkers that doubled as outhouses and have somebody carry away your pee and shit, but you had to pay for that: fifty cents to pee, and a dollar for a dump. Most people just used buckets in their homes and dumped the waste in the ditches that wound through AfricTown, all sloping south toward the Cesspool.

Other than plumbing and utilities, you could get pretty well anything you wanted in AfricTown, if you were willing to pay: knives, guns, wine, whisky, cellphones, milk, cereal, eggs and bread, butane, camping lamps of every size and strength, transistor radios and batteries. You could buy inner tubes and spare parts for bicycles, and you could pay any number of "wheel doctors" a few dollars to fix a broken bike. Most people walked or biked to Clarkson and hauled their staples back. It made no sense to park in AfricTown or leave your vehicle unattended, unless you parked in the Bombay Booty's lot and paid for the car patrol service. Just a few weeks ago, two undercover police officers had come to AfricTown in an unmarked vehicle, which they neglected to park in the secured lot. While the cops were inside Bombay Booty, the car had its tires and wheels taken. The doors were removed. The car radio was stolen. Lula expressed her regrets but said that the best she could do was have the carcass of the car loaded onto a flatbed truck and hauled back to the cop shop, and, of course, give the cops a lift into town. Discreetly, of course. As usual.

Since there was no electricity, people kept perishable goods in old-fashioned iceboxes, coolers and mini-fridges with the electrical cords coiled up. Men hauling carts walked through AfricTown every second day, selling chunks of ice.

There was a school in AfricTown, and its curriculum was based on the Freedom State standardized exams, but many parents kept their children out of it. Police raided it sometimes, arresting children who could not provide documentation of citizenship. And the teachers were not certified educators but parents who lived in AfricTown and knew about math, science, geography, English, history and French. Some of them were highly educated and truly motivated in the classroom. Others were useless. John had survived somehow through Grade 6 by listening to elders and becoming an avid borrower of books at the Clarkson Library.

John had mixed feelings about AfricTown. So far it had allowed him to live undisturbed and not become a ward of the state during his mother's illnesses. It allowed his genius to flower. It allowed him to read thousands of books by battery-powered lamplight in the nighttime and in the early mornings. People let him be, for the most part, except for the name-calling. *Vanilla cake, ice cream, stracciatella, latte boy, cookies 'n' cream*—people had every sort of food name for him, because he was blacker than white but whiter than black. He had learned to deal with that.

As soon as he bought it with his prize money, John carried his video camera everywhere he went, so people would get used to it and act natural and just carry on as usual while he filmed their lives. On his walk from Jerzy Kook Kook to the Bombay Booty for his one-hour-a-day cleaning job before school, John's camera caught a man pulling his toddler out of the sewage ditch she had fallen into and wiping her off. It caught a busker juggling five oranges, and a watering hole where men drank homemade beer sold at twenty-five cents a quart. And it caught a young woman fastening a baby to a sling around her back while holding a bag in one hand and shoes in the other. She looked about eighteen. No makeup, no fingernail polish, but she had a radiant face. Her hair was kept to a short, tight afro. Clean skin and clean clothes. She was walking north, toward Clarkson.

John decided to stop her. People who would watch his documentary needed to see, up close, how hard-working people—or at least some people—were in AfricTown.

"Where are you going, moms?" he asked.

"To work in Clarkson," she said.

"What's your name?"

"Maria Smith. Why are you filming me?"

"For a school project. For a documentary."

"A documentary? Gonna make any money off that?"

"No. I'm a student. Grade 9."

"You want to interview me, it will be fifty cents."

John kept filming. "I pay fifty cents for breakfast. That's a lot."

"Pay me fifty cents, and make your own damn breakfast tomorrow."

John fished two quarters from his pocket and handed them over. She slipped them quickly in her pocket.

"You have two minutes," she said. "I can't be late."

"What kind of work do you do in Clarkson?" he said.

"Clean houses, fifteen dollars a day."

"What's your baby's name?"

"Xenia."

"Where's her papa?"

"No papa around," she said. She spat on the ground. "For all the help I get, that baby might as well have come along by means of virgin birth."

John laughed. "Spontaneous combustion would have been more fun."

She laughed with him. "Anyway. It's just the baby and me. Ain't I enough?"

"I'm sure you're enough. I don't have a papa either."

Maria put her hands on her hips and stared into the camera. "Is that the kind of man you will be? Who leaves his own children?"

"Well, no," John said. He hadn't thought much about being a father. But no. If he ever had children, he would not want to leave them. He had never met his own father, but he did not want his kids to say the same of him. Ever. He said as much to Maria, who reached out and rubbed his head and told him that he was a good boy and should stay that way. John wished that his camera had been able to catch the head rub.

"How long does it take you to walk to work?"

"One and a half hours, each way."

"That's a lot of time."

"It gets me out of AfricTown. Where I work, I get running water, fresh toilets. I can even shower. I wish I could work on weekends too, so there wouldn't be a single day in the week when I had to shit in the pot and throw it in the ditch."

"What do you use your money for? Clothes?"

"No, I get clothes from the women I work for. I can adjust any bit of clothing. Shorten, tighten and hem anything they give me. The clothes I get are always too big. I can take a dress apart and put it back together two sizes smaller. I'm so good that the women sometimes send me home with alterations that I do on Sundays. I charge extra for that."

"So what do you use your money for?"

"Gonna send my daughter to school one day. Hey, your time's up. And, boy, your shorts are dirty, and you got egg on your shirt. You can't go to school looking like that. Don't you have a mother?"

"I change into my clean clothes at school."

"Okay. Clean up real good at school. You want to talk again, it will cost you one dollar. I got film experience now, so my rates are going up."

John watched Maria walk north toward Clarkson. Over her head, and in the distance, past AfricTown and past Clarkson itself, the sun was hitting Flatrock Mountain and its gondolas, one of Clarkson's most famous attractions. White tourists rode up in the daytime to take pictures of the city and Ten-Mile Inlet and, on a clear day, the Ortiz Sea. Young people rode the gondolas at night to dance in an upscale club on top of the mountain. But here in AfricTown, hardly anybody noticed Flatrock Mountain.

It took John ten minutes to walk to the Bombay Booty. He had a key to the door, and he had another to the caretaker's closet, which kept the bucket, the mop and the cleaning solution. Half a cup of cleaning solution, a bucket of hot water, and off he went, rolling the bucket on wheels and mopping. Lula DiStefano did not tolerate dirt on her brothel floors. She had once shown up at the Clarkson Academy, said it was an emergency and hauled John back to AfricTown in her car to make him rewash two floors that had not been cleaned to her satisfaction. Then she made him walk back to school.

John washed the halls of the first and second floors meticulously, and he cleaned the toilets, bidets and sinks, working steadily but carefully for one hour. The floors were made of Italian marble. Imitations of works by the Impressionists covered the walls. Monet, Degas, Renoir, all the sorts of works that would be popular with people in Freedom State. People, that is, who didn't live in AfricTown.

John wanted out of this situation. He didn't want to rely on Lula any longer. She liked having him in her debt, but if he had his way, it wouldn't be for long. John's documentary was going to propel him to the number-one ranking among students at the Clarkson Academy for the Gifted. He would then ask the principal to let him become a boarding student, for free. And to cover his necessities of life: school uniforms and other clothing, books and computer supplies. When his mother was well and living at home again, John could visit her, but he'd be out of Lula DiStefano's clutches.

John finished his cleaning and made sure that even the closet where the bucket and mop were locked was spotless. Then he walked over to Harlan's place. Harlan was one of Lula's personal drivers, and on most mornings that John worked for Lula, Harlan drove him to school. It saved John an hour of walking, kept his runners from wearing down so fast, and gave him time to shower and dress before class.

As he often did, John asked Harlan to let him off at the gate to Ruddings Park, which was in the heart of Clarkson and just a block from his school. With its trees and open spaces and reservoir, the park was the most peaceful place in the city. A two-kilometre footpath for runners and walkers circled the water, and from it, he could watch hundreds of floating ducks. The park was right downtown, so John could see a crush of buildings beyond its trees. Business towers. Government buildings. Telecommunications facilities. Sports arena. Movie theatre. Opera house. John decided to walk around the reservoir to calm his mind before going to school. He had half an hour: plenty of time to loop once around the reservoir trail and still make it to the locker room to shower and change and then get to his journalism class. So he began walking, counterclockwise as the signs instructed. The trail could be a busy one, so signs directed visitors' movement to minimize congestion.

John had been walking for a minute when he heard something behind him. He turned to see a runner approaching extraordinarily fast. He was clearly a distance runner, and he was not sprinting, but he was coming toward John at twice the pace of most joggers. John, who had never seen him before, stood to the side and waved as the fellow drew near. The runner was a lithe black athlete of medium height. He wore a fanny pack strapped to the small of his back, bright yellow track shoes, black track shorts with slits high up the thighs and a white shirt. He was concentrating and working hard, but he nodded to acknowledge John's salutation, and that made John feel good.

John removed his camera from his backpack. He watched the man run for another hundred metres and then slow to a jog and check his watch. John walked faster, keeping the man in sight as long as he could. Then the runner took off again at his high speed. John watched him pull two hundred, four hundred, six hundred metres ahead. It was hard to see him, because he had covered more than half the distance of the reservoir. Soon he would come all the way around and pass John again. John had been walking as fast as he could, but he repressed an instinct to run because he knew he would have looked silly. And either way, the runner would soon lap him. John had walked only one-fifth of the reservoir trail when the runner exploded past him again, then slowed to a jog.

"Excuse me!"

The man looked back at John.

"I was just wondering—what are you doing?"

"Training."

"What kind of training?"

"Intervals. I run two kilometres in five minutes and forty-five seconds. Then I jog for two minutes."

"And then you do it again?"

"Exactly. I must go now."

"Wait, how many times?"

"Today, just six times. Sometimes ten."

"Are you getting ready for a big race?"

The man lowered his voice. "Confidentially, the Buttersby Marathon. But that is just between you and me."

"Do you mind if I film you? I'm making a documentary."

"No, I'm very sorry. Have a good day." He jogged another thirty metres, looked back once at John and then recommenced his insane pace.

John had never seen a runner move so quickly. The sun bounced off the water of the reservoir and caught his body as he rounded the slow curve up ahead. What could it hurt? John turned on his video camera, zoomed in and filmed him for ten or fifteen seconds. It was inspiring to watch the runner move so smoothly in the early morning in the calmest place in the city. It made John want to do something great too. From a distance, the running looked effortless, but John had heard the man breathing. He had seen the sweat on his forehead and the strain in his eyes. The marathoner ran with power and beauty, but it had to hurt like hell to work that hard.

CHAPTER NINE

B EING FIFTEEN YEARS OLD BUT NOT YET FIVE FEET
tall came with one advantage: John was able to sit cross-
legged in a wardrobe box in a walk-in closet of the
Presidential Suite of Bombay Booty. He was reasonably
comfortable. In case the task stretched on and he grew hungry,
he had a peanut butter sandwich. To keep his hands free, he had
strapped to his forehead a flashlight like a miner's lamp. He wore
great big earphones to monitor the sound levels. On his lap, he balanced his computer. His monitor was split into two screens—one for
each of the hidden cameras with microphones that he had planted.
Later, when he was assembling his documentary about AfricTown,
he could splice images together. But for the time being, he had the
laptop on pause and was waiting to hit the record button.

John had planted one camera over a painting above the bed and
the other on a sculpture on the opposite wall. It was risky. But John
had a documentary to make.

He heard footsteps, so he started recording. Two young women
came into view. They stood near the foot of the king bed. They were
girls, really; John guessed they were only seventeen or so, but they
were made up and dressed to look older. One had light brown skin
just a few shades darker than John's.

The light brown girl wore a tan blouse cinched at the waist by
a green belt with a big buckle. Why girls wore belts on their shirts
was beyond John. She was about five foot five. The other girl was

as black as night. She was a few inches taller and wore a short dress that revealed the lower ridge of her butt when she bent over and smacked the bed.

John's teacher, Manzell Reginald, would flip out if he saw any sex in the documentary. John would clean it up while editing. But he had to be here. He had to do this. He had heard about the sorts of mucky-mucks who came to AfricTown under the cover of night. Now he had to find out for himself, film it and show it to the world.

"The man I got tonight," the short one said. "Lula says he's a big shot. Likes his girls deferential."

The tall one laughed. "The fuck that means?"

"Means do what he says."

"Who are you, the Scrabble Queen?"

"I like to read," the short one said.

"I seen you with that cellphone, playing Scrabble, Scrabble, Scrabble every chance you get. Girl, you addicted."

"We're in AfricTown, honey," the short one said. "Girls getting deported left, right and centre. I can think of worse problems than Scrabble."

"Scrabble is for eighty-year-old white ladies in nursing homes."

"Scrabble's just a game, Darlene."

John scribbled in his notebook, *Tall, darker girl—Darlene.*

"You keep on with that game," Darlene said. "I'm here to make some money."

"Me too," the short one said.

"The money is great," Darlene said, "but you know it won't last. You see a single girl here over twenty-four? You gotta have a plan, girl."

"Tomorrow, I'd like to buy a T-bone steak and a red dress. That's my plan."

Darlene laughed. "I'm saving up. One day, I'm gonna take accounting at the Clarkson Community College. Fifteen thousand dollars for a three-year course. All the time people say, 'I like to work with people.' To hell with that. Who needs people? People *do* things to you. Give me numbers and paper, any day." Darlene turned to look at herself in the mirror. "Lula says girls who eat too much turn big-assed after twenty-one."

"You're a year away from twenty-one and a long way from big-assed," the short one said. "I say you're perfect."

"You're a doll, Yvette."

John wrote in his book: *Short, light-skinned girl—Yvette.*

"Hey, kid," Darlene said. "Ask me a number. Anything. Go on. Do it."

"Thirteen times eight."

"Shee-it. That's easy. If I roll thirteen men eight times, that's 104 times I'm getting paid. And in case you wondering, 104 times two hundred dollars is 20,800 big ones. Count it that way, Yvette."

John admired the tall girl. He liked her attitude. He found it hard to believe that she was stuck in a brothel, worrying about whether her ass was too big. He wished he had a sister. Or a brother. Someone who was older, wiser and in his corner.

John had read that if you were mixed but wanted to be black, you had to fight extra hard to establish your identity. You had to out-black the blacks. This documentary was his way of staking a claim.

"Lula says I have to do something extra tonight," Yvette said.

"What?"

"Take his ID and find some papers that make him look bad."

"Don't do it, girl."

"Why not? She's paying me an extra two hundred dollars. Says I'm a good reader, so I'll know if I see something good."

"It's not right, the way she makes the illegal girls do bad shit."

"How many times do I have to tell you, Darlene? I'm from here. I am not from Zantoroland."

Darlene lowered her voice. "Everybody says they're born here, girl. They arrest me, I'll say that too."

"It's true. You don't believe me?"

"Don't matter what I believe. I'm not your problem. If you got handcuffs on, you know what the question is: 'Where's your national citizenship card?'"

"Just because I don't have one doesn't mean I wasn't born here. And Lula's going to help me get a card."

"Good luck with that," Darlene said.

"All I got to do is pay her, and she'll get me a card in no time at all. In fact, I've been taking half-pay for two months. Lula has me on a savings plan. She keeps the other half and says that when I've saved twenty thousand, she's gonna fix me up with a citizenship card and a passport."

It might have been the same for John, with a father from Zantoroland who disappeared before he was born. But he never had to worry about being arrested and deported. Because his mother was white. Freedom Statonian, born and raised. And his father, apparently, had become a naturalized citizen. So John had his citizenship. He felt guilty about that, having something so many others needed.

AfricTown told you all you needed to know about Freedom State. An island continent that was nearly two thousand kilometres north to south and more than half that distance east to west, Freedom State had grown rich by developing tobacco and rice plantations and exporting wood coveted by European furniture makers in the nineteenth century. It boasted one of the world's oldest and most stable parliamentary democracies, and its citizens—if you excluded the residents of AfricTown—were among the wealthiest in the world.

The country had deported all the black people it could after the abolition of slavery, but try as it might, it could not prevent the descendants of its slaves from returning boat by boat, year after year. They were fleeing troubles in Zantoroland and seeking work and prosperity. But Freedom State would not admit, acknowledge or legalize them, so they clustered in AfricTown.

AfricTown, Oh, AfricTown. His country's moral blight. His home.

Darlene cut into John's thoughts. "Savings plan, huh? I'm your numbers girl, and you know what I say to that?"

"What?" Yvette said.

"Fuckin' robbery."

Yvette checked her lipstick in the mirror. "I want that card. Should have got one when I was born. But I'll have it eventually."

"Whatever," Darlene said. "It's your business. But be careful with the big shot."

"I'll be fine," said Yvette. "I've done this before, you know."

"Not this, girl. You ain't done no spying. Keep your eyes open. And if he asks, don't say a word about seventeen. You're twenty-one. Got that? Twenty-one!"

John scribbled in his notebook: *Yvette, 17.* He checked his laptop. Plenty of battery power. The cameras were working fine. He tried to breathe as quietly as possible.

"Get out of here!" Yvette nudged Darlene toward the door. "You got your own work to do!"

Darlene gave Yvette a hug and left. Yvette disappeared from camera range. John could see the king-sized bed, the reproduction of a Monet painting above the pillows—a thousand dabs of paint made to look like water sparkling under a bridge. On each of the bedside tables, a lamp rose out of the back of an ebony-carved elephant. The bedroom looked nothing like the rest of AfricTown. In fact, John realized, it had been made to look like anywhere *but* AfricTown.

John heard Yvette walk into the bathroom and felt uncomfortable listening to her pee. Out of respect, and to save his batteries, he paused the recording. He heard her wash her hands. Brush her teeth. Gargle. And then she sang. John switched the sound back on. This was good B-roll. She was singing a country song: "Constitution." Everyone was singing it lately. It had crossed right over into mainstream radio and was polluting the national airwaves.

We got a Constitution for two, baby, our own book of rules.
Subsection Two, Part Three
Says don't you never go runnin' from me.

How could a seventeen-year-old girl working nights in the Bombay Booty in AfricTown go for country, of all things? "Constitution"?

There were two brisk knocks on the door.

Yvette came back into camera range. John hit record and widened the angle. With his fingers on the computer pad, he could manipulate the cameras to follow the action. The door opened, and a man stepped in. He towered over Yvette. Late fifties. Lean build. Brown eyes, brown hair. He wore a beige turtleneck and black slacks, and he carried a briefcase.

Nobody would believe him, unless he showed the video: John was looking at the prime minister of Freedom State, Graeme Wellington, no doubt about it. John read the papers. He knew the score. And now, he knew he was in over his head. A documentary about AfricTown, yes. But how could he have been so stupid? People were killed for the things they knew. Or sometimes they just went missing. Whatever was about to happen here, John didn't want to see it.

The prime minister stared at Yvette's body. "Not bad," he said.

"Come in," Yvette said. "Make yourself comfortable."

He removed a wallet from his pants pocket, slid it into his blazer pocket and hung the blazer on a coat stand.

"Show me a little more," he said.

She unfastened a button of her blouse. "You like what you see?"

"One more," he added, motioning to her buttons. "Take your bra off, but leave your shirt on."

She turned away from him, and with the other camera, John caught her unfastening her bra and ditching it on the pillow. John had not come for the show. He did not want Yvette to remove her clothes, and he did not want to see her get close to the prime minister. Yvette was built like a woman, but she was only a girl. She could be a senior student in his school. They could be walking down the halls together, talking about their teachers.

"My name's Yvette," she said. "What shall I call you?"

The prime minister snatched her arm. John saw Yvette wince,

and inside the box, he winced too. The prime minister was alone in a room with a seventeen-year-old girl, and he could do whatever he pleased.

"Nobody will know about this. Right?"

"Nobody will know," Yvette said. "I'm a professional."

John noticed Yvette steadying her lower lip. She had not liked being grabbed like that. If a man that big had violence on his mind, how long would it take him to break Yvette's neck or strangle her? If he discovered John hiding in the room, he could do it to him too. He wouldn't leave any witnesses. John tried to settle his nerves by focusing on the computer and zooming in a little closer on Wellington's hand on Yvette's arm.

"That's a good girl." The prime minister released her.

Yvette said, "How about if I undress you?"

"No. Sit on the bed. There, on the edge. Keep your blouse open. Like that. Hang on. I need to do something."

He put his briefcase flat on the bed, opened it and pulled out a file. He flipped through some papers and pulled his Planet cellphone out of his pocket. Those things were cool. You could call anywhere on the planet. No dead zones. He typed out a quick email with his thumbs, sent a message and appeared to be scrolling. Then Wellington put the file back and closed the briefcase. His cellphone rang, and he studied it.

"I have to take this. Wait here. Unbutton the rest of that," he said, staring at her blouse, "but leave it on." He left the room.

Yvette did not unbutton her blouse. Instead, she leapt up and, to John's horror, rifled through the PM's blazer. She opened his wallet but ignored the cash and credit cards. She found the national citizenship card that every citizen of Freedom State was required to have on their person when in public. There was a fine for not carrying it. Yvette looked at the card, and her jaw dropped. "Holy shit," she muttered. John zoomed in and caught it on camera, too: *Graeme Arnold Wellington*. She kept the card but left the rest intact and put the wallet back in his blazer pocket.

Then she walked over and opened the closet door where John was hiding. It was weird seeing her back on his computer monitor as she looked at the very box in which he sat, hidden. He heard a click as she placed the national citizenship card on the shelf overhead. Then she closed the closet, walked to the door to the hall and put her ear against it. She pressed the button in the knob to lock the door, returned to the bed and opened his briefcase. John's camera followed. She opened the manila file, and John zoomed in. Yvette looked at a handwritten message on an otherwise blank piece of paper. John zoomed in, but could only catch a few bits of the note.

Bossman

. . . firmed up the deal with GM . . . we . . . do this on your orders. Off books, $ only. We can keep intercepting bathtubs, return to Z. We pay $2,000 p/k . . . We pay Z—through GM—$10,000 p/k for . . . up to 20 dissidents/year . . .

Please approve ASAP,
Whoa-Boy

P.S. Lula has three for you. Asking 10x the usual fee. Petty cash issues. Talk her down?

John shook his head in confusion. Who was Whoa-Boy? What did it all mean?

Yvette closed the file and returned it to the briefcase. She went to the closet. John could hear her hand patting the shelf overhead, and now she was opening the top flap of John's cardboard box. Maybe to hide the prime minister's ID. John tried to shift but too late. Her hand grazed the top of his head. She opened the box and let out a little cry.

"What the—?" The doorknob turned and caught against the lock. "Who're you?" Yvette hissed.

"John Falconer," he said.

"Stay there or you're dead."

Yvette closed the closet, and John felt the humiliating wetness of urine in his pants. He tried to control his breathing. Could anyone hear his heart pounding? Surely not. The door handle rattled. Then there was a hard knock, and Yvette ran to open the door.

"What the hell is going on?" Wellington said. "The damn door was locked."

"Sorry. It sticks sometimes. That's all."

"Did I hear a voice?"

"Phone call."

"I thought cellphones weren't allowed up here."

"Please don't tell Lula," Yvette said. "I'll make it up to you. I can please you in ways you can only imagine," she said.

She was so tiny. It sickened John to imagine that girl under the weight of the prime minister.

"Where is your phone?" he asked.

"In the bathroom," she said.

"Leave it there," he said. "I don't stand for interruptions."

"You were interested in my blouse," she said. "See how soft it is?" She came closer to him; she had to reach way up to let her fingers slide up and down his shoulders.

Wellington slipped his hand inside her shirt. The way they were standing, John could not see the prime minister touching her, and he was relieved about that. It was bad enough to see the way his hand was moving and know what he was touching.

Yvette reached for Wellington's zipper. "Oh, you're a powerful man," she murmured.

Wellington guided Yvette back toward the bed. Then he bent over to lift his briefcase out of the way. But the briefcase fell open.

"Why is my briefcase open? I closed the latch before I left the room."

On the manila file, the prime minister's name was displayed prominently.

"Were you going through my things?" he said.

"No."

Wellington bent down to gather up the scattered papers. "You nosy whore. You went through my goddamn files." He stood and grabbed her arm. She let out a little cry. "Hurts, doesn't it? What did you see?"

"Nothing."

"Liar. I think you did see something. I think you read my memo."

"No. No, sir. I—"

Wellington struck Yvette, and her head snapped back. She stumbled away, then steadied herself and pressed her hand against her mouth.

John wished he didn't have to watch. But he had no choice.

The prime minister reached for her again and eased her gently against him. Yvette put her head against his chest. Then he grabbed her hair in his huge fist and tilted her head so she was staring up into his eyes.

"You went through my things. That's a violation of privacy." He brought his free hand to her throat.

Yvette lifted her hands to Wellington's and tried to release his grip. John wanted to leap out of the box, to save her. But instead he crouched lower. Help her, he thought. Somebody has to help her. Yvette kicked against the bed frame. The moment Wellington's hands came off her throat, she screamed.

The door opened, and Lula DiStefano burst in.

"No one hurts my girls."

Wellington let go of Yvette, and she fell to her knees, gasping for air. "This bitch went through my things."

Lula looked at the girl. "Yvette, did you touch this man's belongings?"

"Yes," she said.

"Why?" he said.

"I was curious."

"You're not paid to be curious," Lula said. "I'll deal with you later."

Then she turned back to the prime minister and said, "I have to ask you to leave. You'll be refunded. I am sorry for the inconvenience."

"What's your name, bitch?" The prime minister came across the floor at Yvette again. "You said Yvette. Yvette what? What's your last name?"

"I will take care of this," Lula said.

The prime minister grabbed Yvette again and twisted her forearm. "Your last name, you little black bitch."

"Peters," Yvette gasped.

John scribbled into his notebook. *Yvette Peters, 17, threatened by PM.*

"Lula," the prime minister said. "I need you to handle this. Do you read me?"

"Graeme," Lula said, "I run my own show."

John wrote again. *Lula DiS. calls the PM by first name.*

Graeme Wellington's face flushed red. Lula betrayed no emotion whatsoever.

Lula opened the door to the hall, and two tall black bouncers stepped in. "This gentleman is on his way out," she said.

"She read a memo, Lula," the prime minister said. "It wasn't just my name on it."

Lula nodded to the bouncers.

"This way, sir," one of them said, gesturing toward the door.

The prime minister took one last look at Yvette and followed, flanked by the second bouncer, who closed the door behind them.

John stopped taping. He clicked a key to begin saving the video onto a USB. He needed the entire video for his documentary. But for the time being, to protect himself and Yvette, he didn't want Lula to find out that he knew that she had instructed Yvette to go through the prime minister's papers. And he didn't want Lula to know that he might be able to go back to the video to decode the prime minister's private memo. The less Lula thought he knew, the better. As soon as a copy of the video was saved, John stuffed the USB in his sock.

"You said you could handle him," Lula told Yvette, "but you fucked up."

"I tried," Yvette said, "but he was rough."

"You don't know rough."

John returned to the original video on his computer. He deleted the part where Yvette described what Lula had asked her to do, and everything after the PM had told Yvette to unbutton her blouse and left the room.

"How could you be so stupid as to let him catch you?" Lula said.

"You told me to—"

Lula put her palm up. "Not get caught."

"I went as fast as I could," Yvette said.

John saved the edited version on another stick and put it in his pocket. They might search his pockets, but they were unlikely to make him remove his shoes. They would assume that they had it all. Trouble was coming. John prepared himself. He wished his pants weren't wet.

"What papers did you see?" Lula asked Yvette.

"Nothing," Yvette said.

"Do you take me for stupid?"

"I didn't see anything I understood."

"What did you see that you *didn't* understand?"

"Something about a deal. About money. I have no idea what it meant."

"Girl, you're in so deep that ideas don't come into it."

"Whatever it said, I didn't get it and won't retain it. I won't say a thing. But the boy might."

"What boy?"

"There's a boy in the closet. Go look!"

Lula opened the closet door, looked around, and then glanced back at Yvette. "What are you playing at, girl?"

"Open the box," Yvette said.

Before Lula could do so, John pushed out the flaps and stood up.

"Jesus H. Christ," Lula shouted. "What the hell are you doing here?"

John climbed out of the box, laptop under his arm.

Lula pointed at it. "What's that?"

"It's my laptop."

"Come over here! I want you to be nice and close when I slap you upside the head."

John took a step closer, preparing to be hit. Lula drew her hand back and chuckled when he flinched. She dropped her hand.

"Meant no harm, Mrs. DiStefano."

"Cut the bullshit. Do you know this girl?"

"No."

"Did she hide you in that box?"

"No. I was hiding there, and she found me."

"Is that true, Yvette?"

"Yes, Lula."

"That little thing sticking out from the painting over the bed. Is that a bug? Did you plant that?"

"Bug?" Yvette said.

"You keep those big lips shut up until I ask you to speak," Lula said to Yvette. She turned back to John. "So. Is it?"

"Yes."

"Is it taping us right now?" she said.

"No, ma'am. I turned it off."

"When did you turn it off?"

"When the customer left the room a few minutes after he first came in. Before the trouble began."

"Hiding in a goddamn box. You either something ballsy or you got shit for brains. Get into the bathroom and wash up."

"Wash up?"

"Get in that bathroom, and wash your hands and face, and pray that I let you out of here to go change those pants you pissed."

John headed to the bathroom, but he could still hear them talking.

"Stay here," Lula said. "Don't let him go anywhere."

"I got his ID," Yvette said. "Just like you told me. I put it on the closet shelf."

"But you left his briefcase open. Because of you, I have to make nice with the client I just lost."

Yvette said nothing more.

"Bunch of fucking children," Lula said. "It's like a goddamn day-care in here."

As John came out of the bathroom, Lula left and slammed the door behind her.

"I'm in a lot of trouble," Yvette said. "Is this what you do for kicks? Film girls taking their clothes off and—"

"I am not into voyeurism. I'm making a documentary. About AfricTown."

Yvette took a step back. "You're awful young to use such big words."

"Give me a break," John said. "I'm only two years younger than you."

Yvette studied him. "You little bastard. Who's your mama?"

"Mary Falconer."

"Don't know her," Yvette said.

"She cleans houses in Clarkson," John said, "but she lives here and keeps a low profile."

"Low profile," Yvette said. "I could use a low profile right now. Lula will fuck me up good, but she won't put a finger on you, white boy."

"Don't call me that! I'm not white. I'm mixed."

"Mixed awful thin."

"What are you so high and mighty about?" he said. "You're mixed too!"

"Anyone can see the black in me. I may be faded, but you are faded right out."

"My dad was half black. But I never saw him."

"Count my tears," she said.

"I was just explaining. Anyway. Why don't you take off? Disappear."

"Got nowhere to run. Anywhere I run, she'd find me."

"Can I contact someone who could help you?" John reached out to touch her arm, but she pulled back.

"Got nobody."

"What about a mom? You got a mom?"

"Said nobody."

The door flew open and hit the wall so hard that it bounced back off the stopper. Lula strode across the room, and John thought she was going to hit Yvette. Instead, Lula grabbed him by the collar and pulled him behind her out into the hall.

"Boy, you are something stupid."

"It's not her fault," John said. "She didn't know I was there."

"Here's when I want you to open your mouth: when you are answering my questions." She let go of John's collar, and his head smacked the wall.

"Listen up," Lula said, "And look here."

John looked at Lula DiStefano. Tall, regal, powerful. Dark skin. Smooth complexion. Yellow earrings to match her dress.

"Look at me good and straight," Lula said.

He barely saw it coming. She slapped him fast and flat on his cheek. It stung and left his face burning. John had never been slapped by anyone. Not by his mother, not by a teacher at school.

"Next time, I'll slap you right through to Wednesday of next week," Lula said.

His cheek aching, John vowed to himself that he would get away from her once and for all. But Lula wasn't done.

"No more floor washing. I'm firing you from that job, as of now. But I'm hiring you for something else. You are now my personal videographer."

She would find it useful, she said, to have certain incidents recorded. He would provide her with the material, and then he would erase the contents of his computer. If he said a word about this, he would not live to tell the story.

"That clear, little man?"

"Yes," he said. Clear as day.

"Good, because I want you to answer me carefully. Did you record what happened in the room today?"

"Yes, Mrs. DiStefano, I recorded the first part of the client coming into the room."

"I'm going to need that," she said.

He reached into his pocket and handed her the stick.

"That was fast," she said.

"I thought you might ask for it."

"Thinking ahead, hunh?"

He nodded. He did not tell her that he had copied the entire video onto another stick. Older people were clued out when it came to computers.

"You did not see anything today," she said, "and if you did, you have completely forgotten it."

"Yes, Mrs. DiStefano."

"Go on home now," she said. Then she turned and walked back into the room where Yvette was waiting. She closed the door.

CHAPTER TEN

THE PHONE RANG AND RANG IN VIOLA'S HOTEL
room. Five-fucking-thirty in the morning. It was Bolton.
Viola flicked on the lights, sat up in bed and saw
herself in the mirror. Groggy. Overworked. But she could
roll out of bed and be ready in minutes. She'd shaved her head over a
year ago. Why not? She had a beautiful, shapely head, and she refused
to sink hundreds of dollars each month into Cindy's AfriCentric Hair
Salon, where she had once wasted countless Saturdays. How was any
black woman to get ahead if her life ground to a halt for five consecutive hours each time she had to get her hair done? Forget it. Bald
and beautiful was the way to go, although it hadn't done much for
her love life: Viola and her last girlfriend had broken up months ago.

To be given a crack at serious news stories, Viola Hill had to be
perfect on the job. Always on time. Always ready. Invincible. Got the
flu? Don't tell anybody. Having a day when all she could think about
was that she wished her mom were still alive? Swallow that emotion.
Having a rare burst of phantom pain, like a knife ripping through
her thighs? How bloody fair was that, to feel ten-out-of-ten agony
in a part of her body that she no longer even owned? Even phantom
pains she had to mask. She had learned not to scream when they
came out of nowhere. She could not have people thinking she'd keel
over and die. They would never promote her. Viola was sick and tired
of having to be unassailable. But she answered the phone whenever
it rang, because that's what professionals did.

And here was Bolton, all up in her face. Bolton, caffeinated and manic at the tail end of his night shift at the *Telegram*.

"You're in Buttersby, right? To cover the marathon?" He sounded breathless. Instead of letting her reply, he pressed on. "What time does it start?"

"Nine a.m.," she said.

"You're always on my case for a non-sports assignment, right?"

"Yeah," she said. What would it be this time? Chasing a fire truck? Dog bites boy?

"Get over to 1138 Potluck Drive, Unit 3. Woman says her daughter was taken from Freedom State and deported to Zantoroland, where she died in prison. Woman's distraught. Get over there before she calls the local TV station! Interview her quick, take her picture, get a photo of the daughter and send me four hundred words before you cover that race."

Viola had to tip the taxi driver extra before he would let her get into the car at all. Once she convinced him, it was easy. She pivoted her butt from the chair into the back seat of the taxi, reached down, folded up her day-chair and hauled it into the back seat with her. Lifting it over her legs, she stashed it beside her on the seat. She closed the door and had her seat belt on in no time flat. Viola told him where to go, and when they arrived, she paid him to park and run the meter, which would mean less waiting—and one less cabbie to convince—when she was ready to race back to the hotel to file her story.

The mother lived in a townhouse on the ground level, so Viola wheeled right up to the front door. She thumped it with her fist. Six thirty in the morning was not the best time to be banging on a stranger's door.

A woman answered in a bathrobe. Hair a mess. Face puffy from crying. Calves, which were evident under the bathrobe, were puffy too. She was a user, for sure. Viola Hill could spot a user at fifty paces. She had grown up walking past them every day in AfricTown, or running when she felt unsafe. As a child, when she still had the use of her legs, Viola had loved to run.

"Mrs. Peters? I'm Viola Hill, with the *Clarkson Evening Telegram*."

"I thought they were sending a reporter."

"I *am* a reporter."

"You're black," Mrs. Peters said.

"So are you, Mrs. Peters."

"And you're a cripple."

Viola ignored the comment and wheeled inside.

The dingy living room had a lamp or two, a crappy old couch and a TV set. Viola whipped out her notebook.

"You get around fast enough in that thing," Mrs. Peters said. "I only called the paper an hour ago—"

"When is the last time you saw your daughter?" Viola asked.

"I haven't seen her in two years," the mother said. "I didn't like her, and she didn't like me. But I never thought she would end up . . ."

"How exactly *did* your daughter end up?"

"She passed away. In a Zantoroland prison."

"Had she ever been in Zantoroland before?" Viola asked.

"No. Never. I'm from Zantoroland. I never got my residency papers, but Yvette was born here in Freedom State, right here in Buttersby, and that gave her citizenship. I kind of forgot to get her identity card. But she was born here."

"Birthdate?" Viola asked.

"January 24, 2001."

The kid was lucky, or could have been. Like any person from AfricTown, Viola knew that in April 2001, the government had revoked the law granting citizenship to any person born in Freedom State. After that, you were only eligible for citizenship if you were born in the country *and* both your parents were citizens.

"So she was seventeen," Viola said. "Got a photo?"

Mrs. Peters brought her two albums of photos.

"Mind if I hold on to these for a day or two? We'll get them back to you." Viola stashed them in the back pocket of her chair before Mrs. Peters had a chance to object.

Viola got all the basics. Yvette Peters had attended schools in

Buttersby, dropped out in Grade 10, got caught up with some bad kids and started messing around with dope. She and Mrs. Peters had had several run-ins. Yes, Mrs. Peters admitted, the last ones got a bit rough, and she had slapped her daughter a few times too many. She slapped her because she loved her, damn it, and wanted to get her off the path that she, Mrs. Peters, had taken herself in life. But it didn't work. Yvette ran away from home the day she turned sixteen. Later, Mrs. Peters heard through the grapevine that her daughter was a sex worker at the Bombay Booty in AfricTown.

Mrs. Peters had been drying out in a detox centre and had just come home to the latest news. There was a letter in her mailbox from the Zantoroland Ministry of Citizenship. It was dated three days earlier and had been sent by urgent mail. *We regret to inform you that your daughter died of natural causes in immigration custody. Contact us immediately to make arrangements to recover the body at your own expense.* There had also been a message on her phone machine, telling her that her daughter had died and to get in touch immediately.

Viola was scribbling furiously. Eventually, every good interview yielded the quotable paragraph, and soon enough, Mrs. Peters gave it up.

"My daughter gave me a hard time about being from Zantoroland and not getting my papers for Freedom State. I told her I had been here for ages and was getting by, so why rock the boat? Last thing Yvette wanted to do was go to Zantoroland. Someone made her. I know it! Someone dragged her over there. Why did they do that to my daughter? I been calling the newspapers and the government information hotline. I been leaving messages for everyone. I didn't like my daughter, and she didn't like me, but she was my daughter, and I loved her, and now she's dead and I want answers."

Viola had to go. This was a complicated story, and she did not have time to go deeper into it today. She snapped a photo of the grieving mother holding the daughter's photo. She told Mrs. Peters that she'd be in touch again, perhaps later in the day.

"I'm not going anywhere," Mrs. Peters said.

Back in her hotel room, Viola called the Zantoroland Ministry of Citizenship. A man named Chelsea—the jerk refused to give his first name or confirm the spelling of his last—confirmed that they had detained a young woman named Yvette Peters because she had arrived in the country without proper documentation, and that she died in custody of natural causes. When Viola asked what exactly that meant, Chelsea merely repeated, "Natural causes."

Viola checked her address book. She was probably the only reporter in the country who had Lula DiStefano's private cell number. Normally, Viola wouldn't push her luck with Lula, but today it was worth it. She dialed the number.

"I'm sorry to wake you, Mrs. DiStefano," Viola said. "But it's important."

"Who the fuck is this?" Lula asked.

Viola knew that Lula DiStefano never forgot a name or a face or the story that went with them. She acted all rough and tumble and could out-diss any thug on the street, but a little-known fact that Viola might pull out one day was that Lula had studied decades earlier at the London School of Economics.

On the phone, Viola merely gave her name and said she had grown up in AfricTown and that her mother—Rebecca Hill—had been Lula's hairdresser back in the day.

"Uh-hunh," Lula said.

Viola said she had been out on her own for years now and that she was a reporter for the *Telegram*.

"I'm awake now, honey chile," Lula said. "I remember every-thing about you. How are you keeping?"

"I'm fine, thank you. I'm calling about a story we're working on."

"At this hour of the morning, I know you ain't calling to discuss the weather. You workin' for the man now, so spit it out, girl."

"Did a girl named Yvette Peters work for you?"

"Shit, yeah," Lula said. "She was one of my, um, dancers. You get news of her? She disappeared a while back, and we've all been wondering."

"Yvette Peters is dead, Mrs. DiStefano. She died in a Zantoroland prison."

"Zantoroland? Dead? That's awful," Lula said. "Poor kid. She was a good kid. Good heart. But I can't talk any more about this, darling. Don't you quote me, or I'll have my boys rip your kidneys out. And you know I'm good for it."

"Her own mother tells me that Yvette worked at the Bombay Booty. I'm looking at my notes: 'sex worker.'"

"An exotic dancer at the Pit," Lula said. "Clear? You want your kidneys, girl. Most people do, but you got special need of every organ, being you're already in a wheelchair. You come out the other end right good, girl. Reporter now. Well, get going. You got work to do, and I ain't feeling friendly at this hour."

Lula hung up on her. It was strange to be dismissed by someone who had once done so much for her. But that was Lula DiStefano: an angel one moment, and a shark the next.

Viola hadn't spent much time in AfricTown since the accident, and that was twenty years ago. She was run over by the drunk driver of a stolen pickup truck, lost her legs, became something of a one-day wonder in the news. The journalists came in a mob, with camera crews, lights, tape recorders stuck on the end of poles like marshmallows on whittled sticks, pushing into her hospital room until the nurses turfed them out. Viola had never seen reporters at work before. And sure enough, she became one herself.

Now she aspired to write the very sort of news articles that had been written about her, and her mother. Drunk driver in stolen truck runs over mother and daughter in AfricTown. Mother killed, eight-year-old daughter loses legs but survives. Deaths in AfricTown were a dime a dozen and didn't usually attract attention. But the spectacular nature of Viola's loss and survival triggered an avalanche of news. Yes, she was an actual citizen of Freedom State. Yes, her mother was too. That helped, for sure. Fundraising drives were held. Money was raised. Even the people of AfricTown contributed. Lula DiStefano personally contributed fifty thousand. Viola's amputations and follow-up surgeries were all paid for, as was her extensive physiotherapy, her prosthetic limbs and her first wheelchair. Or, as some preferred to call it, her mobility enhancement device. She could walk with prosthetic legs, but they were slow and awkward. So when she had to take notes and balance the notepad on her lap, or when she needed to move fast and had a flat surface before her, Viola preferred a chair. She had two: a regular kicking-about chair for daily living in Clarkson, and a chair for training and racing. Abs of steel, biceps like guns, that was Viola Hill. Every part of her worked just fine, apart from the fact that her body ended with two stumps, mid-thigh.

Viola had just enough to write the story. No time for fancy stuff: seventeen-year-old prostitute from the Bombay Booty, apparently a citizen of Freedom State, ends up mysteriously in Zantoroland, where she dies in prison. Confirmation from the Zantoroland Ministry of Citizenship, confirmation from a source in Afric Town, and a colourful quote from the distraught mother. That was the best Viola could do in two hours. She filed the story, scanned some photos of Yvette Peters, and emailed them with the photo she had taken of the mother. She managed to leave the hotel in time to cover the marathon. It was a morning race. As long as she filed her marathon story by 1 p.m., it too would make the evening edition of the paper.

CHAPTER ELEVEN

A S HE RAN UP THE TOUGHEST HILL IN THE BUTTERSBY Marathon, with Billy Deeds still on his shoulder, Keita Ali slowed just enough to control his breathing. To destroy his opponent's will, he had only to sing a few bars and sound as if he could carry on forever. Keita opted for a country song. He liked country music with catchy melodies and words that told a story. He would sing like the marathoners who had run past his family's church in the Red Hills of Zantoroland. He would sing as if Deacon Andrews and his parents were still alive. He would sing as if he had not been hiding for weeks in Freedom State, and had no reason to wonder what had happened to his sister or to fear for his own life. So, from the hit country song "Ain't Mine," Keita sang loud and clear.

> *I'm so tired of running for you, babe,*
> *Running all time.*
> *But you're running for another heart,*
> *And the heart you want ain't mine.*

"Faggot," Deeds said.
Keita kept singing.

> *I know I'm not the one you want.*
> *I know you'd never die for me.*

But I'd run for you until I caught
Your heart and turned it back to me.

Instead of accelerating, Keita sang louder, while the runner behind him gasped and cursed. "Nigger," his competitor said. Not to worry. "Faggot." Bring it on. "Fagganig." If Keita had his way, Deeds would lose a minute each time he cursed.

Keita sang right up the hill and slapped a few hands on his way. At the twenty-five-kilometre marker, which was the seventeen-kilometre point for the outbound runners, he high-fived a strong, muscular, fifty-something man who was running toward him down the hill. He was moving fast for a man that old. The way things were going, Keita doubted that he would even be alive at that age. But the man thumped like an elephant. He ran as if nobody had ever taught him not to slap the pavement with the soles of his feet. Keita had learned, even as a boy, that you can't afford to run and slap your feet. It wastes energy and degrades the tibia. Keita supposed it didn't matter for middle-aged recreational runners in Freedom State. There weren't any middle-aged athletes in Zantoroland. People in his country didn't run for recreation. You ran to win, or you didn't run at all.

Fifty metres behind the muscular man was a female racer. She looked awfully good. She was black. Or mixed, maybe. His own country had tens of thousands of people who looked just like her. The legacy of nocturnal carousing by its various colonial rulers. She reminded him of home. She was running smoothly, not slapping her feet like the big man in front of her. She was moving much more easily than the man and looked ready to pass him. Keita figured she was running at a 3:10 marathon pace. If all went well for both of them, she would finish an hour behind Keita. Perhaps he would look for her.

A huge smile broke out on her face, and she called out that he was looking strong. She held out her hand. Keita high-fived it as he finished the song. She had a nice hand. Warm, soft, smooth and with a little pressure against his. It was a hand of friendship, one of encouragement and of solidarity.

Now it was time to put some distance between himself and the madman in second. Keita stopped singing and grabbed two cups of sports drink at the next water station. He downed them fast, tossed away the empty cups, grabbed two more drinks, swallowed them too and accelerated. And that was the last he saw of any competitor in the 2018 Buttersby Marathon. He didn't expect the name-caller to hang on to second place. Or third. Keita didn't look back. He knew he had crushed the guy. Crushed him like an ant. It felt good.

THE MOBILE PHONE VIBRATED ON HIS WAIST. DAMN. ROCCO ran on, tempted not to answer. But he had received firm instructions before he had been sworn into his new role in cabinet. He had to keep the phone charged at all times. Have it on his bedside table. Take it along to the crapper. Even in the middle of the Buttersby Marathon, Rocco, who'd worked for four months as federal minister of immigration, had to have his mobile wired to one ear, with a tiny mike clipped on his running shirt. Hell. He looked like a secret service man.

He gave in and pushed the button. "Calder," he said.

"Mr. Minister, are you all right?" It was June Hawkins, his executive secretary. She managed his schedule, organized his life and knew how to reach every government official—in Freedom State and in other countries—that Rocco might need to contact as minister of immigration. She was a darling and totally devoted to the job, but her timing sucked.

"June," he said. "I'm running."

"Happy birthday, Mr. Minister."

"Running right now."

"Just calling to wish you good luck. I thought the race started at ten thirty."

"No, June, I've been at it for more than an hour."

"Well, don't run too hard, Mr. Minister, and remember to hydrate."

"Got it," he said. The woman was so formal. He had asked her a hundred times to call him Rocco, or Rock, but she wouldn't have it. It was just her background. Rumour had it she was born and raised in AfricTown. He'd have to ask her about that, if he could ever get her to relax and have a friendly conversation. AfricTown. It was like a whole other country. An island of poverty, right inside one of the world's richest countries. He had to credit her for climbing up and out. And he had to remember to be kind to her. People expected that of him. He knew what they called him behind his back. Mr. Clean. Because he kept fit. Didn't smoke. Didn't party. Looked like a Boy Scouts troop leader. Sure, he was known to chase a few skirts, but he'd be fine as long as the media had no reason to turn it into an issue.

"Carry on, Mr. Minister."

"Thanks, June. And don't call for another two hours."

"Right-o, Mr. Minister." She hung up.

Rocco hadn't lost his stride. He was feeling good. And he was well under target for a 3:15 marathon. Not bad. He wondered how many fifty-year-olds would finish ahead of him. Well, surely a bunch. Not to mention hundreds of other runners. No matter how fast he ran, a ton of people would beat him to the finish line. That was the thing about marathoning. It kept you humble—

His phone again.

"Calder," he said.

"Rock?" said a voice. Young man. All he had to say was "Rock," and Calder knew who it was. It was Geoffrey Moore, the twenty-eight-year-old smartass who ran the country. Geoffrey was the prime minister's executive assistant. Unelected. Barely out of university. Barely shaving. You could still see the pockmarks on his face from the ravages of adolescent acne. Unmarried. Untravelled, except of course for his doctorate from Harvard University. Nobody in cabinet farted without his say-so. He was a young conservative. Rocco was a conservative too, but it seemed wrong to him that a twenty-eight-year-old should be. At twenty-eight, weren't you supposed to be a Marxist or something? If you started out as a conservative at age twenty-eight, where did you go from there? The only thing left was fascism.

"Whoa-Boy," Rocco said. The PM used that term for his pet, so Rocco replayed it to irk the kid.

"Rock, are you okay? Sounds like you're having an asthma attack."

"I'm in a race, Whoa-Boy."

"A race?"

"Sixteen kilometres into a marathon."

"Good luck with that. Listen up. Anybody asks about the hooker, don't say a word. Not one fucking word."

"Hooker?"

"The girl. The one who died in Zantoroland."

"I don't follow."

"Hasn't anyone briefed you on this?"

Rocco felt a flash of anger. He was the federal minister of immigration, spearheading the government's crackdown on Illegals. A crackdown that wasn't working. A crackdown so ineffective that the same electors who had brought the Family Party to office were now demonstrating weekly outside the Parliament Building. Calling for mass deportations. Calling for AfricTown to be bulldozed. And now, apparently, a girl had died. But when it came to the important stuff, did anyone tell him anything? "No," he replied.

"There was a hooker. Deported to Zantoroland. Died in prison there."

"Was she here illegally?"

"Don't know. It's a real cock-up. Don't say a word, if anybody asks."

"I'm the minister of immigration. Somebody is going to ask."

"Just say that you don't know but will investigate. No. Not 'investigate.' Don't commit to anything. Say that you know nothing about it and have no comment."

"That'll make me look good."

"Good luck in the race, Rock. Gotta go. Some of us have work to do."

Rocco hung up.

Some of us have work to do. Geoffrey sounded like a fifteen-year-old prep school boy. Whiny. Wimpy. But not to be underestimated. The kid lived, breathed, slept, ate and shat politics. He had paid a visit to Rocco not long after Rocco moved into his corner office. Geoffrey had scowled at the rowing machine stashed in Rocco's private bathroom and had advised him to get some art by AfricTown painters on his wall. The idea, he said, was to display a cosmopolitan face while accelerating deportations.

The halfway turn was just four kilometres down the road. Rocco began to descend a long, steep hill. His feet slammed the pavement. Running downhill was as hard as running up. Sure, it didn't leave you winded, but it banged up your knees and quadriceps. He ran a few hundred metres down the hill, rounded a corner and saw that there was still a long descent. Later in the race, it would hurt to run back up this hill.

Three police motorcycles approached from the opposite direction, headlights on, red emergency lights twirling. Rocco could see the race leaders coming. Three guys. One black as night, the other two white as ghosts. One of the white guys had fallen twenty metres behind. You didn't have to be a rocket scientist to tell which runner would win. The black dude looked beautiful. Smooth as a sail. Rocco studied him coming. He was running way faster up this mother of all hills than Rocco was going down it with gravity on his side. The white guy, on the other hand, had his arms pinched up like lobster claws and was listing slightly to the left as he ran. The Kenyan, or Zantorolander, or whatever the hell he was, was in the process of dropping the white dude from Freedom State.

Okay, fine, shoot him. Go right ahead and line Rocco up to face the firing squad. He was guilty. It was unfair to assume the black guy had to be from Zantoroland or Kenya—but what could you do? Freedom State didn't have any decent marathoners. Maybe you ran harder when you were hungry. Maybe it was being in the mountains and training at altitude. Maybe it was the cow's milk over there. Maybe it was just genetic. Blacks were natural runners. Was that such a horrible thing to observe? Did that make him a racist? Was it Rocco's fault that the two fastest marathoners in the world were from Zantoroland, and that a Zantorolander held the world record, and that Zantorolanders had cleaned up in the last Boston Marathon? Was it Rocco's fault that among the world's top ten marathoners were three Zantorolanders, three Kenyans, two Ethiopians and a Moroccan? Wait. That made nine. The tenth was a Canadian. But he didn't really count as a Canadian, because he was black and born in Kenya. Rocco had read about that in *Track and Field News*. Canada, all the way across the world, had been smart about recruiting this immigrant, giving him Canadian citizenship. Now the country of snow and ice had a chance to win a medal in the next Olympic marathon. If only Freedom State could be so enterprising.

Here they came. The leaders were only a few metres away. The one good thing about an out-and-back marathon was that you got to see the leading runners up close, even though it was depressing to think that he was only at the seventeen-kilometre mark when these dudes had already run twenty-five kilometres. By the time Rocco made the halfway turn and fought his way back up this hill, the winner would be across the finish line.

All the runners around Rocco were cheering and clapping for the race leader. Rocco joined in. Man alive, was that black dude moving. Rocco reached out to high-five him. Weirdest thing was, the guy actually high-fived him back. His hand was dry. Not sweating. Okay, this was completely unbelievable. The black dude's name was on his race bib in block letters: *Roger Bannister*. And he was singing "Ain't Mine," that corny country hit that played constantly on the radio.

I know I'm not the one you want.
I know you'd never die for me.

126

But I'd run for you until I caught
Your heart and turned it back to me.

It was a dumb song, but he had a good voice. Why was he singing? Maybe he was trying to psych out his opponent. It was working. The white guy in second was trying to hang on, but it was a struggle. He was five metres back and bent all out of shape. And he was swearing. Well, that was just plain unsportsmanlike!

Rocco was all for keeping the right mix of people in Freedom State. Every voter knew that the Family Party had come to power promising to deport Illegals, to manage its borders more efficiently and to ensure that people of traditional European stock weren't overrun in their own country. Rocco had not been the public face of this campaign. He had been recruited because of his success in business and his reputation for customer service. Two years of free service for any used car that he sold. Customers loved him. He won 60 percent of the votes in his riding and was appointed transportation minister. But then suddenly he was switched into the immigration portfolio. Hell of a job. Nobody told him anything. The Prime Minister's Office ran the show. Rocco would ride out his term and then go back into business.

It was one thing to advocate changes to the immigration and refugee system, and quite another to be uncivil, mean-spirited and rude. What on earth was that second-place man bitching about? What was his problem with the black dude in the lead? Had the black guy been parachuted into the race from overseas to pick up the race money? Well, tough luck. That was sport. You wanted to have a real race, you had to compete with the best. Who was this fellow in the lead? He had no more white in him than an ebony carving, so why was he calling himself Roger Bannister? Maybe he was from Zantoroland. Maybe his parents had named him so, dreaming of bringing a great runner into the world.

Zantoroland. What a dump. Dictatorship. Poverty. The whole country of 4.5 million people was like one giant AfricTown. It was complicated, having AfricTown right on the southern edge of Clarkson, the capital city and crown jewel of Freedom State. Demonstrators insisted on mass arrests. They said the government should put anybody who couldn't prove citizenship on a boat home. If only it were that easy! Where could the government send them? Zantoroland was already bursting at the seams and would never accept a hundred thousand down-and-outers from Freedom State. Rocco was learning that you could only deport so many people. One of his briefing notes explained that Zantoroland, officially, was only willing to take five thousand "returnees" per year. Even arresting Illegals was complicated. You had to detain them, feed them and deal with all the negative publicity related to imprisoning them as if they were ordinary criminals. The only solution was to show the public that the government was dead serious about carrying through on its campaign promises—but to be strategic about it.

The hill was finally flattening out. Rocco had to concentrate on keeping his pace. He had bet five friends that in this, his first marathon, he could beat 3:15. Riding on the bet: a 750-millilitre bottle of eighteen-year-old, single-malt Macallan scotch worth two hundred and fifty dollars. He had to buy one for every friend if he ran slower than 3:15. And if he made the time, he would receive one from each friend. Scotch. Now that was the drink. It left the slightest burn in his gut. Well, scotch would be for another day. Now he had to batten down the hatches and keep the kilometres clicking and hope that his cellphone didn't ring again. Wait. Who was this lovely lady pulling up beside him? What a sight. How did he get to be so lucky? Fit and fifty and out running on a sunny day beside this fine specimen of womanhood.

SERGEANT CANDACE FREIXA WAS DOING THIS JUST FOR FUN. And for training. She was primarily a five-kilometre and ten-kilometre woman, and the two-time reigning champ in both events at the Freedom State Police Games. She had never tried out for an

Olympic team or tested herself against elite runners. She was merely faster than any other distance-running female officer in the country—and faster than most of the male officers too. Police bigwigs liked having a few female jocks on the force. Her bosses bragged to their counterparts in other cities that Candace could whip any cop in their shop—woman or man. Sometimes, they put down money. But it was all in good fun, and it came with great perks. They had sent her to race against cops in track and cross-country meets in Dublin, Amsterdam and New York. It was fun to hang out with fit cops and to get it on once in a blue moon when she knew she would never have to see the guy in Freedom State.

Candace had persuaded her captain to fly her to Buttersby—a good eight hundred kilometres from Clarkson—as a fitness test, in advance of the Freedom State Police Games. She figured she could run 3:10 without too much pain, so she planned to run at that pace or a little faster until the halfway mark and then pick it up if the spirit moved her. She would spend the weekend in Buttersby, go out dancing and if the right guy happened to come along—hot and clean and good about using condoms and all that—and if he didn't open his big fat mouth and say something negative about Illegals in Freedom State, he might just get lucky.

Candace had come from AfricTown, and she had no intention of moving back. Among her fellow cops, she didn't advertise where she came from. She didn't want to have to fend off the inevitable questions. When was she born? How had she gained citizenship? Had she forged her papers? Candace was born and raised in AfricTown, and, yes, so was her mother. Not every person in the community was illegal, although Candace had tired years ago of making that point.

Candace was running down the hill at the seventeen-kilometre mark when the lead marathoners began approaching her from the bottom of the hill. She had the whole hill to watch them coming. The guy up front was an object of beauty. He charged up as if on flat land. His race bib said he was Roger Bannister. She held out her hand for him, just on a whim, and he high-fived her, which made the whole race worthwhile. He was her age. More or less. She glanced over her shoulder to catch another glimpse of him. His ass looked hard, like a fine apple. Sculpted legs. If only hers were that firm. As he ran, he sang. Some corny country song. Candace recognized it.

In the instant that she high-fived the leader and moved past him, she noticed the second-place runner. A white guy. Hurting on the hill. She passed him. What? Had she heard that right? Did he call her a *nigger*? She couldn't believe it. Of course, she had been called a nigger a thousand times in Freedom State, and a thousand times people had assumed she was from away, not born in the country, not a native citizen with a university degree and a job as a police sergeant. But to be called a nigger by a fellow marathoner?

"Fuck you," she said.

At the bottom of the hill, Candace decided to not wait for the halfway mark to increase her speed. She pulled even with a big man ahead of her. About fifty. Good looking. Moving very well, considering his age, although he seemed flat-footed. She ran beside him for a while. Most guys in marathons were cool. He said something, and she looked over. His eyes were roving. This guy was checking her out, in the middle of a marathon.

Curvaceous. Who used that word anymore? It wasn't necessarily even a compliment, although he seemed to intend it so. He mumbled something about his yacht, Macallan single-malt scotch, and what was her number? She took a good look at him. She was on high alert now and not going to take any bullshit.

Just as she was going to let loose the most colourful AfricTown tongue-lashing the man had ever heard, she realized that he was Rocco Calder. Federal minister of immigration. He also happened to be one of the dudes she was ordered to protect, when she was assigned—among dozens of other cops—to do security detail on horseback at demonstrations. The police force used her as a public face. Why not kill two birds with one stone and have a black woman cop highly visible at public events? And Candace used it, for sure. Anything to get ahead. On the police force's tab, she had taken three years of riding lessons. Thousands of dollars of training, for free! So now she wasn't just a cop but also a horsewoman. Anything to get ahead. She wanted to make staff sergeant before she turned twenty-eight.

She pulled ahead of him. Wait till she told her girlfriends that the man known across the country as the Rock had tried to pick her up during the Buttersby Marathon. And that she had brushed hands with the cutest guy in the world, a slender, tight-cheeked black man who had charged like a locomotive up the Buttersby Mountain, singing a country song and flashing a gorgeous smile.

THE RUNNER TO WATCH IN THE BUTTERSBY MARATHON WAS probably from Zantoroland. But who he really was, Viola had no idea. Who in his right mind would register for the race under the alias Roger Bannister? Clearly he was an elite athlete, but Viola had already heard, mid-race, that he had not been registered as such. He had had to push his way close to the front of the crowd of regular runners, starting perhaps a hundred people and twenty metres behind the elite runners on the starting line.

On an international scale, this was a minor marathon that did not attract the fastest runners. What did you expect? It was only offering two thousand dollars for first prize, and an additional two thousand if the winner beat 2:10. Still, the fastest marathoners from Freedom State were entered in this race.

Viola wheeled close to the cordoned finishing line, in the area reserved for media. She positioned herself so that with her camera she could shoot the winner approaching and breaking the finishing tape. Thankfully, she saw no TV cameras. Viola hated TV crews. They showed no respect. TV cameramen and the so-called journalists who went out with them thought they owned exclusive visual access to any and every story. They would just plant themselves right in front of any newspaper person. But Viola had a strategy for that. A whistle hung around her neck right now, and if any smug sonofabitch with

TV equipment on his shoulder situated himself in front of her, Viola would blow that whistle until he moved.

Earlier in the competition, when Mitch Hitchcock—who directed the Buttersby Marathon, and virtually every other major road race in the country—gave her a lift to the big hill, Viola had taken a few shots of the lead runner. In one photo, as he ran up, he high-fived Rocco Calder, the federal minister of immigration, who was running down. Viola made a mental note to look for the minister later. She'd try to catch him after the race, in the tent where they handed out bananas and bagels. He'd be on his runner's high, and she could slip in a question about Yvette Peters.

When Viola had snapped his photo, the minister was already running several kilometres behind the leaders. The lead runner had looked easy and in control, even though some crazy-assed competitor was jawing away at him, calling him a nigger. And worse. Honestly, Viola's country was going to the dogs. What did you expect, with a government elected on a "boot out the refugees" platform? If the country's leaders were going to talk about blacks that way, it only stood to reason that the insanity would trickle down to the population, even to some of its elite marathon runners. This was one reason why she despised the Family Party. In her opinion, it gave Freedom Statonians licence to hate refugees. And her own government fed the prejudice.

Just six months before the Freedom Party was elected, a boatload of refugees had come to shore near the village of Pender's Mill on the southwest coast of Freedom State. They had not been given enough food or water when they were on board, and some had been beaten at sea. No news there. But after they arrived, some of the refugees murdered the captain of the boat. Then they went on a rampage, looting and pillaging in the town. Pender's Mill was hours by car from the nearest police station. Some of the refugees stormed a restaurant to demand food and drink that they could not pay for. There had been fights. Two local men died, as did six refugees. The others were held at gunpoint in a barn until the cops showed up. The incident made national and international news and led even more voters toward the Family Party, which milked the event for all it was worth.

Viola thought she had seen it all. Covered every sport, gone to every game, seen every conceivable thing there was to write about in the sporting world. But never before had she seen a white guy calling a black guy a nigger, mid-race. And what was the black guy doing? Racing up a steep hill as if gravity weren't a factor. Singing.

"Did you see that?" she had said to Hitchcock, who had accompanied her to the mid-race point.

Hitchcock had shaken his head and said only, "That guy in second is such a prick. He's a talented ten-thousand-metre runner, but he'll die somewhere beyond the top of this hill. Bet you he doesn't finish in the top three. But let's get you back to the finish line." He called for the wheelchair van and travelled back with Viola.

Some of the media thought Hitchcock was prickly and arrogant, and called him Bitch Pisscock, but he was a good man. You followed his rules and respected his races, and he treated you decently. Viola had no problem with Mitch Hitchcock.

And here she was, waiting at the finish line. Viola wondered if the lead runner had heard the insult. She had so much to ask that African, or whatever he was, if she could get to him.

Normally, Viola considered long-distance running a major yawn. On a day off, she would rather watch a cricket game, because at least at a cricket game you could have a beer and not worry about missing a thing if you fell asleep and napped for an hour. But this race was different. There was something mysterious about this runner, and Viola was going to find the story.

She was ready, hands on her camera. Hitchcock was standing on the other side of the finishing chute, talking to Anton Hamm, the marathon agent. The guy was about two heads taller and a hundred pounds heavier than Hitchcock. Built like a banyan fig tree. Hands like hams. The man looked like his own name. She shot them twice with her camera, testing the flash. Never a bad idea to have the race director's photo. Why was Hamm here? Did he represent the lead runner?

A boy wandered in front of her. He looked to be about twelve years old, and he had media ID hanging from his neck. This would be the day of strangeness. She waited for a moment, but he parked himself right in front of her, so she had no choice but to let him have it with the whistle. The kid jumped a foot straight up, and then he turned around, looking terrified. It was John Falconer. The whiz kid who had won the essay contest.

"Hey, kid, you've got to move," she said.

"I have to take a photo," he said.

She blasted him with the whistle again. "Move."

"Okay, okay," he said, and he stepped a metre away. "Good enough?" he said.

"More. I can't have you in my field of vision."

"I have to take a photo too."

She raised the whistle to her lips once more.

"All right, already." He gave her another metre or two.

She liked this kid; he had attitude to burn. "How'd you get the media accreditation?"

"Wrote to the race director," he said. He stared at her chair.

"What you looking at?" she asked.

"I was wondering how you get around so well," he said.

"Don't patronize me," she said. "I've never seen a kid covering a marathon before."

"And I've never seen a bald black woman whistling in a wheel-chair, but I wasn't planning to get all dramatic about it," he said. "Anyway, I remember you from the essay prize ceremony."

"So why are you interested in this marathon?"

"The lead runner. I want to put him in my documentary."

"Really," Viola said. "He interests me too."

He said, "Who do you think is going to win this race? A white guy or the black guy?"

"Black."

"How come?"

"Did you see him running up the hill earlier? He was charging uphill, and he wasn't even hurting. The guy who owns the marathon is the one who hurts the least."

"I've already got three hours of footage for my documentary," he said.

"Sounds like it's about more than just the race," she said.

"Maybe I could interview you too," he said.

"Fuck you," she said with a laugh.

"You said before that you were from AfricTown." He turned the camera on her.

"Don't point that thing at me. I'm not your story, fool. I'm your competition!"

"You lost your legs in AfricTown? When you were a child?"

"Later. Shouldn't you be in school or something?"

"I'm excused from class to film my documentary."

"Travelling all on your own?"

"You did, and your legs don't work," John said. "So why can't I?"

"Mouthy little fucker, aren't you?"

He took a few photos of the big man who appeared to be arguing with the race director.

"Who's the giant?" John asked.

"Anton Hamm."

"Who's he?"

"Human trafficker," Viola said.

"Get out!" he said.

"He's an agent for Zantoroland marathoners."

"That's right, I read about him," John said. "The ex-shot-putter. The one with the temper who won two Olympic gold medals."

"You *did* read about him," Viola said.

"We should collaborate," he said. "I could tell you a few things, and you could answer some of my questions."

"I'm a reporter," Viola said, "and I don't answer questions."

"Guess you won't be getting any scoops from me."

The kid was too smartassed for Viola's liking. And he really needed to grow.

"There's just one thing I want to know," the boy said.

"What?"

"You're a reporter and all, so you follow politics, right?"

"You bet."

"Well, about the prime minister?"

"Graeme Wellington. What about him? Spit it out. Not much time, now."

"Does he have some sort of assistant, somebody in his inner circle named Whoa-Boy?"

"I don't know any Whoa-Boy, but he has an EA named Geoffrey Moore."

"EA. What's that?"

"Executive assistant. Okay, lesson is over, Johnny. Move right over. More. More. More. Good. See? The winner is coming, four blocks away. See him? I gotta get set."

The leader looked, well, how would she describe him? Thin, muscular, early twenties. Boyish face. Made running look like an art form. Smooth, effortless, his legs churning, and he was moving faster than a boy like John here could sprint for a hundred metres. What was his real name? What was his story? Not another runner in sight.

Roger Bannister, or whoever he was, crossed the line in 2:09:36. There was a cash prize for winning and another for finishing in under 2:10. She caught him with her camera as he crossed the finish line. Got the look on this face, his arms up, waist breaking the tape. Happy? No. Exhausted? Neither. He looked worried.

She wheeled off to interview him.

LITTLE GUYS DIDN'T LIKE GIANTS TOWERING OVER THEM, SO Anton Hamm gave the fellow some breathing room. In anger management, they had emphasized spatial needs. They had told Anton to visualize a three-metre radius around every person who irritated him. "Do not breach their radius," he had been told. Anger-management people talked like that. With a straight face. *Do not breach their radius.* Anyway, he did have something of a problem. He could admit that. He could easily blow a gasket, only to feel remorseful later. So now, he tried to follow the counselling advice he had received.

Stepping back, he said once again, "Mr. Hitchcock."

Hitchcock did not even turn his head. He kept his eyes on the finishing line and said with false cheer, "Busy just now."

Anton stared at the man. The chain-smoking race director was fifty-something and long-haired and skinny as a fence pole. His strained, pseudo-polite British falsetto really meant, *Screw off.*

Giving Hitchcock extra room was clearly not working. And now there were other people in his way. Anton used his bulk cautiously, wedging himself between minor race officials, pushing them aside without knocking them off balance. The world was teeming with stubborn little people, and the trick was to apply enough force to move them without tipping them over.

"Mr. Hitchcock—"

"I'm managing a marathon here, six hundred volunteers at last count, so it will have to wait."

Hitchcock kept his eyes fixed ahead. Anton double-checked, but there was nothing to see or watch over there—just the empty, cordoned-off corridor through which the marathoners would run to cross the finish line.

Mitch Hitchcock barely cleared five-seven. Anton could have placed his chin on Hitchcock's head. In Anton's experience, the shorter, the testier. Little people were like little dogs. Anton took hold of the race director's elbow. It wasn't much bigger than a turkey bone. Anton squeezed just hard enough to get the man's attention.

Hitchcock yanked his arm back. "Shall I call security?"

"Just one moment."

"You're Anton Hamm."

"And you're Mitch Hitchcock."

"You may have thirty seconds. Starting now. What is it?"

"The guy who's about to win? He's one of mine."

"He's registered as Roger Bannister," Hitchcock said, "and there's no indication he's with you."

"He is. The cheque comes to me, as usual in these cases."

"Look, Mr. Hamm, I set the rules, I let them be known, and I do not divert from them. Unless he's preregistered as one of yours, I can't do that."

"His real name is Keita Ali."

"Well, we agree on one thing—Roger Bannister is a stretch," Hitchcock said. "If you're going to make up a pseudonym, what's wrong with Bob Jones?"

"His name is Keita Ali," Anton repeated, "and he's from Zantoroland. He's mine. The cheque is mine."

"The cheque is his. My race, my rules."

Anton breathed in deeply. *Reflect*, they said in anger management. *Breathe and reflect.* That thing you want to do? If you let the instinct control you, will the consequences help you or hurt you in the long run? *Count to ten. Reflect.* The anger-management people had talked about pros and cons. Anton tallied up the cons. He took the runners in his stable to marathons and other road races around the world, and it would not do to be charged with assault. He got off the last time with a conditional discharge and an undertaking to do community service, which he had done, and to take anger-management classes, which he had done too. So Anton breathed and once more tallied the cons and took a few steps back to restore the safety zone around Hitchcock.

It was not the best time for Anton to pursue compensation for his considerable expenses. The thin young Zantorolander with the ridiculous name Roger Bannister on his race bib crossed the finish line and slowed to a stop.

Anton looked at the clock. His runaway protégé had just broken the course record and there was no other runner in sight. Hitchcock hurried off.

Two of Anton's other protégés from Zantoroland were running the Buttersby Marathon. Neither was doing well. They would not end up on the medal podium, and they would not earn any prize money—money that would normally go almost entirely to him, as their running agent. He had sunk thousands of dollars into flying them to Freedom State, putting them up, feeding them—and he wasn't even going to break even.

On top of that, the Tax Agency for Freedom State was on his case. Letters here, letters there, discrepancy this, discrepancy that, and the most recent and annoying missive said that he had to report to the TAFS main office in Clarkson for a pre-audit meeting tomorrow. If he failed to show up, he would be subjected to a full and complete audit. Anton's papers were a mess. For years, he had dashed off his tax returns. One day, he'd have to hire an accountant to straighten out his records. But right now, he had the most annoying, ball-breaking tax agency in the world taking up his valuable time. What kind of country privatized its own tax agency? TAFS was a for-profit corporation operating at arm's length from the government, and the pursuit of a citizen's taxes had become the pursuit of its profits. When you caught their attention, they came after you like hornets.

To make matters worse, business was tough. In the last year, Anton had brought fifteen Zanfricans—a catch-all term for people from Zantoroland or Africa—to race in America, Europe and Freedom State. He had covered all their expenses—flights, hotels, meals, clothes, passports, visas and race entry fees. Only two runners had won races with respectable payouts. Yes, he was disappointed when one of his runners dropped out or got injured or didn't run as fast as Anton had anticipated. But Keita Ali was the first runner to take off on him. Then the kid had the gall to enter a race by himself and collect his own winnings. Ten thousand bucks, Anton figured he was owed, and ten thousand bucks he would get from that cheating sonofabitch.

Just as his disappointing other protégés were finishing seventh and ninth in the Buttersby Marathon, someone tapped Anton on the shoulder.

He was a copper-toned black man. Medium build. Definitely

not a runner. Dark shades. Baseball cap. In his thirties. Wearing running gear: track pants, running shoes that looked straight out of the shoebox, a big fat running watch and a zippered nylon jacket. About five-ten. Next to Anton, the man was tiny.

"Hey," the man in the track suit said.

Anton was in a suit. Dressed for success. Anton figured the fellow had a brother or a wife in the marathon and had come out to watch. Maybe he recognized Anton. Maybe he knew Anton had won two Olympic gold medals.

"It's Anton Hamm, if I'm not mistaken."

Anton forced a smile.

"I'm Saunders, and I have a proposition for you."

"Make it quick. I have to meet my athletes."

"Is sixty thousand a year quick enough for you?"

Anton stared. Saunders stood there calmly, unblinking. Anton raised his eyebrows.

"We can offer you sixty thousand a year for services that will not compromise your marathon agency work. Indeed, they would complement it. Sixty thousand, plus bonuses for good results, and expenses for one or two of your regular trips to Zantoroland."

"We?" Anton said.

"My associates and I."

"You have associates?" Anton said.

"People of influence. People who can make your life easy—or make it hell."

"Are you threatening me?" Anton asked. He had a mind to take this fellow by the collar and give him a good shaking.

Saunders stood his ground, that calm, stupid grin on his face. For a short man, he seemed unreasonably confident, which Anton found disconcerting.

"I am offering you something that you do not wish to refuse."

"I don't like puzzles, so spit it out," Anton said.

"You travel three or four times a year to Zantoroland," Saunders said.

"That's my business," Anton said.

"Your last tax statement indicated expenses over \$150,000 and that you finished the year with a loss."

"For a little fellow, you're doing a damn good job of getting up in my face," Anton said.

"Consider what you would like more," Saunders said. "Sixty thousand in cash for a minimum amount of work, or having the Tax Agency audit you and your travel expenses." He stepped back and put his hand in his pocket.

"How do I know you're legit?" Anton said.

"You declared most of your expenses as travel. You also listed a business expense called 'wardrobe.'" Saunders studied Anton's suit. "Really, Mr. Hamm. You should know better."

"You half-pint prick," said Anton. "How do you know this shit?"

"Mr. Hamm, calm yourself. You have been called to a pre-audit tax meeting with TAFS tomorrow. If you do not hear me out, tomorrow's meeting will lead to a full audit."

Anton drummed his fingers on his hips.

"Meet me at nine thirty tomorrow morning in the café in the All Saints Hotel on Brunswick Street in Clarkson. You will be in the area because your meeting with TAFS is just around the corner. At noon, correct? I know that they are not yet asking for a full audit, and I trust that you will not give them reason to do so. Let me make this clear. If you do not show up at 9:30 a.m., with a far better attitude, then you will experience the direct consequences two and a half hours later. In the tax office. Good day, Mr. Hamm."

WHEN HE CROSSED THE FINISH LINE, KEITA ALI RAISED HIS arms for the cameras. He felt an almost insatiable desire to lie down in tall green grasses and never get up again, and he fought to silence all the body parts in revolt: the blistered toe, the ache on the right side of his groin, the vibrating hamstring, the stinging hernia and the tantrum-ing heart. At least his body had cooperated this time. It had allowed him to finish a race, with no shakes, nausea or feeling that he might faint. Still, there was something inside him. Some feeling of discomfort. It was stirring now, waking like an angry baby.

To take his mind off his discomfort, Keita played with numbers. 42.2 kilometres. Or 26 miles, 385 yards. Either way, running like this was as close as he could get to dying, without going over the edge. 2:09:36. Two thousand dollars for first place and another two thousand for beating 2:10. The money would keep him going for months. He should have felt relief. Instead, he looked over one shoulder. And the other. No sign of trouble. Nobody looking for him. Perhaps he was safe.

There were hands to shake, photos to pose for and promises of a prize ceremony in two hours. He paid an urgent visit to the portable toilet. In Freedom State, one did not piss behind bushes. In this country, they made one portable toilet available for every twenty runners. So there were 150 portable toilets lined up in a seemingly endless row, and Keita got to them first. Coming out, he could still feel his slamming heart. Without even raising index and middle fingers to his jugular, he knew it was going at about 150 beats per minute. In another minute, he'd be down to 120. Within a day, if nobody chased him and he had no cause to run, he'd return to his resting pulse: 38 beats a minute.

He hated running a single additional step after finishing a race, but he did what he had been trained to do, breaking into a slow jog back out in the direction of the oncoming runners, although none were approaching yet. He ran just outside the fence sealing off the race route, south on a street named Avenue Road. Was it named merely to confuse people who had no business being in the country? Back in Zantoroland, anyone proposing such a street name would be laughed out of the room. Keita could imagine the chuckles: *Yes, of course, and let's name another one Boulevard Road.*

The second-place finisher came into view. The one named Smart. He had a choppy gait; his right knee turned in when he ran.

Had to be a decent fellow. He was the one who had told the name-caller to back off.

"Way to go," Keita said, and the man acknowledged him with a nod as he ran painfully toward the finish.

Smart was coming in at a shade over 2:14. In Zantoroland one-legged runners could hop that fast.

Heading south along Avenue Road, Keita jogged for a minute and turned. By the time he got back, the third runner was finishing in 2:17. There was still no sight of the name-caller.

With the exception of a handful of runners, the five thousand joggers were all still pushing through the marathon, cheered on by marching bands and rock bands and thousands of spectators, pitching like enthusiastic penguins toward the finish line. Recreational joggers in Freedom State carried their life possessions. And the farther back they were in the race, the more they carried. Baseball caps. Water bottles, digital cameras, key chains laden with keys, iPods. Wallet-sized watches with GPS systems. They did this willingly. They found this entertaining in Freedom State.

Keita had chosen a good country in which to hide. It had many cities and a good transportation system. It had one of the best hospital networks in the world. Unless he was hit by a bus, struck by lightning or caught and deported, he had a greater statistical likelihood of staying alive here than where he had come from. That was as much as he could reasonably desire. And there was another benefit to living in this country: after a marathon, they gave out bagfuls of food and offered a free massage.

Keita headed to the food area to collect bagels, bananas, apples and energy bars. He shoved them in a bag. Later, he'd be hungry. This food could last for days. Keita gulped down two bottles of water and one sports drink, but his lips were cracking and still he felt thirsty. His hamstring cramped suddenly, just like it had in the Boston Marathon. What was wrong with him? Was he just nervous? There was no sign of anyone looking for him. No sign of Anton Hamm. He should eat something. Maybe it would make him feel

---

better. He found a firm banana. It made him think of home. It made him think of women on their way to market, carrying platters of bananas on their heads. He and Charity used to try to balance trays on their heads and see how far they could go. Not far. Especially not on bumpy terrain. Charity . . . Still no word from her. Perhaps she had gone travelling somewhere and was simply out of touch by email and phone. If that was the case, Keita hoped desperately that she would return home soon, or at least contact him.

Just then, a black, bald woman rolled up to him in a wheelchair. She looked his age—mid-twenties. Her arms were thick and ripped, like those of a wrestler. She had full lips, dimpled cheeks and eyes that bore right into him. A decal was stuck on the side of her chair: *I dig dykes on wheels.* Back home, gays and lesbians had to be secretive. If they were outed, they were killed. The woman slapped on the brakes, clicked a button on a tape recorder, whipped out a microphone on a yardstick and thrust it toward his mouth.

"Viola Hill, the *Telegram*," she said.

"I saw you training recently," he said. "You were in a racing chair. On Ten-Mile Inlet, in Clarkson. Early morning."

"So that was you," she said. "Well, I'm with the newspaper in Clarkson."

He looked again at her bizarre bumper sticker.

"Could I get your name?" she said.

"Roger Bannister," Keita told her. His gaze fell back on her sign.

"Mister, you got a problem with dykes?"

Keita hesitated. "I have no such problem," he said slowly. "I was just wondering if you could get in trouble for outing yourself."

"Not here, mister. Not from the government, anyway. But thanks for the concern. Your thoughts on the race?"

"The hill in the second half was tough," he said.

"I heard what that guy said to you on the hill," the reporter said.

"What guy?" Keita said. He didn't want any fuss.

"The number-one-ranked ten-thousand-metre runner in this country. Billy Deeds. He called you a nigger. Called you other things too."

"I didn't hear that," Keita said.

"I've yet to meet a black person who is deaf to that word," Viola said.

"When you're focused, you tune out the sounds."

"So why were you singing? What's that all about?"

"Sometimes I sing, as a way of locating my energy."

"So when did you know you would win?" she asked.

"I pulled ahead on the hill at twenty-four kilometres and thought the race would be mine if my hamstrings didn't seize up."

She let out a laugh that sounded like a bark, or a starting pistol. "Right," she said, "the thing about hamstrings is that they own you. Can't run without their say-so."

She knew a thing or two about running. "True enough," he said.

"Cramps bother you often?"

"Usually it's the threat of cramps."

"Have you checked your potassium levels?"

He stifled a laugh. Potassium levels. Ridiculous. For a potassium count, you needed blood tests, laboratories, doctors. He had to get away from her. He knew exactly what was coming.

"You registered under the name Roger Bannister," she said. "But what is your real name?"

"That's it," he said.

"Where are you from?"

Keita felt a pinch in his hamstring. The reporter sitting in front of him seemed blurry. He squinted to bring her into focus. He didn't want to faint in front of her or anyone in this country. Fainting would attract attention and trouble. And now there was something else—a deep, emphatic voice in the distance. Anton Hamm.

"I have to go," Keita said.

Keita looked in every direction but did not see Hamm. He shot an apologetic look at the reporter and turned to go. It now felt more tiring to walk than it had to run during the race. The cramping flared again in his hamstring. Keita limped into a massage tent marked with a sign Athletes Only. He needed to be alone. He needed to lie down. He needed to escape the inevitable questions.

Inside the massage tent, a young woman smiled at him.

"Could we close these?" he said.

"Sure," she said, drawing the curtains fully around them. "Massage today?"

"Definitely," he said.

The therapist had red hair and brown eyes. She shook his hand firmly.

"I'm Paula," she said, then she stepped out of the curtains to allow him a moment of privacy. He slipped out of his shirt and socks, climbed onto the massage table and lay face down, letting his brow and cheekbones sink into the doughnut-shaped face rest. It was heated. So were the cotton sheets under his belly. The warmth soothed his ribcage and seeped through his body.

Paula returned, placed one hand on the small of his back and began to slide the heel of the other palm along his hamstring while covering the other half of his backside with a heating pad.

"Problems today?" Paula's hands pressed down firmly on his neck, back, buttocks, hamstrings, calves and feet. In an instant, she located a knot in his left hamstring and placed some weight on it.

Keita tried to breathe through the pain. "I'm tired all over," he said, "but you've already found one sore spot."

"No wonder," she said. "I hear you broke the course record."

"Uh-huh." Keita had wanted to set the record. Now all he had to do was collect his winnings and get out of town before anybody caught up with him. But after marathons, race officials took their time about handing out prize money. They wanted to have most of the runners across the finish line before they held the prize cere-mony. For Keita, that would mean a two-hour wait. As much as Keita found the marathon a dance with death—an exploration of just how much pain a person could tolerate—the suffering lasted only a little more than two hours. He couldn't understand how any recreational runner could keep going for four hours.

Paula leaned deeper into his upper leg. Keita groaned.

"You've got a sore ham," she said.

As she massaged, Keita relaxed under the pressure of her hands. He thought of his mother and father and the last time he'd seen them together. They were having tea on the two chairs on the front porch, debating about whether plane trees were native to Zantoroland or a foreign species. Yoyo said he could spot an invader any day of the week. What did he know, his mother said, being a foreign interloper himself? Keita remembered the sound of their laughter. It was like a duet. The laugh they made together was Keita's purest notion of home. Home had a door, and as it opened and Keita walked through it, he felt an ocean of tears welling inside him. So he walked back out and closed the door gently behind him, and he came back to Paula, who was talking still about the tightness in his hamstrings.

"The left is tighter than the right," she said. He sank into the pressure and allowed her to cause him pain without tensing his muscles.

"When I run hard, it tightens up and starts to cramp," he said.

Paula slicked her hands with massage oil. It sounded like people doing it in bed. He hadn't been with a woman in ages. In this country, he wondered if he ever would. She slipped over to his other leg. The one that didn't hurt.

"So are you on the national team?"

"No."

"Well, you beat all of them today. Just exactly where are you—?"

"Kintermore," he lied. Kintermore was located one hour to the west. Whenever people asked where he was from, he named a different city in Freedom State—but never Clarkson.

"Kintermore? And before that?"

"It's a long story," he said.

"We've got time," she said, but he did not reply. She spent a few minutes working on his good hamstring and then asked if he wanted her to return to the sore leg.

"Sure," he said. He could feel her palm digging into a knot at the top of his thigh.

"So, have you been saved?" she said.

"Mmm," he moaned. Keita wondered if Paula would be interested in seeing him later that day.

Miraculously, she asked, "Are you free this evening?"

"I believe so," Keita said. He had been planning to leave town on the eastbound intercity bus leaving that night, but if luck smiled down on him, he could always leave in the morning.

Her hands slid down to his calves. "This calf is quite loose," she said. "Amazing, after a marathon. You should see the calves I meet up with."

"Only the hamstrings cause me trouble."

"There is a solution," she said.

"And that is?"

"Are you ready to take Jesus into your heart?"

Keita flipped over on the table and looked straight at Paula. She was smiling and confident. Just behind her was a large poster on a stand. He had missed it earlier: *Christian Massage Centre*.

"Pardon me?"

"Are you ready for Jesus? There's a gathering at the Church of the Redeemer tonight."

His twitching hamstring escalated into a full-blown cramp. He was low on liquids. That was the problem. Dehydrated. As they said in this country, short on electrolytes. He swung his legs off the table and put his weight on the cramping leg.

"I just came for the massage," he said. "I didn't see your sign."

Her mouth collapsed into a frown.

"Is Roger Bannister in there?" A loud male voice announced itself outside the curtain.

It startled Keita, but at least it was not the voice he had been fearing.

"Is that you?" Paula asked him.

Before Keita could answer, the voice continued. "The race winner. I want the race winner. Is he in there?"

"He'll be out in a jiffy," Paula said.

Keita would leave on the night bus, after all. "Thanks for the massage," he said.

Paula pulled back the curtain.

* * *

THE RACE DIRECTOR HAD LONG GREY HAIR AND WORE JEANS and sandals. He was slim, tanned and wrinkled. The word "hippie" came to mind. When he was a boy, Keita had heard from Yoyo that hippies were long-haired, anti-war Americans and Canadians who in the 1960s and 1970s ditched their jobs, took drugs, listened to electric music and believed in "free love." Hitchcock directed Keita to his tent nearby and offered a chair. But sitting would pitch his hamstring into a full-fledged revolt. Keita couldn't afford to fall. Someone might call an ambulance. And then there would be questions: Who was he? Where were his papers?

"Could I have a drink with fruit, sugar, something with . . ."

"Electrolytes," Hitchcock said.

"Exactly," Keita said. "My hamstring is revolting."

"Hamstring revolting, is it?" Hitchcock chuckled. "Right, then." He ripped open his tent flap and shouted for his aide to bring him three bottles of electrolytes. They came in a minute. Hitchcock put one bottle in Keita's hand, but Keita hesitated, so Hitchcock took the bottle, unscrewed the cap and handed it back. "Drink, man," he said. "And sit down."

Hitchcock studied Keita intently. He reached forward. Keita flinched as if he were expecting to be hit and dropped the bottle.

"Take it easy there. I couldn't hurt a flea," Hitchcock said. "Steady. I'm going to help you." He opened another bottle of the drink, placed it in Keita's hand and brought it gently but firmly to Keita's mouth. Tipping the bottle up, he told him to drink.

Keita felt hot. He felt cold. He couldn't control the trembling. His vision was blurry.

"We've got one or two angry people outside," Hitchcock said. "Because you swept in and scooped up the prize money. But it's a free country. Prize goes to the fittest, and you were that today. The second-place finisher is the third-ranked marathoner in this country. Ran in the last Olympic Games. The guy who finished fourth, Billy Deeds—he was the one bad-mouthing you up the big hill—is the best ten-thousand-metre runner in this country. He's one helluva runner, but he blew a gasket today. What did you do to him out there?"

Keita didn't want trouble, so he just said, "I ran faster than him." He decided to risk the chair. Better to battle the hamstring cramps than to faint dead on the floor. He sipped the sweet liquid again. He wished he could lie down, take the drink in an intravenous line and sleep. He shivered. He just had to collect his prize money and get to the bus. If his hamstring would cooperate, he could sleep for the whole ride.

"Did you hear him insulting you on the course?"

"No."

"Do you mind me asking where you are from?"

"Kintermore," Keita said.

"Do you take me for an idiot?" Hitchcock said.

Keita felt it wise not to answer.

"What's your name?" Hitchcock said. "And don't waste my time telling me it's Roger Bannister. I wasn't born yesterday. Roger Bannister was the fastest miler in the world—about sixty-five years ago."

"Does my real name matter?" Keita said.

"If you want your prize money."

"If I tell you my name, will you let the name Roger Bannister stand as the race winner? I mean, in the printed race results?"

"No can do."

It felt like a clamp fastened itself around Keita's left buttock and began to tighten. Keita shouted, stood to lessen the pain and saw tiny fragments of light spinning around before his eyes. The next thing he knew, he was lying on the floor and smelling beer on the breath of Mitch Hitchcock, who was checking for a pulse.

"Talk to me," Hitchcock said.

"I'm talking," Keita said.

"Shall I call a paramedic?"

"Please don't. I'll answer your questions. No paramedic and no police."

"Easy there," Hitchcock said. "I don't call the cops on my runners. God love ya. Bend your legs." Keita obeyed. Hitchcock slid a blanket under Keita's head. "I think we'll leave you right here. Have another sip."

Keita turned to the side, sipped the drink and then eased onto his back again.

"I'm Keita Ali. I'm from Zantoroland."

"I figured as much."

"A man is looking for me, and I'd rather not have you use my name."

"If you want the prize money, you'll have to use your real name."

"Could I take it in cash?"

"We use cheques. Accountability concerns. And I'm very sorry about this, but if I'm going to give you the prize money, I have to identify you correctly to the media. So you can either take the money and be identified, or decline the money and remain anonymous."

"I need the money." Keita sighed. He'd seen a private cheque-cashing service in Clarkson, but it took 15 percent of the total. "Could you cash the cheque for me and give me the money?"

"It would look like I was taking a kickback. The cheque's good. Don't you have ID?"

"No."

"How did you get into this country?"

"I'd rather not say." Keita finished his drink and asked for another. He felt ready to stand again.

"There are people outside who want to talk to you. Listen." Hitchcock put a finger to his lips, and they paused for a minute. "That's the reporter in the wheelchair," he said under his breath. "Watch out for that one, man. She never gives up. If she had legs, she'd outrun you."

"What's her name again?"

"Viola Hill."

Keita could hear the reporter interviewing Billy Deeds. He was saying that the prize money should be for citizens. They were the ones who were running for this country. They were the ones who would honour the country in the Olympics. They were the ones who relied on prize money to keep up their training regimens.

Viola asked Deeds why he had called the race leader a nigger.

"I didn't say any such thing."

"I heard you. He was dropping you on the big hill, and you used a bunch of nasty words on him, so how do you call yourself a sportsman?"

"You're starting to piss me off."

"Well," Viola said, "he sure whipped your ass."

"Hey," he said. "I've got my citizenship card. Have you seen his? He shouldn't be taking prize money from legitimate runners unless he has a citizenship card."

Hitchcock grinned at Keita.

"Don't let it bother you," Hitchcock said. "The guy likes to rant. And nobody but me is allowed to rant."

Keita smiled faintly. He didn't know why, but he was beginning to like Mitch Hitchcock.

"I also heard him calling you names on the course," Hitchcock said. "Want to file a complaint?"

"What did you hear?"

"Don't play me for a fool. Deeds was out of control, ranting and swearing. What was that about, anyway?"

"I don't know. He doesn't like me."

"Do you want to file a complaint?"

Keita looked alarmed. "No fuss, please."

"All right," Hitchcock said. "No fuss. You look like an honest sort."

Keita waited for Hitchcock to reveal his intentions.

The race director continued. "Trouble with this country is that decades have gone by since we produced a top-ranked marathon runner. And how did you get here without ID? Did Anton Hamm bring you in?"

"I'd prefer to collect the prize money and just leave quietly," Keita said.

"You showed up at my race at the last minute," Hitchcock said. "That's right, it's *my* race. I started this race thirty years ago. I have fought for every cent of its funding. I don't care if you're a Zantorolander, Egyptian, Algerian, Moroccan, Ethiopian or Kenyan. I give you a drink when you faint in my tent, hold off this pack of first-rate angry assholes outside so you can rehydrate in peace—and you want to avoid my questions?"

Keita smiled. He was able to get up to a chair and sit down without a resurgence in his hamstring. "I'm sorry if I was rude."

"You can stay in my tent until the prize ceremony, and I'll keep the devils out."

"Thanks."

"Do you even know who Roger Bannister was?"

"He ran the first sub-four-minute mile in 3:59:04 on May 6, 1954, in Oxford, England."

"Why'd you take his name?"

"When I was a boy, we had back issues of *Track and Field News* at my school."

"I'll be damned. Back issues of *Track and Field News* in Zantoroland. Regardless, because you are unknown to us and because you were running under an absurd pseudonym, three race officials insisted that you couldn't possibly have won this race legitimately in two hours, nine minutes and thirty-six seconds. It's the fastest time posted this year in the country. I had to go back to the computer to check your progress over the checkpoints."

Thank God for computer chips, Keita thought. The computer chip attached to his shoelace had tracked him as he ran across all twenty of the computerized rubber mats placed along the marathon route.

"I didn't believe you could have run that fast either. I guessed you were a cheater," said Hitchcock. "But your chip turned up good. You passed every single time check. Did you drink during the race?"

"Some."

"Not good enough. You need electrolytes. You need a coach."

"I run for pleasure."

"The pleasure of money."

Hitchcock let Keita stay in the tent. Keita heard him hollering out the door that the winner was recovering from dehydration.

When the time came to receive his medal and cheque, Keita followed Hitchcock outside. He looked to his left and then his right, took a step and walked right into Anton Hamm. The man had a chin that pointed sharply, like an accusation.

Keita drew in a quick breath. He tried to step back, but Hitchcock was right behind him.

"You little fucker," Hamm said.

"I'll make it up to you later," Keita said.

"Nobody takes off on me when I've flown them around the world," Hamm said.

"Language, language," Hitchcock said.

Hamm snatched Keita's forearm and twisted the skin to make it burn. "I have a bone to pick with you."

"Hey," Hitchcock said. He came up beside Keita.

"Look," Keita said, "I have some problems, but I will—"

"Problems indeed," Hamm said. "You owe me ten grand."

"Let go of him or I'll call security," Hitchcock said.

"No security, please," Keita said.

Hamm squeezed sufficiently to show Keita how easily his wrist could snap. "I'm warning you, and just this one time. Ten grand. In U.S. dollars. To cover my expenses and my trouble. I want four K by April 25 and the rest by July 1."

"Hey, hey, hey, no touching the runners," Hitchcock said. "I'll have a police officer here in seconds if you don't leave the premises this instant."

Hitchcock was a small man, no larger than Keita, but when he gave Hamm a forceful shove, the giant let go of Keita's wrist and backed off.

"Ten grand," Hamm said. "Ninety days. Are you getting my message?"

"Last warning, or I use the radio right here on my hip and call the police," Hitchcock said. "There are fifty of them right over there. So leave, and leave now."

To Keita's astonishment and relief, Hamm turned and left.

"No police, please," Keita said to Hitchcock.

"No need for them now," Hitchcock said.

AFTER THE PRIZE CEREMONY, THEY RETURNED TO THE TENT. Hitchcock gave Keita an envelope.

"Don't lose it," he said. "It's your cheque."

"Thanks." Keita borrowed the race director's phone and tried one more time to call his sister. Still no answer.

Hitchcock grabbed another bottle of sports drink and led Keita out the back door of his tent. Viola Hill was waiting.

"Here comes trouble," Hitchcock said.

"Keita, I need to know. Are you from Zantoroland? Or an African country?"

Keita smiled and walked past her. She spun in her chair and caught up to him.

"Keita. Listen. I will lose my job if I can't answer the basic questions. You won that race, and sports fans deserve an answer. Are you an African?"

"No," he said.

"Then Zantoroland," she said. "Just look at me for a moment, and smile if you are from Zantoroland."

He looked at her. He smiled.

"Thank you," she said. "How can I reach you?"

"That's quite enough, Miss Hill," Hitchcock said. He gave the handle of her wheelchair a little shake.

Then he put Keita in a car and drove him to the bus station. There, he bought the ticket for Keita. One hundred and thirty dollars for the eight-hour bus trip to Clarkson, leaving at 11 p.m.

"Got any money, other than that cheque you don't know how to cash?" Hitchcock asked.

"There is food in my bag."

Hitchcock stuffed some bills into Keita's hand and suggested the pub beside the bus station. "Try the shepherd's pie."

"Thanks."

"Remember. When you're back in Clarkson, get in touch with me. I'll introduce you to the national team. They train in Ruddings Park. Weekend mornings, seven o'clock."

"I'll think it over," Keita said.

Hitchcock paused for a moment, letting his eyes rest on Keita. "For an uncoached runner, you've got potential. Nobody just goes out there and posts a 2:09 marathon. No team, no coach, no backup. Come on. Run with the team!"

Hitchcock gave Keita his business card, shook his hand and left.

There were decent folks around. Keita felt lucky to meet them. He could use a little good fortune, and he could use a friend.

CHAPTER TWELVE

WEEKS EARLIER, AFTER KEITA'S FIRST NIGHT in Clarkson—in a forty-dollar-a-night motel that did not demand ID because he paid cash up front—he had gone running in Ruddings Park. A jogger recognized him as being of the same Faloo ethnicity and asked him to stop. Keita did so briefly, but he didn't give his name or tell the man where he was staying. He listened, though, when the man told him not to travel in cars. Not if he wanted to avoid the immigration cops. They stopped people in cars all the time, the man said, and always demanded the national citizenship card. If you didn't have it, they detained you until they could figure out where to deport you. Some people, he said, spent years in detention centres.

Keita thanked the man and said he had to keep moving. The man asked if he could run with Keita, just for a kilometre. He hadn't run with anyone since leaving Zantoroland, he said, and he missed it. Sure, Keita said. He began running again, slowly to accommodate the fellow.

"So," the jogger said, "have you heard of ZRA?"

Keita said he hadn't.

"It's Zantorolanders Refugee Association. We want the government of Freedom State to hear our voices and to stop deporting people who are found without papers." The jogger tapped his shoulder familiarly, like a friend might have done back home. "We need people in the movement."

Keita nodded noncommittally.

"By the way, you run beautifully. Are you an elite marathoner?"

"I was. Now I'm just running to stay alive."

"You could be a role model for our cause."

"Sorry," Keita repeated, "but I can't help you right now." And with that, he accelerated and left the jogger behind.

KEITA WAS HEEDING THE ADVICE NOT TO TRAVEL BY CAR. Though his muscles were aching, he was sitting at the back of a bus in the Buttersby station, waiting for it to depart for Clarkson. He had killed several hours in the pub, where he sat in a corner, facing a wall, nursing tea and shepherd's pie and hoping to avoid attention. Nobody knew his name or a thing about him, or cared if he was cold or hungry or afraid, but he feared that everyone noticed him.

Keita had boarded the bus the minute the doors opened. The less he was in public view, the better. He chose a window seat near the back. He had barely sat down when a boy—perhaps only twelve years old but travelling alone—took the seat beside him.

To take his mind off his troubles, Keita had turned on his iPod, put the buds in his ears and listened to a country song about a man with a broken heart.

> I got the gotta have you
> God I want you
> Don't you wanna love me blues
> Wait all day for you to call my name
> But baby baby baby baby
> You ain't got the blues the same
> No
> You ain't got the same.

Keita found it odd that here, in one of the richest nations of the world, bad grammar seemed acceptable in music. Still, the words and music were catchy, and he hummed along until a woman across the aisle gave him a nasty look. He stopped and unplugged the iPod. He had to be careful. One did not hum or sing in public in Freedom State—neither while walking around the street nor while sitting on a bus. People in this country took it as a sign of mental imbalance. To Keita, that itself was insanity.

Keita opened the *Clarkson Evening Telegram* he had bought before boarding and flipped through the news. He scanned an editorial that criticized the government for having curried votes during the election campaign by promising something that it must have known would be impossible to deliver: the bulldozing of AfricTown and the deportation of every Illegal in Freedom State. On the back page, Keita found a story by Viola Hill, the woman who had tried to interview him after the race, about a seventeen-year-old girl named Yvette Peters who had been deported to Zantoroland even though she was born in Freedom State. One line stood out: "An official from the notorious Pink Palace, who identified himself as Mr. Chelsea, claimed that the young girl died of natural causes."

Keita studied one of the photos of the girl, taken when she was ten or so. Pretty. Brown complexion. A wary smile. Another photo showed her at age twelve, standing with her mother. The girl probably died in the same building as his father.

Keita wondered how many people had been killed in the Pink Palace, and how many loved ones—like Yvette's mother, and like him—had to go on living anyway. Keita did not want to look at the photos anymore, but he was drawn back into the details of the story. There wasn't much. The mother said the girl had run away from home at the age of sixteen. Strange. In Zantoroland, children often lost their homes or their parents; they did not run away from them.

A line in the story riveted Keita.

"Immigration Minister Rocco Calder, who was interviewed after finishing the Buttersby Marathon, said he had no comment on the matter. Asked if he had any knowledge about how Yvette Peters had come to leave Freedom State, he said, 'Absolutely none, and I can guarantee you that.' As for whether the mother had a right to an answer about what happened to her daughter, he said only, 'In such circumstances, it is only natural that a mother would want answers.'"

Answers. Keita had not been able to ask any questions about his father's death, let alone get answers. He knew he had escaped Zantoroland just in time. In Freedom State, he had kept trying to get in touch with his sister, but he had received no replies to emails sent from Internet cafés. Anxiety knotted like a ball under his sternum. He found it easiest not to think about all that he had been through. Thinking could be detrimental to purpose. Sometimes it was better just to carry on. Usually he could avoid thoughts about his mother and father, but it was impossible to not think of Charity, because she was his only family, and she was still alive. Somewhere. But where? And why wasn't she responding to his messages?

Keita put down the news section and picked up the sports pages. There was rugby on the front page, football and cricket on the next, a bit of tennis, and when he turned to the back page, Keita found two photos of himself at the Buttersby Marathon. In one, he was high-fiving a recreational runner. In the caption, Keita read:

Federal Immigration Minister Rocco Calder encourages winner Keita Ali, who registered under the alias "Roger Bannister." The minister finished more than an hour behind Ali, in a time of 3:15:29. Calder placed twentieth out of 825 runners in his 50 to 55 age category, but as he stood after the race with a beer in one hand and a bagel with cream cheese in the other, he muttered that he owed five 750-millilitre bottles of single-malt scotch to friends who had bet he wouldn't crack 3:15.

Above the main article was a photograph of Keita with his head turned as he crossed the finish line. He appeared to be looking for someone. His face didn't reflect the thrill of victory. Worry framed his eyes and furrowed his brow.

It had not occurred to Keita that people in this country would fuss over the alias he had chosen. He realized he'd been naive. Just a few weeks in the country and he'd already been photographed and named in a newspaper. It was going to be hard for him to stay hidden long. He wanted to hide as long as he could. He wanted to stay alive. But he had doubts about how long he could manage that, given that racing made him visible.

Keita stretched out and dozed off. When he awoke, he smiled at the boy sitting beside him. There was something comforting about being beside the youngster. Keita fell asleep again and woke hours later to the odd sensation that he was being examined. He cracked open an eye. He was slumped in his seat and his T-shirt had pulled slightly up, leaving his lower belly exposed. The boy had turned on the overhead light, and was peering at the golf-ball-sized lump of flesh protruding from Keita's navel.

Keita sat up and tugged down his shirt.

"What's that?" the boy said.

"A hernia," Keita said. "A little bit of my insides sticking out at the navel."

"Does it hurt?"

"A bit."

"Are you sick?"

"No."

"Gonna get it fixed?"

"What's the big deal?" Keita said. "Don't you have a navel?"

"Yeah, but mine doesn't look like that. It's flat. That's you, isn't it?" The boy was pointing to the back of the sports section on Keita's lap.

Keita spoke quietly. "I'll tell you a secret, if you promise not to tell anyone."

"Let me guess," the boy said. "You won that race?"

"It is me. But as I said, that's a secret."

"Not much of a secret, if it's in the newspaper."

"It's a secret that the guy in the newspaper is me."

"Huh. Anybody could see that. Does anybody else on this bus look like they're straight out of Africa?"

"I'm not from Africa."

"I'm making a documentary film on AfricTown and Zantoro-landers in Freedom State. Want to be in it?"

"No."

"Come on."

"No."

"You already are. I already filmed you."

"When?"

"Okay, full disclosure," the boy said. "I'm not a stalker or anything, but I said hello the other week when you were running in Ruddings Park. I watched you win that marathon today and filmed you while you were standing beside that woman in a wheelchair who works for the *Clarkson Evening Telegram*. And I just used the term 'straight out of Africa' to get you going. To break the ice. My teacher says that a good interviewer should strike with a question that's so uncomfortable it is virtually incendiary."

Keita took a second look at the boy. *Incendiary*. "Any other 'incendiary' questions?"

"Did you know you were high-fiving the federal minister of immigration?" The boy unfolded the newspaper and pointed to the photo.

"I saw that photo," Keita said.

"He's a refugee cowboy."

"What?"

"He's the guy who goes after illegal refugees. I had to do a project on him for our civics course. Given how fast you left that race, I'm figuring you don't want to be high-fiving Rocco Calder. He is not your friend. But he's a jock, so he'll respect you for having beaten him."

Keita studied the photo. The camera had caught the minister smiling, one hand high-fiving Keita and the other giving a thumbs-up. In the background, behind the minister and just entering the photo frame, was the woman who had also high-fived Keita.

"Since you know all about me, tell me your name."

"John Falconer."

"Why aren't you in school?"

"This term, I'm making a film."

"And in this country, children are allowed to travel unaccompanied?"

"I'm fifteen."

Keita could see there would be no debating with this boy.

"Where do you study?"

"I attend a gifted school in Clarkson. But I live with my mom in AfricTown."

"In AfricTown? With your mother?"

"Sure. When she's well. It's not just black folks in AfricTown. Others live there too. A few other white people. Mixed, too, like me. And it's not all people without legal documentation, you know."

"And your mother. You say she's not well?"

"She's in a psychiatric hospital."

"I'm sorry to hear that," Keita said. In his childhood, he had imagined Freedom State to be a land of riches and comfort where people had big houses, luxury cars and more than enough food.

"We'll get through it," John said. "What about your family in Zantoroland?"

"I don't have any family left in Zantoroland," Keita said.

The boy nodded quietly and gave him a sympathetic look.

"Gifted," Keita said. "What does that mean?"

"You have to be smart to get into it."

"You're not shy about it."

"I'd be a misfit in a normal school," John said, then returned to his line of questioning. "Do you have a place to live?"

"Here and there," Keita said.

"Why don't you come to AfricTown? Are you, like, without documentation?"

"That's a personal question."

"If you need to hide," John said, "it's the place to go. Thousands of people who look just like you—though you have to watch out for police raids."

"The police raid AfricTown?" Keita asked.

"Sometimes. But we can usually see them coming." John explained that sentries with walkie-talkies kept watch over the road from Clarkson to AfricTown. "If you came to AfricTown, you could fit right in. Some hide there for years. Others, for a lifetime. I could show you around."

"I'll think it over," Keita said.

"I will tell Lula DiStefano all about you. She's the furthest thing from an angel, but she runs AfricTown, and I bet she would let you stay."

Keita had heard of her. Even in Zantoroland, people knew of the so-called queen of AfricTown.

When he first got on the bus, Keita had hoped that the seat beside him would remain empty, so he could take some time to think quietly about how to locate his sister. But the boy brimmed with such energy that it comforted Keita. His last unhurried chat had been with his father, when Yoyo had told him to contact the marathon agent. But what would he say now?

Keita was sure of only two things. His father would have wanted him to do whatever was necessary to stay alive. And to find his sister.

"So why did you leave Zantoroland?" John asked.

"Political violence."

"Care to elaborate?" John asked.

"Against dissidents, and against the Faloo people." Keita swallowed.

"Are you a Faloo?"

"Yes, through my mother. But my father was a Bamileke, from Cameroon."

"What happened to them?"

"Not . . . not right now."

"What about other family members? Siblings?"

He paused again. "My sister, Charity, is studying at Harvard University, but I have not been able to reach her lately."

"I've got a cell," John said. "Why don't I try her for you right

THE ILLEGAL

now?" Keita gave him Charity's number. John dialed, but the phone just went straight to voice mail, as it always did.

"What do you miss about Zantoroland?"

Keita had to hand it to the kid—he was persistent. Keita shared a memory of watching his sister copy-edit the articles their father wrote for international newspapers and being offered five cents for each typo she corrected.

"Is she proud of you?"

"She would say I frittered away my youth in pursuit of an adolescent dream."

"That's rough. But you are both pursuing your dreams."

"Charity is. I will never be able to run for my country again, nor will I be in the Olympics."

"Why not?"

"To do so, you need a country."

"Maybe this will become your country."

"Unlikely," Keita said.

"Tell me more about what you miss. What was fun about your childhood?"

Keita sat back in his chair. "Once a week," he said, "we would deliver a newspaper all over the city. We had to carry it everywhere, jumping on and off the tro-tro—a cross between a bush taxi and a bus—to drop it off at stores and newsstands. Our last stop was always at the Yagwa market, where we would each buy a mango and eat it right there. We had to wait until after we'd delivered the last newspaper, because the juice made our hands so messy. As we ate, we would watch women carrying fruit on platters on their heads, and Charity would usually find a reason to chide me. Older sisters are like that. 'Running is useless,' she would say. 'The most famous Zantorolanders are runners,' I would reply, 'and they ran their way into fame and jobs.' And then she would stun me with some line that seemed to come straight from a textbook: 'You are more than just another black male body. Use your mind. Elevate yourself.' And I would say, 'Would you just elevate that half of the mango into my hand, if you are not going to eat it?'"

165

John laughed. "At least you have a sister."

Keita paused and looked out the window. Dawn had broken. The highway was getting busier, and instead of farmland, he now saw office towers and apartment buildings. All the tall buildings in the city of Yagwa were confined to less than a couple of square kilometres. Here, they stretched endlessly.

"How long before we get to Clarkson?" Keita asked.

"About forty-five minutes."

"Do you think I could borrow your laptop?" Keita asked. "I want to see if my sister has emailed me."

John turned it on, entered a password and handed over the laptop. Keita opened his email, expecting nothing. Instead, he found two messages sent earlier in the day. Each had been sent by one George Maxwell in Zantoroland, and each had the subject line "Re: Charity." Keita sat up, startled. He quickly opened the first message.

Dear Brother Keita,

I am required by my jailers in Zantoroland to write to you.

In case you need convincing that this is me, when you were ten years old, you received a brand new pair of Meb Supreme track shoes. You were not allowed to wear them except when you ran, although you wore them to sweep the church the day Deacon Andrews was killed.

Keita, someone in the Pink Palace impersonated Dad and sent me an email from his computer, saying there was an emergency and he needed me immediately. I used up my savings to fly home but was arrested at the airport and have been detained for weeks.

I am using my jailers' computer and am not at liberty to say much. But I need your help and know you will do all that you can.

Charity

His sister, in Zantoroland? Jailers? Not possible! Keita desperately hoped this was a prank, but he feared—somehow he knew—that it was not. And he believed he knew what was coming next. He checked the second email.

Dear Mr. Ali,

The Republic of Zantoroland has detained your sister, Charity Ali, on suspicion of treason. I have been asked to act as an intermediary. Should you wish to secure her release, you must wire $15,000 in U.S. funds to us, at a bank account to be provided later, with a payment deadline of June 22, 2018. Please confirm that you have received this communication. Undoubtedly, you desire to ensure your sister's safety.

George Maxwell

Panic rose in Keita's throat and sweat covered his forehead. He wished he could get out and be alone, so he could scream and pound his fists into the earth. But he couldn't escape, he couldn't scream and he felt trapped in the back of the bus.

The boy was nudging him. "Keita. Keita. Are you okay? Is it bad news?"

"Awful."

Keita sat limply. The boy took back the computer and looked at the screen.

"Is this for real?" John said.

Keita nodded.

"What will you do?"

"Whatever it takes," Keita said.

He had to think. He had always believed that Charity was the smarter sibling. But now he had to think for both of them. John offered Keita a napkin and a bottle of water. Keita took the bottle and gulped from it.

This changed everything. Now he had to stay alive not just for his own sake but for his sister's. And he had to buy some time.

"Can I have that back?" he asked the boy. Keita typed:

Dear Mr. Maxwell,

I have no residency documentation or right to work. I do not have $15,000 or access to a bank account.

Keita Ali

A reply came minutes later.

Dear Mr. Ali,

Congratulations on winning the Buttersby Marathon today. And on setting the course record. There are numerous other road races in Freedom State. Run those races, and run to win. Once you have done so, we will instruct on the means of transaction.

George Maxwell

S AUNDERS WAS WAITING IN THE DINING ROOM OF THE All Saints Hotel, flipping through the business pages of the *Telegram*. He barely raised his eyes to look when Anton entered the room.

Anton sat down and put his hands on the table. He clasped them and stared at his blackmailer. Anton did not smile, but he did not scowl or say anything rude.

"Good morning, Mr. Hamm," Saunders said. "So pleased that you could join me. I recommend the *omelette aux asperges et saumon*."

"Just coffee," said Anton, who thought about how good it would feel to snap Saunders' neck.

"In every relationship, there is giving and taking," Saunders said.

Anton smiled. Exactly. In every relationship, there was someone giving and somebody on the take.

Saunders laid it out. He and his associates would offer Anton sixty thousand in cash yearly, plus expense money, and make arrangements for the Tax Agency for Freedom State to accept Anton's illegal tax returns for the last two years. In exchange, Anton would provide information about Illegals from Zantoroland who were hiding in Freedom State.

"I get passports and visas for all of my runners," Hamm said.

"We are not interested in your runners. Carry on as usual with that. We just want you to bring information to us about certain Illegals in Freedom State."

Anton said he didn't know anything about Illegals. Saunders explained that he would be directed to pick up information here and there, to verify the odd detail and to pass it on. The tasks would be clear and specific.

"And what will you do with that information?"

"Why should you care?" Saunders said. "You'll be paid good money to work a day or two a month, plus travel time."

Anton considered the situation. What if Saunders and his people were the ones who had initiated the tax investigation? Well, whether they had cooked it up or not, there was a good chance the investigation would bite Anton hard. TAFS could audit him. Seize his assets. Revoke his business permit. If Anton played along, he might escape a tax nightmare.

"All right," Anton said. "I'm in."

Saunders slid a thick brown envelope across the table. "Your first monthly instalment," he said. "In cash. Instructions are inside. We know that you are going to Zantoroland tomorrow. Take this along." Saunders passed over a second envelope, which felt thick with bills. "That envelope is not for you, and you are not to open it. Go to the offices of the Ministry of Citizenship. Ask for George Maxwell. Give him the envelope. He will have something for you and explain the next steps."

"All right." Anton Hamm stood and walked toward the door.

Saunders called after him, "By the way, your appointment with TAFS has been cancelled. You are free to spend the day with your protégés."

Anton kept walking.

IN ZANTOROLAND, ANTON ASKED A TAXI DRIVER AT THE airport to take him to the Ministry of Citizenship. The driver chuckled.

"You mean the Pink Palace?"

"It's called the Pink Palace?" Anton said.

"It is a black hole for Zantorolanders."

This was news to him. Anton's experience of Zantoroland was training camps, road races and hotel lobbies.

"Many go in but do not come out," the driver said.

"Really?" Anton said. He wondered what else he had failed to notice in the country.

"But you, sir, have nothing to worry about. You are a nicely dressed businessman. And you are the right colour."

Anton looked out the window. A boy was hauling a wagon loaded with bunches of live chickens, each bound by the feet. He also had a pile of oranges. One of them fell off the wagon. The boy stooped to retrieve it.

"Where are you from?" the taxi driver asked.

"Freedom State."

"Yes, nothing to worry about."

An hour later, in a windowless room on the third floor of the Pink Palace, George Maxwell rose slowly from a comfortable chair to greet Anton. The man was bigger than Anton had been when he was throwing the shot. Not taller—George Maxwell stood no more than six feet—but as round as a cannon ball. Easily 380 pounds. Maxwell's shaking hand was meaty and thick, and even if he had wanted to, Anton could not have crushed it.

"Have you a business card?" asked Maxwell.

What was it with Zantorolanders and their business cards? On top of that, you could never begin a conversation in this country without talking about family. It was a complete waste of time, but there was no way around it. Anton gave Maxwell a business card and readied himself for the routine.

"Sports agent," Maxwell said. "Very good. You have come to the right country."

"I have something for you," Anton said, reaching into his pocket.

Maxwell put up his palm. "Let us first speak, as friends. How is your wife?"

Anton didn't have a wife. A few months earlier, while he was

171

travelling with his runners, his live-in girlfriend had carved up his couch and left it in pieces, along with a trail of sawdust. She also left behind a brief note. *#1: I told you the couch was ugly. #2: To hell with you and your temper.*

"My wife is fine," he said. "Perfect health. And yours?"

"She is wonderful," Maxwell said. "And how are your children?"

"We have four, and they are well," Hamm said.

"Four children!" Maxwell said, smacking the desk. "Good man. Busy man. They are in school?"

"Yes."

"Good students?"

"Yes, and yours?"

"Thank you for asking. I have two, and they will be good students, I expect, when they enter school. They are at home with their mother. We have another on the way."

Anton glanced up at a portrait of the president.

"So you have brought me an item of business?" Maxwell said finally.

Anton gave him the sealed envelope.

"And here is something for you," Maxwell said.

Anton took the envelope and prepared to slip it into his jacket, but Maxwell stopped him. "Open it now, please."

The envelope contained a long piece of foolscap with fifteen handwritten names. The page was not addressed to anyone nor was it signed by anyone. Beside each name was an address. Anton looked at the first one. *Sibiri Tom, male, age 25, 271 Carstairs Avenue, Apartment 418, Clarkson.*

"What is this?" Anton said.

"Mr. Hamm, if you could please read me what you see on this paper."

Anton read out the list of names. It seemed like a waste of time.

"Very good. Copy each name and address in your own hand-writing, with pen only. Do that now, please."

Anton wrote down all the information. It took him ten minutes. When he was finished, Maxwell took back the original.

"Go to every address and verify that the person lives in the building," Maxwell said. "Speak with the superintendent. Look on the list of names in the lobby. But do not go to the door of the person or ask for that person directly. Confirm with a check mark the names for which you have been able to verify addresses. And then provide this information to Mr. Saunders in Freedom State."

"Do I look like a courier to you?" Anton said.

"Discussions are to be between you and Mr. Saunders. But those are your instructions. And let me tell you something about Mr. Saunders," Maxwell added. "He does not tolerate errors or lax behaviour." Maxwell pushed himself upright and smiled. "But you are a perfectionist. A person does not win gold medals in two Olympic Games without being one. I must congratulate you. Gold medals, twice! For the shot put, correct?"

"Yes."

"We have no shot putters in Zantoroland," Maxwell said. "Only distance runners and marathoners. We have few resources, so we must concentrate them efficiently. And you, Mr. Hamm, can do the same."

CHAPTER FOURTEEN

THE DOORBELL RANG. IVERNIA BEECH CONSIDERED leaving it unanswered. Her house was not presentable. Unread newspapers and wet socks littered the floor of the mud room.

The bell rang again. The trouble with being old was that people would wait eternally. They knew she might not hear the first ring. They knew it might take her some time to get to the door.

Near the entrance, she stopped to adjust a portrait of her with her late husband and their son, Jimmy. The photo was taken in happier times, decades before Ivernia and Ernie won the lottery, moved to Clarkson and bought the house on Elixir Bridge Road. In the photo, Jimmy was still a young man. He stood between his parents, with his mop of hair and bowtie, weight shifted onto his left foot. Ivernia remembered the day the photo was taken. That same evening, Ernie had brought home a bottle of Châteauneuf-du-Pape. Ivernia had made a roast to go with it, and later they had made love. Ivernia tried to remember the last time she had made love.

Hard as it was for Ivernia to contemplate that she had aged, she was even more bewildered to think that her son was now over fifty years old. Jimmy was only twenty in the photo. Shortly after it was taken, the University of Freedom State suspended him for retyping an almost forgotten short story by Anton Chekhov and handing it in as his own work. Even at that age, Jimmy could fool one woman out of five with his poor-me, bad boy grin. But he was no match for his English prof, who happened to be a Chekhov scholar.

After college, Jimmy had occupied himself with one bankruptcy, two marriages, three affairs and countless years of unemployment. Ivernia and Ernie should never have told him that they had won the lottery. They should never have moved to Clarkson and bought the five-thousand-square-foot home. They should have hidden their wealth. Jimmy would have been none the wiser. They had underestimated their son's venality. Over the years, Jimmy had launched endless schemes to wrest money from them. The efforts had intensified after Ernie died.

The bell rang again. Ivernia hoped it would not be one of those perfectly coiffed neighbours coming to ask her again to sign a petition calling for Elixir Bridge to be turned into a gated community to protect it from riff-raff, refugees and robbers. Ivernia dreaded meeting strangers and having to explain herself. Widowed, old, living alone, she found cookies and wine for dinner just fine, thank you very much, and if she died soon because her diet was so awful, well, that wouldn't be such a bad thing. Ivernia abhorred the idea of a long, drawn-out illness. A swift death would be good.

A face pushed up against a tiny glass window in the door. "Mother. I see you in there. Open up. Please. There is someone here to meet you!"

Jimmy hollered as if she were not only half deaf but also an idiot. Ivernia fumbled with the chain and the two deadbolts. Had she not had the locks changed recently, Jimmy would have let himself in. The boy had no respect for boundaries.

Ivernia opened the door. An attractive blonde woman in a business suit stood on the step. She was slender, about thirty, holding a briefcase and giving a shy smile. The woman offered her hand. Ivernia shook it.

"Mrs. Beech, I am Sondra Pasieka. I trust that you received my phone messages."

Ivernia didn't tend to pick up phone messages.

"I am a social worker with the Office for Independent Living," Sondra said. "We were to meet this morning, about the incident."

The incident. By which she meant the car accident. She was good. Polite and tactful.

"You may come in," she said to Sondra. For Jimmy, who stood to the woman's side, she pulled a five-dollar bill from her purse and said, "Get yourself a coffee while Miss Sondra and I meet."

Jimmy took the money. "Mother, that's rude."

There was no negotiating with her son, so Ivernia made her case to Sondra. "I had a four-thousand-dollar Inuit carving of a polar bear. Last time my son came here, he stole the bear and sold it to a pawnshop."

Without responding, the social worker entered her mud room. As Ivernia prepared to close the door on her son, Sondra cleared her throat.

"He is a party to the claim against your independence, Mrs. Beech, and as a family member, he has a right to be informed of the result of this process."

"He can sit in the hall while we meet in the study. Leave your shoes on. I haven't got around to sweeping today."

Ivernia glanced at her living room on the way to the study in the back of the house. Nothing too small in there and nothing worth stealing. After the last incident, Ivernia had removed all valuables that could fit into a pocket and hidden them in a box in her bedroom. She didn't need them out. Nobody came over anyway, except her son.

"Do you mind if I ask a few questions?" Sondra said.

"For what purpose?"

"To see if you have sufficient cognizance to care for yourself."

"I'm only cognizant in the mornings, so let's get cracking," Ivernia said.

Sondra brought out a clipboard with a form to fill out.

"Your full name?"

"Ivernia Anne Beech."

"What is the date and time?"

"Is it cheating to check my watch?"

"No rules against that."

"Well, it is Monday, March 19, 2018, and it is 9:30 a.m. That is to say, it is 9:30 a.m. in Clarkson, the capital of Freedom State. Would you like to know the time in Japan or Australia?"

"I am sorry if this is a demeaning process. I'll go quickly."

Ivernia had to say the place she was born—Buttersby, Freedom State. She had to give her address—37 Elixir Bridge Road, Clarkson—and her telephone number. She had to identify where she kept her bank accounts—Bank of Clarkson, Elixir Bridge Mall branch. Next, her birthdate: April 2, 1933. Finally, she had to name her son and give his date of birth: James Matthew Beech, June 15, 1966.

Sondra said that Ivernia had passed the spot test.

"What's next?"

Ivernia would forfeit her driver's licence for three months and have to be retested to get it back.

"Right," Ivernia said.

She would have to pay seven thousand dollars for the repair of one car and three thousand for the other.

"Yes, I understand," Ivernia said.

But she would face no traffic charges, given her age.

"But being old also presents a problem," Ivernia said.

Sondra cleared her throat. "That is true."

For the time being, Ivernia's bank assets would be frozen. She could not sell her house or car, and based on the latest estimates of the cost of living for a person of her lifestyle, Ivernia would receive a monthly cheque—drawn from her own bank account—of two thousand dollars, until such time as her fitness for independent living was confirmed.

"How do I establish my fitness for independent living?"

"In about two months, a review board judge will meet you to review your circumstances. And then the matter will be decided."

"What is the worst that this office can do to me?"

"It can control your assets, order you to be moved into an

assisted living facility and award power of attorney over your health and finances to an independent arbiter or a family member."

Ivernia wanted to throw up her hands and say that she might as well just off herself right now, because she would not go into some assisted living facility to sit with drooling, senile people in an airless lobby while musically challenged nine-year-olds showed up to play Christmas songs on ten-dollar recorders.

"Mrs. Beech," Sondra said. She smiled. "You can beat this thing. Although this process has been triggered, it is not a sure thing that you will lose your independence."

"What do I need to do?"

It came down to four factors. If Ivernia wished to satisfy the judge in two months' time, she should clean her house and yard and pay attention to her hygiene and clothing.

"They care how I dress?" Ivernia said.

"The board does need to know that you can care for yourself," Sondra said.

"What else?"

Sondra said it would please the review board judge if Ivernia could show ties to her community.

"But most of my friends have died." Ivernia almost added *lucky them*, but caught her tongue.

"Perhaps you could join a book club or a bridge group," Sondra said.

Ivernia sniffed. "If I find volunteer work, would that get the Office for Independent Living off my back?"

"It would help," Sondra said. "Finally, if you have a friend or relative move in, that would show you are taking steps to ensure good self-care."

Ivernia thanked Sondra for her advice and escorted her to the front of the house, where she discovered her son removing silverware from her dining cabinet. She recovered two serving spoons and a pie fork and locked the door behind both of them.

* * *

EIGHT YEARS EARLIER, AFTER BUYING THEIR HOME IN Clarkson, Ivernia and Ernie had donated $300,000 to the Clarkson Library. The library made quite a fuss over them, and the CEO—a kind gentleman named Ken O'Neill—had repeatedly stated that if the library could ever do anything for them, all they had to do was pick up the phone. Now, after meeting with Sondra, Ivernia did just that, and days later she began working as a volunteer.

Ivernia had two responsibilities at the library: to make sure that a first-aid room was properly supplied with a bed, sheets, pillow, apple juice and tea; and to sit at a desk in a far back corner issuing new library cards. To qualify for a library card, a person had to show two pieces of identification and pay ten dollars. A new law also required any prospective library card holder to establish that he or she was a citizen of Freedom State or at least in the country legally. Indeed, this was to be required of any person receiving any publicly funded service, from health care to welfare.

Ivernia was given two shifts a week. She settled into a routine. Sweeping the first-aid room and ensuring it was properly stocked was easy because it was rarely used. The rest of the time, she sat alone at the card-issuing desk under a sign that said New Cards. On a typical shift, she had only a few cards to issue, so she spent her time scouring the stacks and bringing back books to read. The latest, *Dying for Dimwits*, said that any idiot who did his or her research could pull off a successful suicide. The author was a middle-aged Aussie with a full head of hair and decent teeth. He wrote: "We want you to have a long life. However, if you are reading this book, it is likely that you would like to take the timing of your demise into your own hands. If you really must off yourself, do us all a favour by researching the matter properly. Any idiot can die. But it takes a well-informed person to plan to die without causing others unnecessary perturbation." The book went on to review some of the most sensational ways in which celebrities had either killed themselves or made a poor showing of it. Ivernia skipped that part. It didn't interest her to laugh at the misfortune of others. She did read the list of suicide techniques that were neither advisable nor efficient. Do not crash your car, the book said, because you could hurt someone and increase insurance costs for all those left behind. Do not jump off a bridge because you could land on another person. Over the last decade, the book said, at least a dozen pedestrians or hikers had died after being struck by suicide jumpers. A successful suicide required the unequivocal avoidance of personal agony, third-party misfortune and lawsuits.

Ivernia didn't, especially, want to die. But she didn't want to live without autonomy or dignity.

Ivernia found that working at the library improved her mood. Many people who came to the library needed more than books. They needed email connections and jobs. They needed to use the toilet or to get out of the rain or the sun without being accused of loitering. They needed a safe place to relax or to fall asleep in a chair by a window. Ivernia wondered how many of these library patrons had come from another country.

The newspapers were full of stories about the hardships faced by refugees. Just last week Ivernia had read about the fate of passengers on another two ships—leaky bathtubs, really, crammed to the gunwales with refugees—in international waters just off the coast. The Coast Guard had blocked them from entering the waters of Freedom State and forced them to turn around and head back to Zantoroland. There were three hundred people in the two boats, which had been at sea for a month. Thirteen had died of dehydration or cholera. When the refugees arrived back in Zantoroland, a riot broke out and police moved in. Six more men died.

When she wasn't reading, Ivernia developed new ways to show compassion for the people who came to her desk without documentation. The library required Ivernia to photocopy and file ID showing a new customer's name, citizenship and address.

On her first day of work, Ivernia had to reject five people who did not qualify for a library card. The next time she came in, Ivernia was approached by a black woman who carried her possessions in a frayed pillow case. She looked to be about sixty, but she walked with less confidence than Ivernia. She asked for a library card.

"Do you have ID?" Ivernia asked.

"No, I don't have any of that." The woman began to turn away.

"Wait a minute."

The woman turned to face her. Ivernia typed a memo and sent it to the printer. It said:

Date: _____

To Whom It May Concern:

I hereby attest that I, _____, am a citizen of Freedom State and reside at the following address _____.

Sincerely,

_____

Ivernia helped the woman fill in the blanks.

"Where should I say I live?" the woman asked.

"Put down 33 Old Clarkson Road," Ivernia said.

"Where's that?"

Ivernia spoke quietly. "Bus station, but who cares?"

The woman signed the form. She didn't have ten dollars, so Ivernia paid for her.

The woman held the new card against her bosom. "God bless you!"

Ivernia wrote to Rocco Calder, minister of immigration, complaining about the punitive treatment of people without legal status. To make it a crime for public institutions to serve the undocumented simply isolated people and drove them into poverty, she wrote. From then on, people who came looking for a library card received one, regardless of whether their papers were in order.

CHAPTER FIFTEEN

A FTER TAKING THE OVERNIGHT TRIP FROM BUTTERSBY and disembarking in Clarkson, Keita entered the bus station that he had been using since he had gone into hiding in Freedom State.

The Clarkson bus station allowed him access to a locker, with in-and-out privileges, for thirty dollars a month. It also offered a hot shower with towel service for five dollars. Keita stood for ten long minutes under the stream of hot water. He had to present himself well at all times. It horrified him to think that poor hygiene or odour might draw attention to his paperless status. People who smelled and looked clean always got more respect. Keita hadn't showered since the day before the marathon. Nobody would see him or arrest him or deport him in the shower, so he lingered and allowed himself to think.

He would not live to an old age. He might not make it to thirty. It didn't matter. He just needed to stay alive long enough to run again, to run as many times as necessary to help his sister. He prayed for strength. And in the noise of the pounding water, he cried.

Keita turned off the shower, wrapped the towel around his waist and over the hernia and approached his locker. The facilities were run by a short black man. He stood at four foot ten and called himself My Hero, and he had muscles from head to toe. My Hero was offering Keita a second towel.

"Here, man. An extra. No charge. Just take it, from brother to brother." Keita took the towel and began to dry himself off. He waited for a moment of privacy, but My Hero planted himself with crossed arms and stared.

"You're in shape, dude," he said. "Fine shape."

My Hero was as dark as Keita. He kept his hair cropped short like a soldier's and had an arrow tattooed on each forearm.

Keita dried his feet.

"You got calf muscles like grenades," My Hero was saying. "Little bombs you got there. I'd say you're a runner."

"You got me there," Keita said. He ditched the towel and dressed quickly.

"If I was you, I'd run to AfricTown," My Hero said.

"I beg your pardon?"

"Most folks who come by here ain't what you'd call regularized. You in a hunting ground, smack-dab in the middle of Clarkson. You need to run to the caves, boy. But seeing as they ain't no caves in Freedom State, all you got is AfricTown. You can blend in there and hope they don't catch you."

Keita put his running clothes in his small knapsack and shouldered it. He put the big knapsack with the remainder of his clothes into his locker and shut it. "Got to go." He smiled at My Hero, said goodbye and left.

Keita's first priority was to set up a bank account with the four-thousand-dollar cheque from the Buttersby Marathon in his pocket. If he could deposit the money, he could wire it to Charity's captors.

He was wearing dress pants, a dress shirt, white socks and dress shoes. Charity would have scolded him for undermining his overall look with the socks. *You look like a clown.* But Keita had forgotten dress socks, and now he had other priorities. At all times, he had to be prepared to run.

Keita found an intersection with a bank on every corner. First he saw the Bank of Montreal, the J.P. Morgan Chase Bank and the Bank of Freedom State. But he selected Family Credit Union, because the building featured a sign that advertised it as a "People's Bank" and showed a photo of an employee greeting customers representing every conceivable racial group.

Three tellers glanced in his direction and returned to their business. He asked a woman at the reception desk if he could speak to someone about opening an account.

"Certainly," she said, motioning for him to sit.

He waited ten minutes until a man in a blue suit came to meet him. The man had a ruddy face and walked with a deliberate, heavy stride, legs wide apart, suggesting he had an irritation in his groin.

"James Bell. May I help you?" the man said, offering his hand.

Keita shook it and gave his name. "I would like to open an account."

Bell led Keita to a coffee counter. "Coffee?"

"I will have it with six milks and two sugars, please."

The man suppressed a grin, poured a few ounces from a coffee thermos, passed over a bowl of milk and sugar packets, and said, "Here, you can mix and match."

They moved to a tiny office, which had a desk, a computer, a filing cabinet and one extra chair. Bell invited Keita to sit across from him.

"What kind of account would you like to open?"

Keita looked Bell in the eye. "May I speak frankly?"

"Of course," Bell said, sitting back, straightening his tie.

He was built as thick as a football player. How did people in this country get so solid? Keita wondered. Bell had a square ring on his middle finger. Back home, Keita had heard that in the Pink Palace, if an interrogator intended to do you harm, he would slide a ring off one finger and onto another. A bad omen. Bell's big square ring tapped the countertop.

Keita looked up and began. "I have a cheque for four thousand dollars from the Buttersby Marathon, and I wish to use it to open an account."

"That shouldn't be a problem."

Keita lowered his voice a notch and held the man with his gaze. "But I have no ID."

"Have your valuables been stolen?" Bell said.

"They were taken from me, but not in the sense of an ordinary theft."

"Have you called the police?"

"No."

"Are you a citizen of Freedom State?" Bell asked.

Keita's eyes drifted to the office door. Nobody barred it, and no police officers waited outside. Keita strove to keep his voice even and calm.

"If you examine the cheque, you will see that it is valid."

Bell tapped his ring against the table again. It made Keita jump in his seat.

"Sir," he said firmly. "I can't help you if you don't have full identification. For starters, I would need your passport, driver's licence, birth certificate and national citizenship card."

Surely there was a way to work with this gentleman. In Zantoroland, slipping a fifty-dollar bill under the table would solve the problem.

"Mr. Bell," Keita said, "let me assure you that I am trustworthy and that this cheque is valid. I see that you are a bank for the people. I am not asking for a loan. I just want to deposit my money."

"It's against the law for me to open a bank account without your full identification," Bell said. "Technically, I am supposed to report anyone who attempts to open an account without papers." He cleared his throat and tightened his tie.

The man's smile, handshake and coffee had meant nothing. Absolutely nothing. Keita could be deported tomorrow or receive news that his sister had died, and it would make no difference to James Bell. Keita's knees ached from the bus ride. His thighs still burned from the marathon. It was best to walk before he had to run. Best to leave before he overstayed his welcome.

Keita rose from his chair. "Thank you for your time and for the coffee."

Now that Keita was leaving, the banker brightened considerably.

"Thank you for considering us, sir, and have yourself a wonderful day." He extended a thick hand. It was a hand that had been strengthened by a gym membership and fed by hot cereal in the morning, lunch at midday and meat every night.

Keita reached out for the obligatory shake, but to him, the banker's cold palm felt like a wall. The wall had a door, and the door had a lock, and the lock needed a key. Some people had keys to this world, but Keita was not one of them.

CHAPTER SIXTEEN

T HE PRIME MINISTER HAD DECREED THAT OFFERING cabinet ministers chauffeur-driven limos did not conform with the Family Party's tax-cutting values, so Rocco drove himself to work. Rocco didn't mind. It gave him time to think. This morning, he had his mind on the "fireside consultations" that the PM and his sidekick, Geoffrey Moore, had made him set up so that it would appear he was doing something about Illegals in Freedom State.

It was Geoffrey's brilliant idea that Rocco should invite concerned citizens from all walks of life to small, informal discussions. In the intimacy of his corner office with the gas fireplace, Rocco would solicit their opinions about what to do, and he would put it all in a stupid report that would go absolutely nowhere and fail to impress a single government critic but allow the government to claim that it was soliciting public input.

In the last twenty-four hours, Rocco had decided whom to invite to his next fireside consultation. He put the fix in to secure that good-looking woman who had beaten him at Buttersby: Candace Freixa. He had looked her up on the results board after the race. She was a cop. Who better to contribute than a black law enforcement officer? And he had invited Ivernia Beech. He remembered her as the funder of the national student essay prize, and he knew that she was a lefty. Lately, she had written him a letter complaining of the "draconian measures" used to deport people without proper papers, asking, Did the government not realize that some of these deportees might face death in their own countries? She would not in a million years vote for the Family Party. But Rocco needed at least one social misfit to attend each session, so he'd had an aide call her up. He could have his meeting and get the PM's aide off his back.

Rocco parked in the outdoor lot behind the government office known as the Freedom Building. He checked his watch: 7:05 a.m. Plenty of time. The PM liked all of his ministers to be in their offices by 7:30. First thing in the morning was the PM's favourite time to come calling. Some mornings, Rocco heard laughter coming from other offices down the hall. Four cabinet ministers had played with the PM on the rugby squad that won the World Cup thirty years earlier. But Rocco was not one of them. He didn't regret it. Thirty years ago, Rocco was dropping out of university and setting up his first used car dealership. He had been careful with his money. He did not need this job. If his career in politics went belly-up, well, worse things had happened.

Rocco closed the door to his Volvo station wagon, turned and found himself face to face with a young boy. White. Or maybe not. His hair was loosely curled, but you couldn't exactly call him black. About twelve? Lost? He wore a school uniform. Rocco caught the letters on the boy's blazer: *Clarkson Academy FTG.*

"Sir," the boy said, reaching out his hand.

Rocco shook it, because that's what you did when you met a future voter.

"John Falconer, sir," the boy said. "We met before. Congratulations on your performance in Buttersby."

"Now I remember you," Rocco said. "You won that essay competition, and you live in AfricTown."

"That's right, sir. You promised me an interview."

Come to think of it, Rocco *had* said that he would meet the boy. John was an energetic one. Like a puppy. Best to get this over with. "What do you wish to talk about, and can we wrap it up in ten minutes?"

"Sir, I am writing and directing a film documentary for a special Grade 9 project."

"How about if we walk and talk?"

They took the stairs up one flight to Rocco's corner office. John explained that he wished to shadow him over the next month.

"Shadow me?" Now they were in his office. While Rocco opened the fridge and poured a glass of apple juice, the boy stepped back to videotape him. Rocco frowned.

"It's just for school," John said. He swung the camera around to film the far side of the office. He walked toward another door.

"Your own bathroom? Multiple stalls and sinks, all to yourself? How cool is that? Man! A rowing machine. Who gets to have a bathroom big enough for a rowing machine? I bet that keeps you in good shape, sir. I bet you could run that marathon in three hours, if you set your mind to it."

The kid was getting annoying. And Rocco had things to do. "About the shadowing. You'll have to submit a request in writing."

"Sir, why is the Family Party deporting people without documentation?"

"Every country has a right to self-determination. That includes enforcing the rules of citizenship."

The kid lowered his video camera. "Bathroom break," he said, and he disappeared into Rocco's private bathroom.

Rocco heard the kid piss. He heard a tap running. After the toilet flushed, he heard the window opening. The building was a century old. You could lift up the window and jump right out, if, say, the PM's executive assistant was undermining your sanity. If you felt depressed about the stream of illegal refugees arriving by boat on the nation's thousands of kilometres of unprotected coastline. Why was that kid opening the window? Rocco hoped the boy was just checking out the sights, and that he wouldn't do anything stupid. Rocco had just begun to move toward the bathroom door when Graeme Wellington and Geoffrey Moore walked into his office.

Rocco turned to greet his boss and his nemesis.

The prime minister sat on the corner of Rocco's desk. He always did that. It was his pretense of humility, lowering his height so that he would not appear to be looking down on you. Rocco was six feet tall but seemed like a midget in comparison to the PM, who was six-six. The PM was the tallest man in his cabinet, and Rocco the shortest male. Every man in the cabinet had to be tall and slender. Even the media had commented on this, derisively referring to cabinet as "Rugby Central." The PM's unelected aide took the comfortable corner chair.

"Prime Minister," Rocco said.

"Good to see you at it early in the morning, chap," the PM said. "How goes the battle?"

"Well," Rocco said.

"I hear congratulations are in order," the PM said.

"Sir?"

"Don't underestimate me, Rock. I make time for the sports pages. I hear that you ran a marathon the other day. The Buttersby Marathon."

"Yes, sir. I was aiming to break three hours and fifteen minutes, but came in twenty-nine seconds too slow."

"Exactly how long is a marathon?" the PM asked.

Rocco wondered if Wellington was pulling his leg. He chose to play it straight.

"It's 42.2 kilometres, sir—or 26 miles, 385 yards, if you prefer imperial."

"That must have taken training. Good on you, Rock. Fit as a fiddle. Rock, sit down."

Wellington waited for Rocco to sink into the chair behind the desk, and then looked look down into his eyes. "So. How's it going with the boats?"

Before the Family Party took power, about seventy-five ships had been landing, unauthorized, in Freedom State each year. That represented about five thousand Illegals annually. Rocco's department was tasked with cutting down the number of ships dropping refugees on the shores of Freedom State. Rocco hadn't made a dent in those numbers, although lately he had heard that the Coast Guard had redirected a few ships back to Zantoroland. Oddly, those orders had not come from Rocco's office, but he wasn't about to flag that for the prime minister.

"Rocco?" the PM said.

"It has been a struggle to reduce those numbers. We are working on it."

"Soldier on, Rocco," the PM said.

Rocco knew exactly what was up. Reminding him of his failure to intercept the refugee boats was intended to soften him up for a request. Or an order. The PM liked to frame his orders as if they were requests.

The PM cleared his throat. "You heard about this cock-up involving the prostitute from AfricTown."

"Geoffrey called me about it while I was running the marathon, and I saw the story in the *Telegram*."

"So did we. And we were none too pleased to see you quoted in that article," Geoffrey said.

Rocco ignored Geoffrey and addressed the prime minister. "I didn't give the reporter anything. I don't have anything to give."

"Do you have any details about the dead girl?" Wellington asked.

"Not a thing. My department's Deportation Squad was not involved."

The PM reached down and touched Rocco's arm. "Are you quite sure?"

"Shall I have my people double-check?"

"Not just now," Geoffrey said.

"She came from AfricTown," Wellington said.

"So I heard," Rocco said.

"We already have one reporter stirring the pot. But she's a light-weight, and I want this story to die." The PM stood and cleared his throat. "Rock, I need to ask something of you."

"Here to help, sir."

Geoffrey stood up to come closer to the PM. Rocco knew the little prick was scheming to get him fired.

"How about going to AfricTown?" Wellington said. "Tonight. Have a good time. Watch a show. Go to the Bombay Booty. Would you like that?"

"Why?"

"We've set it up for you. Go see the show. If you meet a girl named Darlene, say, around midnight, you can ask about the girl who went missing. Who she was. What happened to her. That would be very interesting to us, if you happened to find that out."

"Sir?" Rocco said. "I'm not convinced this is a—"

Wellington clapped Rocco on the shoulder. "Settled. So, are you already planning your next marathon? Running for hours must take concentration. Good stuff. Stay fit, stay focused. Geoffrey?" The executive assistant stood to attention and followed his master out the door.

Rocco rubbed his temples. "Good dog, Whoa-Boy," he muttered. The PM was setting him up. But for what, exactly? Maybe Rocco could turn this to his advantage. The PM had something to hide.

The bathroom door opened. Nearly gave him a heart attack. He'd totally forgotten: the kid from the Clarkson Academy.

"About that interview," John said. "I have just a few questions and—"

"No time now." Rocco put up his hand. "On your way out, make an appointment with June."

"Yes, sir." The boy turned to leave.

"Wait. What have you been doing all this time?"

"Sir. I heard people come into your office. I didn't want to interrupt your business."

The kid was savvy. Rocco, too, had learned how to read each situation, back when he was starting his sales business.

Rocco sent the kid off, and changed into his running gear. Beside the window in his bathroom, a door opened to a set of stairs—an old-style fire escape—leading to an alley behind the building. It was one of Rocco's favourite features of the office. He slipped out the back and headed in the direction of Ruddings Park. His quads ached as if someone had pounded them with a cricket bat, but he needed a run. His morning had already been shot to smithereens, and he had to clear his head. He was going to have to outmanoeuvre the PM and his lackey. Fine. He had always enjoyed a competitive challenge.

AT THREE THAT AFTERNOON, JUNE, HIS ASSISTANT, PUT A call through to Rocco's office. The caller had a smooth, suave voice, richly accented—possibly from Zantoroland.

"Sir," said the caller, "just a call to inform you of the modalities of this evening's visit."

Rocco was given an ID number to use at the Bombay Booty, and he was told that his driver would have a password to enter AfricTown without complications from the thugs who patrolled AfricTown Road, stopping cars and demanding tolls that they cooked up on the spot depending on the make of the car and the look of the driver.

A year before the election that brought the Family Party to power, Geoffrey Moore had driven to AfricTown one night on his own, without going through proper channels. He had not even informed Lula DiStefano. He might have a Harvard degree, but he was still as stupid as a mama's boy. On an isolated stretch of AfricTown Road, three men had wandered out of the bushes and onto the road and blocked Geoffrey's car. When he refused to pay a toll, they smashed his headlights, side-view mirrors and back window. He was ordered out of the car and made to remove his shirt, pants and shoes. When Geoffrey swore at them, he was ordered to take off his socks and underwear. Only then was he allowed to turn around and drive back to Clarkson.

Geoffrey was so enraged that after he returned home he hired a film crew to hide on AfricTown Road and record similar thuggery. Clips from these encounters had formed the centrepiece of the

Family Party's election campaign. In the ads, young masked black men were seen thumping cars with baseball bats and dragging men onto the road. *Do you believe in law and order? Vote against illegals in Freedom State. Vote for the Family Party.*

As Rocco prepared to leave his office, June put her hand on his arm.

"Not a word, June."

"You're venturing into my backyard, so I have a word of advice." She looked at him with calm confidence. No judgment.

Rocco could see that she wanted to help him. He was lucky to have her. "Shoot."

"Bring your runners."

"Pardon?"

"You're a marathoner, so bring your running shoes in case you have to leave quickly."

Rocco met a driver in an anonymous car outside his office at seven that night. Rocco had come prepared for trouble. He wore a comfortable shirt, a blazer he could ditch, loose pants with running shorts instead of underwear and—as June had suggested—running shoes. If the driver didn't show, or if Rocco had to get out early, he could always run home.

They proceeded to AfricTown. The driver gave a code number when the roadside thugs stopped the car, and magically, the thugs let them through. The car drove south on AfricTown Road, passing an endless row of shipping containers converted into windowless homes for entire families. Children wandered across the road, unsupervised. People lugged pails of water to and from water taps. A man banged nails through a corrugated tin roof. Teenagers relieved themselves openly on the side of the road. A woman fried fish on a barbecue grill by the roadside, while customers waited in line.

The car dropped Rocco in a lot outside the Pit, the dining and entertainment hall next to the Bombay Booty, both of which were owned by Lula DiStefano. Lula was said to take a piece of every dollar that changed hands in AfricTown. Rocco arranged to meet the driver at the same place for a lift home.

Rocco got one of the best seats in the house, with a clear view of the stage and, beside it, a sunken wrestling ring. He ordered a salad with grilled chicken. He allowed himself one small potato. No butter or sour cream. He had sparkling mineral water instead of wine. Lula's selection of single-malt whisky was probably terrific, but when you had the likes of Geoffrey Moore plotting your downfall, you had to stay alert. The night's performance featured a Jackson Five look-alike group. They were good. With their afros and colourful clothes, they danced as if their lives depended on it. The lead singer—a kid who looked about eight—belted out "I Want You Back." He wore a purple porkpie hat and vest and looked just like Michael Jackson the night he performed on *The Ed Sullivan Show*. The Jackson Five had appeared on the show the year after Rocco was born, but he had seen clips of it. Rocco wondered if the impersonators were from AfricTown. He had heard that Lula DiStefano encouraged local talent.

Next came a jazz quartet. Also very sharp. After that, a burlesque show. And then, the infamous wrestling match. Two muscular black men, naked except for tight-fitting, leopard-spotted shorts, approached each other on the edge of a giant snakepit. In the pit were rattlesnakes. If you didn't believe it, you could walk over to the edge before the show began to see them writhing and hear them rattling. You could place bets on one or the other wrestler, who fought in the ring around the pit, trying to throw each other in. That was the object of the match. Men stood at the pit's edge, ready to throw a ring buoy to the losing wrestler. And ready to haul him out in a nanosecond and yank off any snakes that had curled around his legs or torso. Man, what a show. The crowd turned electric when the wrestling began.

The wrestlers crouched like sumos, reaching for each other, slapping away intruding hands. Then their heads slid into place on each other's bodies like cars parking. Their arms locked, their knees bent, and then they were pushing, grunting. Suddenly, one man grabbed the other man's head, tripped him at the ankles and flung him into the snakepit. The winner raised his arms as the loser was fished from the pit, and dozens of clients applauded wildly. Rocco could feel his meal turning in his stomach.

He had an ugly feeling about this evening. The PM was not paying for a night out to reward the immigration minister for a job well done. He wished that he could finish with his obligatory visit to the Bombay Booty. But he had hours to wait for his appointment. Rocco spent it watching more wrestling, standing between matches to peer down into the snakepit, and brooding about his job as "Minister of Nothing" until it was finally time to go.

Rocco walked out of the Pit and down a long hallway. When he arrived in the Bombay Booty, he paid a visit to the men's room. Marble floors and granite countertops. Gleaming taps and faucets. On the counters, platters held soaps, razors, shaving cream, deodorant, even sealed toothbrushes, toothpaste, mouthwash bottles and condoms. Patrolling inside was a black man in tight-fitting jeans and a T-shirt. He wore white sneakers with white socks and had clean hand towels draped across his arm. He opened the toilet door for Rocco, turned on his water tap, even pumped soap into his cupped hands. Jazz played from speakers in the bathroom, and there were photos of naked men and women—all black, all gorgeous—on the walls. There was a name under each. *Harry. Josiah. William. Miriam. Delilah. Marvena. Doris. Darlene. Yvette.* Rocco took a second look at Yvette. The girl who had disappeared and ended up dead in Zantoroland. She looked young. Shy smile. Deep cleavage.

The attendant offered a towel, and Rocco took it and dried his hands.

Nodding at the photo of Yvette, the man said, "You can have anything from the menu except that dish."

"Why not that one?" Rocco answered.

"Sold out," the man said.

Rocco headed out of the bathroom. He had heard that you could swing either way in this joint. If you were coming to "fuck," you wanted a woman. If you were coming to "buck," you desired a man. Well-heeled white women from Clarkson also showed up to fuck or buck in AfricTown. Yes, sir, Lula DiStefano was an equal-opportunity huckster.

Rocco approached a desk and provided a sheet of paper with the identification number he'd been given. A young black woman with a low-cut dress gave him a big smile, said her name was Emma and asked if he could just give her the briefest moment to check something. Sure, he said.

When she returned, she said that his date was in the building and would be able to see him soon.

After a short wait, he followed Emma up two flights of stairs. "I hope you are okay with stairs," she said. He told her he was a long-distance runner, and she replied, "Oh, we do like marathon men."

She opened a door and waved him inside a room. "You are welcome to remove your clothes if you wish. Or you can leave them on for now. There's a shower. And there is a king bed, which you are welcome to rest in. Darlene will be with you in about twenty minutes. You'll find reading material by the bedside. Have a lovely time." She left and closed the door behind her.

Rocco checked out the room, which was as luxurious a bedroom as he had ever seen. It had a walk-in closet with many coat hangers, shelves above, and oddly, a large box—it looked like a garment box for moving house—on the floor. He hung up his clothes, leaving his wallet in his pants, and closed the closet door. He took a shower in the marble stall and brushed his teeth at the sink. Rather than climbing into bed naked, he put on a large, soft bathrobe and sat in a chair, forgoing the soft-porn magazine for *Sports Illustrated* and the *Economist*.

Eventually, he heard a knock and saw the door open gradually. "May I come in?"

An attractive young black woman, perhaps twenty years old and wearing a tight shirt and hot pants, entered the room.

"Hello," she said. "My name is Darlene. I understand we are to call you Bob."

"Yes, Bob will be fine," Rocco said. "Good to meet you, Darlene."

"Aren't you the polite one?" she said. "I like a man with manners. Emma said you were a marathon man. Say it ain't so, Bob."

Rocco grinned. He felt a stirring in his loins as she stood over him and placed her hands on his knees.

"Could I persuade you to remove that robe?" she said. She stood up and patted the bed. "And come join me here?"

He stood and walked to the bed. He did not remove the bathrobe, which betrayed his erection.

"I see that Marathon Man responds well to commands," Darlene said.

Rocco thought he heard a cough coming from elsewhere in the room. "What is that?" he said.

"What?"

"That sound?"

"Sometimes sounds come from other rooms, Bob. But let me assure you that we are alone here, and that's just the way I want it."

Rocco excused himself to go to the bathroom. When he came out, he said, "How about if we just talk?"

A pained look crossed the woman's face. It was clear to Rocco that he was no longer a perfect client. Now, he was weird. Only a fool came to talk instead of doing what any self-respecting heterosexual male would do with a beautiful woman in a brothel.

She straightened her shirt, got off the bed and sank heavily into a chair. "Champagne?"

"Hunh?" Rocco said. He hadn't noticed any champagne.

She pointed to a small fridge by the wall. Rocco jumped to his feet, opened it, and removed the champagne and a can of soda water.

"Let me pour you a glass." He uncorked it and poured it into a long, fluted glass.

"Aren't you having champagne, Bob?"

He pulled opened the can of soda water and poured it into a glass. "I'm in training, so I can't."

"Training." She snorted. "So did you win your last marathon?"

"Win? I just run for fun."

"I've been hearing about another marathoner. Keita someone . . . but calls himself Roger Bannister. Man cleaned up at the Buttersby Marathon."

"I was at that race too."

"You give him a run for his money?"

"No."

"How far you finish behind him? One hundred metres, maybe? Or two hundred?"

"I finished an hour behind him."

"An hour! What'd you do? Stop for beer and have a nap?"

"I'll have you know lots of runners finished behind me."

"If someone put me in a race like that, I'd take the subway. Yes siree. Run a hundred metres, take the damn subway to the last block of the race, get off and run the last hundred metres. Why run if you have a perfectly good subway? But if y'all are going to run, you need to use both legs. You can't be losing by a whole damn hour. That ain't no race. It's a whupping."

"At my age, it's not about winning," Rocco said.

She narrowed her eyes. "What is this about, Bob? Why you go to all the trouble and money to book a room with me, if you don't want what most guys want? Are you in the wrong room? Do you want to get bucked tonight?"

"I'm not into men."

"You like the ladies?"

"Yes."

She sipped her champagne and pretended to pout. "But just not me."

"Well, it's just . . ."

"Let me guess."

Rocco didn't know what to make of Darlene. First, she was all friendly. But now that there was to be no sex, she was getting familiar.

"Okay, guess," he said. He had time. It was only half past midnight. As long as he was out by one o'clock, he'd be fine.

"You're a college teacher, and you're writing a study about prostitutes in AfricTown," she said.

"I'm not a college professor."

"You're a cop."

"Nope."

"You're too old to be a student."

"True."

"You want to talk about your wife."

"God. No."

"Are you sure you don't have a wife who doesn't sleep with you anymore?"

"I'm divorced."

"Sorry, Mr. Bob. So tell me what your thing is."

"I want to know what happened to Yvette Peters."

Darlene sat up in her chair. Her smile disappeared. "How you know about her?"

"It's in the newspaper."

"Are you a journalist? A TV reporter?"

"No, I am not. Do you see a notebook? A TV crew?"

"So what are you doing in a bathrobe in this bedroom?"

"I just want to know what happened to her."

"Can't tell you."

"She was a friend of yours."

"Now you sound like a cop."

"I swear on my mother's life that I am not a cop."

"Sure, I knew her. We all knew her. She was here and then she was gone. What do you want me to tell you?"

"Why was she deported?"

"Talk to the government about that. Hell. That's it. You is government. I got you now. Don't I? Don't I?"

"Yes, that's what I am."

"So you here to arrest me too?"

"I am not a cop, and I don't arrest people. I want to know what happened to Yvette."

"Well, you'll have to ask someone else. Because I can't help you."

Darlene stood and walked to the bathroom. Then she turned and motioned to Rocco to follow her. Did she have kinky stuff in mind? He followed her into the bathroom, where she closed the door.

"She got it on with Mr. Big, and then out the door she went," Darlene whispered.

"Yvette did?"

"Yeah."

"Who's Mr. Big?"

"You're government. Who is biggest?"

Rocco had trouble believing it. "You're saying she slept with someone here in the Bombay Booty—someone powerful—and then she was deported? Why?"

"That's all I can say. Who are you, anyway?"

"You're not supposed to ask that question."

"And you're not supposed to pay for pussy and get an interview. On the way out, they gonna ask if you sexually satisfied. And if you say no, guess what happens to my paycheque? So you coming in here asking a lot of questions is hard on my budget."

"Hey, Darlene, let's get right to it. I need you to talk to me. How much would that take?"

She paused. "Five hundred dollars."

"I don't have five hundred in cash," he said. "I can give you three hundred."

"Where it at?"

Rocco stood up. His erection was gone like a groundhog into its hole. He walked out of the bathroom and over to the closet and riffled through the bills in his wallet. He fished out six fifty-dollar bills and put his wallet away. Then he returned to the bathroom and gave the money to Darlene.

She put it in her bra.

"So," he said. "About Yvette?"

"She was gonna make some money and pay Lula to get her a citizenship card."

"Why didn't she have one?"

"Said she was born here, but never got one. Hey. Let me ask you something. Do you think I could be a accountant?"

"Anything's possible."

"I would like to hold people accountable. I reckon people have a lot of accounting to do for the things they done, to me and others."

"Are you good with numbers?"

"I know that three hundred dollars is sixty percent of five hundred," she said.

Rocco grinned. Perhaps he could funnel some money to her later, if she would tell him more about Yvette.

"You gotta help me, or I'm dead meat," she said.

"Why?"

"I know too much."

"What do you mean?"

"Something bad happened to Yvette, and it could happen to me too. If I get out of here, could you help me? I mean, help me hide?"

"What exactly are you talking about?"

"Help me hide."

He felt for her. What could be the harm in giving her his number. "You're good with numbers. Can you remember this?" He said his number and asked her to repeat it.

But Darlene said, "What's that sound?"

"What sound?" he said.

"Shh!" she said.

He heard sirens. Police sirens. It sounded like a hundred of them, wailing. He whipped open the closet door and was dressed in a minute. Rocco was good like that.

"It's a raid, Mr. Bob. Take the back door. I'll show you. But when I call you later, you better pick up."

Rocco felt his veins fill with adrenalin. He could not afford to get caught in AfricTown. Goddamn that Geoffrey Moore. Sending him here, setting him up. He would not let himself get caught.

There were back stairs. There was a basement. There was a secret underground tunnel. Getting out of there involved some crawling that ruined his clothes. He passed through two other buildings and came out in a grove of trees a few hundred metres away from AfricTown Road. He knew which way was north toward Clarkson, and there was a footpath parallel to the road, beaten by who knew how many hundreds of others who had fled just like him.

The police were swarming AfricTown's Bombay Booty. But they would not catch Rocco. He had the cover of night, and if push came to shove, he could always run.

CHAPTER SEVENTEEN

FTER THE BUTTERSBY MARATHON, KEITA PAID for three more nights in Clarkson, switching motels every day. He didn't want to keep spending money that he needed to save to help Charity, and worried that an overly scrupulous motel clerk might report him to the police. After visiting an Internet café and receiving an email from John Falconer, who said that Lula DiStefano had invited him to visit, Keita changed his strategy. He took a small knapsack with just enough clothes to keep him going for a few days, stuffed the rest back into his bus station locker, and began walking south.

He crossed railroad tracks that seemed to demarcate the city limits. The road passed an abandoned field and, up ahead, rounded a bend out of sight. There were no signs on it and few cars. A couple of hundred metres to the west of the road, a footpath led through a wide hole in a massive, barbwire fence. Wide enough for two people to pass each other on their way through. Every pedestrian was black or mixed. Almost everyone was carrying something: shoes in hands, bags on shoulders, knapsacks on backs, sacks of flour or rice on heads. Keita hadn't seen many black folks on the streets of Clarkson, but there were hundreds here, passing through that hole at a steady pace.

Keita's instructions had been to begin walking the footpath from Clarkson around noon. He was to look for an older man who answered to the name of DeNorval Unthank. Unthank would head north from AfricTown at the same time that Keita left Clarkson, meet Keita on the walking path and escort him safely to AfricTown.

In the first kilometre, he saw no one who corresponded to the description of DeNorval Unthank, so he continued on. Most people greeted him. *Hello. Good afternoon. Good day. Be with God.* A boy tried to sell him bottled water. An adolescent carrying a duffle bag tried to sell him a pair of running shoes for ten dollars. A woman sat by a makeshift table selling watermelon and barbecued corn. One young man stopped him, pointed a gun at him and told Keita to turn over all his money. Keita was in the process of saying that he had no money (he did not mention his cheque or his cash, which was zipped into a secret pocket inside his shirt) when an older woman carrying a huge purse walked up and swung it at the man.

"Junior, leave him alone." Then she looked at Keita. "Don't pay him no mind. That ain't real. It's plastic. He ain't right in the head. He tries this on everybody, till he gets to know them."

Keita thanked the woman.

"Don't thank me," she said. "Thank the Lord. But I'll take five dollars for my troubles."

Keita told her he had fallen on hard times and did not have any money to spare.

"Well then, next time," she said. "Once you find a job, you can give me five dollars one day."

"We'll see," he said. And he kept walking.

By the second kilometre, Keita saw a long line of shipping containers to the west of the path. Some were hooked up to electrical power lines that ran overhead, but the hookups looked makeshift. The containers were painted wild colours, just like the houses of Zantoroland: pink, purple, green, blue. Some were striped or polka-dotted. Some had murals depicting famous runners or cricket players. Most were single containers, but sometimes they were stacked two or three high. Keita watched a woman toss a rope ladder from a square hole cut into a third-floor container and lower herself to the ground. People sat in chairs outside the containers, watching the pedestrians pass. The containers appeared to be houses, drinking holes and places where women set up to wash clothes. Sometimes, in the gaps between them, Keita would see a patch of grass covered with clothes spread out to dry. Nearby, next to water taps popping out of the ground like mushrooms, women would be washing, wringing or spreading out clothes.

The public toilets were abysmal. The first one Keita visited was so disgusting that he turned away, choosing to wait. This place looked poorer than Zantoroland. In his own country, even villagers with no education and minimal income kept clean homes and outhouses. It was hard not to think of home as he walked south on the trail beside AfricTown Road. But Keita didn't want to let his thoughts wander. He had to stay level-headed, and he had to find a way to get money as fast as he could to Charity's captors.

A teenage boy sat by his father, whose eyes were clouded over and bluish, like marbles. A few pairs of shoes were laid out on a rug at their feet along with a sign that said Shoe Doctor.

"Mister," the boy shouted to Keita. "Shoe polish? Shoe repair?"

Keita smiled apologetically and pointed to his new running shoes.

"But in your bag, surely you have a pair of nice shoes? Polish, just two dollars. Repair, more."

Keita shrugged and kept walking.

Finally, after about three kilometres, he saw a tall, thin, silver-haired black man with a white goatee walking toward him on the path. A bright red cloth was slung diagonally across his chest and belly, and as the man drew closer, Keita could see, protruding from it, the head of a baby.

"Keita," the man said, extending his hand.

Keita shook the hand, which was relaxed and gave his a friendly squeeze. It felt instantly comforting, like that of an uncle.

"You must be DeNorval Unthank," Keita said.

"Sent by Lula DiStefano, and at your service. Sorry I couldn't meet you at the start of the road. Been a busy day."

"What's your baby's name?"

"Xenia," DeNorval said. "Five months old. But she's not my baby. I'm just helping out."

The baby gurgled. She stared at Keita. Keita smiled at her, and she broke into a smile too. DeNorval patted her bum.

"She's dry, and she's been fed, so we might as well keep walking and get you where you're going." DeNorval turned to join Keita on the walk south.

Keita didn't think he had ever seen a man carrying a baby on his back or chest in Zantoroland.

"I trust that nobody's given you a hard time so far?" DeNorval asked.

Keita told him about the man who brought out the plastic pistol and the old lady who stopped him. DeNorval laughed and said they worked as a team. The man threatened, and she intervened, and half the time they made off with five or ten dollars in thank-you money.

"So where is the child's mother?" Keita asked.

"Studying math. She's just seventeen. We have a little school in AfricTown. Not much. But she can't go there, because she has no papers and sometimes police raid the school. But we have people in AfricTown who give lessons, so on Thursday mornings she studies with them. On the other days, she cleans houses in Clarkson."

"And you?"

"I'm just an all-around helper. Since I wasn't doing anything for a few hours, except walking out to meet you, I offered to take Xenia. I don't mind. Lovely baby. And anyway, babies and I understand each other."

They walked for a while in silence. Up ahead, on the right, Keita saw two men working to make a connection between the top of a shipping container and an electrical wire. A stepladder was perched on the container roof. One man steadied it, while the man on top looped a cable around the electrical wire.

"Dangerous work," DeNorval said. "People die every year trying to siphon off electricity. But they need it for lights, refrigeration, fans."

Keita asked if DeNorval worked for Lula DiStefano.

"I'm in AfricTown at her pleasure. Occasionally, when she requires services in addition to my usual work, I comply. Today she wanted someone to get you reliably to the Pit, so here I am."

"The Pit?"

DeNorval explained about the Pit and the Bombay Booty. He said that all visitors to AfricTown were supposed to check in with Queen DiStefano or her representatives. She liked to meet distinguished guests.

"Distinguished?" Keita asked.

"Don't kid yourself. The whiz kid, John Falconer? He's your friend, right?"

"We met on the bus and spoke for a few hours."

"He mentioned you had won the Buttersby Marathon. Word spreads fast around here. So, yes, Lula wishes to meet you."

Keita nodded his appreciation. He was curious and asked about the shipping containers. DeNorval said thousands of people lived in them in AfricTown. Cut holes for ventilation, stacked them end to end, side by side or one on top of the other if they could afford it. Lula DiStefano obtained used shipping containers from port authorities in Freedom State and Zantoroland, DeNorval said. She had them hauled to AfricTown and rented them out. And occasionally she prevailed on the authorities to install more public water taps.

"So what do you do in AfricTown?"

"We don't generally ask what people do in AfricTown," DeNorval said. "You can safely assume that most of it is not what someone would want written down and shown to anyone."

"I see," Keita said.

"But confidentially," DeNorval said, "I greet newcomers sometimes. I am sometimes asked to house guests for a short time in my premises. Baby Xenia and her mother are staying with me, for a while. And I'm a health adviser."

"What is that?"

"Got a cut? An infection? A broken finger? A tooth that needs pulling? I can deal with minor emergencies."

"You are a doctor."

"I was trained in Zantoroland. For a time, I was chief of the ER at Yagwa Hospital. But I had to flee and I have no certification here. So I just call myself a heath adviser."

DeNorval Unthank was not a fast walker, and it took an hour to cover the rest of the way to AfricTown. But Keita did not mind. He had nowhere to go and nothing to do except meet Lula DiStefano. Unthank was a good conversationalist. If he had been a physician in Zantoroland, he must have had reason to flee. Keita wished his own father had fled while there was still time. This man who was greying and gaunt—perhaps he could become a friend. An ally. But never a father. Parents could never be replaced. When they departed, they left a hole that never went away. Keita tried to imagine what his father would advise him in this new situation. *Be aware. Stay alive. Help your sister.*

DeNorval steered Keita off the main path. "A little detour, to the Red Square."

"What's that?"

"You'll see. We'll be there in a minute. I have to drop off Xenia with her mother."

A few hundred metres to the west of the main footpath, they came to a series of shipping containers, painted bright red and forming four sides of a square. Outside were water taps and a stand with a soap dispenser. What looked like a hundred men, women and children were lined up outside, waiting patiently by a sign marked In. Near another sign marked Out, people exited the square in ones and twos and walked away. DeNorval stepped to the front of the queue. People moved aside and let him by with smiles and greetings.

"Hello, DeNorval. Good afternoon, DeNorval. Good day, DeNorval." One young man called him Dr. Unthank, but Unthank corrected him.

"It's just DeNorval, please," he said. "You can wash your hands here," DeNorval said to Keita, going first. He soaped his hands thoroughly, rinsed them and shook them dry.

Keita did the same. Then they stepped into a courtyard formed by the containers. Inside, in five long rows of folding chairs, people sat with plates on their laps. On those plates, Keita saw rice or macaroni, Brussels sprouts and scoops of chili. All along one side of the courtyard, a team of men and women served food from huge cooking pots suspended over firepits with red coals. At the exit was a barrel filled with apples. Each person took one on the way out.

"We serve lunch here, Mondays, Wednesdays and Fridays, but there are a few rules. You have to wash your hands, be orderly, take only what you are given, not bring any drugs, alcohol or weapons, show up sober, be courteous and help clean up. You also have to bring your own plate and cutlery."

"What does it cost?" Keita asked.

"It's free."

"Who pays for it, then?"

"Lula. She says the rent she charges for the containers includes a food tax, which she uses to pay a team of people to go to market and buy groceries."

A woman came up and tapped Keita on his shoulder. "Are you Keita, the runner?"

Keita was stunned to be recognized. "I am."

"I have a teenage son. Thirteen. Very fast runner. Can you teach him? He wants to be a famous marathoner."

"I would help if I could," Keita said, "but I don't have a place to live yet, and I don't even know if I'll be living here."

"Please live here," the woman said. "We need someone like you to teach our boys to be great. Like you."

"I'm far from great," Keita said.

"You won the Buttersby Marathon," she said. "Two hours, nine minutes and thirty-six seconds!"

"Thank you," Keita said, "but—"

DeNorval steered Keita away. "Come. Meet Xenia's mother."

They approached a young woman serving rice from one of the big cooking pots.

"Maria, meet Keita. Keita, this is Xenia's mom."

She had a child's face, for sure. She smiled shyly at Keita, took Xenia and strapped the baby onto her back.

"DeNorval likes to carry her in the front, where he can see her, but I like to carry her behind me."

"What did you do in your math lesson?" DeNorval asked her.

"Long division," she said. "Thank you, DeNorval."

"Don't mention it," he said.

DeNorval led Keita to a chair, where Maria brought him a plate of food. As he ate, children and teenagers gathered around. Touching his running shoes. Admiring his calves. Asking him to teach them to run.

He asked where people could run in AfricTown.

"Nowhere," DeNorval told him. "There is only AfricTown Road, but cars speed on it, and there's no shoulder for pedestrians."

After lunch, they walked out to the road, accompanied by thirty children who walked barefoot or in sandals and tried to impress Keita by sprinting past him and doing pushups and burpees.

"It would take many people to build a running trail beside this road and to see that children trained on it safely," Keita said. "But it is possible."

DeNorval smiled, put his hand on Keita's shoulder and said that it was good to see him thinking.

"By the way," Keita said. "Who set up that lunch system?"

"It's a little project of mine," DeNorval said. "All I have to do is organize the volunteers."

A TALL YOUNG BOUNCER AT THE PIT RECOGNIZED KEITA'S name. "I heard you tore up all those other runners in the marathon, man," he said. "Good running. Miss Lula said to take care of you this evening till she is ready to meet you herself."

The bouncer, whose name was Jake, escorted Keita to his table and told the server that this one was on the queen bee. Keita found himself in a large lounge with a stage for performers and several dozen tables.

"Don't go near any white customers," the bouncer said. "They're here for fun but don't want to be recognized. If you get within even a few steps of one, I don't care if you're a nice guy and Miss Lula's guest, I'll have to throw you out."

"Got it," Keita said. He looked down into the pit. "Are there rattlers in there?"

"Western diamondbacks. Imported straight from New Mexico."

"Venomous?"

"Want to jump in and find out?" the bouncer said.

Keita said he would just sit and watch the show. He couldn't have approached a white man even if he wanted to. They sat together in a cordoned-off area, ringed by security guards.

Now the wrestlers caught Keita's eye. They locked arms, pulled, pushed and tried to knock each other off balance, until one tripped the other and sent him sailing into the pit. The loser screamed as he disappeared into the bed of writhing snakes. After they fished him out, a man injected serum into his flank, and four helpers carted him away on a stretcher. A few spectators threw money at the victor, which he snatched up while strutting and waving to the crowd. Keita wondered when the victor would wrestle again—and when he would lose. Even the best wrestler must lose eventually.

A tall, medium-set black woman in her late fifties approached the table. She bent down and kissed Keita on the cheek.

"I'm Lula DiStefano. Welcome!"

She had trim abs and arms, and she looked like she ate salads and went to the gym every day. She had eyes like drills that bored into Keita.

She reached out her hand to shake Keita's and held it a moment longer than necessary. She was sizing up his hand, his grip, his fingers. Keita had the sensation that she could read his thoughts just by squeezing his fingers. But he was unsure.

"Thank you for letting me come to AfricTown."

"I hear you beat two thousand runners in the Buttersby Marathon. That you set a course record. And that you are some hot thing in a race."

Keita smiled.

"I never met a marathon man before. Does it hurt much, running that fast for so long?"

"It's all about how well you tolerate pain," Keita said.

Lula let out a barking laugh. "I hate pain, but I ain't averse to dishing it out."

"I have never intentionally dished it out," Keita said, "except to beat other runners."

"Tell me about that!" Lula said. "How do you beat them?"

"You wear a runner down, and just when he or she is nearing the point of cracking, you sing. If a runner is suffering and you can sing to him, I can pretty well guarantee you will break his spirit."

"A man in the streets of AfricTown comes to beat you up and take your money, singing won't get you far. In fact, if you open your mouth to sing, he'll spot your gold fillings and steal them too."

"Singing and running are my only weapons."

She frowned and played with her fingernails.

"Not much of an arsenal. You good enough to win the Olympics?"

"No. And I'm not thinking Olympics. I'm thinking day to day."

"John Falconer, is he a friend of yours?"

"We met on the bus."

"He sure runs his mouth. Sometimes I think there's a prime minister fixing to bust out of his pint-sized body."

"He is eloquent, that's for sure," Keita said.

"I take care of him, now. His mama ain't well. So every day, I make him sit his ass down in my office and do his homework. But I'm the last thing anyone wants for a mama. Never had children, never wanted them and would have kilt them if I had had them anyway."

Keita laughed uneasily. Lula DiStefano exuded endless energy, but it was hard to tell how she channelled it: to love people, or to harm them.

Lula caught the waiter's eye. He came over and asked what they'd have. When Keita hesitated, Lula stepped in for him. "A grand Caesar salad and steak frites for monsieur. Medium, Keita?"

"Pardon me?"

"Do you take your steak rare, medium or well done?"

Keita had never ordered a steak in his life, so he guessed: "Medium, please."

When they were alone again at the table, Lula took his hand. She examined his palm and fingers. "You got perfect skin. As we say, black don't crack. But you're too young for even the tiniest crack. You are not a day over twenty-five. Right?"

"That's right. I'm twenty-four."

"And you have never done one whit of farming. Boy, you ain't even dug yams."

"I grew up in the city. Yagwa. We didn't have any land."

"Your momma and daddy? Still on this earth?"

"No," Keita said.

"Siblings?"

"One."

"Where she at?"

"She was studying till recently at Harvard." His voice caught when he thought of Charity and how she might be suffering.

"Smart one. But, hey. I'm smart too." Lula sat up and cleared her throat. "So what can I do for you?"

Keita hesitated. Whatever favours Lula granted would come at a cost. But what choice did he have? He asked if he could stay in AfricTown and whether Lula could assist him in cashing a cheque.

"Are you illegal?"

"Yes."

"Zantoroland?"

"Yes."

"Faloo."

"Yes."

"In trouble at home?"

"I haven't committed any crimes, if that's what you mean."

"How much is the cheque for?"

"Four thousand dollars."

"From whom?"

"Buttersby Marathon."

"Very good," she said, smiling. "I can cash that for you. From you, I'll just take five percent. And I'll set you up for a few nights, at no charge."

"I don't mean to be ungrateful. But I cannot afford to give away even five percent of the cheque."

Lula removed her glasses and stared down the rim of her nose at Keita. "You're pushing it. I'm letting you stay here because you're young, polite, good-looking and you kicked some Freedom State ass in that marathon. I'll cash your cheque for a one percent fee. This time. You would pay twenty-five times more on the street."

"I know. And I do appreciate—"

"Where is it?"

Keita pulled it from his backpack and gave it to her. Lula reached into her purse and removed a wad of cash. She peeled off forty one-hundred-dollar bills and handed them over.

"After you finish dining on my tab, leave a forty-dollar tip for the server."

Keita promised to do so.

"After three nights here, you need to find somewhere else to hide. You'll have some profile, having won that race. I can't afford to have you bringing trouble to AfricTown."

"I'll get a place to stay soon," he said.

"For a fee, I could arrange a passport for you."

"Passport?"

"Making you a citizen of Freedom State."

Keita's only illegal act ever was existing in Freedom State without a right to do so. He didn't feel right about buying a phony passport, but he couldn't help asking.

"How much would it cost?"

"Twenty thousand dollars."

"I can't afford that. I have urgent business with the little money I do have."

"Well, keep it in mind. In the meantime, keep your eyes open, young man."

"What do you mean?"

"People are pissed about that working girl who got deported," she said. "Problem was, she was born here. But she died in Zantoroland, in custody. You hear about her?"

Keita said he had seen the item in the newspaper.

"Top is gonna blow," Lula said. "People gonna rise up. You seen a volcano? Watch out for a human eruption, soon. There will be more raids here, of that I am sure. And we will be in the streets, marching and demonstrating."

The last place in the world Keita needed to be was in the middle of a political demonstration ringed by police officers.

Lula seemed to sense his reticence.

"When you leave here," Lula said, "go uptown and find some sweet woman in the suburbs. You're gorgeous and pure. She'll fall for you. Take my word for it. White women in Freedom State are always falling for authentic black males. Even when they ain't authentic."

Lula reached over the table and stroked his cheek briefly, then she stood to leave. Keita placed the fingers of his right hand gently on her sleeve. She pivoted to face him.

"Lula, I need to make some money."

"Don't we all?"

"I need to make it urgently. It's not for me. It's for someone else."

"Heard that before, honey. Didn't you just make four grand winning that race?"

"But I must make much more, and soon."

"Are you willing to kill?"

"No, of course not."

"Steal?"

"No."

"Carry drugs across borders?"

"No."

"Are you willing to break any kind of law?"

"My existence is a violation of the law."

"Other than existing. Which you can't help."

"I need to make thousands of dollars, quickly."

"Then win some more races. Your salad is here. And your steak is coming. When you finish, ask the waiter to have someone escort you back to DeNorval's place."

As he prepared to leave the Pit between wrestling matches, Keita saw a middle-aged white man get up from his table and walk to the edge of the snakepit. He walked with an athletic confidence that seemed familiar. Keita had seen the man before. He was a runner, Keita was sure of it. But he had no time to give it more thought. A man from the restaurant escorted Keita south past stalls of women selling grilled fish, men selling watches and clocks, and boys selling soap and hot water to people who wanted to stand in a curtained bathtub and wash. They passed more shipping containers, these ones interspersed with wooden shacks with corrugated tin roofs.

They stopped at two containers joined to make an L. One was painted purple, the other orange.

"It's here," the man said.

Keita knocked at the door. No answer. He knocked again. Still no answer. He let himself in and found that he could turn left toward a door marked Strictly Private or right toward one marked Health Adviser. He knocked on the door to the right, but still there was no answer. He pushed the door open and stepped into a sitting area: four empty chairs. Old magazines on the coffee table. A cloth screen blocked off access to the room beyond. Keita pushed it aside.

A man was lying on his side, knees curled up around his chest, while DeNorval wiggled a finger deep inside his ass. Keita let out a shout.

"Knock next time," DeNorval said. "Step back and wait in the waiting room."

From the sitting room, Keita heard the patient gasping.

"All done," DeNorval said. "You can wipe yourself with this and get dressed."

The man grunted. "So, Doc. Find anything in there?"

"I don't like the feel of your prostate," DeNorval said.

"And I don't like you feeling it, Doc."

"What is your status?"

"Same as yours, Doc. Why the hell else would I be seeing you?"

"Do you have any money?"

"No."

"Some say saw palmetto can help control prostate size."

"What the hell is a saw palmetto?"

"A small palm. From its fruit, you can take an extract used for medicinal purposes."

"Fucking AfricTown. You see a fucking doctor without papers who tells you to fix a pain in the ass by sucking on a palm tree."

"So you don't want me to get you some sample capsules?"

"What the fuck. Go ahead and order them."

"Come back in a week. That will be ten dollars."

"For sticking your finger up my ass and promising a palm tree?"

"Ten dollars. We all have to eat."

"Well, I don't have ten dollars."

"Then I won't have any saw palmetto for your enlarged prostate, and don't come here next time you need stitches, or antibiotics, or dressing for cuts, or a tooth pulled. You or your kids."

There was a pause. The patient swore softly. "Here. Take your goddamn bill. How fucked up is that? Ten dollars for a poke up the ass."

Emerging through the curtains, the patient stopped and took a look at Keita. Sandals, black gym pants and a T-shirt that said *Go F Yourself*. Clean-shaven. Buzz cut. Brown eyes. He was a light-skinned black man—clearly of mixed race. About thirty years old. Skinny as a hydro wire, walking with a limp.

"Ten dollars," the man said.

Keita looked at him quizzically.

"Ten dollars, I said. You watched the peep show. It oughta be worth that."

Keita shook his head. He had no intention of giving the man ten dollars.

"If you don't give me ten dollars, I'll mash your fucking face into a pulp."

"Well, then, at least I'm in a doctor's office."

"Smart one, are you? What's a matter? You're not from around here. It won't kill you to part with ten dollars."

"I don't have any money to spare."

"Look at your shoes. Now look at mine. See this hole here at my big toe? Now look at this heel. Worn right through. Do you got that? Hunh? Tell me. Who's in the more urgent need here? What we need here is a redistribution of wealth. So how about that fucking ten dollars?"

DeNorval came from behind the curtains. "Howard, no harassing my patients. Get out of here."

"Some shithole office," Howard said, "and you're not even a fucking doctor." He left the office, still ranting.

"Sorry about that," DeNorval said. "You've just seen the underside of my work."

"Looks like you know all about prostates, anyway," Keita said.

DeNorval grinned. "But how can I help you? It's not a medical matter, is it?"

"Well, there is the small matter of a hernia."

"Let's take a look."

DeNorval gestured him into the examining area, and Keita stood with shirt raised. The health adviser prodded, poked and tapped the golf-ball-sized protuberance. He asked if it had changed size or shape lately. Keita explained that it had grown over the last few months.

"You should get this fixed, but it can wait," DeNorval said. "I couldn't do anything for you here. You would need surgery. But you would have to pay."

Keita asked how much it might cost. DeNorval said he could be looking at ten thousand dollars, easily. Keita explained his other problems: how while running, he sometimes became dizzy, or faint, or completely ran out of energy, or felt an uncharacteristically intense thirst.

"The hernia might cause pain. But it doesn't explain what you're describing. What helps alleviate those symptoms?"

"When I stop running, and drink lots of water, and rest."

"Let me run a little blood test on you."

Keita looked around. The room was not filthy, but it did not have the antiseptic quality of a proper hospital room. "I would rather not."

"It would just take a minute. And it might give us valuable information. In fact, I would like to take your blood, just a drop, five or six times at key moments over the next few days. What do you say?"

Keita said, "Maybe later."

"As you wish. Housing, right? You've come for help finding a place to stay?"

"Yes."

DeNorval offered Keita the use of his guest room.

"That would be fabulous," Keita said.

The doctor cleared his throat. "Let me clear up some possible misconceptions," he said. "I am gay. Indeed, I am in Freedom State because I was outed by a medical rival at the Yagwa Hospital. You know what our country does to gays, right? Torture? Execution? You are aware?"

Keita nodded.

"I had to leave fast after he outed me, and I paid seven thousand dollars for passage on a ship to Freedom State. By some miracle, I arrived alive and got here. I am gay, Keita, but I am not interested in jumping your bones. I have a deal with Ms. DiStefano. She refers to me people who need unofficial medical help and a place to stay. She has given me lodgings. Very decent, for AfricTown. I have a spare

room, and the deal with Ms. DiStefano is that I share it, at my dis-
cretion and on a very short-term basis, with trustworthy people who
are in a desperate situation. So. I cannot help you with the hernia,
other than to tell you where to get treatment. I have a theory about
your other problem, but for the time being, you do not wish to have
your blood tested. For the next few days, I can offer you a clean
single bed in a clean, simple room with access to a private, locked
outhouse that is cleaner than just about any outhouse you will find
anywhere in AfricTown."

DeNorval led Keita to a curtained-off section of the shipping
container that formed the living quarters. It had two single beds,
one for DeNorval and the other for Maria and her baby, pulled up
against opposite walls. There was a small, circular table, a portable gas
stove hooked up to a propane tank, and lights and a small refrigerator. From the refrigerator, DeNorval brought out a tuna salad, red
peppers, apples, bread and water.

"You like? Hope so, because it is all I have. That, plus milk for
the child."

"I just ate," Keita said, "but I'll sit with you."

Maria came in then with her baby. She spread a cloth on her
bed and changed Xenia quickly. Then she gave the baby to Keita,
wordlessly, and he held the child as if he'd been doing it all his life.
Xenia lay calm and smiling in his arms. Maria returned minutes later,
shaking her wet hands. She smiled at Keita and took the baby back
to offer her a bottle. Xenia pushed the bottle away to stare at Keita.

"She likes you," Maria said. "She doesn't like everybody. She
must know that you are good."

"I've not held a baby for years," he said.

Maria handed the baby back to him, along with the bottle. Keita
offered it, and Xenia grasped it with her tiny hands and drank. For
the first time in a month, Keita felt at home.

Keita sat with DeNorval and Maria as they ate quickly and
without ceremony. DeNorval said it was a long walk to Maria's
cleaning job in Clarkson. Since their kitchen was about to turn into

the bedroom that he shared with mother and daughter, DeNorval offered to show Keita to his room.

Keita felt grateful and safe as he settled onto the bed. But just as he was closing his eyes, he heard sirens and the sound of people shouting. He rose and tucked his bag under his arm, ready to run. At the front door of the shipping container, he encountered John Falconer. John was with a young black woman who said her name was Darlene.

"Police raid," John said. "You'd better get out of here."

"One moment, then." Keita left his bag with John and Darlene and ran to the outhouse. He relieved himself and ran back again.

"What about Maria, Xenia and DeNorval?" he asked.

"They have gone into hiding," John said, "but you have to make tracks. Afraid you have to go back to Clarkson. This is not a safe place tonight. Come. I'll show you the way."

OUTSIDE DENORVAL'S HOME, JOHN WAITED UNTIL KEITA was visiting the outhouse before slipping a 100-gigabyte memory stick into the outside, zippered pocket of the runner's knapsack. Darlene raised her eyebrows as if to say, *I hope you know what you're doing.* The stick contained not just the footage of the minister's encounter with Darlene that night, but also the visit by the prime minister to the Bombay Booty. It was an extra—just a private backup system in case anyone managed to separate John from his belongings.

On the trail back to Clarkson, Keita walked so fast that John had to run two steps out of ten to keep up. He urged Keita to slow down so as not to overtake the tall man who was walking a hundred paces ahead of them, also away from the cacophony of police sirens and loudspeakers. John told Keita that the man was the minister of immigration, Rocco Calder.

"What is he doing here?" Keita asked.

"Not sure, but he's in a hurry to leave," John said.

John did not feel he could offer Keita a full account of how Lula DiStefano had asked him back to the Bombay Booty to videotape the minister in the room with Darlene. "Insurance" was what Lula had called it. She wanted fifteen more water holes dug, a new school built and a reliable power line installed to feed electricity to AfricTown. What she didn't want was police raids impeding her business, she said. And she wouldn't stand for any more of her young protégés airlifted to Zantoroland and killed in prison there. Since John had footage of the prime minister and his immigration minister cavorting in AfricTown, and she had the PM's citizenship card too, Lula said she might prevail. Indeed, her last point to John had been "Pressure without pain is pointless."

"Don't you have school tomorrow?" Keita said.

"What are you, my headmaster?"

"It is late," Keita said. "Don't you need to sleep?"

"I decide my own schedule."

Keita chuckled. "It is a very long walk to Clarkson, and when we get there it will be the middle of the night."

"I could stay with you and then just go to school."

"Thank you, brother," Keita said. "But I can take care of myself. Go home now."

John had not been called "brother," or any other gentle word, for a long time. His mother, when she was healthy and at home, called him Johnny. When she was curled up like an embryo in Wintergreen Psychiatric Institute, she didn't call him anything at all.

"I know the immigration minister, the dude up ahead," John said. "I've been in his office. Maybe I could get him to issue a permit for your sister."

"You must not talk of this, to anyone," Keita said, stopping abruptly. "Let me be clear. If this is done wrong, my sister could die."

"Okay, okay. I won't say anything."

They walked in silence for a while.

"So tell me about your father," John said.

"I don't want to talk about it."

"Look," John said, "my mother is in a crazy ward. Locked up. I don't want to talk about it either, because I can't fucking stand the image of her rolled up in a ball, unmoving and unable to talk. When I see her like that, I fear that I did that to her. But the wiser part of me knows that's not true. Right?"

"A child is not to blame for his mother's health problems," Keita said.

"I told you something I never tell anyone. So now you can talk to me. Tell me about your father."

Keita felt the same grief well up in him that he had faced on the massage table after the Buttersby Marathon. That time, he had closed the door, gently but firmly, on his sadness. This time, he held it open a crack to let his story seep out. He spoke. Reluctantly, at first. But he gathered steam as he went and soon found himself telling John everything.

He was so absorbed in the telling that he had finished the story before he noticed that the boy had been holding his hand for several minutes.

"I get nightmares," John told him.

"Me too," Keita said.

"It's weird," John said. "I can't explain it. In my dreams, my mom and I are walking along the streets of Clarkson. I know it never snows here, but in this dream it's very cold and the streets are full of snow. Outside one of the finest jewellery shops, my mother jumps onto a snowbank and tries to take off her clothes. I pull her off the snowbank and plead with her to let me take her, fully dressed, to the psychiatric hospital. 'But they'll only let me in if I'm crazy,' she says, 'and how will they know that unless I arrive naked on a winter day?'"

"I hope your mother gets better soon," Keita said.

"Me too," John said. "What's your dream?"

"In my dream," Keita said, "I am a child. A boy, just your age. I am wandering around Yagwa, eating figs and cookies that have been sent to me by the president. I am looking to buy a wagon, while my father is being held in the Pink Palace. Wagon vendors refuse to take my money or sell to me, and they keep saying, 'How could you dare think about amusing yourself with a wagon when your father is being tortured in the Pink Palace?' They stand there smirking when I say, 'They won't stop hurting him until I come with a wagon.' Like the president, they keep insisting that I eat more figs and cookies. I cannot ever get the wagon. I cannot stop what they are doing to my father. He is in the Pink Palace and I am in the market, and we are separated by only a kilometre, but in my dream it is much too far to run."

CHAPTER EIGHTEEN

K EITA STUDIED THE ENTRANCE TO THE CLARKSON Library. Such thought and money had gone into the creation of the building! Pools of water everywhere, huge plate-glass windows and vines crawling up the walls. It was a building that invited him to sit down and rest. Perhaps to sleep. After reaching Clarkson, he had spent the night in an all-night burger joint, where there were newspapers to read and tea cost only a dollar—but it had not been restful. Now, standing on the far side of the street, Keita watched every person who walked in or out the front doors of the library. He was terribly thirsty again, and a little dizzy. Perhaps it was only the lack of sleep. Still, this task was important, so he tried to focus. It appeared that people were allowed to enter the library freely. Some people had their bags checked on their way out, but that was just to determine if they were trying to steal books or newspapers. They were not asked to show ID.

Keita walked up to the entrance and pushed through the turnstile. Nobody stopped him or questioned him or looked at him at all. A good sign. Up ahead, to the right, was a bank of fifty computers, each on its own desk. It looked like a huge classroom. He saw young people with odd rings looping through their lips and eyebrows, children who looked barely old enough to kick a football, people in business suits and even a nun in her habit. A boy of about sixteen got up from a computer and walked away. He owned a belt, but it did not appear to work properly. His pants were hanging below his buttocks, leaving his underwear partly exposed. He seemed to be aware of it, because he spread his legs wide and walked bow-legged. Was he right in the head? Keita also saw people who didn't appear to have showered or changed clothes in days, and who looked like they were carrying their belongings in bags or carts. Homeless people. Some of them were white. This he found hard to believe.

He slid into the chair vacated by the boy with the tumbling pants. He tapped the keyboard and saw that he needed a password to go online.

He glanced around. To his right was a young black man with dreadlocks and rings on every finger. He poked furiously at a computer keyboard using only his thumbs and middle fingers. It looked like he was using both hands to pluck a mbira. Keita loved the thumb piano, and hadn't seen one played since he left Zantoroland.

"Excuse me, sir," Keita said.

"Peace," the man said, continuing to type.

"How do I get online?" Keita asked.

"You got two choices, brother. Divine intervention or a library card."

"At this moment, I'm short on divine intervention," Keita said.

"I hear you, brother."

"So how about the library card?"

Mbira Man pointed with his chin at the reference librarian. "Whatever you do, don't go to that man."

"Isn't he the librarian?" Keita asked.

"Purebred Aryan! You could have five pieces of ID, but he would still turn you down. In this world, there are people who spend years learning how to *not* help a man. He is that sort of person. Set him loose from your mind, man. Set him loose like a bad dog. Okay, brother, retrain your mind. Swing around in your chair. Follow me."

Mbira Man pointed with the longest index finger Keita had ever seen. "See way back there, in the corner of the library? That there grandma?"

Sitting at a simple desk was a grey-haired white woman. She was talking to a patron, while two others waited in line to see her.

"That there woman is Missus Beech. Look like a little ol' nothing. Don't be fooled. Ain't easy for a white person to be saintly, but she closing in. That there woman is your camel, passing through the eye of a needle. Yes, sir. She a friend of the people, brother, so make her your friend too."

"Thank you."

"That will be ten dollars."

"But I don't have ten dollars to spare."

"Well then, give me ten the next time we meet. Meanwhile, take this—"

It was a card with just a few words: "*One Love*, by VanderVann. Look for it. Buy it. Read it."

"What is *One Love*?" Keita asked.

"My novel."

"You're writing a novel?" Keita said.

"All up here, man," Mbira Man said, tapping his noggin.

"And who is VanderVann?" Keita asked.

"That's me, brother."

Keita approached the desk at the back of the library. Mrs. Beech sat under a sign that said New Cards. Keita hadn't seen many old people in Freedom State. In Zantoroland, old people could be found everywhere. Picking fruit or cooking spicy fish by the roadside or minding grandchildren or great-grandchildren. But in Zantoroland you would never find an old woman working in a public building.

He waited for his turn to see Mrs. Beech. A sign said you required a national citizenship card and proof of residency to apply for a library card. But the woman seemed to welcome those who did not look like citizens. The people in line ahead of him were not white or well dressed, and in some cases, they did not even appear to speak much English, but she was kind to each one of them. She looked familiar.

When Keita's turn came, he sat down opposite the woman. He

saw that her hands trembled. Blue veins wormed across the back of her palms, and brown spots made her hands appear freckled. Behind her, Keita noticed a purse with a book sticking out of it. He cocked his head to read the title: *Dying for Dimwits.* What a disturbing title. Did the people of Freedom State believe that people of low intelligence should commit suicide?

"Are you here for a library card?" she asked.

"Yes, but I don't have . . ."

"We won't worry about what you don't have," she said. "Have a little faith, and all will go well." She slid a piece of paper across the desk to him.

"Fill in your name and sign at the bottom," she said.

The paper, which was typed, said, *I hereby attest that I, _____, am a citizen of Freedom State and reside at _____.*

Keita left the address blank but printed and signed his name as Roger Bannister.

She took the paper back, stared at him and said, "I thought so. You are the singing runner!"

Keita was not sure what to say.

"You showed me such decency. I was in a scrape on Aberdeen Road."

"A scrape?" Keita asked.

"Car accident. I dinged up two nice cars, quite badly. Some woman was screaming at me, and along you came, running and singing that country song."

"'Ain't Mine'?" Keita asked.

"Yes! I hate that song. But never mind. You stopped to help me in a moment of need. You told me your name was Roger Bannister."

It was only two weeks, but Keita did not remember what the white woman who caused the accident had looked like, except that she was old and frail and seemed shocked by the mayhem she had caused.

"My name is Ivernia Beech, and I am here to help you in any way possible."

The old woman dropped a pencil. As she bent over to retrieve it, her purse fell open and her book yawned. Keita couldn't help reading: "There is really no reason to botch a suicide attempt if you go about it properly. If you have an IQ of 60 or less, just give up and close the book, because you have no hope of offing yourself properly. But if you passed Grade 5, you should be good. Keep reading if you would like to die at your own hands."

With clean water, roofs over their heads and every imaginable device to make their lives easier, why would white people in rich countries want to kill themselves? In Zantoroland, mothers died in childbirth and children were born with and died of HIV/AIDS. People died of diarrhea, typhus and malaria, and even from infections resulting from cuts. Others, like his father, were ordered killed by those who purported to lead the country. But he had never heard of people in his homeland killing themselves. Perhaps only those who did not fear a premature death sought to accelerate the process.

"There you go," Ivernia Beech told him. "You should be good now."

"Roger Bannister isn't truly my name," he said in a low voice.

She gave him a knowing smile. "You may use the library card now to surf the Net. Or to borrow books. I've made out your address as 41 Moore Street. Is that okay?"

"Where's that?"

"Heaven knows." She laughed. "I made it up. Treat this like your library card for life," she said. "Don't lose it, because I won't be here forever."

"Thank you."

"Anything else I can do?" she said. "I would really like to help you."

"No, thank you. You've already been so kind." Keita couldn't stop running his finger over the smooth, laminated card. Perhaps this was how every refugee managed to make the transition into a legally recognized life: by obtaining a library card and using it to build a wider base of identification.

He walked back to the computers and took a spot again beside Mbira Man, who was still typing with thumbs and middle fingers. Keita entered his library code and checked his email. Three messages awaited him.

The most recent was from John Falconer, who used a peculiar email address: mostgifted@freedomstate.fs.com.

Thank you for walking with me during the night. And for talking. Could we meet for a proper interview, for my documentary? I could be useful to you too.

Yours truly,
John Falconer

P.S. I hope my email address doesn't sound boastful. "Gifted" was already taken so I had to take "Mostgifted."

Keita opened the second message. It was from Viola Hill.

Dear Keita,

I got your email address from the race registration form, hope you don't mind. I am the reporter with the Clarkson Evening Telegram. *We met after the Buttersby Marathon. May I meet you for an interview? It is urgent.*

Thank you,
Viola Hill

Keita had no time to think about media interviews. Next, he found an email from Mitch Hitchcock.

Dear Mr. Ali,

We met at the Buttersby Marathon. I gave you refuge in my director's tent and kept you away from Mr. Hamm. I have just been appointed director of the Freedom State Olympic Marathon Team. It is a six-year term, designed to take the team through the next two Olympic Games. We could use an athlete of your talent on the team. Could we meet to discuss at your convenience? Just name the place, date and time, and I'll see you there. Lunch on me!

Cheers,
Mitch Hitchcock

Keita was so preoccupied with trying to stay hidden and finding a way to help his sister that he found it almost impossible to contemplate Hitchcock's suggestion. But yes! In the best possible outcome, Keita and his sister would be reunited in Freedom State. They would not have to hide and would be allowed to stay in the country. Charity could build her career and her life, and Keita could finally run free. He couldn't imagine a more beautiful way to be welcomed into the country than to be invited to run for the Olympic team. But none of this seemed within reach. He couldn't waste his time fantasizing about the impossible. Where was his sister? Why had he not heard from her again, or from her abductors?

Keita checked his junk folder and found two other emails. The first was from Anton Hamm.

You got away from me at Buttersby. Nice run. You made $4,000, which belongs to me. I require payment of $10,000, with a first instalment of $4,000 by April 25 and a final payment of $6,000 by July 1. If you comply, I shall wash my hands of you. If payment is not forthcoming, there will be consequences. You will meet with a royal beating if the first deadline is not met, and a suitable collection of your bones will be broken if full payment is not made by the *final deadline. After which, I will see to it that you end up in the hands of deportation authorities. Rest assured that your reception in Zantoroland will be indelicate. When we first met, I concluded that you were a man of intelligence. I am now doubting my original judgment, but invite you to confirm it.*

As Keita closed Hamm's message, he felt an onslaught of nausea. Hamm was after him. Charity's captors were after him. Everybody wanted a piece of him.

And there it was. The message he wanted. Buried among spam about lottery prizes and penis enhancement. The final message came from George Maxwell.

Dear Mr. Ali,

Just a reminder to provide $15,000 by June 22. This amount is required, in full and on time, to secure the safety of your sister.

George Maxwell

Keita swallowed, afraid that he would vomit. His computer keyboard and screen became so blurry that it was hard for him to log out of his email account. He wished for a bed. A floor. Any surface on which to rest his body. Even with his eyes closed, he felt dizzy. He felt his body follow the pull of gravity. From a distance, he heard a woman's voice call out, "Good God, is he all right?"

WHEN HE CAME TO, KEITA WAS LYING ON A COUCH IN THE first-aid room of the Clarkson Library, with Mrs. Beech sitting on a chair pulled up next to the couch, holding an ice pack to his forehead.

"You gave yourself a nasty bump on the head," she said. "Do you know who you are?"

"Yes," he said.

"What is your name?"

"Keita Ali."

"Is it, really? Where are you?"

"Freedom State."

"Can you be more specific?"

"Clarkson Library. You are Mrs. Beech."

"That's good. Since you've got brain function, you may call me Ivernia."

Keita tried to raise himself up on an elbow, but he felt unusually tired. He couldn't walk a kilometre, let alone run a marathon.

"You seem agitated," she said. She left but returned a few moments later with a bottle of apple juice. She popped off the lid, inserted a straw and brought it to his lips.

"May I have water, instead?"

She brought him two mugs of water, which he downed quickly. He asked for another two mugs, and two more after that.

"I should be okay soon," he said.

"When was your last proper meal?" she asked.

"I've been eating here and there," he said.

"Take this. If you don't eat it, I'll revoke your library card."

Keita ate Mrs. Beech's egg salad sandwich on rye bread. Then he ate her two pickles, her apple and her three oatmeal raisin cookies.

"I don't think I've ever had such pleasure watching somebody else eat my lunch," she said.

"I'm fine now and would ask permission to leave the library."

"This is not a police state," she said. "Though it has tendencies in that regard. But this is my first-aid room, and you are free to leave."

"Mrs. Beech, thank you. By the way, the computer I was using. Was the account . . . ?"

"Yes, it was shut down. I closed it after you tumbled off the chair."

He looked at her steadily, and she returned his gaze. If she had seen anything, she was letting him know it would be their secret.

"Thank you, Mrs. Beech."

"Signing out any literature today? You are allowed three books the first time you use a card."

"Not today, thank you very much. I've had enough reading for one day."

"How old are you, if I may ask?"

"Twenty-four. And you?"

"I am eighty-five, sorry to say."

"In my country, old people are venerated. They are wise. We know that and treat them well."

"I lost my husband years ago, and now my son wants me put away."

"Put away?"

"Into an old age home."

It was good, speaking with a man young enough to be her grandson. You could ask him out for lunch without any risk of the invitation being taken the wrong way. It wasn't at all like that with men in their seventies or eighties. Show them a spot of kindness, agree to two consecutive lunches, and suddenly you were fending off marriage proposals. Since Ernie died six years ago, she had held up a stop sign to three men. And they hardly even knew her. Eventually, she had stopped going out, even for a bagel, with any single man in her age bracket.

"Come to my house for tea," said Ivernia. "My shift's almost over."

"I would love to accept. I've never been invited into the home of a Freedom Statonian. But I have to decline, because I must look for a place to stay."

"Come to my home, and we will work it out."

In any city or town in Zantoroland, a foreigner would have trouble walking the streets for two hours without being invited into somebody's home. The poorest people in the world brought in strangers, it seemed, and the richest people in the world kept them out. Keita decided to accept this kind invitation. He would go to Ivernia's house as soon as he recovered a few items of clothing from the bus station. If he was lucky, perhaps she would let him wash his clothes.

"I don't do fancy," Ivernia said. "I don't have time for it. This is what I have at home: crackers, cheese, salami, apples, grapes and an inexhaustible supply of cookies. Oh. And tea. I may not have a pot roast in the oven, but I will always, always, be able to serve you cookies and tea."

CHAPTER NINETEEN

O N THE FAR SIDE OF RUDDINGS PARK, PEOPLE with placards were gathering outside the Freedom Building. A crowd was the last thing Keita needed. Police could come to bust it up, or tear gas or arrest demonstrators. All the demonstrators appeared to be white. Well dressed. They jabbed their signs to the skies: Illegals Get Out; Go Home; and Bulldoze AfricTown. A man with a loudspeaker initiated a call and response.

"What do we want?"

"Deportations!"

"When do we want them?"

"Now!"

Keita stood just one block away, transfixed.

"Mr. Prime Minister," the man with the bullhorn called out, "we know that you can hear us. We know your lackeys are listening. You promised to deport Illegals. You made this promise, and so we elected you. But how many have you deported?"

"Not enough!" someone in the crowd hollered back.

"Have you torn down AfricTown?"

"Not one shack!"

"Illegals don't pay taxes. They drain our resources. They are violent and criminally oriented. Out with Illegals!"

"Out with Illegals!"

Keita felt a nudge against his back. It came from a man of about forty, white, tall, with a sign that said Boot Them Out!

"Who are you?" the man said.

Keita just stared at him.

"What are you doing here? Do you have your papers? Are you an Illegal?"

Keita looked behind the man. From the south, more demonstrators were coming. He looked up ahead, to the north, where the crowd was thick. But to the east, there was an empty street. Keita dashed for it, at a speed no demonstrator could hope to match. Two blocks down, he turned north. Nobody was following him, but he ran hard anyway, continuing north for a full kilometre before he swung west again, turned north once more and continued along Aberdeen in the direction of Ivernia Beech's home.

The shops disappeared about a kilometre north of Clarkson's downtown core and were replaced by houses and apartment buildings and parks. At least the city planners had thought to include green space. Keita ran into Serena Park, which continued for eight kilometres northeast. The park followed the road and was about a kilometre wide, with a running and biking path through the middle of it. Keita noted that unlike Ruddings Park in the central city, where runners and joggers at least waved to each other, here nobody greeted anyone else. To Keita, it seemed the height of rudeness to pass someone walking or running on a path and to not say hello. But he didn't want to draw attention to himself. Even at an easy pace, he overtook other runners as if they were standing still. To his far right, a forest bordered the park. He left the path to explore it and saw footpaths continuing into woods that were thick and deep. Good places to hide, he noted. At the end of Serena Park, Keita turned right onto Elixir Bridge Road. It was a quiet, eastbound street. A ravine ran behind the houses on the north side. Many homes had driveways blocked by wrought-iron gates protecting as many as four or five cars. He noted the big garages and imagined how many people from AfricTown could sleep in each one.

37 Elixir Bridge Road was perched on the edge of a ravine. It was rectangular and three storeys high with a white stone exterior. It had a two-car garage and a mound of earth on the driveway. Keita could think of much worse places to hide. Still, it stood out from the other houses with manicured lawns. The grass needed cutting, and weeds abounded in the bed of untended earth that might have been a garden. As Keita approached the front door, he heard a woman's voice call out from the house to his right.

"Yoo-hoo. Yoo-hoo. Are you expected, sir?" She emphasized the "sir."

Keita ignored her and knocked on the door.

"You, sir, over there. By the door. Black man! What is your business here?"

He knocked again. If Mrs. Beech did not answer the door, he would have to run.

Out of respect to Mrs. Beech, he felt it best to not reply to the neighbour. But she would not relent. She stepped inside her house and came right back out with a small canister, which she pointed at him. As she marched closer and Keita knocked once more, he glanced back and saw that the canister was labelled *Bear Spray*.

"Apologies, madam, no need for distress. I will be on my way." Keita retraced his steps over the granite blocks implanted like elephantine teeth in the walkway between the front door and the gate.

As he reached the end of the driveway, another voice called to him. "Roger. Roger Bannister. Where are you going?"

He turned and saw Mrs. Beech standing in her open doorway.

"I knocked," he said, "but this lady—"

"Come back," Ivernia said. "I'm hard of hearing, and you have to use the doorbell. Lydia, everything is fine, and there is no need for bear spray."

"Who is this man?"

"My friend," Ivernia said, "and he is coming in. Lydia, you may go now."

Lydia still looked suspicious but turned to leave. Ivernia grabbed Keita by the wrist, pulled him into her home and bolted the door.

"Don't mind her," she said. "One of the crazies. There are more and more like that in Freedom State. Even, unfortunately, on good old Elixir Bridge Road."

"Is this your home?" Keita asked.

"It is a bit much for one person," Ivernia said.

"You live here alone?"

"Yes, I have since Ernie died," she said, "although I keep him here with me in an urn. A few people object to the fact that I live alone, and the neighbour you met monitors every arrival and departure. But what can you do but carry on in the best British tradition?"

Keita smiled. To his knowledge, his father had never set foot in Britain, but when homework needed to be done or discipline summoned, he too had been fond of puffing out his chest and saying, "Let's just carry on in the best British tradition." He told this to Ivernia, who smiled and said she'd learned the expression from *her* father.

Inside the house, Keita slipped off his running shoes and put down his small knapsack.

"Would you like to use the powder room?" she said.

Keita changed quickly into street clothes and then joined Ivernia in her kitchen.

She looked straight at him. Blue eyes, and white hair that was cropped and hanging slightly untended, almost like that of a child. No lipstick. Half-moon bags under her eyes.

"I don't cook anymore," she said, "but I have crackers and tinned oysters."

"Tinned? Do you mean smoked?"

"Yes."

"My father used to eat smoked oysters at our kitchen table every Sunday. On Ritz crackers. With a mustard sauce. It was one of his few extravagances. That, plus roasted peanuts."

"I have peanuts too," Ivernia said. "Let me roast them for you."

"Could we sit and talk first? I have something urgent to discuss."

She pointed to a chair and they sat at her table.

Keita took a deep breath and told her about the death of his father, his flight to Boston and Freedom State, and the abduction of his sister.

"I am ashamed to ask for help," Keita said, "but it is not for me. It is for her."

"Are you able to get the money by winning races?" she asked.

"Perhaps," Keita said. With the dizziness and the cramping, he was starting to doubt himself. Would his body betray him again?

Ivernia explained about her accident, and how she had lost her licence and control of her assets. "I can't give you any large amount of money," she said, "while my assets are frozen. But here's how I can help you."

As Ivernia prepared a snack, they came to an agreement: she would give him room and board as well as five hundred a month in cash, if he would make three meals a week for her and tend to gardening and other tasks totalling eight hours a week.

"You have nobody who does these things for you?" Keita asked.

"Who would do it? My son is useless."

"Surely he is not as bad as you say."

"I say that my son is useless, and it's true."

After they finished eating, Ivernia and Keita decided that he would begin his first task right away, transferring the mound of earth from the driveway to the gardens in the backyard. It took him about two hours to cart the earth to the back in a wheelbarrow and spread it where Ivernia indicated. Between the tenth and the eleventh trip, he stopped to peer at a metal cylinder hanging like a lamp from a post in the veranda at the back of the house. Tiny embossed letters circled the brass container: *Ernie Beech, 1923–2012. Passable cook, good plasterer, great husband.*

"I'm afraid it's not much," Ivernia said, when she showed him the bachelor's suite in her basement.

But it was as perfect as Keita could have imagined. It had a kitchen with fridge and stove, a bathroom with a shower, sink and toilet, and a bedroom with a window looking out on the backyard. The bed even had sheets, a blanket and a pillow, and next to it, a night table with a lamp and radio. The bed was firm, and the sheets were clean. He was relieved to have a safe space to sleep, which would allow him to intensify his training.

"How can I ever thank you?" he said to Ivernia.

"I am an old woman, Keita. I can't help every person who is in a bad way. But I can help you."

His father's screams were seeping through the walls of the Pink Palace and echoing in the waiting room where Keita sat. The president's men offered Keita tempting plates of fresh oranges, pineapples and coconut water, which he refused. After hours of waiting for his father's return, Keita was unbearably hungry and thirsty, and he began to weaken. Would having just a little food and drink constitute betrayal? As he brought one solitary section of the fresh orange to his mouth, his father cried out again, and suddenly, the fruit was transformed into a rank and rotting sardine. Keita dropped the sardine and was then ordered to get down on his hands and knees to lick the floor clean. Then he awoke, thrashing.

He finally fell back to sleep, only to dream of having no place to stay in Freedom State and being bounced from flophouse to brothel to park bench until he finally had no choice but to take refuge in a massive sewer. It was a cavernous culvert deep underground. You could sleep in the concrete vault, but you knew that the sewage could come flooding in at any time, and when it came, it came torrentially. Each time he woke, he tried to distract himself so that the nightmares would not resume when he fell asleep. But they kept coming back.

Keita rose before dawn and ran for two hours. It was the time of day that police officers and immigration officials were least likely to be looking for Illegals, but he stayed off the roads as much as he could, running instead in Serena and Ruddings Parks. He gradually relaxed and let his mind drift, and he even sang, and began to feel immeasurably calmer.

By the time he had returned and showered and dressed, Ivernia was making tea and toast, and she invited him to join her. As they talked, she dunked her toast in her tea.

"The very best thing in the world to dunk is a madeleine," Keita said. "And Zantorolanders make the best madeleines in the world."

"Proust wrote a sort of ode to the madeleine and the way it ignites memory," Ivernia said. "Did you know that?"

"Do I know it? My friend, the finest bakery in Yagwa posts quotes from *Remembrance of Things Past* on its walls. On Main Street, a quote from that very book is etched into a beautiful pedestrian walkway: 'She sent out for one of those short, plump little cakes called "petites madeleines," which look as though they had been moulded in the fluted scallop of a pilgrim's shell. And soon, mechanically, weary after a dull day with the prospect of a depressing morrow, I raised to my lips a spoonful of the tea in which I had soaked a morsel of the cake . . .'"

"The writings of Proust are displayed on the sidewalks of Zantoroland? Imagine!" Ivernia said.

In this country, they seemed to hang their utensils overhead. Mr. Beech's ashes were in the urn hanging in the veranda, and here in the kitchen, seven pots and frying pans hung from hooks screwed into a ceiling beam. When Ivernia made tea, she covered the teapot with a sort of woollen coat. You knew you were in a wealthy country when they dressed both dogs and teapots in coats.

Keita shivered, and Ivernia noticed immediately.

"You're cold," she said.

Keita said he was frequently cold in this country. Ivernia disappeared for a moment and returned with a yellow long-sleeved cotton sweater with a hood. She said her husband used to wear it when he was sitting on the veranda in cool weather, and she might as well put it to good use.

"How long ago did he die?" Keita asked.

"Six years."

"I'm sorry."

She smiled at him. "I've gotten used to some things. To getting up and going to bed alone and not having him around."

"I don't know if I'll ever get used to not having my parents around."

They drank their tea quietly. Silence with another person took a certain depth of trust, and Keita was surprised at how easy it felt with Ivernia.

USING IVERNIA'S COMPUTER, KEITA EMAILED HIS SISTER AND George Maxwell. No answer. In the afternoon, he went out for his second run of the day and spent an hour stretching to loosen his sore muscles. For dinner that night, he offered to make Poulet Chez Yoyo.

"What on earth is that?"

"A dish my father taught me. I need two breasts of chicken, with the bone in. Carrots, potatoes, Spanish onion, garlic, a dozen big ripe tomatoes, olive oil, white wine, fresh basil, rosemary, curry, salt, pepper, two plantains and peanut butter."

"Peanut butter?"

"Trust me."

Ivernia had the ingredients delivered to her door. Then she sat in the kitchen and watched intently while he worked. First, he chopped the onions into fine pieces and sautéed them in olive oil. Then he diced the dozen tomatoes—it only took a minute to reduce them to a runny mound—and added them to the frying pan to simmer on a low heat. He browned the chicken breasts in a separate frying pan, put them to the side, and washed and scrubbed the potatoes and carrots and cut them into small pieces. Once the tomatoes had been reduced in volume by about half, he added three tablespoons of peanut butter and stirred in the spices. Then he added the carrots, potatoes and chicken and cooked them until done.

While they ate the fabulous Poulet Chez Yoyo, Ivernia had two glasses of wine. Keita stuck to water.

"I see that you eat slowly and chew your food carefully," she said.

"Yes, I can appreciate it more that way."

"Do you never drink?" she asked.

"Rarely."

"Why not?" she asked.

It would interfere with his training, he said. But in truth, he knew lots of runners who drank, at least from time to time. Mostly, he didn't drink because he was afraid he would not be in control of his faculties at the very moment he might need them. He couldn't forget that he was in hiding, and that he might be found at any moment.

The doorbell rang. Ivernia sighed, pushed herself up from her chair, walked to the door and opened it. Keita heard a voice before he could see the man.

"Mother, if you just gave me a key, this would not be necessary."

"Could you come another time?"

"Smells good. Who's cooking? You have company, don't you? Who is it?"

"Jimmy—"

Keita heard footsteps in the hall, and Ivernia's son walked into the kitchen.

"Hello," Keita said to a man with long grey hair pulled back in a ponytail.

Jimmy wore jeans and a leather motorcycle jacket. His tiny blue eyes were almost buried under a protruding brow. It was as if his brow were a cliff and the eyes were birds hiding underneath the ledge. Keita had imagined that Ivernia's son would be boyish. But that was silly, of course, because she was an old woman. Though her son was dressed like a busker, he was pushing sixty.

"Who are you?" the son said.

"Roger," Keita said. He stood up to shake the son's hand, but the man turned away.

245

"Mom, who is this?"

"Ivernia," Keita said. "Thank you very much for the dinner. I shall leave you to your visitor." Suddenly, it seemed paramount that the son not discover that Keita was living there.

Ivernia put her hand on his shoulder. "Sit down. I haven't served coffee yet. Or dessert."

"Mother," Jimmy said, "what is this man doing here?"

"I prepared for your mother a delicious dish," Keita said, "with chicken, vegetables and peanut . . ."

Jimmy put his palm up. "You ate, I got it. Mother, is this a home invasion?"

"I'll show you a home invasion," Ivernia said. She left the room, returned with a broom and whacked her son on the knee.

"Ouch. Oh come on, Mom, stop that."

"Get out, Jimmy. You cannot bust into my house and boss around my guests."

"Okay, okay. Who is he? Just tell me that and I'll go."

"Roger," she said.

"Roger who?"

"Roger Bannister."

"Very funny. How did he get in here?"

"He came up the stairs."

"Up the stairs? He broke into the basement and came up to get you?"

"Jimmy, he lives here. He lives with me. He is renting a room in the basement. And you are on your way out."

Ivernia took her son's arm and led him out the door. Keita was astonished. In his country, you had to worry about thugs and politicians showing up at the door. Here, sons invaded their mothers' homes, and mothers hit their sons with brooms! Keita did not tell her that in his own country, a son behaving so rudely to his mother would be shunned.

★ ★ ★

246

WHAT IVERNIA DID NOT TELL KEITA WAS THAT HER SON HAD contacted government authorities on numerous occasions. Jimmy had not held a proper job in thirty years, but he could fire off letters of complaint with the best of them. And he was not above firing off another.

After they had finished washing the dishes, Keita said good night and went downstairs to his room. Minutes later, the doorbell rang again. Ivernia went to the door and looked through the peephole. A police officer!

"Is everything all right?" he said, when she opened the door.

"Yes. Why wouldn't it be?"

"We had a report that you were acting irrationally and had an unwelcome visitor." He checked his notes. "A black man, possibly from AfricTown."

"My son must have called you. I am fine, and there is no invasion."

"Then why did he call?"

"My son is angry because I won't let him stay. He wants to take over my bank accounts and house and run my life. He is pushing sixty years of age, and he has the emotional development of a six-year-old."

The officer smiled. "Sounds like my staff sergeant. Sure you're all right?" He searched her face.

"I'm just peachy, apart from the fact that I'm five steps from the grave and my arthritis is acting up." Ivernia did not actually have arthritis, but it seemed like a convincing thing to say.

The officer smiled. "Well, madam, it's good to know you're okay, and now I have one less thing to do."

"Always good to hack away at that to-do list," she said.

"Keep your doors locked," the officer said. "You can never be too safe."

"I've never felt safer. Good night."

CHAPTER TWENTY

I N THE COMMUNITY PAPER AT IVERNIA'S HOUSE, KEITA noticed an advertisement for the 5K Clarkson City Fun Run, which offered each of the top male and female runners a five-hundred-dollar gift certificate to a running equipment store. That seemed like a good bet, and a place to start.

Anton Hamm would have to wait. First, Keita had to rescue Charity. He would make a bit from his monthly salary from Ivernia Beech, but that was far from enough. To earn the rest from races, he would have to keep well fed, rested and fit. Keita needed new shoes and knew they would help him avoid injury, but he didn't want to touch his savings.

The next day, Keita paid ten dollars to enter the race and get a bib and a computer chip for his running shoe. He edged to the starting line, where a thousand runners waited for the starter's gun. The key to a local race was to win, but not by such a margin that he drew much attention.

The gun went off, and Keita spotted a lithe black man among the front runners. Smooth stride. Landing easily on the balls of his feet. Damn. Keita had competition. He ran right behind the pack of front runners to get a good look at them. He could tell almost everything he needed to know by watching the runners for four hundred metres. Two looked like high school students who would fall off the pace within a kilometre. Two others were already breathing hard and slapping the pavement. But the lithe runner meant business. No socks in his racing shoes. An easy, smooth gait. Arms pumping efficiently. Keita couldn't hear his breath.

By the second kilometre, the four Freedom Statonians had fallen off the lead, and it was just the African, with Keita keeping watch a few metres behind. At the midpoint of the race, Keita decided to surge up a hill and throw in a 2:45 kilometre, to see if his competitor could follow. The man was young. He looked like a university student, perhaps brought over on scholarship. He stuck right to Keita's shoulder. Keita then ran a 2:40 kilometre, and he was hurting, and when it was nearly done, with just five hundred metres to go, the competitor was still on his shoulder. One hundred metres from the finishing line, the opponent kicked and Keita could not respond. The other runner pulled ten metres ahead and crossed the finish line first. The winner fell into a light jog after the race, heading back out in the direction of the finishing runners—the third-place runner was more than a minute behind. Keita ran out with him and shook his hand.

"Good race," Keita said.

"Thanks, man, you're damn fit too."

"On scholarship?"

"Yes, in Texas. I flew into Freedom State for a week, to visit my aunt. She paid for the trip."

"What do you run in Texas?"

"The 5K is my specialty," the fellow said.

"Just my luck," Keita said. "Where are you from?"

"Kenya. You?"

"Zantoroland."

"On scholarship?" the fellow asked.

"Just living here now, trying to stay fit."

"Well, take my word for it, you made me run hard today."

"Obviously, I didn't make you run hard enough."

"You're the marathoner who won at Buttersby, aren't you?"

Keita nodded.

"Runners are talking about you. You're the one who skipped out on Anton Hamm, right?"

"He isn't too pleased," Keita said.

"Well, he has a terrible reputation, so you did well to leave him."

The Kenyan from Texas scooped up the prize. Unfortunately, there was no second prize, although volunteers barbecued hamburgers and served coffee and pop.

A woman moved in beside Keita to take a hamburger and gave him a smile. He had seen her before. Young, confident, coffee-coloured complexion. He had seen her cross the finish line: first female finisher and fourth overall.

"Good run," he said. "Congratulations."

"Right back at you. You were second, right?"

"That's right."

"What time did you run?"

"Thirteen minutes, fifty-six seconds," Keita said.

"You broke the course record by almost four minutes," she said.

"Technically, the guy who broke the course record was the winner."

"You broke it too; you just didn't win."

"What was your time?" Keita asked.

"Seventeen minutes, fifty-seven seconds."

"So you broke the course record too."

"I did."

"So you get the five-hundred-dollar gift certificate?"

"Actually, eight hundred. They threw in another three hundred for breaking the record."

"You can get a whole lot of stuff with that."

She smiled. "It's a good prize. But I've pretty well got the shoes and stuff I need."

"I'd been hoping for that prize too, but a better man came out today."

She smiled and put her hands on her hips. "Didn't you win the Buttersby Marathon in some crazy record time? You high-fived me on the big hill. I was fifty minutes behind you at the finish line."

Keita suddenly remembered her and the way her hand touched

his during the marathon. He laughed. "Are you training for a particular race?"

"I've got my eye on a fifteen hundred metres later this summer. I'm doing some longer races these days, for endurance."

"Do you get much for winning?" he said.

"Kudos from all my bosses and hopefully a promotion down the road. Got any tips for me? On how to run faster?" She gave a friendly smile.

"Sure. When you are tired and ready to give up? That's the time to go faster."

She touched his elbow. "You're funny."

"Or you could follow a strategy that works well for me," he said.

"And what might that be?"

"Start out real slow, and then slow down."

"Right, like you know anything about that." She laughed easily and energetically in a way that caused a stirring in Keita's groin. "Say, would you like to go out for an easy jog sometime? On a weekend, maybe?"

"Perhaps sometime," Keita said.

"Okay, perhaps I'll catch you a bit later," she said, sliding away into the crowd.

Keita ate another hamburger, drank three bottles of water, and left.

Later that day, he found a handwritten note in the open, outside pocket of his knapsack. *Congrats again on the run. Give me a call if you'd like to go for an easy jog sometime. Saturday mornings are good. I don't need this, so enjoy. Candace Freixa, 555-588-2345.* Folded into the note was her gift certificate to the running equipment store.

CANDACE DIDN'T THINK HE WOULD CALL. HE HAD SEEMED shy, and he had given the impression that he barely noticed her. Guys talked her up all the time. They stared at her breasts, checked out her ass, but that's all they cared about. If a guy was hitting on Candace

Freixa, then he was almost certainly the wrong type of guy. But something in the way the marathoner held himself, looking into her eyes, not gazing at her chest, and the way he laughed when she said she knew he had won the Buttersby Marathon, made her think he would be fun to get to know. Okay, that might have been too much, folding the gift certificate into his pocket. But no harm done.

Candace had grown up in AfricTown among pickpockets and had picked a few dozen pockets herself by the time she got caught at age thirteen and taken to youth court. Fortunately, she was let off with a warning and paired with the world's best social worker. If it hadn't been for that social worker, Candace might never have joined a track club or even finished high school. Or studied criminology. Or become a police officer, with a decent salary, on the community patrol. Riding a bike. Riding a horse. Walking the streets. They used her for all the roles that made her visible. *See?* her police force seemed desperate to trumpet. *See the black woman in uniform? See how we are a multicultural police force?*

Candace had been on the force for five years and had made sergeant. Well, with some luck, she'd get off the security detail soon. People often assumed she was Portuguese, like her mother. But her looks worked in the police force. They loved the black in her. She was ethnic, young, had a BA and an MA, and knew lots of people in the worst parts of town—all these things made her a catch in their eyes. These days they had her attending some press conferences, and she assumed they were grooming her for a role as a public face of the police force. Already, she had taken advantage of professional development opportunities to ride a horse, learn martial arts and pass a test as an advanced markswoman. She would bide her time until they let her transfer. Public Affairs. That would be an ideal job for a people person like Candace. Staff sergeant of Public Affairs in five years—that was her goal!

Her phone rang at eight the next Saturday morning. Someone was calling from a pay phone. Nobody used pay phones any more. Germs! And who didn't have a cellphone? Usually, if her phone didn't display the caller as someone she knew, she let it go to her answering machine. But this time, she answered, hoping.

"Hello, Miss Candace," an accented male voice said. "We met at the 5K race."

Miss Candace? Who spoke like that? "Sorry, I didn't catch your name."

"Keita. The marathoner. We met at the 5K race."

"Oh, now I've got it. Hey!"

"Thank you for the gift certificate. With it, I bought four pairs of shoes. And twelve socks. Pairs, I mean. And two pairs of running shorts and a watch."

"That's a good haul. But why four pairs of shoes?"

"All the same kind. Hard to find, and they had a special, twenty percent off, so I wanted to capitalize on the opportunity."

She giggled. "Good thing. We all have to capitalize on opportunities." She let that hang in the air.

He cleared his throat but said nothing.

"Well, were you calling for a reason?"

"To thank you . . . for the gift certificate."

"Anything else?" Damn. Too pushy. Far too pushy. Could she just back off and give him some room?

"Would you like to go for a run, and then—how do you say it—a Tim's?"

It was funny to hear this cute, slender-as-a-rake fellow with the Zantoroland accent and polite diction asking her if she wanted to accompany him to the cheapest coffee chain in the world. Tim Hortons had been popularized a continent away, in Canada, before spreading around the world and even across Freedom State. Everybody in Freedom State loved Tim's now, and if you showed up at peak hours, you could wait fifteen minutes just for coffee. Well, Candace didn't have time for that. Forget it. A job, her professional development courses, her training, a leering boss who had to be backed off every day . . . Candace had no time for lineups at Tim's. Except, maybe, this one time.

"Sure, Keita, I would love that. When did you have in mind?"

"I have to do some housecleaning for a friend, so how about today at three, at the Freedom Gates entrance to Ruddings Park?"

What sort of guy would call up a woman and expect a date the same day? But then, this wasn't really a date. It was a run and a coffee. Why not?

"I happen to have the day off, so sure, I can meet you then."

"All right, Candace, I will see you at the aforementioned time and place."

She giggled again. *Aforementioned?* "Okay, Keita, see you then."

HE TURNED UP ON TIME, IN HIS RUNNING GEAR. HE WAS NOT tall—about five foot eight, she guessed, just three inches taller than she was. Three inches was a good height differential for . . . love-making. Stop it. Stop it right now. He was as slender as she remembered, but his calves and thighs looked as hard as rocks. Many guys wore formless shorts that dropped down to the knee. Ug-*ly*. But Keita's shorts were the real thing, revealing much of the thigh and slit at the sides for comfort. Thin as he was, he also had a rounded, ample ass that Candace thought would hold up well under inspection. He kept a small pack strapped to the small of his waist.

"You rarely see elite athletes with a fanny pack," she said.

He reached out to shake her hand and then kissed her lightly on each cheek. He was from another continent, that was for damn sure. But it was charming. No real pressure to the kiss, but at least it was a *real* kiss—not an air kiss, which was disgusting and fraudulent.

"It's for my key plus some change for Tim's, and sometimes I put an apple in there."

She hoped that he wouldn't run her into the ground. Some guys could be strange about running with a woman. They'd either kill themselves to keep up or try to run her ragged. But she had a strategy. If some dude was getting too competitive, she would just back off the pace. Slow down. Let him run ahead.

He noticed that she was holding her car key.

"I'll put that in my fanny pack if you want," he said.

Candace liked an observant guy. And she let him do it.

He had virtually no hair on his legs. She wondered if his ass was that smooth. She hadn't been laid in . . . how long was it now? Stop it, Candace, stop it right now. We're out for a run here. A pleasant, friendly run in Ruddings Park, with the promise of a coffee afterwards. A run and a coffee, and that's all.

They broke into an easy jog, just right for warming up.

"I usually run alone," he said. "So why don't you set a pace that's comfortable for you?"

She gave him an A-plus for that, and set out at a pace of 4:20 per kilometre—slow enough for easy conversation. Ruddings was one of the most beautiful parks in the world. Some local arts dealer had persuaded the park authorities to purchase a dozen large serpentine sculptures from Zimbabwe, so the striking, curved forms would come into view from time to time as they ran the ten-kilometre path circling the park.

"Would you like to run two loops?" he asked. Each loop had two big hills and passed at points through dense woods.

"Two loops sounds great."

She asked him if he minded running slowly. No, he said, it was perfect like this.

"How could it be perfect," she asked, "when you can run a sub-2:10 marathon?"

"For me," he said, "this run is a perfect warm-down."

"Warm-down," she said. "What do you mean?"

He explained that he had just completed the core of his workout by running intervals on the track around the park reservoir. At first she felt a flash of anger—how dare he call her out for a run that was to be only his warm-down? But they kept running, and she liked his smile and that he asked her about her running history.

"Funny how my workout is your warm-down," she said.

"Where I come from, I could not even make the national team."

"And where are you from?" she said.

"It's a long story," he said. "Tell me about yourself."

She didn't want to tell him that she was a police officer, particularly not if he was going to hold back himself. Nothing turned some guys off faster than hearing she was a cop. A lot of guys were intimidated by a black woman with a decent job. And she wasn't interested in that kind of guy.

"Do you have family here?"

"Yes, I grew up in AfricTown. My father was a black man from Brazil," she said, "and my mother is mixed, Portuguese and black."

Candace told him that she grew up with her brother and grandmother in AfricTown and that people assumed her mother was part black because what the hell else would she be doing raising kids in that part of the city. But the truth was that AfricTown was all she could afford, and at least in that part of Clarkson, her kids would not stand out or be teased about being mixed. Candace's mother became the secretary at her high school, which Candace hated, because she knew everything about every boy that Candace even looked at. Candace told Keita that she'd had a little scrape with the law when she was a young teenager.

"Folks said I had quick hands, and I became a little too adept at the art of pickpocketing. Social worker got me off. Tough as nails, but heart of gold. She read me the riot act and scared me. So I joined the cross-country team and started studying in earnest."

"And what do you do now?" he said.

"I'll tell you about it," she said, "when you tell me more about you."

After the run, Keita took her to Tim Hortons and bought her a coffee. She offered to cook him dinner. He said he would be delighted to join her—but what about clothes? Well, she said, she could drive him home, wait for him to change and then drive them back to her place. But he said it would be better if she gave him directions and he came back in two hours. And this he did, exactly as promised.

★ ★ ★

SHE SERVED HIM SPAGHETTI, WITH HOMEMADE SAUCE MADE from tomatoes that she had grown in her own garden. And salad. And bread with cheese. And fruit. She figured that a serious marathon runner wouldn't go in for crappy desserts. He ate it all. When they finished, she sat beside him on the couch and put her hand on his forearm. It was all the encouragement he required. He stood to take her into his arms, and Candace took him into her bed.

When Candace woke up in the morning, she discovered that he was gone. She had no idea where he lived, or how to reach him.

GETTING TOGETHER WITH CANDACE HAD BECOME A PROBLEM he couldn't ignore.

Yes, she had made him feel that taking her out on a run and then for the coffee and then coming home to her meal and her arms was the most natural thing in the world.

As they ran, he had found it difficult to think of anything but her body. Her sounds, too, had intoxicated him. Her breathing quickened in the final kilometres of the run. She kicked up the pace to 4:00 per kilometre, and as she pushed close to her limits, working on hills, she panted and gasped, and he could not stop imagining the sounds she might make if she were spending herself on him.

When they tumbled into her bed, all he knew was that he had never felt so hungry in his life. And her hunger had met his.

While she slept, he had washed up for her while fantasizing about the next time that he might touch her again. Occasionally he poked his head into the bedroom to hear her gentle snores. But people in this country had so many things. He had no idea where to put away her knives and forks. Frying pans. Pots. As he was looking for a place to put the glasses, he opened a bottom drawer and noticed a thick telephone book and, behind it, a police badge. He turned over the badge. *Sergeant Candace Freixa / Clarkson Police Department.*

He left quickly, quietly opening her front door. He jogged the ten long kilometres back to Ivernia's home, looking over his shoulder the whole way.

As Candace entered the kitchen the next morning, she noticed that Keita had washed her dishes before leaving. What other guy would take her for an easy run, listen to her gab about her youth and mother and father, invite her out for coffee, love her utterly and then do the dishes? He had put them away in ridiculous places in her cupboards—forks, knives and spoons in the middle of a frying pan in a cupboard meant for plates. She'd tease him about that, next time. She took a step toward the coffee maker and saw that a drawer had been left open. The one with her badge.

CHAPTER TWENTY-ONE

I F DARLENE COULD JUST EARN A FEW THOUSAND MORE dollars, she would disappear and never be found by anybody who might like to do to her what they had done to Yvette.

Darlene wasn't stupid. She had eyes and ears. She knew the score. She'd seen Yvette after the prime minister left. While they had tea in the staff room, Yvette told her the whole story. Yvette was rattled and said she wouldn't mind spiking her tea with rum. But neither of them had any. There was a no-smoking rule in the Bombay Booty, so Darlene had slipped out the back door of the brothel and was standing in the dark in a grove of trees, about to light a cigarette, when a vehicle marked *Reliable Security Services* pulled up and stopped just a few feet away.

Darlene closed her cigarette lighter and watched Lula walk over to the driver. They were so close that if Darlene had emerged from the trees, she could have touched them. But she stayed right where she was. Still, she saw that Lula leaned over and spoke through the window. And that a man got out of the car, dressed in a security officer uniform and wearing handcuffs on his belt. Lula pointed him to the stairs at the back of the building. Darlene held perfectly still as they walked right by the place where she was hidden.

"Yvette Peters," Lula said, "you hear? Don't let her out of your sight until she's on the plane. Yes, the usual authorization."

* * *

DARLENE DIDN'T HAVE A BOYFRIEND, BUT SHE DIDN'T HAVE a pimp either. That was one of the perks of working at the Bombay Booty. Lula took care of everything. All Darlene had to do was satisfy the men who came into her bed, act like she enjoyed it and keep her mouth shut. Outside work, Darlene had her routines. After her Tuesday and Thursday morning workouts, she would stop in at the Bleeding Heart grocery store in south Clarkson—the neighbourhood was falling apart because it was by the railway tracks bordering the city, and thus close to the route taken by people walking to and from AfricTown—and buy herself a package of Smarties.

Darlene was shaking the Smarties out of the package into her hand and turning right on Liberation Street when she sensed that she was being followed. She sped up, turned the next corner and ran. A car shot ahead of her, blocking the intersection ahead, and a black man with a gun on his hip jumped out.

"Easy way or hard way, honey. You decide," he said.

"Who are you?"

The man pulled a purple pistol from his belt. The neighbourhood had gone so far to seed that he didn't seem to care that they were in broad daylight.

"The fuck you doing?" Darlene said.

"Pointing a Ruger .22 calibre semiautomatic pistol in your general direction," he said.

"Put that thing away," she said.

"The easy way is that you stand real nice and answer my questions, and the hard way is that I shoot you now. Stand over there," he said, motioning to an office building with a brick exterior.

"No need to get excited," she said.

"Do it," he said, pointing the gun at her.

Darlene stood with her back to the building. He aimed above her head and shot off a bullet at the wall. A spray of crumbling brick fell over her.

Darlene flinched. "No need for that," she said.

Now he opened the trunk of his car and pointed his pistol at her.

"Hard or easy, Darlene Wood. You decide."

He knew her name. "Easy," she said. "Let's go easy."

"What happened to Yvette Peters?" the man asked.

"First, just tell me who you are."

"Saunders. Now talk. What do you know about Yvette?"

"She was my friend. I'm sure you know where we work. Here one day, gone the next."

"Who did her in? How did she disappear?"

"How do I know how my best friend ended up dead in a country she'd never fucking seen before?"

"What did you last talk about?"

"How much we loved sex."

"I'm running out of time." He stepped in close, grabbed her forearm and squeezed. It hurt like hell.

"We talked about who she was going to see that night."

"And who was that?"

"I don't know. Sometimes we imagined the guys we would be doing. Would they have big dicks or small? You, for example, surely have a tiny dick, to leave room for such a big asshole."

He punched her in the mouth. Darlene bled from the lips and tongue, and one of her teeth fell out.

"One more wisecrack and you die."

"All right," Darlene said. This time, she believed him.

"Did you hear anything about what happened when she was with her last customer?"

"No."

"The last customer—a man I happen to be representing right now—thinks he saw a recording device in the room."

Darlene shook her head.

He twisted her arm again. "I can kill you here, fast. I can do it nice and slow in your living room. On your red couch. 201A Stewart Street, right? You'll find your place a bit messed up. If you ever make it back there. Nice hiding place, for the money. Under the mattress. Very original."

"Okay, okay. Let go and I'll talk."

He let go.

She was feeling cold, suddenly, and her entire body was trembling, but she was trying hard not to show it.

"I heard the conversation was taped," she said.

"Who has it?"

"I don't know. Some guy took it."

"What guy?"

"Don't know his name."

"What did he look like?"

"Don't remember."

Saunders pressed the pistol against her temple. The cold metal dug into her skin.

"I heard it ended up with that marathon guy. The black dude who won the Buttersby Marathon."

"Name?"

"Keita Ali."

"From where?"

"Zantoroland."

"Illegal?"

"How would I know? I didn't ask for his passport."

Saunders pointed his pistol at her again. "If this doesn't add up, I'll come back for you, put this in your mouth and pull the trigger." He closed the trunk of his car, got in and drove off.

Darlene did not go home. She was no fool. She waited for the car carrying Saunders, his gun and his fist to go out of sight. Then she took a taxi to a women's shelter in a far end of town. She didn't plan to stay there long enough for anyone to find her. Darlene was sorry to have given up Keita Ali. She had no way to get word to him. Maybe they wouldn't catch him.

She hadn't had the chance to go beyond Grade 9, and she'd wasted her teenage years working for Lula, but all that was about to change. Darlene Wood could take a hint. She would leave town as fast as she could.

CHAPTER TWENTY-TWO

A S HE DROVE TO WORK, ROCCO DRUMMED HIS fingers on the steering wheel. Diminishing returns. A simple economic concept. You had it good, once, but things got less and less pleasurable with every passing day. That pretty well summed up what Rocco felt about his job. Minister of immigration! He had had more control over his life running a used car business. And given the way the Prime Minister's Office ran the show, micromanaging every hiccup, Rocco had had more influence on the country selling cars too.

What kind of prime minister would try to frame one of his own cabinet ministers? The visit to AfricTown had been a set-up, for sure. The PM had intended to see Rocco stung in that police raid. Had Rocco been caught with his pants down in AfricTown, his name and face would have been splashed all over the media, he would have been criminally charged with "being party to an act of prostitution," and he would have been fired from cabinet and bounced from government.

Now that Rocco knew that a certain "Mr. Big" from the governing party had been to the Bombay Booty on the night the girl disappeared, he believed that his own arrest—had it taken place—would have been a way to steer attention away from the teen prostitute who died in a Zantoroland prison. Or to frame *him* as Mr. Big. There had to be more to the story, but no one was talking.

★ ★ ★

John Falconer knew just how to read the guy.

"Not you again," Minister Calder always said when he saw John in the government parking lot. But John kept coming, and each time, the minister relented, let him come upstairs and gave him details for the documentary.

"It's just a school assignment, right?" the minister would say, while John filmed him. "I can give you five minutes and not a second more. I have a meeting."

Five minutes always led to fifteen. In John's opinion, the minister of immigration had nothing to do but attend meetings. It was harder to be a Grade 9 student. The minister always offered him candies and soft drinks, and showed him charts. How many refugees were estimated to have come in the country illegally over each of the last five years. How many illegal ships were impounded. How many ship captains had been arrested for trying to dump Illegals on the shores of Freedom State.

"So why do you think they keep coming here, from all over the world?" John asked.

"Because they have it made in Freedom State. Services, electricity, clean water, a booming economy. They have every opportunity to abuse our generosity."

"The children in AfricTown, attending substandard schools or no schools at all, and sleeping in garages and on the street—are they abusing your generosity?" John asked.

"Son, that's what you would call a bleeding heart question. You would have to talk to their parents. Why did they bring them here? Why are they working illegally in an underground economy, not paying taxes and not registered as citizens of this country?"

"But why would you fault a child for what their parents have done?" John said.

"I'm not faulting any children, but their parents have to take responsibility for their actions. The Family Party is about family responsibility. We are for minimal government but for maximum family responsibility for their own matters."

On the morning of the fireside consultation, John was waiting as usual at the side of the parking lot, out of sight, in the shadows under the fire escape. He had decided to ask if he could shadow the minister for the day and then stay on for the fireside consultation. The poor man could not say no—at least not to John. Maybe that's what it took to become a good journalist. You kept at the story until people gave you what you wanted, or relented and finally told the truth.

The minister pulled up at his usual time: 7:10 a.m. He opened the door, got out, grabbed his briefcase, and was about to lock his car when a tall man crossed the parking lot with the purpose and speed of a linebacker. John had seen that man before. Anton Hamm. The sports agent. The minister was six feet tall, but this man dwarfed him. He was almost as tall as the prime minister. But Hamm was younger and more athletic, with a bullet-shaped head. He wore a suit but moved like a runner. He looked like a brute. John turned on his camera.

"Mr. Minister," Hamm said, standing so close to Calder that the minister had nowhere to go.

"To what do I owe this pleasure?" Calder said. He tried to move, but the big guy pinned him against the car.

"Name's Anton Hamm," the big man said. "I have a pressing question."

"If you will give me some breathing room," Calder said.

Hamm backed away a few inches. "Tell your people that I want my payment, and I want it now."

"I don't follow," Calder said.

"Sure you do. Your people have had me do some favours. You know what I am talking about. We had an understanding. I haven't heard from them lately. And I want my payment."

"What is the nature of your understanding, and with whom?" Calder said.

Hamm stepped closer and seized Calder's arms. "Mr. Minister, don't fuck with me."

"I don't know what you're talking about."

"Deliver the money, and you'll have nothing to fear."

"Are you threatening me? Look at me," Calder said. "Look me in the eye. Go ahead. Do it. Now listen. I have no idea what you are talking about. You seem to be onto a scam, but it doesn't involve me. Why don't you tell me about it?"

"Fuck this," Hamm said.

John filmed the former shot putter in the suit running back across the parking lot and out of sight. And then he swung the camera back to the minister, who was straightening the arms of his jacket. This was not a good time to approach him, John could tell.

JOHN RETURNED A FEW HOURS LATER, WHEN THE MEETING was scheduled to start and others began arriving. While the minister was shaking someone's hand, John called out with nonchalance, "Minister, I'm just here for the school assignment and will stay out of the way."

The minister frowned, but he was soon locked in conversation with a police sergeant who introduced herself as Candace Freixa. He was saying he was sure they had met before, and she said, yes, briefly, during the Buttersby Marathon. He asked how her race had gone, and she said very well. He asked if he had been passing her or she him, and she smiled and said she wasn't entirely sure. And what did she run that day? he asked. Oh, she didn't remember, she said.

"Sure you do," he said. "Every marathoner remembers their time."

"Two hours, fifty-eight minutes and forty-seven seconds," she said.

"Wow, you really took off on me. It's amazing that you finished under three hours. Who does that? You must have been blood doping," he said, stepping closer.

She pulled back.

In fairness, at least the minister had not slept with Darlene in the Bombay Booty. John had to give him that much.

He sat on a couch at the back of the room as the minister gathered the committee members in a seated semicircle. They made their introductions. John gave his name, his school. There was a murmur when he said Clarkson Academy for the Gifted.

"Best school in the country," the minister said.

Ivernia Beech looked at John. "Well, don't hide in the corner. Come sit beside me."

John shrugged and moved to sit with her. She shook his hand and said she hadn't seen him since the prize ceremony for his essay. He smiled and asked if he could interview her for his documentary. She flicked her fingers as if to chase off a fly.

"I'm too old to be on camera," she said. "Nobody wants to see the wrinkles on this face."

"I do," he said. "I really do, and you could make a difference in my life."

"Well," she said, "you never know. Maybe something good will emerge from this meeting."

The discussion started. A black businessman said that Freedom State was the best country in the world and that he had never experienced discrimination. He said Illegals should not be given a free ticket to take advantage of the rules of civilized society. A woman who said she was head of the chamber of commerce basically said the same thing. The others all reiterated that something had to be done about Illegals, who were taking over the country.

"And AfricTown," one of them muttered. "It's a disgrace."

"Bulldoze it and see what comes out," another said.

Candace Freixa, the police sergeant, let out a cough to redirect the conversation. Every person in the room looked to her. She said quietly, "You are speaking of my home. I was born in AfricTown and grew up there, and many good people gave me a helping hand."

Silence fell over the room, until the minister cleared his throat and asked Ivernia for her thoughts.

"I am a widow, eighty-five years old, born and raised in Freedom State." She went on to say that she didn't understand why these people had to be referred to as Illegals. "To identify a human being as illegal is to diminish his or her humanity," she said. "Why don't we call them people without documentation?"

The minister said that it was not for the committee to challenge the basic vocabulary used by the government of Freedom State. They were there to address the problem of illegality in the country.

Then he gave a slide show—basic statistics about tax revenue loss, economic stress and criminality associated with Illegals in the country. He and the others then spent half an hour going over all the problems—the boats laden with refugees and the difficulty of securing agreement from countries to which Freedom State wished to deport Illegals. The minister checked his watch, said they would have to wind up soon, picked up his phone and spoke with June, who came in a few minutes later with a tray of cookies.

The minister said he wished he could run as fast as that black runner who went by the alias Roger Bannister.

"What made you think of him?" Ivernia asked.

"Probably an Illegal," the minister said. "But don't get me wrong. I admire the guy. He's one helluva runner. He high-fived me on the big hill at the Buttersby Marathon. I was running down, and he was on the way back up, and still he was going twice as fast."

One of the other committee members cooed about how cool it was that a minister of the Freedom State government was fit enough to run a marathon, and in a very respectable time too.

"Strangest thing in that race. Heard a white runner giving the black guy the gears, calling him the *n*-word."

"Really?" someone said.

"I'm not for rude and insulting language," the minister said. "I have nothing against this fellow. I wish him well. But I should point out that few valid refugees come to Freedom State. Most Illegals are economic migrants. They want a better life. I can't blame them for that. But if they want to come here, they should get in line just like any other immigrant."

John stepped in. "Mr. Minister, just how many immigrants did Freedom State accept from Zantoroland last year?"

"Well, as I think you know, we have closed legal immigration from that country because we have so many troubles with Illegals."

"So they can't really come in any legal way, then," Ivernia said.

"For now, no."

"Mr. Minister," Ivernia said, "some of your so-called economic migrants are in great danger. When you are deporting people you deem to be illegal, you might be sentencing them to death. I wish you would think about that when you sign your deportation orders."

The minister looked vaguely alarmed. Three other people rushed to his defence, saying Ivernia was being harsh and there was no reason to personalize the situation.

"You want impersonal? How's this? If you want to increase tax revenue, declare a general amnesty and regularize the situation of people without documentation, then bring them into the national economy—entitling them to work and obliging them to pay taxes."

"Economics are never that simple, Ivernia," the minister said.

Ivernia stood. All eyes turned to her. She pointed shyly to the bathroom and said, "When you reach a certain age, some things can't wait."

ROCCO HAD SAID GOODBYE TO EVERYONE BUT CANDACE BY the time Ivernia Beech emerged from the bathroom.

"You should check under the sink in there, Minister," she said.

"Why?" Rocco asked.

"You may find an Illegal," the woman said, and then she too was gone.

Rocco grimaced, but when he saw Candace laugh, he tried to act like he appreciated the old woman's humour. God, was that running cop beautiful.

"Candace, I've got a few things I'd like to talk to you about. How do we integrate the police force into AfricTown, that sort of thing. Do you have time for coffee?"

"Sorry," Candace said. "Got another meeting." And she was gone. That fast. As if she couldn't stand to be in his presence.

Alone again in his office, Rocco felt deflated and lonely. He'd just been blown off by a hot woman. And earlier today, he'd been shaken down by a thug, which was humiliating and troublesome. What scam did that idiot think the minister was into? And since Rocco knew it wasn't him, who *was* behind the scam? He could report the assault to the police, but that would bring him more aggravation than benefits, and it would lead the PM to question Rocco's ability to manage his affairs. For now, Rocco had better just sit tight.

He locked himself into his marble-floored bathroom, donned his exercise gear and rowed for thirty minutes. Exercising got him wondering again who that mystery runner was. If he were truly an elite marathoner, he'd be running the Chicago Marathon and the Boston Marathon—he wouldn't be pissing away his time in Freedom State. So what was he doing here, anyway?

His cellphone rang. He ignored it and kept rowing. Part of him wanted to have a beer with the guy, ask how he trained, and find out what had brought him to this country. The phone rang again. Finally, Rocco got up to answer it.

"Calder," he said, wiping off the back of his neck.

"Mr. Calder. My name's Darlene. We met in AfricTown. I helped you get out. You said you would help me."

"I can't talk at work. I'll call you back."

"Promise?"

"Yes."

"When?"

"Today. I'm in a meeting now. I have to go."

"Wait. I didn't give you the number yet."

"It's on my cell. That the one?"

"Yes."

"Okay, later."

Darlene. It would be dangerous to meet her—but even more dangerous not to. As long as he didn't do anything stupid—touch her, sleep with her. As long as he did nothing that could destroy his political career, meeting Darlene might actually give Rocco some ammunition. He needed something the PM didn't have. Something Geoffrey Moore didn't have. Shit was going to fall, and he didn't want to get rained on.

CHAPTER TWENTY-THREE

A FEW NIGHTS AFTER HIS DATE WITH CANDACE, Keita ran to an all-night Internet café, where in his email he found another message from Anton Hamm. The subject line was "Pay Up!" Hamm gave Keita a new deadline: he still owed four thousand dollars on April 25 but the remaining six thousand was now due by May 7. Anton Hamm had to know that there was only one race in Freedom State offering a big purse before May 7: the Grant Valley Half-Marathon on May 6.

Keita was already planning to run that race, but if he won—and he *had* to win—the twelve-thousand-dollar prize would not be going to Anton Hamm. He would have enough, with his winnings from the Buttersby Marathon, to pay his sister's ransom immediately. He sent an email to George Maxwell.

Dear Mr. Maxwell,

May I have news of my sister? Reassurance that she is okay? Ask her, please, what nickname did she go by as a child?

Keita Ali

Keita received the correct reply within minutes.

Dear Mr. Ali,

You called her "LouBelle." We will provide the banking information prior to your deadline of June 22.

George Maxwell

Maxwell and his co-conspirators were no idiots. They knew that June 22 was the day after the annual Clarkson Ten-Miler—offering the best prize money in Freedom State. If he did not raise that money, he'd never see his sister again.

Keita had to question his own judgment. Out of loneliness, he had let down his guard and slept with a woman who turned out to be a police officer. She knew his real name. But if she had known who he was before their night together, could she not have arrested him earlier? And how stupid could he be? In the long term, no woman could be attracted to a man like him, who had no roots, no permanency.

Keita left the café and ran back to Elixir Bridge Road. His hernia ached, and the dizziness he had been feeling lately while running was back. He wanted only to climb into bed and sleep. How could he win the Grant Valley Half-Marathon feeling this rotten? He would have to run it in under sixty-one minutes to have a chance of winning, and he did not feel capable.

When he let himself in the front door, Ivernia startled him. She was sitting in the front hall, waiting.

"It's two in the morning," he said. "Why are you up?"

"I sat here all evening waiting for you. Worrying. And I waited for you earlier this week, too. You said you would make meals three times a week, but for days you have forgotten the deal."

Keita was not prepared for this. "I have had a stressful time, and the meal escaped my thinking."

"Well, it didn't escape mine. Are you or are you not able to live up to your end of the bargain?"

"Yes, for sure," he said, but he did not feel it. He felt capable of living up to no obligations whatsoever. All he felt was the need to win some races and to get together the money for Charity.

"Is that all you have to say?" she asked.

"I'm sorry."

"You don't sound sorry."

"I wish I had remembered to cook your meal. But you have food here."

"That's not the point."

"You could have fixed yourself something to eat. You've been doing it all these years."

She slapped a newspaper down on the coffee table, startling him. "Exactly. And I hate that. I don't feel like eating alone anymore. I can't stand the thought of it. You said you would cook for me. I was counting on it."

"I'm an imperfect house guest. Do you want me to leave?"

"Leave? Are you crazy?"

"I am truly sorry that I forgot about the meals. I'll make it up to you."

"I hope she was worth it."

"Pardon?"

"You heard me. When you're out this late, there could only be one reason. So was she worth it?"

"I thought so initially," Keita said. "But I cannot afford to take such pleasures. In retrospect, it would have been better not to go out." He grinned. "I should have stayed in and washed my socks."

"You should have stayed in and washed *my* socks."

They laughed.

"When is your next race?" Ivernia asked.

"In about three weeks, I will run the Grant Valley Half-Marathon."

"I'll come out and cheer you on."

CHAPTER TWENTY-FOUR

VIOLA HILL COULD FEEL HER TRICEPS BURN AS SHE crested the hill at the end of her first loop of Ruddings Park. On Sunday mornings, the park's Perimeter Road was closed to traffic, so she flew past walkers, joggers and slow cyclists. People didn't anticipate a wheelchair athlete racing up behind them, so she kept her whistle hanging from a string around her neck. One loop to go. Ten more kilometres. She could cover that in less than thirty-five minutes and would have the afternoon free to dig into her story.

That story about Yvette Peters was her ticket to success. Who was that girl? If she was born in Freedom State, why was she deported so rapidly? Had there been no effort to check her identity? Viola knew that in every story, there was somebody getting screwed and somebody doing the screwing. Peters had been screwed. And then deported. And then executed. Fine. But who did it to her? It had to come down to some sort of decision in the immigration department. But who wanted to see her gone, and why? She needed an interview with the immigration minister. She had called the schmuck five times already.

Viola coasted down a hill, negotiated the curve at the bottom and came into a flat, isolated section of the park. A couple of hundred metres ahead on her left, a van was parked illegally on the side of the road. The driver's door was open. It was not a park vehicle. And the road was supposed to be closed to traffic today.

She coasted, slowed down and put the whistle in her mouth. Then she saw it. A commotion on the grass, just beyond the van. One man was kicking another, who was down on the ground. The aggressor was shouting. Viola let it rip: two super-shrill blasts of her whistle, followed by two more. The attacker scrambled into the van, and then it screamed down the road.

Viola pulled up beside the victim. Slim black man. Face down, with hands around his head and knees pulled up under his chest. He rolled onto his back. Groaned. His face was bleeding. Keita Ali! In his running gear. No knapsack. No way in hell's half acre had this sonofabitch been rolled for a dollar.

WHEN ANTON HAMM THREW HIM TO THE GROUND, KEITA tried to imagine that it was a friend roughhousing with him in the schoolyard. Hamm went for his stomach and his face. Keita raised his forearms to protect himself, and Hamm kicked them too. Kicked so hard he lost his wind and could not breathe. Was Hamm going to kill him? Was this it? Had he been interrupted in the last run of his life? Hamm kept shouting. It was hard to concentrate, to pick up the words, amid the pain of the blows.

"Deliver, you bastard," he shouted. "Ten thousand dollars, or you will never run again."

Keita heard the shrieking whistle. A whistle, but no cars and no voices. He waited for the sirens, for the officers, for the handcuffs. Now they would send him home—if you could give that name, *home*, to the country that had killed your father and kidnapped your sister. He would be no good to Charity if he was in prison too. They would both end up dead. Their bodies would be deposited naked in the square in the heart of Yagwa, but nobody would come for them.

"Hey, man, are you alive down there?"

A woman's voice. It seemed vaguely familiar. He could not place it.

"Earth to Keita Ali or whoever you are, do you read me?"

Keita heard the squeak of a brake and a grunt, and then he felt a body crawling up to him, pushing his shoulder.

"For you, I got out of my wheelchair and hauled my ass over wet grass. So would you do me the service of opening your eyes and telling me whether or not you plan to live or die?"

Keita opened his eyes. He felt warmth on his face. He wiped it off and looked at his hand, red and wet. He was bleeding from his lip and eyebrow. He rubbed his face again and looked at the woman who was lying on the ground beside him. A black woman. Her legs ended in stumps at her upper thighs. Her arms were sculpted like a weightlifter's. She was in training gear.

"Let's start with basics," she said. "Do you know who you are?"

"Keita Ali."

"Is that truly your name, or did you make up that one too?"

"It's real."

"Do you know where you are?"

"Ruddings Park."

"Do you know who did this to you?"

"No."

"How about this. Do you remember me? Viola Hill. *Clarkson Evening Telegram.*"

Keita did remember. She had written the story about his race in Buttersby. And about the girl who had been wrongly deported to Zantoroland. Since then she had emailed him repeatedly, asking for an interview.

She flipped open a cellphone and took his picture. He was too weak to protest.

"Shall I call 911?"

He was suddenly very cold: it was just fifteen degrees Celsius at seven thirty in the morning, and he was lying on the wet morning grass wearing nothing but shoes, shorts and singlet. He told her that she would be doing him a grave disservice by calling the police.

She asked if he could get up. He struggled to his knees, while she rolled over twice to reach the side of her chair and hoisted herself back up on the seat.

"You are in shape," he said.

"Yes, Mr. Roger Bannister, I am in shape, and at this moment in slightly better condition than you. Here"—she pulled a knapsack from the back of her chair, removed a water bottle and a cloth and handed these to him—"I come prepared for all eventualities," she said. "If you don't wish to attract attention, rinse the blood off your face and apply some pressure."

Keita took the bottle. The water stung, but he squirted and wiped until his face felt clean.

"That guy really pummelled you," she said. "How do you feel?"

"Sore," he said, "but nothing broken."

"It was Anton Hamm, wasn't it?"

Keita said nothing.

"You're lucky he didn't kill you. Why was he beating up on you?"

"Don't know."

"You lie! What did he want?"

"No idea."

"He wants money from you, doesn't he? But he doesn't want to hurt you too bad, because you're his meal ticket. Is that it?"

It didn't hurt any more to walk than it had to lie down and take the blows. As he walked and then began to jog along the road, Viola Hill wheeled along beside him.

"Come on, why did he do this to you?"

"Private matter," Keita said.

"Buddy, I just spared you the worst part of a mugging."

"Thank you. But you write for a newspaper, and I know what that means. My father was a newspaper man."

"Not the famous Zantorolander journalist Yoyo Ali?"

"Yes. He was my father."

"You're kidding. What do you mean, *was*?"

"He died recently."

"How did he die?"

"He was murdered."

"Jesus. That's awful. I'm so sorry. Does the world know about this?"

"No. But . . . I have to go now."

"Why was your father murdered, Keita?"

"Look, I'll answer if you promise not to write anything about what happened to me today. If this gets out, people will think I can't run anymore, and my sister's life could be in danger."

"All right, talk."

"My father was working on a story. Something to do with corruption tying Zantoroland to Freedom State."

"What kind of corruption?"

"Not sure. Freedom State officials were paying off their colleagues in Zantoroland. Something to do with refugees."

"That's it?"

"That's all I know."

"Who was he writing it for? Someone must have details."

"There was a Canadian journalist who knew my father for many years. They were good friends. He might have an idea."

"Name?"

"Mahatma Grafton."

"Where is he?"

"I think he's an editor with the *New York Times*."

"What's your relationship with Anton Hamm?"

"He was my agent. But I fled from him, and now he says I owe him money."

"Why did you flee?"

"He would have sent me back to Zantoroland, and I would have been killed."

"Why?"

"Being the son of a dissident is like being the dissident himself."

"Who killed your father?"

"His body was left in the fountain of the public square in Yagwa. Check with Amnesty International. This is how the authorities in

Zantoroland always dispose of the bodies of their dissidents. And now they have jailed my sister, Charity."

"Unbelievable. What do they want from her?"

"They want me to pay ransom money."

"How much?"

"Fifteen thousand dollars."

"So Hamm is after you for money, and so are the Zantoroland officials?"

"Yes. But you can't write about that. My sister's life is at stake."

"Holy shit."

Keita began to pull ahead of her. "I really must leave you now. Thank you for saving me."

With that, Keita Ali headed off across fields that Viola could not traverse in her wheelchair.

CHAPTER TWENTY-FIVE

OCCO AGREED TO MEET DARLENE IN THE SAFEST place that he could imagine: the running path by the reservoir deep in the heart of Ruddings Park. There couldn't be recording bugs there. And if anybody was following them, Rocco would notice. He wore his running shoes, shorts and shirt. He carried his house keys and five hundred in cash in a fanny pack. And no ID.

Darlene showed up on time. She wore runners too, and sweatpants and a sweater with the hood pulled up.

"What do you want?" he asked.

"Citizenship papers."

"Can't help with that."

"Yes you can. You're the fucking immigration minister. And I also need money."

"Why?"

"My money was stolen from my apartment. I can't even go get my clothes. They'll be watching my place."

"Who?"

"Lula. Or the government people. I'm not sure. Some guy stole my stuff and came after me with a gun."

"I was threatened recently too."

"Really?" she said. "Was the guy black?"

"No, he was white and huge."

"Serves you right. You sent away my friend. And she died in Zantoroland."

"I didn't send her away."

"Somebody did."

"Yeah, and I'm trying to find out who. But you have to tell me what you know."

"The story's yours—in exchange for my papers."

"You think I just dash off passports and citizenship cards on a notepad? I can give you money, but that's it."

Rocco pulled five hundred dollars from his fanny pack and gave it to Darlene.

Darlene said she had been out back behind the Bombay Booty smoking under a tree the night Yvette entertained the prime minister.

"The prime minister?"

"It was Graeme Wellington. Believe me."

Darlene told him about the man in a car marked *Reliable Security Services*. She'd gotten a good look when Lula went out to speak with him. Tall, about six-three. White. Four-inch scar like a pickle carved down his right cheek. Brown hair. Buzz cut. Maybe forty, forty-five. Solid build, like he did time in the gym.

"He went straight upstairs and came back down in five minutes, with Yvette in handcuffs. The girl was crying, but not resisting, because there wasn't a thing she could do."

"Is that it?" Rocco asked.

"No, that ain't quite."

A week later, Darlene said, Lula took her aside. "I want you to treat a client extra special, extra nice. Give him everything he wants, and more. This a man we have to please."

Darlene knew better than to ask why. She just got ready and went to meet him. He was the man with the scar running down his cheek. She gave him what he wanted and then got him talking.

"Hope you satisfied," she had told him.

"Hell, yes," he said with a grin.

"Better than you get at home?" she said.

"Since I live alone."

"I ain't seen you here before," she said. "Maybe you could ask for Darlene again, so Miss Lula know I'm popular and desired around here."

"Don't know if I'll be coming back."

"Expensive, I guess."

"It's not that. A freebie for me, here."

"You extra important?"

"Not in the grand scheme of things. I'm a runner."

"You run marathons?"

"No. I run people to the airport. Then someone else takes 'em right through security and gets 'em on planes."

"You police?"

"No. Private security, but I do just as good as any cop when it comes to deportations. I'll say something nice about you on the way out. And have yourself a good night," he said.

Darlene said to Rocco, "That's what the fucker who took away Yvette Peters said to me. *Have yourself a good night.*"

Rocco wasn't sure about any of this. How credible was she? She had told him the company name on the vehicle used to seize and deport Illegals. She'd mentioned that the guy was private security, not a cop, and it was true that the government used a private contractor to take deportees to the airport. He didn't know what this was all about, but he knew one thing for sure. He had recently, and discreetly, interviewed the head of security for his own immigration department, and not a single person working for him had issued or carried out the order to deport Yvette Peters.

"I got something else for you," Darlene said. "But I need papers."

"I told you—I can't do that."

"You know the time you came to see me? In the Bombay Booty?"

"What about it?" Rocco said.

"It was videotaped. The whole thing. On Lula's say-so."

Rocco stared at Darlene. "If that tape gets out, or if the PM gets hold of it, my career is over."

"I have an idea about how to get it. How about those papers of mine?"

"Your papers are looking a little more possible."

"And don't worry about the prime minister. He'll be keeping his own mouth shut," Darlene said.

"Why is that?"

"He was videotaped too. On the night he was with Yvette."

CHAPTER TWENTY-SIX

T HEY MET IN THE MEDIA TENT BEFORE THE START of the Grant Valley Half-Marathon.

"Whatcha doing here?" John asked.

"I was going to ask you the same thing," Viola said.

"I'm doing what you're doing," John said. "Research."

"Fine. As long as you do not get in the way of my camera, enjoy it."

"Did you know that Yvette Peters was deported right after she was alone in a room with Prime Minister Wellington in the Bombay Booty?"

"Get out," she said.

"I can prove it."

"Tell me more."

"So, what will you give me, if I give that information to you?" he said.

"I'll explain things to you that you don't understand," she said.

"I understand everything, except, well, who is paying off whom in the Freedom State government, and why our government would be in cahoots with the people in power in Zantoroland."

"Anything to stay in power," she said. "Let's talk after the race."

"Deal."

When John left the tent, Minister of Immigration Rocco Calder was walking right by.

"Mr. Minister! How are you doing?"

"John. You are everywhere."

"Still working on that assignment," John said. "Good luck in the race."

"I'll see if I can beat that Roger Bannister fellow," the minister said.

"Dream on," John said. "Wait, Mr. Minister. Let me take a clip of this." He aimed his video camera at the immigration minister. "Mr. Minister, can you win this race?"

The minister smiled. "I can win the race against myself," he said. "I hope to run the half-marathon in less than ninety minutes. If I can beat that time, I'll be happy."

"Anything you'd like to say to Keita Ali? I hear he has registered."

"Tell him that I wish I could run with him."

"A losing proposition, Mr. Minister. If he runs well, he'll finish half an hour ahead of you."

"Then I'll have to train harder."

"Hey, Mr. Minister, one other thing?" John checked a piece of paper in his pocket. "In the immigration business, what does the acronym IRBL mean?"

The minister frowned. "Illegals Returned Before Landing. Look, I've got a race to run."

"Okay," John said. "Thanks, and good luck!"

Viola emerged from the tent and wheeled in between them. "Mr. Minister, I am Viola Hill, *Clarkson Evening Telegram*."

His face clouded over, but she pressed on. "Why was Yvette Peters deported to Zantoroland? The girl was born and raised in Freedom State."

"I don't know," he said.

"Come on, Mr. Minister. I'm just doing my job. Why did you sign the deportation order?"

"I did no such thing," he said.

"Sure you did," Viola said. "The only way to deport someone is for you to sign the order."

"Not true. And I signed nothing."

"Then who did?" she said. "Who can explain what happened to this girl? People want to know."

"I can't help you. Gotta go."

Rocco Calder pushed into the throng of runners lining up for the start of the race.

"Way to scare him off," John said.

"Are you kidding?" Viola said. "I've got him on record insisting that he did not sign the deportation order. That means someone else did it. Only so many people are authorized."

"Yeah?"

"Stick with me, kid. You'll pick up a thing or two. Let's talk later about that proof of yours."

"I have it on a USB," John said.

"Calder's denial?" she said. She pointed to her notebook. "Big deal. I've got the fastest handwriting on the block."

She wheeled off before John had time to explain what he had meant.

KEITA ATE A BANANA AND TWO SLICES OF TOAST WITH PEA-nut butter, and then he took the bus with Ivernia to the town of Grant Valley, fifteen minutes west of Clarkson. He got off the bus, left his bag with Ivernia and headed out on a jog to warm up. It was a hot day: thirty-two degrees Celsius in the morning, and humid to boot. He kept the jog short and then began stretching. He jogged some more, did a few wind sprints and then pushed his way forward through the throng of runners waiting for the start of the race. It took him about five minutes. Sometimes people moved gracefully to the side and let him pass, seeing that he looked like a serious runner. Others gave him a hard time, staring and frowning.

"Excuse me," he said to one woman, who said, "Sure," and moved to the side. They looked at each other for a long moment.

"Keita," Candace said. "You should be way up front."

"Trying to get there," he said.

"I hope we can talk," she said.

He lifted a hand so she could see him wave as he moved through the crowd.

"Good luck," she called after him.

Keita couldn't understand her kindness. If she was a police officer and had hidden that from him, she could not have good intentions, could she? Keita banished the memory of her in bed. He had to get to the starting line.

BIG RACE. HUGE CROWD OF RUNNERS. EVERYBODY FIGURED they could run that far. Just 21.1 kilometres, but a good test of fitness. Rocco figured he could run the half-marathon in ninety minutes. So that was his target. But who knew how he would handle the heat? The race was set to start in ten minutes, and his phone was vibrating again.

"Calder," he said into it.

"Rocco. Geoffrey here. What's all that noise? Sounds like cattle."

"I'm lined up to run the Grant Valley Half-Marathon."

"I figured as much. Can you get a good look at that Roger Bannister or Keita Ali guy?"

"He runs a bit faster than me," Rocco said.

"We want to talk to him. If I come to the race, can you point him out afterwards?"

"Geoffrey boy, you don't get it. There are five thousand runners corralled behind the starting line. He's going to finish half an hour ahead of me. By the time I get there, he will have showered, had a massage and two beers, and gone home."

"Don't they have a prize ceremony afterwards?"

"Yeah."

"Don't the victors have to stick around for their prize money?" Christ, this guy was annoying. "Yeah."

"Well, what's he look like?"

"Thin, black, too short for a job in cabinet."

"Very funny. Meet me at the end of the race and point him out to me."

"You won't need me for that," Rocco said. "He'll be onstage getting a medal. Anyway, what do you want to do with him?"

"Just talk," Geoffrey said.

"The end of a race is not a good place to talk," Rocco said.

"Meet me there." Geoffrey hung up.

Damn. Who was running the immigration department, anyway? Rocco tried to shake off his annoyance. Ninety minutes. That was his goal today. He would have to run at a pace of 4:15 per kilometre. He would need to reach kilometre 10 by about forty-two minutes. He could do it. Right? Already bloody hot weather, though. Note to self: drink more than usual.

Rocco pushed closer to the starting line. The race official raised the starter's pistol. In the other hand, he held a megaphone and issued last-minute instructions that were completely unintelligible.

Well, what do you know? To Rocco's right. Roger Bannister.

THE GUN CRACKED. THE RUNNERS BEGAN MOVING. IT TOOK Keita ten seconds to cross the starting line. But then they were off.

Keita dodged and darted, squeezing between recreational runners. He shot past them, fixed his eye on the race leaders up ahead, and tried to get into a smooth groove. Half-marathons brought out fast runners, especially for a twelve-thousand-dollar prize. It was a long shot that Keita would win. But the good thing about racing a half-marathon was that he would recover quickly. Racing a full marathon really took it out of your legs. But a half-marathon—he could run that and bounce back in two weeks. To win this race, Keita would have to run sub-sixty-one minutes. That meant running faster than 2:50 per kilometre. Keita pulled down the first kilometre in 2:40. He kept that up for the second kilometre, and slid in behind the pack of five leading runners.

Keita was paying a price for the fast pace. Trouble breathing.

And for the first time in his life while running, he had a headache. Every step jarred his skull. He tried slowing down his breathing, but he gulped and gasped for air as if he were coming up from under water. He tried shorter, shallow breaths, but that didn't work either. He concentrated on trying to inhale in ways that filled out his diaphragm, inhaling through the nose and exhaling through the mouth, but he felt on the edge of hyperventilation.

In the first kilometres, he sat right behind the leaders, letting them break the wind. But he didn't feel that he could run much faster. His legs felt heavy. Dead. At kilometre 10 he heard Hamm shout at him from the sidelines.

Kilometre 17. He had pulled into the lead and slowed to a 2:50 pace, and noticed, rounding a corner, a group of three runners less than fifty metres behind him. You could make up that distance very fast on a dying runner.

At kilometre 18, his face felt hot, his body was trembling, and he wished he could stop then and there to take a pill for his headache. Mitch Hitchcock pulled even with him on the back of a police motorcycle and studied him. Keita was sure that he saw concern in Hitchcock's face. Keita grabbed a sports drink from the table at kilometre 19 and took a sip, but it did not make him feel better. Two runners were right on his ass. By kilometre 20, they had pulled even with him.

One was Billy Deeds. "Got a song for me today?" his competitor said.

Keita didn't like the look of his chief rival—he seemed strong, and he did not appear to be suffering.

Ivernia was on the sidelines, cheering for him.

"Ain't that sweet," Deeds said. "Roger Bannister and his mother."

Deeds pulled ahead as if Keita were standing still. He had only one kilometre left. Less than three minutes, but he couldn't hold on to the pace. Deeds pulled even farther ahead, and two more runners blew past Keita. He was aware that he was slowing dreadfully. He was swaying too. He heard someone shout, "Help that runner!" Now he was barely jogging. Three other runners flew past. He could see the finish line just a hundred metres ahead, but he could barely put one foot ahead of the other. A race official came out to him, but Keita could not understand what he was saying. Walking now. Forty metres. Twenty. There was the finish line. Not quite over it. Down.

Sure, Mitch thought, runners had bad days. Sometimes a runner felt sick and finished as much as ten or twenty minutes off the mark. Or just dropped out. Runners fainted, got heat prostration, had cramps. Mitch thought he had seen it all. But Keita had been running fast, at a sub-sixty-one-minute pace, right up to kilometre 18. Might he get out-kicked at the end? Sure. Might some other runners finish the last kilometre more quickly? Entirely possible. But to slow to a jog and then a walk, and then to stagger and sway like a drunk man and fall right on the finishing line? You almost never saw that with elite athletes. The smart kid from the Clarkson Academy was running toward him, shouting, "Please, sir, he's my friend and he needs an ambulance." Mitch jumped into action.

Viola had a spot right before the finishing line. She saw him coming. He looked like a toddler who hadn't quite learned how to walk, zigzagging, almost stumbling and finally pitching forward like a blind man. Was it the beating he had received? No, it couldn't be. She had heard the radio reports. Keita Ali had been with the leaders through kilometres 4, 10 and 15. He had taken the lead at kilometre 15. The competitors caught up to him at kilometre 18, and then he just died. What was going on?

She dictated into her tape recorder: "Mystery runner Keita Ali, clearly the most talented runner in the bunch today, ran into problems at the Grant Valley Half-Marathon. He staggered like a drunk man in the last metres and was passed by seven runners in the last kilometre. He was drooling. His eyes were rolled back. When he reached the finish line, spectators shouted for an ambulance. He fell so abruptly that his body was on the line—not over it—when ambulance workers carried him off, motionless, on a stretcher."

Maybe Viola lost, in that moment, any semblance of objectivity. Maybe it was a fluke. But as the marathoner she sought to describe on the page was carted out of her field of vision, she felt a sudden wave of phantom pain. Once more, the knife ripped right through her thigh. She screamed. Turned a dozen heads. And then the sensation was gone.

IVERNIA IDENTIFIED HERSELF TO THE PARAMEDICS AS HIS next of kin, and even though that drew a strange look from Mitch Hitchcock, he made room for her in the ambulance.

"He would not wish to be taken anywhere where he will be documented," Ivernia told him.

"Sorry," Hitchcock said, "we're going to the hospital."

"At least take him to a hospital that is out of the way. Somewhere where people won't think to look for him. Please."

"Out of my control. How are you related?"

"He works for me."

He looked at her with surprise. "Really?"

"Yes," she said. "Long story."

"He's got talent. Do you realize where he could go, if he had support here in Freedom State?"

"I don't think he wants to go anywhere," she said. "He wants to win because he needs the money."

"He finished eighth today," Hitchcock said, "so no money in that. And he wasn't really even eighth. He had to be lifted off the finishing line. Technically, he didn't finish the race at all."

Ivernia took another look at Keita, who was lying on the gurney, his mouth covered because an EMT was pumping oxygen into him. He had an IV drip. He was breathing. And his heart was beating. But he was unconscious.

* * *

CANDACE PULLED RANK. SHE WAS NOT SUPPOSED TO DO IT, but she did it anyway. It had felt good to run the half-marathon in 83:08. It hadn't hurt all that much. On a cooler day, she could have run two minutes faster.

It had been a good effort today, but any positive feelings dissipated when she crossed the finish line and heard that Keita had collapsed at the finish line and been rushed to the hospital. She asked for the race director, but he was gone. She asked for the assistant race director, and some official tried to stall her. She brought out her badge and identified herself as a sergeant with the Clarkson Police Department and said she needed to speak to the assistant race director pronto. That got action.

From him, she found out that Mitch Hitchcock had accompanied Keita to the Freedom Hospital. She hailed a cab and changed into street clothes in the back seat. The driver watched through his rear-view mirror. But she couldn't care less.

Waiting in the emergency area were Hitchcock and, to her surprise, Ivernia Beech. Candace sat down beside the older woman to wait.

"Are you two friends?" Ivernia asked.

"We've met," Candace said. "I heard he had some troubles, and I was worried. You know each other too?"

"We do," Ivernia said. "I got in by saying that he worked for me, but I'm not really here as his employer."

"I'm not really here as a police officer," Candace said.

"I figured as much. He is very handsome."

Candace blushed.

A couple of hours later, a doctor in scrubs came into the waiting room looking for next of kin. Three people stood up. The doctor looked quizzically at Ivernia, Mitch and Candace, and motioned to Ivernia, who said she was like a mother to him.

"If you don't mind," Mitch said. "As the director of the race where Mr. Ali has hurt himself, I really must join you."

Candace stood. "Clarkson Police," she said, flashing her badge. "I guess it will be a full party."

KEITA, FOR HIS PART, WASN'T FEELING SO BAD NOW. HE wanted to have the IV detached. He wanted to leave. A hospital was not a safe place to hide.

The doctor came in and said that three people wished to join them for a conversation.

"Who are they?" Keita asked.

"An older woman, a guy with a grey ponytail, and a lady cop. I can tell the cop to wait, if you wish."

"Does she look like she has come to arrest me?" he asked.

"She's in civilian clothes. I think she just ran the half-marathon too. She probably isn't planning to arrest you, if she was prepared to sit patiently for two hours in the waiting room."

"Okay," he said. "Let them all in."

"IT'S THE HERNIA, RIGHT?" HE SAID TO THE DOCTOR, A TALL black man.

Keita wondered how he had come be a doctor in this land. Was he born here? Had he come from elsewhere? He didn't seem to have a foreign accent.

"I saw your hernia, and another physician checked it out too. It is enlarged. You should have it operated on. But it is not your chief issue here."

"It has been growing, and I've been feeling sick lately when I run. It wasn't this big before. Are you sure—?"

"Yes," the doctor said. He cleared his throat. "Mr. Ali, you could have died today."

"Shit," Mitch said. "Don't tell me it's his heart."

"His heart is fine," the doctor said. "Mr. Ali, you have diabetes. And today you suffered from dehydration. It's not to be ignored."

"What do you mean?"

"If you don't get this under control, it could lead to diabetic ketoacidosis."

"Which is what?"

"If your blood sugar rises too high, and if you suffer from serious dehydration, you could fall into a coma and suffer cardiac arrest. You need medicine to control the levels of sugar in your blood. You need it, starting today."

Nobody said a word. Keita looked at the faces of the three who had come to see him. He saw Ivernia trying to be calm and strong. She took his hand.

"Are you quite sure?" Mitch finally said.

"Positive. Nobody goes to levels that high without being diabetic. And he responded immediately when we put him on an insulin drip. Plus fluids and electrolytes."

Keita swallowed hard. "Can I keep running?"

"Yes—*if* you go on insulin and get your blood sugar under control."

Keita dropped his eyes. Whatever this treatment meant, he knew he did not have the money for it.

"I'm a runner too, by the way," said the doctor. "Ten kilometres is my max. I am blown away that you could run a sixty-three-minute half-marathon while suffering from dehydration. It would take me sixty-three minutes to jog half that distance in perfect health." He paused, seemed to read Keita's mind. "You're wondering about cost. I don't know what situation you are in, but we will worry later about the hospital bill. My first job is to treat. Others can worry about money. We can get you some free supplies. Enough to keep you going a few months. Keep the stuff refrigerated, that's all. Maybe you can work out a solution after that."

"I'll help him with the needles," Ivernia said.

"Okay," the doctor said. "I'll set you up with a nurse. It might take another hour or so. Have some water and relax, and we'll get you out of here before the day ends."

"Doctor?"

"Yes."

"If I take this insulin, the problem will go away?"

"It can be controlled. Lots of high-performance athletes manage diabetes, with the help of medication."

"Thanks."

"You're welcome. We've run some blood tests already, to figure out the right level of insulin."

"Doctor," Keita said.

"Yes?"

He lowered his voice. "I have to be out of here very, very soon."

The doctor raised his eyebrows.

"It's true," Ivernia said. "He's in danger."

"I'll do what I can," the doctor said, and he left the room.

"Handsome man," Ivernia said.

Mitch and Candace laughed.

"I've got to get going, now that I see you're alive," Mitch said. "I want you to come see me, but I know you're not going to do that. So I'm going to come to you. I want you to train with the national team. If you can get your health back on track, you could be one helluva marathoner."

"I appreciate that, and maybe later, but right now I'm facing a crisis. Someone needs me, and I can't let that person down."

"I think he needs to consider the matter when he is feeling better," Ivernia said. "No more pressure."

Mitch stood. "Okay, okay. We'll talk when you're feeling better. And by the way—we'll take care of your hospital bill and look into getting that hernia fixed."

Candace stood as well. She asked if she could have a moment with him. Mitch and Ivernia nodded and left the room.

"How you doing?" she said.

"I needed to win that race today."

"Right now, you need to focus on your health."

He took her hand.

"You got the wrong idea about me," she said.

He looked at her. "You didn't tell me you were a police officer."

"I am not after you—in that way," she said.

He smiled. "I have a lot of problems. Too many to tell you about."

"Try me."

"I'll call after things get under control."

"Or you could let me help you," Candace said. "You know how to reach me." She kissed him on the cheek and left the room.

CHAPTER TWENTY-SEVEN

I T HAD BEEN A GOOD RACE. HOT AS HADES OUT THERE. Rocco must have lost two litres of sweat. He drank at every water station, did not answer the cell while running and finished the half-marathon in ninety-four minutes. Not as fast as he had been hoping, but he didn't suffer too much. He was fifteenth in his age group—men fifty to fifty-five years old—and that made him feel pretty good. Overall, he finished 250th, which was not bad in a race of five thousand.

Rocco checked the race results posted on the bulletin boards. He was looking for the finishing time of Candace Freixa. He hadn't seen that babe once in the whole race. Maybe he had beaten her today. Maybe she had wilted in the heat. He watched for her, too, in the finishing area, where they served food and drinks, but she was nowhere to be found. He looked again at the race results board and finally found her name. She had beaten him by eleven minutes. Damn, was she fast.

He checked the top of the bulletin board. No result for Keita Ali. Weird. He checked the bottom of the board. It listed the runners who did not finish—each name had a big *DNF* beside it. Keita Ali was one of them. What had happened?

Someone tapped his shoulder.

Geoffrey. In shades and a Tilley hat that made him look like a Canadian tourist.

"Taken away by ambulance," Geoffrey said.

298

"What?"

"Keita Ali collapsed and was taken away by ambulance."

"What happened?" Rocco asked.

"No idea. Try to find out, would you? And meet me in the office tomorrow. Bossman and I have a few things to go over."

Geoffrey spun on his heel and walked away. Rocco thought again about the next election. Two more years, and he would be out of there.

In the morning, Rocco got to his office early. June was waiting for him. She stood close to him and whispered, "Since you're interested in that runner fellow, I want you to hear the message that some guy left on the Illegals hotline. Nobody else has heard this."

On Rocco's initiative, a five-thousand-dollar reward had been offered to any citizen who reported an Illegal, provided that the report led to the individual being caught and deported. Not many legitimate tips came through the hotline, but this man seemed determined. He identified himself as Jimmy Beech and said, in an angry voice, that an Illegal using the name Roger Bannister was mooching off his mother, Ivernia Beech, at 37 Elixir Bridge in Clarkson. The message ended "I should be entitled to my five-thousand-dollar reward for this and would appreciate receiving it at your earliest convenience."

Rocco shook his head. He didn't buy Ivernia Beech's politics but admired her activism. Too bad the old woman was stuck with a meddling son. She deserved better. But at least Rocco now knew where Keita lived.

"The prime minister is asking to see you now," June said. "In his office. Shall I delete the message?"

"Good thinking," Rocco said.

As Rocco walked along the fourth-floor corridor, a black man with opaque sunglasses emerged from the PM's door and walked quickly toward him. The man was walking purposefully, but Rocco was tired of mysteries. He stood right in the man's path.

"Excuse me, who are you?"

"Who are *you*?" the man said back.

"Rocco Calder, federal minister of immigration."

"Saunders," he said, "and I'm just leaving."

"Saunders who?"

"It's just Saunders."

"What do you do?"

"This and that," Saunders said.

He had one helluva attitude, and he was not the least bit intimidated by Rocco.

"Who were you just meeting with?" Rocco asked.

"Ask them," Saunders said, slipping past him and hurrying to the stairwell.

"Hey," Rocco said.

The man did not answer or slow down.

Rocco knocked on the PM's door. Inside, he found Wellington and Geoffrey.

"Who was that guy?" Rocco asked.

"And good morning to you too, Rocco," the PM said.

"The black guy who took off like a shot. Wearing shades."

"Sit down," Geoffrey said, "we need to talk."

Rocco took a chair.

"What can you tell us about this Keita Ali?" the PM asked.

Rocco told him much of what he knew: Keita was apparently from Zantoroland, and he had used an alias to run in Freedom State; he was a talented runner who had collapsed at the Grant Valley Half-Marathon; apparently, he was not registered as a citizen or legal visitor, and his visa to enter the country had expired. All these things Rocco had learned by having his people dig through the files in the immigration department.

"Where does he live?" the PM asked.

"No clue," Rocco lied.

"We want you to help us find him," Geoffrey said.

"I'm told he was taken to a hospital after the race," he said.

"He checked out of the Freedom Hospital late yesterday afternoon," Geoffrey said. "He left no address."

"Guy's fast," Rocco said.

"We need to talk to him," Geoffrey said, "so have your people look, and meanwhile, scour the files."

"And Rocco," the PM said.

"Yes."

"Sorry about the mix-up in AfricTown. We had no idea that a police raid would be conducted."

"It happens," Rocco said.

"Did you get anything out of Darlene?"

"You know what? Not a single thing! I was just settling in when the raid began. So there was no time. I did catch the wrestling, though. Man. Gotta watch out for snakes."

"There's trouble brewing in AfricTown," the PM said. "They're unhappy about those raids we've been conducting, and they are raising hell about Yvette Peters. Lula DiStefano is threatening to stage a demonstration and name people who have visited the Bombay Booty lately."

Rocco cleared his throat. "That could mean a lot of trouble, for a lot of people."

"Just be prepared," the PM said.

CHAPTER TWENTY-EIGHT

I NSIDE THE FREEDOM BUILDING, VIOLA USED HER PRESS pass, rolled into the elevator, went up a floor, got out and wheeled along the corridor. She was looking for the office of Rocco Calder.

When she found it, she rolled past his secretary and straight into his office, stopping near his desk. Calder was behind it.

The secretary followed, chastising her. "Excuse me, you can't barge into this office." But then she saw Viola's face, and everything changed.

"Hey, June," Viola said.

"Viola Hill." June laughed. "Been a very long time. You really got the stuff in that chair. Move like greased lightning." June had grown up in AfricTown, and like Viola, she had escaped.

"Working girl's got to move," Viola said.

"You fast in that thing," June said. "Ripped arms too. You working out, child?"

"When I ain't chasing immigration ministers."

Rocco got up and came around his desk. "Ms. Hill. To what do I owe the honour?"

"Sorry to barge in, Minister, but I've been calling and calling, and it just can't wait."

"June," Rocco said, "please, close the door behind you."

"Yes, sir," she said. "Viola, go easy on him." June flashed her a grin.

"Sure thing," Viola said.

When they were alone, Calder said, "She's been working for me for two years, and that's the first time I've heard her talk naturally."

"Don't you ever speak naturally, Mr. Minister? All alone, with the boys?"

"Not really," Rocco said. "Not much these days. Anyway, I saw you at the half-marathon, taking notes, interviewing people. You never stop, do you?"

"I saw you running. Ninety-four minutes, right? Not bad for an old white guy running in the heat."

"At least you didn't say 'old dead white guy,'" Rocco said, laughing. "I guess we're both just working with what we've got."

"Mr. Minister, we all grow. But not everybody loses their legs."

"When you put it that way," he said. "I'm sorry if I sounded callous."

"Don't worry," she said. "I work on being callous every day. But I sure didn't feel callous when Keita Ali fell on the finishing line."

"Me neither," he said. "At the starting line, the guy was stuck in the thick of the runners, just like me. He couldn't even get up to the front to start with the elite guys."

"He was beaten up not long before the race."

"That's awful."

"Tell me about Yvette Peters. And Zantoroland."

"I cannot speak on the record. I told you that last time, and you quoted me anyway. I caught hell from the PM for saying I had nothing to do with the girl's deportation. If the PM walked in here now, I'd be thrown out of cabinet."

"This is off the record," Viola said.

"Completely?" he asked.

"Completely. I'm going to Zantoroland, and I need to figure a few things out."

"Okay, but first you tell me something."

"Okay."

"Who is Saunders?" Rocco asked.

"Black man, not six foot, thin, attitude as big as his head, packs a revolver?" she said. "That the Saunders you mean?"

"I didn't know about the revolver."

"Grew up in AfricTown," Viola said. "Now he's a freelance thug. Tells secrets about people in AfricTown. He's paid by your own government and anyone else who wants the inside scoop on what goes down there."

"He was just in with the PM," Rocco said.

"Well, I'll be damned," Viola said. "That is a very interesting fact."

"An off-the-record fact. Are we clear?"

"Clear."

"The PM says there's gonna be a demonstration soon by Lula what's-her-name," Rocco said.

"DiStefano. Also good info. Saunders must be the PM's snitch. Okay, my turn for questions."

"Go ahead."

"You came into office swearing that you'd turn boatloads of refugees right back to Zantoroland."

"My government did. I only moved into this portfolio recently."

"You were going to get tough with Illegals and intercept their boats in our territorial waters and send them right back home before they even landed in Zantoroland?"

"Right."

"And you know how for its first two years in office, your government has been unable to send significant numbers of Illegals back to Zantoroland?"

"Yes. That's not going so well."

"It's well known that traditionally, Zantoroland has only agreed to accept small numbers of the refugees that Freedom State wanted to send back. Why have two big boatloads of refugees suddenly been intercepted in Freedom State waters and been turned back to Zantoroland? Why is Zantoroland now allowing that?"

"Beats me. They told me to crack down on the big numbers, and I've been unable to do it."

"Whose permission is needed to deport someone to Zantoroland?" she asked.

"Normally my signature is needed. Or that of my deputy minister, but he never signs without my say-so. Or the minister of justice."

"Anyone else?"

"The head of the Immigration and Refugee Board."

"And who is that person?" Viola asked.

"The prime minister," Calder said. "Not many people know that. But the PM took over that role when we came to office."

"So when Yvette Peters was deported . . ."

"You're the reporter. You'll come to your own conclusions. But I will swear on my own life that I did not sign her deportation order."

"Thank you, Mr. Minister."

"Off the record, right?" he said.

"Yes," she said. "Off the record. Thanks for helping." As Viola swung her chair around to leave, she said, "I've been interviewing scores of Zantorolanders here in Freedom State. Some have close ties to what is going on in their home country. Word on the street is that there's some sort of secret arrangement between our two countries, which has us shipping dissidents back to Zantoroland."

"I know nothing about that."

"Would that have to go through cabinet?"

"No. The PM's Office could handle it. The PM's Office handles everything."

TODAY, IT SEEMED THAT EVERYBODY WANTED A PIECE OF Rocco. Mitch Hitchcock was next in line.

"Congratulations, Mr. Minister," he said when he was seated in Rocco's office. "I see you ran the half in ninety-four minutes."

"Thanks," Rocco said. What did this joker want? The man had recently been named to head up the men's Olympic marathon team for 2020. What kind of Olympic coach dressed like a hippie?

"It's about Keita Ali," Hitchcock said.

"How did one Illegal end up occupying my whole morning?" Rocco said. "What's with that guy?"

"I just want to help him," Hitchcock said.

"Nothing in it for you, is there?"

"It's not about me, but I would bask in his glory if he ran well in the Olympics."

"Olympics? For Freedom State? Isn't he an Illegal?"

"Minister, every country in the world makes exceptions for world-class athletes who wish to run in the Olympics."

"Is he good enough to race in the Olympics?"

"He's running already at an elite level, without any support in this country."

"And you want . . ."

"Would you consider granting him citizenship so that he can race for Freedom State?"

"Has he agreed to that?"

"No, but he will."

Rocco sat up in his chair. The fellow ran beautifully. Once in a while, you had to bend the rules and let someone stay in the country. What a public relations coup it would be, if Keita ran in the Olympics—for Freedom State. By the time the next Games came around, Rocco hoped to be out of politics. He'd be running a car dealership again. Talk about a perfect corporate sponsorship!

"I'll think it over," Rocco said.

CHAPTER TWENTY-NINE

IVERNIA RUMMAGED IN HER CLOSET FOR CLOTHES. Plain flats. Pressed black pants. White blouse. A lime-green scarf and a thin coffee-coloured jacket. Lots of tooth brushing, mouthwash, red lipstick and a hint of blush. She arrived at the Office for Independent Living fifteen minutes early, found Room 301, checked in at reception and sat in a waiting room that felt like a doctor's office.

There were two other people sitting in the plastic chairs. One man and one woman. Both alone. She wondered if she looked as old and frail as they did. A TV screen was attached to the wall, and it played cartoons.

When her name was called, she stood up and turned to the other two. "Good luck."

Ivernia was led into a windowless room with the Freedom State flag in the front left corner, a portrait of Prime Minister Wellington on the front right, and the judge's desk in the middle. Ivernia sat in a small chair facing the desk. When the judge came in, she stood up and was invited to be seated again.

"Ivernia Beech?" said Judge Rosalie Highcomb, checking her papers and not looking up.

Highcomb was about forty. White. No nonsense. No rings. Ivernia wondered how this woman enjoyed making decisions about the lives of old people—their freedom or loss of independence. Did she think, ever, that she would one day be old?

"Yes," Ivernia said.

"One moment," the judge said, reviewing her notes. "At the accident, there was no personal injury to anyone, correct?"

"That's right," Ivernia said.

"And you made restitution for the damage caused to the cars, correct?"

"Yes."

"The report says you have a volunteer job at the Clarkson Library. How'd you swing that?"

"I applied," she said, "and met with a bit of luck."

"You also have attended meetings held by the immigration minister. All very topical. Good for you."

Ivernia cleared her throat. She didn't want to say thank you.

"You received praise from Mrs. Pasieka, the social worker who visited your home," the judge said. "However, I am concerned by some of the details in your file. When you had the accident, you damaged two cars, one after the other, not simultaneously. Second, your son Jimmy has written numerous times to all manner of government employees, including to this office, attesting to your incapacity to go on living alone. He says that you have given shelter to an Illegal. Is that true?"

"A man has come to take care of some domestic tasks, such as cooking and gardening. He stays in the basement."

"Is he an Illegal?"

"I did not ask," Ivernia said.

"Employers in Freedom State are required to obtain proof of citizenship or visitor documentation from their employees."

"It didn't occur to me that this applied to domestic services—gardeners and the like."

"You must know that it violates the laws of this nation to give employment, housing or professional services to an Illegal."

"I see," Ivernia said. She did not want to overplay her naiveté.

"Mrs. Beech, I am concerned about the soundness of your judgment, but I also hear alarm bells when a son argues so adamantly on this score. I am going to put you on six months' probation. In that time, you are to register any worker hired by you. You are to ensure that any tenant you take in is a citizen of Freedom State or legally entitled to be here. I am reinstating your driver's licence, but you will lose it forever if you are found to be at fault for any other accident. You may continue to live alone, but your assets will be managed in trust for another six months. If at the end of six months there have been no more accidents or traffic violations, and if you comply with all of these conditions, you shall have your assets unfrozen, and this case will be closed. But if you are in violation, the Office for Independent Living will proceed to guide you into assisted living facilities with permanent loss of your driving licence, sale of your property and supervision of your assets. Is that clear?"

"You are saying that I still don't have access to my own money, and that if I don't behave, there will be big trouble."

"You'll still have a monthly allotment of two thousand dollars."

"I would prefer complete control of my own assets."

"You shall receive the stipulated allotment. After six months, if you have abided by my conditions, your assets will be yours to manage again."

"Am I free to go?"

"Yes. And you are welcome."

"It may seem rude that I am not thanking you," Ivernia said. "I don't wish to be rude. So let me explain. This is my life. I live in my home. My assets are just that: my assets. So I don't wish to thank you for allowing me to have—in part only—what I have not ceded."

"I will increase it to three thousand and see you in six months."

"There is only one reason I am here before you," Ivernia said. "It is because of my age. Otherwise, I would not be forced to submit to this humiliating procedure."

"Mrs. Beech, you smashed two cars and did not appear coherent in the eyes of the police. You've shown some community ties, but— from your son's report *and* your own testimony—you appear to be flouting our immigration laws."

"I find it offensive that you are doling out my own money and autonomy, like a bean counter. I want my freedom back."

The judge gave the tiniest smile. "You have heard my decision. You are free to contest it in a court of law. Good day, Mrs. Beech."

WHEN IVERNIA GOT HOME, SHE FOUND KEITA ON THE PORCH, tying his shoelaces and about to leave on a run. His heart tests had come back clean. He was injecting twenty units of insulin daily. He had learned to monitor his blood sugar level with a glucometer several times a day: fasting level before breakfast, two hours after one or two key meals each day, and before and after exercise. He had learned to strap a bottle of sports drink to the small of his back when he ran, so he could take in some carbohydrates if the insulin and exercise were driving down his blood sugar. Ivernia had watched him several times measure out the insulin and inject it.

Good thing Ivernia no longer had her nose in *Dying for Dimwits*, because it would have been easy indeed for her to fast for two days, take several of Keita's insulin pens from the fridge, inject a massive dose, go to sleep and never wake up. But it was too soon to die. She wanted to help Keita. She wanted to see him reunited with his sister. She wanted the satisfaction of shaking the Office for Independent Living off her back.

"How did it go today?" Keita asked.

"A partial victory," she said, and told him about it—except for the detail about not being allowed to give refuge to a so-called Illegal.

He jumped up and gave her a hug. "We both have to have faith," he said.

She asked how he was feeling, now that he was running again.

"Fine," he told her. "No more problems."

He said he had one other race to train for: the Clarkson Ten-Miler. It was the most popular race in Freedom State.

"What is the purse?" she asked.

"Twenty-five thousand dollars for first place," he said, "and fifteen thousand for second."

"Can you do it?" she said.

"I must."

She asked how far he was going to run now. For two hours, he said, and then he had an errand to take care of.

After he left, Ivernia napped for half an hour and then got up to make tea and read the newspapers. She was deep in an article explaining that Zantoroland seemed to have changed its mind and was now allowing refugees to be returned, when a deep voice shouted at her door. "Police! Urgent!"

Ivernia cracked open the door to one of the largest men she had ever seen. He was not a police officer. He put his hand on the door frame and pushed it open farther as if she were not even there. She stumbled back, and he stepped in and closed the door behind him. He locked it.

"You must leave now," she said, "before the alarm goes off."

"Where is Keita Ali?"

"Who?"

He sighed and walked past her into the living room. And the kitchen. And the family room. But Keita kept all of his things neatly stored in his basement suite. He looked up the stairs toward the second floor.

"If you don't leave this minute, I will call 911."

"Right," he said, his feet crashing down on creaking wood as he took the steps two at a time.

She grabbed the phone. The line was dead. Rather than chasing the man upstairs, she ran to the front door, but he must have heard her. He tore back downstairs and across the living room faster and had her arm in a vise grip before she could step outside. He closed the door and locked it, and this time he kept her with him, holding her arm, as he went upstairs and walked through every room. Downstairs again, he looked in the kitchen cupboards.

"Careful of my china," she said, but she knew he was searching for running gels, energy drinks or water bottles. Keita hadn't left his extra running shoes at the door, thank goodness. Then he opened the door to the basement and took her with him downstairs.

At Keita's locked door, he banged hard, banged again, and then he bashed it open with his shoulder. Stepping inside, he yanked Ivernia into Keita's room.

"I hate old ladies who lie," he said.

"And you're a paragon of virtue?" she said. "Break and entry. Forcible confinement. Vandalism. When the police get hold of you—"

"Shut up," he said, clapping a meaty palm around her mouth. She bit it. "Ouch. Fuck!" He pointed his finger at her. "Keep it up, and I will lose my temper."

Ivernia did not fear dying, but she did not want to die at this man's hands.

"I know who you are," she said.

"He owes me money."

"Why don't you take it to the police?"

"It's the last time I ask nicely: where is he?"

"I have no idea. Aren't you ashamed?"

"I'm not the one who ran off with ten thousand dollars."

"Some gold medallist! My husband couldn't believe that a man from Freedom State had finally won an Olympic gold medal in track and field. He said you probably took steroids, and I actually defended you."

"I won twice," he said.

"Why don't you put your experiences to good use?"

He shoved Ivernia up against the wall and pounded his giant hand above her head.

"I won the goddamn gold medal twice for this country, and I get no respect. Did I get a single sponsorship when I won gold? No. Not a single dollar."

"Mr. Hamm, why don't—?"

"Don't you tell me what to do. I've had it. Had it up to here." Anton grabbed Keita's chair and hurled it to the floor.

"Now you listen here," she said.

Ivernia saw him shift his weight but did not see his fist coming. She felt a sudden dullness in her head and then her face on the floor, which was cold and gritty. The blow had caused her to bite down hard, and she moved her sore tongue around her mouth.

Hamm rummaged through Keita's belongings, and a thick envelope tumbled out of a drawer. Ivernia watched him open it. Cash. He thumbed through it. One thousand. Two thousand. Three thousand.

"He has more than that. Where the hell is it?"

Ivernia attempted to get up from the floor, but she could not even pull her legs up beneath her. She heard banging on the window and looked up. Lydia! Her neighbour was on the back lawn with a cellphone to her ear.

"Calling 911!" Lydia shouted.

"Fuck." Hamm grabbed Keita's money and ran up the stairs.

He sounded like an elephant crashing through the house. Ivernia heard her door open, and then he was gone. She wanted to say *No police*, but she couldn't get the words out.

CHAPTER THIRTY

ANTON HAMM RECEIVED A TEXT FROM SAUNDERS telling him to book a flight to Zantoroland within the next three days and saying that he would be paid and reimbursed promptly. Anton ignored it.

Then came a handwritten message in his mailbox. *Book the ticket today. Will see you tomorrow.*

He didn't care. Let Saunders come after him. Anton was done with the threats and the blackmailing.

At seven the next evening, Anton bought himself a chicken Caesar salad at the Lox and Bagel on Aberdeen and then walked to the alley behind the shop where he had parked. It was quiet back there. As he buckled himself in, a car pulled up behind his, preventing him from backing out. Who the fuck? Anton got out. His size alone usually led people to cooperate. But the car didn't move. Instead, the driver's door opened. Well, well.

"You," Anton said.

"Good evening to you too," Saunders said.

Saunders was cocky for a small guy. Anton did not trust any man under six feet tall. He also didn't appreciate the blackmailing. And he didn't take kindly to being bossed around by a black man. Frankly, Anton didn't give a good goddamn anymore what the Tax Agency would do to him.

"Don't even think about it, asshole," Saunders said.

"What?" Anton said.

"I know what you're thinking. You're ticked off that you haven't been paid, and you're thinking about vigilante justice. Aren't you?"

"Aren't you Mr. Know-It-All."

"I know that you've got nothing but hairy armpits and a big fist, and I've got this—" Saunders revealed the nose of a purple semiautomatic pistol.

"Tough guy," Anton said.

"I could waste you here and now. And nobody would care."

Anton stood with his weight on the balls of his feet. He wanted to reach out and snatch the gun out of Saunders' hand. Saunders had no idea how fast Anton's hands were. Or maybe he did. Maybe he'd figured it out exactly. The little prick was standing two arm's lengths away. If he knew how to use that thing, he'd have time to shoot before Anton got to him.

"Well, I have your money," Saunders said. "And I have a new assignment."

"I will take what you owe me. But no more assignments."

"Keita Ali," Saunders said. "Heard of him?"

"If you're asking the question," Anton said, "you know the answer."

"Where is he?"

"Don't know," Anton said.

"How can that be? You set up his visa. Which has expired. You are responsible for his time here and for getting him out on time."

"He took off. I've been looking for him."

"I bet you have."

"What do you plan to do with him, if you find him?" Anton said.

"That's not for you to ask."

"Well, I don't know where he is," Anton said.

"Go to Zantoroland tomorrow, and see George Maxwell. He has people on the ground here, and he should know where this Ali is. This envelope is for you. It has cash for your expenses. And this other envelope is for Maxwell."

"Fuck you."

"I've been patient with you, but now you are starting to piss me off," Saunders said. He raised his pistol. "Stand against that brick wall."

Anton leaned against the wall. No way this midget would shoot him. Saunders took aim. Just to the right of his head, brick exploded.

"Give me my money, and leave me alone," Anton said. "I'm giving you one last chance. If you don't, I will hunt you down. And when I find you, I will put my hands around your neck and wring it like you're a chicken."

"You fail to appreciate a certain imbalance of power."

"Lock your doors, Saunders, and keep that little protector of yours nearby."

Saunders raised the pistol again. "Move your hands from your body, and spread your fingers."

"No need for that."

"Move them now, or I'll send hot steel into your belly."

Anton lifted his arms.

"Hands out," Saunders said.

Anton spread his arms wide against the wall.

"Right hand or left hand?" Saunders said.

"This is stupid," Anton said.

"Last request, or I shoot you twice. Right hand or left?"

"Left."

Saunders aimed the pistol at Anton's left hand, squinted, adjusted slightly and fired. Again, a bullet blasted into the brick wall. But this time it took the tip of Anton's left pinkie with it. He looked at his hand and saw blood, ragged flesh and bits of white bone.

"You shot my finger!"

"Just the tip. This here's a Ruger .22 calibre semiautomatic. It's good for fingertips, but it can also kill."

"I'm bleeding here."

"What, do you need medical attention?" Saunders reached forward and patted Anton down. He pulled the phone from his pocket and dialed. "There. I've called 911 for you."

Saunders handed the phone to Anton, got in his car and drove away.

Anton jammed his bleeding hand into his right armpit. He could hear a siren. It was coming for him, and he would be obliged to lie through his teeth.

CHAPTER THIRTY-ONE

THINGS WERE NOT GOING WELL FOR ROCCO. The fireside consultations had been farcical. Candace had turned him down for a date. Ivernia and scores of other people were writing letters to the editor of the *Clarkson Evening Telegram*. They had been reading the pieces by Viola Hill and wanted to know: why were boatloads of refugees being redirected back to Zantoroland? They also asked about Yvette Peters. Everyone had an opinion. To top it all off, Geoffrey had convinced the PM to revoke some of Rocco's powers. As of June 22, Rocco wouldn't be able to sign permits granting interim legal status to refugees. That would be handled by the Prime Minister's Office.

Today, the boy wonder John Falconer showed up again at his office, uninvited, at 7:10 a.m. Rocco was going to tell him to get lost, but the kid dropped a little bomb.

"I was there, the night the prime minister was in the room with Yvette Peters."

"Son, you're telling a tall tale."

"And I was there the night you were with Darlene too. The night of the raid."

"That's quite enough, son."

"Don't treat me like a child."

"You have an overactive imagination."

"I recorded it, Mr. Minister. You did *not* go to bed with that girl. You sat and talked. She took you into the bathroom and—"

"Enough. Have you discussed this with anyone?"

"Just you."

"You're saying you recorded this?"

"I'm saying I recorded you, and the PM—I have it on a USB—and there are a few things I do not understand."

"Why should I talk to you? What do you want? Why is everybody coming at me?"

"I want answers. For my documentary."

"I cannot be in your assignment. Not that part of it!" Rocco said.

"You'll be in it whether you like it or not, Mr. Minister. So you might as well put your best foot forward."

Rocco sat down at his desk and laid his head on its surface. He was finished. Not only in politics, but perhaps in sales too. Who wanted to buy a minivan from a guy who'd been caught on tape in a brothel?

"Mr. Minister," John said in Rocco's ear. Rocco jumped. The kid was certifiably sneaky. "Mr. Minister, we need to talk about Keita Ali."

"Everybody wants to talk about him."

"He is my friend, and he is in a bad way."

"What does that have to do with me?"

"I will do something for you, if you do something for him."

"What are you saying?"

"I will get the USB back to you. You may destroy it. You can do whatever you want with it."

"Then hand it over."

"Not yet."

"Why?"

"First, you have to help me."

"What do you want?"

"A minister's special permit for Keita Ali to stay in this country. I looked it up. Last year your office issued one special permit. The year before, two."

"He would still have to go through the proper process. And you would have to return the recording to me and tell me what you know."

"Easy," John said. "But there are a couple of things I need to figure out. First, who is Bossman?"

"Bossman is the term Geoffrey Moore uses for the PM," Rocco said.

"And what is DOA?"

"Deport on Arrest."

"ILD?"

"Information Leading to Deportation."

"Thanks. That helps. I need you on camera now."

"Fat chance."

"Do you want the USB?"

Rocco sighed. "An interview about what?"

John flipped on his video camera and sat in the frame with the minister. He gave the time, date and location. He named the minister, and he named himself.

He asked Rocco if he had any knowledge of the deportation of Yvette Peters or any involvement with it. The answer came back: "Categorically not." John asked who was responsible. The answer: "I don't know."

John then read aloud parts of the message from Whoa-Boy to Bossman that he had videotaped Yvette reading before the prime minister caught her looking at his documents: "'Bossman. I firmed up the deal with GM . . . Citing NS we can bypass CO and do this on your orders. Off books, $ only. We can keep intercepting bath-tubs, return to Z. We pay $2,000 p/k for each IRBL. To cover Z's A + R costs. . . . Also . . . We pay Z—through GM—$10,000 p/k for ILD for up to 20 dissidents/year on the lam here. GM fingers them for us. Points us right to them. Every one of those suckers, we can DOA. Good results. Minimal cost. Win win. Please approve ASAP. Whoa-Boy. P.S. Lula has three for you. Asking 10x the usual fee. Petty cash issues. Talk her down?'"

John looked at Rocco, his head tilted.

"NS is National Security and CO is Cabinet Office," Rocco said.

"Z is for Zantoroland," John said, "but what is p/k?"

"Per capita."

"OK. But what does it all mean?" John asked.

Rocco said it looked like someone was sending cash to Zantoroland officials on two levels: two thousand dollars for each "Illegal Returned Before Landing" and ten thousand for "Information Leading to Deportation" of each Zantorolander dissident hiding in Freedom State.

"What is A + R?"

"Assimilation and resettlement," Rocco said. "Basically, it's money in the president's pocket."

According to the memo, Rocco said, Lula was in on the action too. She was also getting paid for information about Illegals hiding in Freedom State.

John sat back. "Man. What a scam. What a story." He turned off the video camera.

"Now give me that USB," Rocco said.

"I can't."

"We had a deal!"

"But I don't have it."

"Who does?"

"Keita Ali."

"What is *he* doing with it?"

"He doesn't know he has it. I put the USB in his bag."

"He has until noon on June 21. And that's it. If he gets it to me by then, I will give him a special permit. But if he does not bring the video to me by then, he is out of luck. And you are out of a deal."

CHAPTER THIRTY-TWO

K EITA HAD BEEN OUT FOR HOURS. FIRST, AT AN Internet café, he had contacted George Maxwell to ask about his sister. He said he was getting ready for a race and asked for the details about the bank into which he had to make a deposit by June 22. Then he went to Ruddings Park for a thirty-kilometre training run. When he finally returned to Elixir Bridge Road, five police cars with flashing lights were parked outside Ivernia's house. Keita turned right around and kept running until he got to AfricTown.

"WHAT'S IN IT FOR ME?" LULA SAID.

"I can't offer you anything today," Keita said, "but if you protect me and I succeed in athletics, you will always be able to call on me for assistance."

"How long do you want to stay?"

"One month. Enough time to train for the Clarkson Ten-Miler."

Lula stood up. She told him that she would put him in two shipping containers arranged in a T shape for maximum space. She'd set him up with a cook, DeNorval Unthank would see to his medical needs and he'd be given food so he could stay healthy and train.

"I need a safe place to run," Keita said.

"The only people who run in AfricTown have somebody after them with a knife," she said.

"Well, I have to run somewhere."

Lula agreed, but said Keita had to render a service in return.

Lula was planning a demonstration at Ruddings Park. She had organized protests before, but they'd never drawn much attention or media coverage. It would be different this time, she promised. She wanted all of her AfricTown people out there to support her, and since he was a famous runner, she might want him to say a word or two.

"I can't come to a political demonstration," Keita said.

"Relax. All you gotta do is run up on stage in your shorts and wave. It will give all the ladies a thrill, and it will give me cred."

Keita said, with great hesitation, that he would do his best.

"Oh, and you'd better win that race," Lula said.

ON KEITA'S FIRST TRAINING RUN AROUND THE NEIGHBOUR-hood, he saw that he was not alone. In the densely populated core of AfricTown, people carrying buckets to and from water taps, balancing platters of fruit on their heads and walking barefoot to school stopped to cheer him on.

"Keita Ali, Keita Ali, go for gold, Keita Ali!"

There was no gold to run for, but it was hard to explain that. He was running for cash to get his sister out of prison, and there was only one race left with a big purse.

Lula had ordered one of her aides to drive a Volkswagen Beetle fifty metres ahead of Keita when he ran. On top of the Beetle, a tinny loudspeaker broadcast: *Attention for Keita Ali. Attention for the champion of AfricTown. Look out, Olympians, here comes Keita Ali.* Children stood by the roadside and clapped, and they ran after Keita, sprinting alongside him for a few metres at a time. Offering him water and slices of oranges, which he sometimes took just to please them. Occasionally a teenager would surprise him by keeping up with him for more than a few metres. There were no true runners in AfricTown. It was not at all like Zantoroland, where it seemed that a child in every household ran seriously. Perhaps, if Keita managed to get himself straightened out and able to stay in Freedom State, he would start up an AfricTown running club. Get somebody to donate shoes and running clothes. And see if there was any talent waiting to be discovered.

He ran every day on the undulating AfricTown Road but dared not venture into Clarkson.

John came to see him and filmed Keita running. He brought greetings from Ivernia and the insulin from her fridge. Keita had to ask Lula if she could keep it cool in a part of AfricTown that had electricity. John explained that Anton Hamm had broken into Ivernia's house and stolen Keita's cash. The police had responded to a call about a break and enter and an assault. Once they got there, they started asking questions. It turned out that Jimmy Beech had placed fourteen calls to the Clarkson Police Department over the last few weeks, and when the cops came out for the B and E, they finally decided to investigate. They charged Ivernia with harbouring an Illegal and confiscated all his possessions. She'd been released, but she knew she was being watched.

And there was more. John explained about the videotaping at the brothel, and passed along the message from Rocco Calder. John said he had put the USB in Keita's bag, but assumed the police had taken both during the raid on Ivernia's house.

"But my bag wasn't at Ivernia's."

"What?"

"Most of my stuff's still at the bus station. As a precaution. I only left a little at Ivernia's place."

"Keep it there till the race," John said. "That USB is as good as a citizenship card. Better, maybe. But it's only good until June 21. Why don't you go see him right away?"

"It's too risky," Keita said. "What if something goes wrong? I'll be of no help to Charity if I get arrested."

Keita and John agreed to the plan: he would run the race, and if things went well, win the money and have it sent to Charity's captors. And then, immediately after the race, he would go see the minister to obtain his special temporary residency permit. John, for his part, would tell the minister to expect Keita on June 21.

"He'll need the USB," John said.

"I'll be sure to have it with me. Can the minister be taken at his word?" Keita asked.

"It's your only shot," said John.

WHEN MITCH HITCHCOCK CAME TO SEE KEITA IN AFRICTOWN, he was on a training run. Mitch was amused to see the security car riding ahead of Keita, and all the children running and chanting behind.

"Nice set-up here," Mitch said. "But we could give you better training facilities in Clarkson."

"This is the best I can manage, for now," Keita said.

"How is the insulin working?" Mitch asked.

Keita said he had no more headaches, cramping or dizziness. No hyperventilating. He had tested himself on a hard run: ten kilometres at a 2:50-kilometre pace on the broken AfricTown Road. No problems. His body had not betrayed him. Mitch asked again if Keita would like to train with the Olympic marathon team. No, Keita said. It would not be safe to train in Clarkson. Mitch agreed to let Keita enter the Ten-Miler without having to pay the two-hundred-dollar entry fee. Keita would have to register under his own name, but his registration could be confidential until the day of the race. Nobody would know before then that Keita was to take part.

"How are you doing with those problems of yours?" Mitch asked.

"I will be doing a little better if I win that race," Keita said.

"I'm afraid this may be your last chance," Mitch said.

"What do you mean?" Keita asked.

Mitch explained that the government of Freedom State was quickly moving to close a loophole regarding Illegals. An amendment to the Act to Prevent Illegals from Abusing the Generosity of Freedom State had been tabled. This would make it illegal for the director of a sports event to provide a financial reward to any competitor who was neither a citizen of the country nor a visitor with a valid visa, or who had entered the competition under a false name.

It would take a few weeks for the amendment to pass through Parliament, Mitch said. But it was coming soon.

Keita would have to give this race all he had. Everything depended on it.

CHAPTER THIRTY-THREE

WHAT PAINS THEY TOOK TO COMPLICATE AN old woman's life! Ridiculous. She had been arrested. Fingerprinted. Photographed. Charged with harbouring an Illegal. And once she was released, she received a notice from the Office for Independent Living. Her file was once more under active review.

Somebody had even gotten to the library. It came to her boss's attention that Ivernia had been handing out library cards to bogus applicants. She was fired—a volunteer!—and banned from the building.

When Jimmy came to visit, she refused to let him in and spoke to him only through the locked door.

"Why'd you do it, son?"

"You were harbouring an illegal alien. Do you realize how dangerous that is?"

"What's your reward for having tipped off the police?"

"Mother. Please."

"How much is it?"

"I won't see a cent unless they catch him, convict him and deport him."

"Go away, Jimmy, and don't come back."

"Mother! As fate would have it, I'm short of cash and I was wondering . . ."

Ivernia turned away and walked down the hall until she couldn't hear her son at all.

CHAPTER THIRTY-FOUR

K EITA HAD HEARD FROM HIS FATHER THAT IT WAS no easy feat to attract a crowd to a demonstration. You had to overcome political apathy, offer demonstrators an incentive and make it easy for people to congregate. And you needed decent weather. It seemed to Keita that Lula and her followers had figured out what it took to bring people out. But this crowd was not assembled to hear speeches. They had come for something else entirely, something of Lula's own making. She had dangled a promise—proof of government officials breaking the very laws they were promising to enforce.

"Some of these movers and shakers might have left something," she had been quoted as saying in an article by Viola Hill. "We want to make sure these items are returned to their rightful owners."

Attending Lula's political demonstration at the gates of Ruddings Park, adjacent to the offices of Prime Minister Graeme Wellington and his cabinet, violated common sense. Keita had no business being near demonstrators or the police who had come out to watch. But Lula expected to see him.

Keita's father had taught him how to count heads in a crowd. You climbed to a high spot—a rooftop or a tree—and picked out a manageable segment of the crowd. You counted every person in that segment. And then you multiplied the number by the approximate number of such segments in the crowd. From a third-floor café overlooking the Freedom Gates—the main gates to Ruddings Park, adjacent to the government building—Keita had just estimated four thousand people. But the crowd was swelling by the minute.

Against his better judgment, Keita left his vantage point and wandered down to the street. He saw hot dog vendors. Ice cream sellers. Teenagers walking about catching the sun. And there, on a homemade platform, Lula stood with a megaphone and three young women. All black. All wearing high heels, hot pants and halter tops.

"What do we want?" she shouted, and then she handed the megaphone to the woman next to her.

"Water!" the woman hollered.

"What don't we get, that everybody else in the country enjoys?"

"Sewers!"

"Instead of handcuffs?"

"Teachers!"

"Show us your tits," a man called.

"That's why we came," another man shouted.

"We have many supporters," Lula said from the platform. "And we entertain many visitors. The women of AfricTown receive visitors of every size, shape and colour. Some of our visitors walk the halls of power in this country. Some get so lost in the heat of the moment that they forget their things. Socks. Underwear. Watches with engraved initials. Even ID. If the raids don't stop, and if we don't receive clean water, we will show you what some of these big men left behind. Things like pieces of paper. Like ID."

A roar went up. Another man shouted up at the stage, "Shaddup and show us your tits!"

Keita saw a group of black men tackle the heckler and a larger group of white men descend on the black men. A white man drew a knife. A black man revealed a gun. The two groups backed away from each other. Meanwhile, the audience thickened with people arriving from every direction.

"What do we want?" Lula shouted.

"Justice!" the young women next to her responded.

The people stirred, impatient for action.

Keita wandered to the outer edges of the crowd. Police officers on horses were stationed in pairs every fifteen metres or so. One officer on a horse moved toward him. He froze.

"Keita. It's Candace!" She signalled to her partner that everything was okay and then trotted over to Keita.

Candace leaned over her horse's neck. She had a holstered revolver, a baton and a helmet with a glass mask that was pushed up to reveal her face. She looked young and attractive, even with all that equipment.

"Not a safe place for you," she said.

"You think it will turn violent?" he asked.

"If Lula trots out any government members' ID, officers will move in."

"For what?"

"They've been told to just do it and justify their actions later. Possession of stolen property. Demonstrating without a permit. Why don't you go while you can?"

A roar went up from the crowd. Keita could see another fight breaking out. Candace's police radio crackled.

"Gotta go," she said.

"Show us your tits!" a man shouted.

"Pigs out there," Candace said. She gave Keita a wave and turned her horse to go.

"Mr. Prime Minister," Lula shouted through her megaphone. "Mr. Wellington. We know you can hear us out here. And you know that we have come to demand change. We know you are at your fourth-floor window, looking out at us. Come speak to us. We have some items in our lost and found. We shall release them to the public, if you do not speak to us."

A large contingent of black women in the crowd began chanting: "Welling-TON, Welling-TON, we want you, Welling-TON."

There was no response and no movement from the doors of the Freedom Building.

Lula addressed the crowd again. "We shall give them a few minutes. Prime Minister Wellington's knees must be pretty busted up from rugby. And the building has a lot of stairs. In the meantime, props to sister Viola Hill for writing about this story for her newspaper. Sister Hill, do you have something to say to the crowd?"

IN THE THICK OF THE CROWD, NEAR THE STAGE, VIOLA HILL was taking notes. She looked up and waved—no, she did not wish to come up on stage. For one thing, ten steps led up to the platform. More importantly, Viola was not a community activist. She was here to report the story, not to become it.

"Come up here, Sister Hill," Lula said.

"No," Viola called back up, "staying down here, thanks."

"Just one minute, folks, while we fetch Viola Hill," Lula said.

Fuck them. There was no way Viola was getting up on that stage. She would lose all credibility with Bolton. They might not let her keep covering the story. But then four black men reached down to place their hands under her chair.

"Ma'am," the lead male said.

"Just leave me right here, please," Viola said.

"Sorry, ma'am, Mrs. DiStefano's order."

"I don't give a flying fuck what your orders are. It's my ass you are putting your hands under, so let go."

"Sorry, ma'am." The men bent over, hoisted her and carried her up the steps. They put her down beside Lula.

"Viola Hill, you have done us such an honour by writing about this tragic situation. Could you tell us what you know?" Lula handed her the mike.

Viola was met with loud cheers from a vocal section of black women in the crowd. "You go, girl! Stick it to the man!"

Viola wanted to tell the crowd that anything she knew could be found in the pages of the *Telegram*. She cleared her throat.

Then a bottle of Coca-Cola sailed through the air, crashed and shattered into a million pieces less than a metre away. Suds bubbled up next to her. Someone shouted, "Dyke faggot gimp freak!"

Another cried, "Get that lesbian nigger gimp off the stage, and show us some tits!"

More bottles sailed through the air. One struck Viola on the shoulder. Stuck in a wheelchair on a rickety homemade stage! Goddamn that Lula DiStefano. Viola didn't care how important she was. If she could have stood on her own two feet, she would have punched that woman's lights out. The men who had carried Viola jumped down off the stage.

"Take me too," she called to them, but they ignored her and gave chase to the first bottle-thrower.

Viola saw them ripple through the crowd, like wind through weeds, as the offender fled and the men followed. Eventually, Viola lost sight of the perpetrator. Instead, she saw Keita Ali. He was waving to her and pointing. *Look out*, he seemed to be telling her. Others were making similar gestures. "*Look out!*" a thousand people were calling now. Suddenly, a volley of bottles, cans and rocks bore down on her. Viola dove out of her wheelchair and crawled head-first down the steps.

VIOLA'S WHEELCHAIR REMAINED ON THE PLATFORM. JOHN kept his video camera rolling. The images wouldn't be worth much, because he was getting shoved and pushed in the crowd, but he was certainly catching some good sound effects. He'd captured Lula challenging Prime Minister Wellington to come out and speak to the crowd. He'd got some angry male voice screaming obscenities at Viola after she was introduced to the crowd. He got voices warning, "*Look out, look out!*" He caught an angry man yelling through his own megaphone.

And now there was the sound of a young man beside him, saying, "No, John, don't film me, please, just come this way. This is no place for a boy to be."

John spoke into the camera. "That was Keita Ali, the runner, trying to steer yours truly away from the riot. We are going to try to escape now. We are trying to get to the perimeter of the crowd."

Whistles blew. Police yelled through their own megaphones: "*Disperse. This is the police. If you do not leave, you will face arrest.*" The last sound that John captured, before he was knocked to the ground, was Lula.

"Mr. Prime Minister, we are waiting for you. But our followers cannot wait any longer. They all long to know what is in our lost and found from the Bombay Booty in AfricTown. The first item is a piece of official government identification belonging to—"

John struggled back up. Police officers had rushed the stage. And behind him, hundreds more uniformed men had blocked the park exits.

BLINDS COVERED ALL THE WINDOWS, IN CASE THE DEMONSTRAtors in Ruddings Park had it in their minds to spy on them with binoculars. And since everyone knew the prime minister's office was on the fourth floor, it was Geoffrey's idea to set up a war room on the eighth. They would have an even better view of the demonstration below, and they were less likely to be spotted peering through the blinds.

Geoffrey had three different cellphones going. He had a line to the Clarkson police chief, so that they could discuss containment. And although it was highly unlikely that the crowd would storm the Freedom Building, there were five hundred soldiers on standby inside the Parliament Building just across the street. Geoffrey also had a line to their chief plant in the demonstration, Saunders, whose job was to beat up on white people—also plants—in the demonstration. In case things got nasty, they would need photos of blacks attacking whites to justify the police intervention. Geoffrey could stage a chess match like nobody's business.

"Let's send Rocco out to address the crowd," the prime minister said. "We should appear calm and accessible."

"There's nothing for him to say, Bossman," Geoffrey said. "He's going to stand out there and make a fool of himself."

"He's a fool anyway," the PM said.

"Yes, but if he goes out there and makes an ass of himself, people could really get riled up. He might have trouble getting out of there. He could get hurt. Or the officers escorting him might get hurt. Then we would have a major incident. Not worth the risk."

"I don't like this. We look indecisive."

There was a knock on the door. Geoffrey opened it to Rocco Calder in his gym wear.

"Out for your constitutional?" the prime minister asked.

"I was running in the park, saw the disturbance and thought I would come right to the office."

Geoffrey snickered.

Rocco wanted to call him a half-pint mama's boy, but instead, he walked up to stand beside the prime minister, body-checking Geoffrey on his way. Just a little shoulder, to throw the jerk off balance. The prime minister didn't even notice. He was busy peering out the blinds.

"Mr. Prime Minister, I think I should go down there."

"And do what?"

"Give a statement. Tell them that we are considering their requests and will have a response in a matter of days."

"You can't go down there, Rocco."

"Why not?"

"It's not safe," the prime minister said.

"Sir," Geoffrey broke in. "There it is! A projectile. Straight down there, to your right. Time to unleash the first wave."

"Get the police chief on the line," the PM said.

"I've got his chief of staff right here," Geoffrey said, pointing to the cellphone.

"Tell them it's time to break up the demonstration. Lula claims to have the ID of government officials. That would constitute stolen property. Arrest the bastards, search them and confiscate their goods."

"Sir," Rocco said, "there's no need to crack heads over this. I'm sure we can contain this and disperse the crowd with a promise to investigate."

"Too late," Geoffrey chirped again, "heads are already cracking."

BASTARDS. CANDACE HAD PREDICTED IT. HER RADIO CRACKLED. Officers were instructed to hold their ground and to arrest anyone seen throwing rocks, speaking into a megaphone or attempting to run away. She saw children, women and men running as the police pressed in. She saw the instigators drop their rocks and cans and attempt to blend in with the crowd.

She spotted Keita running nearby with two officers in pursuit. She silently wished him luck. But her partner, Devlin James, a smartass cocky bastard who was good on his horse, gave chase and caught up to Keita. Devlin whacked him on the shoulder and jumped down to distribute his own brand of justice. By the time Candace reached them, Devlin had zip-cuffed Keita and was demanding ID. Good thing she outranked him.

"Let him go, Devlin."

"He was fleeing."

"He threw nothing. He caused no harm. And I know him. He's a good sort. A marathoner. Let him go."

"I'm taking him in."

"Cut through those zip-cuffs and let him go, and that's an order."

"Cut him free yourself," Devlin said and rode away. She could see that she had made a permanent enemy of him, pulling rank in front of a civilian. Some guys couldn't take being outranked by a woman.

Candace got down from her horse. With her Swiss Army knife, she cut through the zip-cuffs.

335

"I told you to get out of here."

"I was trying to do that."

"Well, try harder. But stay away from Freedom Gates. That's where the police are concentrated."

"Thank you."

"Call me!"

He ran. She watched, and nobody caught him this time.

CHAPTER THIRTY-FIVE

G RAEME WELLINGTON COULD NOT MEET LULA AT the Bombay Booty. Or in the Prime Minister's Office. He suggested that they meet in the back of his limo, but she said that a black driver could not be trusted just because he said "yes sir, no sir." She told him to meet her at Patty's Doughnuts in downtown Clarkson.

He wore shades, although he knew that if anybody stopped to look, his tall frame would give him away. She wore tinted glasses and a sun hat that made it hard to look into her eyes unless you got close and stared. And nobody would. There was something about her that people didn't mess with. It wasn't that she was as unflinching as a rugby winger scoring a try. It wasn't that she was as dark as night, and as hard to read. It wasn't her voice, which rang out like a military commander's. It was, as Graeme himself had said thirty years earlier, something to do with her aura.

He hadn't been invited to enjoy that aura since she was young and beautiful and on the verge of creating an enduring business in AfricTown. Even when Lula drew him near, something about her exuded, *I dig you, baby, but if you double-cross me, I'll tear you apart.*

She was one of the only people who knew. And maybe the only living person. His parents had died long ago, and he had no siblings, and he had long ago cut off most ties to his past. He got by, saying that he spent a lot of time in the sun, playing rugby and tennis and all that, and that there were Italians in the family. Swarthy, he would say, to anyone who asked. But long ago the media had stopped asking about his dark good looks. He had, after all, been in politics a long time. Grooming himself for office during decades in opposition. Even his own wife did not know.

Certainly, the rugby team that he had led to the world championships didn't know. Three decades earlier, it was still a whites-only team. No mulattoes, quadroons or octoroons. He had passed over to the other side, and with flying colours.

Now Lula stirred her tea and said, "Graeme, I can't have this."

"We'll come to an arrangement," he said. "We always have before."

"You're all up in my business, raiding for real and arresting my own people."

"Let's just map out a peace treaty."

"We better. Because you, Mr. Prime Minister, have as much to lose as I do."

"I'm asking you to stop demonstrating."

"And I'm asking you to stop raiding AfricTown. And I want goddamn electricity and water services, right to the south end. You keep denying us, and it will come right back in your face. Have you no shame?"

"None of that," he said. "We agreed."

"Okay. No more comments about your shame, wherever it is buried."

"I mean it, Lula. I will walk out of here and send raid after raid, and your business will be shut down."

"Political suicide," she said. "I would tell the world where you've been at night."

"Let's not get personal."

"You always say that. It *is* personal for me, Graeme."

"If I call off all raids and commit to electricity and water services over, say, the next two years—"

"Two years?"

"Can't do these things overnight, Lula. Anyway, if I commit

to that, I need some commitments from you. First, I need my ID back."

"I might be able to help with that."

"And I need the USB back."

"What USB?"

"Don't give me that poker look," he said. "I know you, Lula. I know how you lie."

"Of all the men I took into my bed, you're the only one I regret," she said.

"You didn't mind it at the time," he said.

"You had the equipment," she said, "and you had some decent moves—not bad for an octoroon."

He raised a finger to his lips, his expression firm. "One more word, and I'm out of here."

"You can threaten all you want, but I know you're not going to walk out that door till we've settled up," she said.

"Not one more word," he said.

"Fine, fine. Lay it on me, white boy."

He stood up to leave. She grabbed his hand and pulled him down. "Okay already."

"I want the USB, and you know what the hell I mean. I heard about it, and my source is good."

"Saunders!" she said. "His days are numbered."

"I want it, and I know who has it."

Lula sat back and cracked her fingers. "And who, pray tell, is that?"

"The Roger Bannister fellow."

"The runner," Lula said, with a sudden smile. "Keita. You know him?"

"I do now. Why has every Freedom Statonian heard of this Illegal? Why is he not on a plane out of this country?"

She smiled and said nothing.

"I want the USB," he repeated, "and I want him too."

"Can't give him to you quite yet," Lula said.

"You've given me others, and we've paid you dearly. What's the problem?"

"Not yet, I said."

"Non-negotiable," he said.

"He has my protection until the Clarkson Ten-Miler."

"The what?"

"He has a big race he has to run. June 21. Right in Clarkson. For a road race, it's the highest purse in Freedom State."

"What's the payout?" he asked.

"Twenty-five thousand dollars to win. Fifteen for second. And five for third."

"Peanuts."

"Not if you're a refugee," she said. "After the race on June 21, you're welcome to him."

"What are you advocating, Miss Support the Poor and Downtrodden?"

"I want peace again in AfricTown. No more raids. No more bullshit about taxation. No more deportations. I don't care where you catch your other Illegals, but leave me alone in my own territory. And I need that electricity and water. I'm giving you two years. If it is not in place before your next election campaign, every citizen in this country is gonna know who yo mamma was."

He stood to leave. "Lula. Always a pleasure. I believe we have an agreement." He shook her hand. "Your skin was so soft, once."

"Yeah, and you knew who you were, once. Was it worth it, Graeme? Are the silk sheets smooth out there in the white man's world?"

"I guess you'll never know."

CHAPTER THIRTY-SIX

VIOLA HILL DID NOT WANT TO BE PART OF ANY pack of journalists and felt best about a news story when she alone was writing it. Still, it offended her that nobody else seemed to care about the death of Yvette Peters. A black sex worker from AfricTown had been deported to Zantoroland, where she died in prison. Out of sight, out of mind. But not for Viola.

"Why should I send you to Zantoroland?" Bolton said. "Airfare, hotels! It's not a page one story."

"So this girl's life and death only matters as a news story if it lands on page one?" Viola said.

"I have a limited travel budget. Why should I eat into it to get a couple of paragraphs that will end up buried on page twenty-three?"

"I want to find out who deported her, who killed her, and why. There had to be some sort of coordination between the governments of Freedom State and Zantoroland. That is a news story, and once I get it, every other media outlet in Freedom State will be chasing it."

"I can give you airfare and two nights at a hotel in Zantoroland."

"I need four nights."

"Three, then. And you'd better file a page one story."

Viola knew that Yoyo Ali had been killed for working on a similar story, and that the government of Zantoroland persecuted other dissidents. For security, she announced her travel plans to every person or group that mattered: the Freedom State embassy in Zantoroland, Immigration Minister Rocco Calder, Amnesty International and PEN International. She told John. And in her car, which was retrofitted for a paraplegic driver, with accelerator and brakes activated by hand controls on the steering wheel, Viola drove to AfricTown to speak with Keita about her trip.

She found him running on the AfricTown Road, with a security car driving ahead of him and hundreds of children scattered along the roadside to cheer him on and offer him water. Viola waited for him to finish his run and then met him at his container.

While Keita untied his shoes, wiped the sweat off his face and drank, Viola told him she was going to travel to Zantoroland.

Keita put his bottle down and looked at her urgently. "Maybe you will get word of my sister. Maybe you can do something to help save her."

"It should shake them up to find out that a journalist from Freedom State is onto her case."

"Or maybe you will be in danger too," he said.

Viola asked for more details on the story Yoyo had been writing at the time of his death.

"All I know is that it had something to do with officials in Freedom State bribing their counterparts in Zantoroland," Keita said. "Go to my house. Look for the teapots on the kitchen shelf. My father kept notes on political stories in the yellow teapot."

"How will I get into the house?"

"Easy. I will give you the key."

The last thing Viola did before travelling to the airport was to use a paint scraper and olive oil to remove the *I dig dykes on wheels* bumper sticker from her wheelchair. Every bit had to disappear before she showed up in Zantoroland.

IT OCCURRED TO VIOLA, AS SHE WAS BEING SERVED TEA AT 32,000 feet, that refugees on an overcrowded fishing boat might take three weeks to travel the distance that she was covering in three hours. Three weeks for the refugees—if they made it at all. Viola wondered how bad it was in Zantoroland for people to risk their lives on those boats. You'd have to be convinced that you would die if you stayed home and had nothing to lose by trying to leave.

Viola had checked the numbers before she flew to Yagwa. According to Amnesty International, the Zantoroland authorities had executed at least twenty dissidents and had incarcerated dozens more in the year 2017 alone. In addition, the government or its mercenaries were killing members of the Faloo business class, and even friends of Faloos among the Kano majority. This had incited even more Zantorolanders to attempt the passage across the Ortiz Sea.

After landing at the Yagwa airport, Viola haggled successfully with a taxi driver and then checked into the Five Stars International Business Hotel. Soon after, she wheeled outside to look for another taxi. She had the name of Yvette Peters' grandmother and the name of her neighbourhood.

On the street, while she waited, a group of eight boys surrounded her.

"Where are you from?"

"Give me money."

"What happened to your legs?"

The boys started patting her stumps, touching her head and asking why she had no hair, and demanding American dollars.

As she wondered how she would get rid of them, a man who looked about twenty years old approached and smacked the boys, cursed at them and sent them running. Viola found herself looking into the clean-shaven, baby face of a man whose irises were so dark that they appeared to merge with his pupils.

"Victor Jones, at your service," he said, shaking her hand. "And what is your name?"

"Viola Hill."

"What does Madam fancy? A visit to the President's Promenade? Lunch Chez Proust? A nice strong Zantoroland man to take you into his private room and give you a little hah hah hah?" With this, Victor shook his hips suggestively.

"Hah hah hah?" Viola said.

"You don't appreciate hah hah hah? Not to worry. What is your fancy?"

"I want to find someone named Henrietta Banks. She's in her late fifties and lives in the Latin Quarter. Can you help me with that?"

"Victor can find anybody," he said. "Twenty dollars, American."

Already he was in the street, hailing her a taxi and berating the driver who pulled over until he reluctantly got out and opened his back door, muttering that there was no room for the lady and her wheelchair.

Viola pivoted into the back seat, grabbed her wheelchair, folded it flat and hauled it in with her.

"Room enough? Let's go."

The taxi driver demanded more money, but Victor launched into another tirade, so Viola got off with a two-dollar fare.

Once they reached the Latin Quarter, and she was sitting in her wheelchair on a potholed street lined with shacks bearing scribbled signs for Shoe Doctor, Witch Man and Crocodile Powder for Male Bone, Viola found herself surrounded by street urchins. Victor had disappeared. He came back a minute later and shooed away the crowd.

Victor pushed Viola along the potholed road—it was soft earth, and hard going, and Viola was pleased that she did not have to wheel herself alone.

She told him that she was a journalist and wanted to interview Mrs. Banks.

"Do you write for a famous newspaper?" he asked.

"The *Clarkson Evening Telegram*," she said.

"The *New York Times*. The *Guardian*. *Le Monde*. *El País*. The *Clarkson Evening Telegram*. One day I, too, hope to write for one of the great newspapers of the world."

"Yeah, right," she said.

"You don't think I am smart enough?"

"The *Telegram*'s not smart enough for you," she said. "Get a job at one of the other papers you mentioned. And put in a good word for me."

"Henrietta Banks lives on Snailpath Road."

"You know her?" she asked.

"Everyone knows Mrs. Henrietta," Victor said. "You want to ask about her granddaughter, right?"

Viola whipped out her notepad, but it was hard writing during the bumpy ride. She taped him instead. "You have heard of Yvette Peters?"

"All in Zantoroland have heard about her. Deported. Killed. We saw it online. Everybody goes to the Amnesty International website to find out about people getting killed in Zantoroland. We have a great, great country. Beautiful mountains. Fast runners. Kind citizens. But our government is corrupt—it kills people," he said.

"Who is being killed?"

"Returnees, who are refugees who got sent back here. Dissidents. And Faloos and their sympathizers."

"Is that why so many people are trying to leave in fishing boats?"

"Of course. I would leave too, but I have my brothers and sisters. And my grandmother. If I left, nobody would be here to look after them."

Within a few minutes, they arrived at a wooden shack with a corrugated tin roof. The thin metal door hung on weak hinges.

"This is where she lives," Victor said. "Shall I come in?"

"No, but meet me when I am done."

"I shall be waiting," he said.

HENRIETTA BANKS LOOKED WORLD-WEARY AND WISE, BUT she said she was only fifty-two. She pushed Viola's chair into her house and said that she must be a very good journalist indeed.

Why was that? Viola said.

Because, Henrietta said, she was the first one to find her. And also, Viola was black and in a wheelchair, but still she had a good job writing for a newspaper in Freedom State.

Viola smiled.

"Would you like to see a picture of Yvette?" Henrietta asked.

"Yes."

Viola spent an hour with the grandmother and then travelled with Victor to Keita's house. She gave him the key. He seemed nervous, unlocking the door for her.

"This is the house of the slain journalist," Victor said.

"How did you know?" Viola asked.

"Yagwa is a small city," Victor said, "and he was well-known."

They entered the bungalow.

"Small house," Viola said. "One room with a kitchen."

"It's good for Zantoroland. Clean. Nice beds. Pots and pans. Good people lived here. You can tell."

Viola looked at the two typewriters on Yoyo's desk, the family photo showing Keita and Charity at about eight and nine years old, the old running shoes arranged in a neat line under Keita's bed, and the kitchen shelf with all the teapots.

"Hand me the yellow teapot, Victor," Viola said.

She took it from his hands, placed it on her lap and fished inside. She came up with folded notes, which she opened and scanned. Yoyo had a source. He'd given him, or her, a code name: Twain. Yoyo's notes said Twain had given him information on payment for the most recent batch of dissident refugees to be removed from Freedom State and deported back to Zantoroland: for eleven refugees sent back in February, twenty-two thousand U.S. dollars were carried by a mule from Freedom State to Zantoroland and delivered to George Maxwell in the Ministry of Citizenship. Of the eleven, four were red-caned and seven killed. Twain said Zantoroland enlisted spies on the ground in Freedom State to find out where refugees were hiding. The only ones Zantoroland really wanted back were the dissidents.

Viola considered stuffing the papers into her bag. But if she were caught, she could be in trouble. So she read the key details quickly into her tape recorder.

Victor interrupted her. He had seen a man looking in the window. What man? she asked. He was gone now, Victor said. But she feared that they had been followed. The taxi driver who had promised to wait was also gone. Viola and Victor wheeled and walked together to the Fountain of Independence and the Pâtisserie Chez Proust before they saw a taxi.

"It is a beautiful fountain," Viola said.

"Nobody touches it or goes near," Victor said, "because this is where the dead are left. After Yoyo Ali died, people began calling it the Fountain of Blood."

Viola shuddered. She bought a madeleine and tea for Victor and herself at Chez Proust, paid him and tipped him extra, and said goodbye. Then she took a taxi to her hotel and began writing.

The story, along with her photo of the bereaved grandmother, ran the next day on page one of the *Telegram*.

GRANDMOTHER NEVER MET HER MURDERED
GRANDDAUGHTER

Henrietta Banks says she would rather have died than learn that her seventeen-year-old granddaughter died in prison in Zantoroland a day after being deported from Freedom State.

Banks, 52, who lives alone in a one-room shack in the Latin Quarter of Yagwa, Zantoroland, never saw her granddaughter until her body turned up at the Fountain of Independence in Yagwa. The victim was naked and had a bracelet on her wrist iden-tifying her: Yvette Peters. Prostitute. Belongs to Henrietta Banks, Latin Quarter. *Banks knew only from photos what her granddaughter looked like. Peters was the only child of Banks' only daughter, who lives in Freedom State but with whom Banks has lost touch.*

347

Banks said that Peters was born and raised in Freedom State and had never set foot outside the country until she was deported to Zantoroland. After Peters died, Banks said, neighbours carried the girl's body to Banks' home. She had been garroted, which, according to Amnesty International, is a common method used in Zantoroland to kill prisoners and intimidate their families and acquaintances.

Banks buried her granddaughter in a tiny plot of land behind her home.

"How dare they write that awful word on her wrist," Banks said. "I was so hurt, so hurt, so hurt. Even if it was true, did she deserve to die in prison and be dumped like a criminal in the square? The girl was seventeen years old. If she sold her body to get by, somebody made her do it. Why did Freedom State hate her? Why did they deport her? And why did they kill her here? People are afraid to talk in Zantoroland when these things happen. But I am not afraid. I am too old for fear. If it is true that my granddaughter was a prostitute, who was the last man she saw in Freedom State? What does he know about her?"

The Zantoroland Office of the Attorney General did not return Banks' telephone calls. This reporter was escorted from the premises when she showed up at the building—nicknamed the Pink Palace, and widely reputed to be a place where political prisoners are tortured—where the attorney general, the minister of citizenship and other cabinet ministers work.

Freedom State Immigration Minister Rocco Calder declined comment other than to say that he would "look into the matter" and to insist that he never issued or signed a deportation order for Yvette Peters.

GRAEME WELLINGTON WAS PANICKING NOW. HIS PEOPLE had expended a great deal of effort and money to set up the return of significant numbers of Zantoroland refugees. It was particularly gratifying to turn them around and send them back home before they'd even landed in Freedom State and begun sucking life out of the economy. But all this nonsense over Yvette Peters was threatening the whole operation. If Graeme's Zantoroland contacts got nervous, or if the world press cottoned on to this story, there could be trouble.

And now, what the hell, that disabled dyke was writing about the story as if her own sister had died.

In Freedom State, things had to be done a certain way. But Viola Hill had already taken herself out of the picture by going off to Zantoroland. Why not, Geoffrey said, keep her out of the picture?

Graeme put in a call to his people.

THE MORNING AFTER SHE VISITED HENRIETTA BANKS AND was turned away from the Pink Palace—they were rough with her and booted her off the premises—Viola received one of the most surprising emails of her life. It was from Anton Hamm, and it was a confession.

He said he had been carrying cash bribes to Zantoroland for a man named Saunders, who had connections high up in the Freedom State government. In return, Zantoroland officials provided the names of Zantorolanders hiding illegally in Freedom State. Hamm said he was paid and promised a break on his taxes in exchange for carrying this information back to Saunders in Freedom State. Saunders was a psycho who worked under the table for the federal government and who had recently shot Hamm in the hand. Hamm wanted out. He planned to tell everything to Immigration Minister Rocco Calder, whom he had originally suspected of masterminding the arrangement, but who, he now knew, could not possibly be responsible. Anyway, in case something went ape-shit wrong, Hamm wanted Viola to have the goods. There. Was she satisfied? She was free to quote him.

From her hotel room, Viola called Mahatma Grafton at his desk at the *New York Times*. He confirmed that Yoyo had been on to a story when he was killed. He had found something out about an exchange of money and refugees between Freedom State and Zantoroland. Yoyo had been circumspect about it. He said he would have to get himself and his son out of the country before he could publish. Yoyo had believed he could sell the story to the *New York Times* and that this would boost his career enough to allow him to continue as a journalist overseas.

"Did his son, Keita, get out of the country?" Grafton asked.

"Yes," Viola replied, "he did." But she didn't want to say anything more.

"Good," Grafton said.

Viola said that in Yoyo's notes, she had seen mention of a man named George Maxwell in the Zantoroland government. Maybe he would talk to her.

"I wouldn't do that," Grafton said. "If I were you, I would get on the first plane out of Zantoroland. The government does not take kindly to journalists."

"Well, I'm here now," Viola said. "What are they going to do? I'm a citizen of Freedom State."

"My advice is to leave now."

Viola thanked him and said she would be in touch. She hung up the phone. She was nervous. She had brought a second cellphone—a tiny model for travellers. She double-checked that it was fully charged and that all her emergency numbers were grouped together for speed-texting, and then she securely attached five one-hundred-dollar U.S. bills to it by rubber band.

All was well. All was together. She put the miniature cellphone and money in a ziplocked bag and shoved it inside a secret pocket she had sewn inside her shirt.

Viola was still arranging her notes and figuring out what exactly to ask George Maxwell when two men burst into her room. One of them showed Viola a gun with a silencer and said he would kill her then and there if so much as a peep came out of her mouth. Understood? She nodded.

As she wheeled out of the room, they followed, giving her orders. They took the elevator down and crossed the lobby to the outside. There they opened the back door of a black sedan. She hoisted herself into the vehicle, hauled her wheelchair in after her and waited for them to close the door.

After a short drive, they parked at the Pink Palace and told her to get out. There were six steps leading up to the main entrance. They made her go up the stairs on her own, ass on one step and then on the next, dragging the wheelchair with her. She didn't want to show the fuckers that she cared or was intimidated or was wondering if she was about to die.

She was put in a room with a man in a military uniform, a gun prominently on his hip.

"Are you taking me to see George Maxwell?" she asked.

He laughed and said any number of people working in the Pink Palace might be going by the name George Maxwell. It was the name given to any operative working behind the scenes on behalf of the government.

She was shocked but tried not to show it.

The guard turned and left her alone in the room, locking the door behind him. Moments later, he returned, took her purse and left again. Damn. It looked like Mahatma Grafton was right. She should have taken the first plane out. But she was so damn close. Viola would either get her story or die trying.

AFTER HOURS OF WAITING, VIOLA BEGAN TO SHOUT AND demand to be taken to a toilet. Nobody came. Another hour or so went by, and she heard men outside her room. The door opened. A young, uniformed soldier came in and took her to a bathroom. Viola was allowed to relieve herself while he waited outside the partially closed door. She removed the ziplocked bag from the pocket inside her shirt, flipped open her cellphone and texted Bolton: *Imprisoned at Pink Palace in Yagwa.* She hit send but could not get any reception. She turned off the phone and put it back into her shirt.

The soldier was talking with someone in the corridor, so Viola stayed longer in the bathroom to listen.

"Boss gets back tomorrow. Just hold her till then."

"Let's put her in with the other one, then, until we know what to do."

They took Viola to a holding cell. The walls were bare. Toilet with no seat, and sink in the corner. Window above. One single mattress, no sheets, no pillow, and on it sat a young woman. She was black, in her mid-twenties, dishevelled, and she had a black eye, with a cut above it still oozing blood.

The woman saw Viola entering in her wheelchair.

"It will be a tight fit," the woman said.

"I'll make do," Viola said. She climbed down to the floor, folded up her chair, pushed it against the wall, crawled over on hands and bum, and hoisted herself up to sit beside the woman on the mattress. "It goes where I go."

"Who are you?" the woman said.

"Viola Hill, and I know who you are."

"I doubt that."

"How about this: Charity Ali. Harvard student. Twenty-five years old. Daughter of Yoyo, the journalist, and I'm sorry for your loss, and brother of Keita, the marathoner, currently illegal in Freedom State. Keita, by the way, is a friend and gave me the key to your house. I may have been arrested because someone saw me reading the notes your father had kept hidden in the yellow teapot on the kitchen shelf."

Charity stared at Viola. "How do you know—?"

"Tell you in a minute. Is there cell service in this building?"

"How would I know? I've got nothing but the clothes on my back and bruises up and down my body."

Viola tried to use the phone again, but still she failed to find a signal. She turned it off to save the battery.

"Your brother has told me about you, so we might as well be friends," Viola said. She reached out with her hand.

Charity's face softened. She let out a faint sob and leaned over to throw her arms around Viola.

IN THE MORNING, THE CELL DOOR FLEW OPEN. A YOUNG MAN stood with a much older official who was dressed in a suit. He was massively rotund, and he seemed in charge.

"Why are they together?" the man in the suit said.

"We thought it might be best. Keeping the two women together. Apart from the men."

The older man smacked his junior on the head. "Fool! Move the disabled one, now. Bring her to my office."

Minutes later, Viola sat in her wheelchair in front of a fine mahogany desk.

"Are you George?" she asked.

"You may call me Mr. Maxwell, if it gives you comfort to put a name to a face. Not that it matters."

He asked all the expected questions. Name, nationality, place of employment. She answered truthfully. They probably knew the answers anyway. Viola wondered if Bolton would do something when he noticed that she had gone missing. If he noticed.

"Why have you brought me here?" she said, interrupting the interrogation.

"You were spying on our government. You have no visa to work in this country."

"I am not a spy. I am a journalist. And I was not being paid by anyone in your country. I do what journalists do. We go places. We travel. We write about what we see. This is not called spying, where I come from."

"Here it is called spying, and that in itself merits capital punishment."

"You're kidding."

353

He stood up, moved around the desk, bent over and looked her in the eyes. "How does it feel, knowing you will soon die?"

His words shocked her momentarily into silence. "Since you are so decided on this course of action," she said, "why don't you tell me what the hell is going on in this country? Why did you kill Yoyo Ali?"

"For the same reason that we are going to kill you," he said. "You ask too many questions."

"So you have nothing to lose by telling me what he found out."

"True! He found out about certain commercial arrangements we have been solidifying with Freedom State."

"Which are?"

"We tell them which refugees we want back. Exiles. Dissidents. We know where they are in Freedom State. We are not stupid. We monitor these things. We tell them where to find these criminals—"

"Criminals?"

"That's right. It is a criminal offence to leave Zantoroland without permission. So we explain where to find these criminals, and the good people of Freedom State send them back to us. And they pay us, because we need hard currency and they need our goodwill."

"What's in it for Freedom State?" she asked.

"In exchange for the dissidents and the cash, we allow them to send some boatloads of refugees back home. Here. Where they came from."

"You're shitting me," she said.

"People in Freedom State are rich, but they are so vulgar," he said.

"You're calling *me* vulgar? Why have you kidnapped Charity Ali? What's in it for you?"

"Fifteen thousand dollars, due in just a few days."

"What's so special about fifteen thousand?"

"It adds up. Here and there, a president can amass a healthy fund through such practices."

"You kidnap and ransom for the president's pleasure?" Viola said.

"The Faloos ruled this country for seventy-five years," Maxwell said, "and now it's our turn to eat."

DAYS WENT BY. HOW LONG WOULD IT BE BEFORE BOLTON asked questions? If she ever got out of here, things would change at the newspaper. She would move up or she would move out. Viola tried to focus on the story she would write, and on the story that Yoyo had been hoping to publish, during the days upon days of eating bread, water and lukewarm noodles.

In her cell, there was no way of telling if it was day or night. Every day, she tried to make conversation with the woman who brought her food. Yes, Viola was indeed in the Pink Palace. Yes, the woman in the other cell was still alive. And finally, yes, today it was June 20. Viola knew that Keita's big race was the next day. Would he win? Wire the money to Zantoroland? Would the authorities here release Charity? And what would happen to Viola? Would she be freed too? With every hour that passed, it seemed less likely.

The next day, Viola asked a young guard to let Charity and her sit out on a balcony to get some air. She promised him a hundred dollars American. He told her to speak to him when she had the money. She asked him to come back in an hour. When she was alone, she pulled the ziplocked bag from the secret pocket in her shirt. She removed one of the five hundred-dollar bills and put the rest back.

VIOLA SAT ON THE BALCONY WITH CHARITY, LOOKING NORTH at the Ortiz Sea. If she could have seen for hundreds of kilometres, she would have spotted a dozen or more fishing boats at sea, carrying refugees north. If she could have seen more than a thousand kilometres, there would be Freedom State. The sunlight burned her eyes.

"Keep a lookout for anyone coming from inside," Viola said. She faced the sea and held the cellphone close to her body. Finally, she

LAWRENCE HILL

had a signal. She had Amnesty International, PEN International, the Freedom State consulate in Zantoroland, Mahatma Grafton, Mike Bolton, Minister Calder and Calder's assistant June Hawkins all lined up on group speed-text. She sent a message to all of them.

Imprisoned in Pink Palace in Yagwa, Zantoroland, with Charity Ali, daughter of slain journalist Yoyo Ali. Lives threatened. Please help.

CHAPTER THIRTY-SEVEN

OVER AND OVER, JOHN EMAILED HER. AND called her work number. He even called her editor, Mike Bolton, and found out that she had not returned from Zantoroland. Viola was missing in action.

Bolton ran an article on the front page of the *Telegram* about his valued reporter disappearing. But there was no word from any kidnappers.

Viola was John's competition, but she had also become his friend and co-conspirator.

John was quite sure that with his information and hers, they could produce a killer work of journalism. He had a plan for how they could both benefit. The minister had arranged to see Keita. In his office. Before noon on June 21. There was an understanding. Keita was to bring the USB in exchange for a temporary permit. John wanted to be there. He wanted Viola to be there too. Together, they could assemble the pieces of this big story. But Viola was nowhere to be found.

MITCH HAD RECEIVED HIS INSTRUCTIONS FROM IVERNIA, who had received hers in a note that Candace delivered from Keita. Ivernia had made arrangements with her bank. The paperwork was in place. If Keita won or placed second in the Clarkson Ten-Miler on June 21, Mitch would issue the cheque to "Keita Ali, payable to Ivernia Beech" and accompany Ivernia to the bank, where she would sign the cheque on Keita's behalf and wire fifteen thousand dollars immediately to a Zantoroland bank account registered under the name George Maxwell.

CHAPTER THIRTY-EIGHT

I NEED TO SPEAK TO THE MINISTER."

June Hawkins had been the immigration minister's executive secretary for only two years, and in that time she had turned away hundreds of people.

"I'm sorry," June said, "but the minister is not available."

He leaned over her desk. If he wanted to kill her, he could wring her neck on the spot.

"It's important," he said. "Vitally important." He had a huge bandage on his left hand.

"I could schedule you in next week," June said.

"No time. Please give him this"—he passed her a letter—"and tell him that Anton Hamm will be back to see him soon."

June opened it, as she did all the minister's correspondence.

Dear Minister Calder,

I'm sorry about threatening you. I was wrong. It wasn't you. I have been screwed now over and over by someone dealing with deportations. Man named Saunders has been paying me to . . .

June skipped over the details. Minister Calder could absorb them later. But her eyes were drawn to the last part of the letter.

. . . I want out. Can't do this anymore. Motherfucker shot me up, and I can't handle it. I didn't pay my taxes, and I'm screwed but I don't care. You need to know what is going on right under your nose. Tell Saunders and his people to leave me alone. I hope you arrest all those bastards.

June walked into Rocco's office and dropped the letter into his inbox. As she turned to leave, her pen slipped out of her hand. She stooped to retrieve it and saw, attached to the undersurface of the minister's desk, a strange object. Half the length of her index finger. As thin as a pencil. Hard plastic shell. Wires inside.

It was the first time she'd seen one, but June was quite sure it was an electronic listening device.

CHAPTER THIRTY-NINE

Rocco Calder took a taxi to the Clarkson Academy for the Gifted. The century-old brick building was located on the University of Clarkson campus and was world-renowned. If you graduated with good marks from the Academy, the rest of your life was set. Or so it was said.

Rocco noticed the headmistress's office stank of Limburger cheese.

"Can I help you?" a receptionist said. Middle-aged. Grey-haired. Little makeup. Brown bag on her desk. Thirty thousand bucks a year, max.

"I'd like to have a word with John Falconer," Rocco said.

"I'm afraid he's in class, sir."

"It's urgent."

"Are you his father?"

Rocco hesitated. "No, I'm—"

The headmistress came out of her office. She was suave, attractive, mid-thirties, dressed in a black suit, with red pumps and red lipstick. Good looking, and probably brainy too. He wondered if she had voted for the Family Party. In the last election, the party had captured more votes than expected from young, professional women.

"Why hello, Minister Calder, I'm Brenda Tolmer. And to what do we owe the honour?"

"I'd like a word with one of your students, John Falconer, please."

"Is there a problem?"

"No. None. He has been, um, interviewing me recently, and I need to make an important correction."

"Highly impressive that one of our Grade 9 students got to you," the headmistress said. "He must have been persuasive."

"Yes."

"We've been finding him, if I may say so, a wee bit distracted lately."

"How so?" Rocco asked.

"Head in the clouds. Seems constantly to be reviewing film in his video camera. We'd hate to see him get off track. Kid's as smart as a whip, considering his background." She stepped in a little closer. "First student we've ever had from AfricTown. Full scholarship too."

"He definitely has potential. And so, may I have a word with him?"

"Let me page him."

THEY MET IN THE OFFICE OF THE VICE-HEADMASTER, WHO left the room but kept the door open.

"Just checking to see if you really study here," Rocco said.

The boy smiled. "So what brings you here? Do you want to see my private bathroom and rowing machine?"

"Very funny."

John brought out his video camera.

"No," Rocco said. "Not this time. No taping, nothing."

John stretched his feet out on the couch. "Okay, then. What's up, bro?"

"I have reason to believe that my office is being bugged. I have no doubt who is behind this. And I need your help."

The boy was paying attention now. He liked to be asked to help.

"The PM and his sidekick will know, thanks to their bug, that I plan to meet Keita Ali on June 21. And they've been asking me about him. Repeatedly."

"They'll try to deport him straight away."

"If Keita gives me what is promised, I will give him a temporary residence permit allowing him to stay here while applying for refugee status."

"Still seems dangerous," John said.

"It's more dangerous if he does not come to get it."

"So, where do I fit in?"

"The PM will turn up at the meeting, I know it. Do you think you could videotape the whole thing? In a . . . clandestine manner?"

"Now you're talking."

CHAPTER FORTY

MILE 1. SEVEN RUNNERS IN THE LEAD PACK. Keita was tucked in at the very back of the group. It was a windy day, and he didn't want to do any more work than necessary. They'd covered the first mile in 4:34. Keita hoped that nobody picked up the pace. It was too fast to maintain. There were two Zantorolanders, three Kenyans, Billy Deeds—the lone white guy from Freedom State—and Keita.

Deeds was full of bravado. "Come on, you pussies," he shouted. "Don't tell me this is the best you got. Put on a show for Roger Bannister."

Keita ignored the taunt. True, Deeds had beaten him in the half-marathon because Keita passed out. But now the problem was under control, and Deeds was the least of his concerns. Just looking at the way he ran, Keita was sure Deeds did not have more than five more miles in him at that pace. 4:34 was fast.

Keita had tested his blood early in the morning, and again two hours after eating and one more time right before the race. Each time, his glucose levels were normal. DeNorval had been coaching him well about how to manage diabetes. DeNorval had also told him to drink fluids with electrolytes and carbohydrates at the race's five-mile mark. A low blood sugar level, DeNorval warned, would feel even worse than a high one. But the latter was unlikely, now that he was injecting twenty units of insulin a day.

Keita's legs felt loose and easy. He hoped they stayed that way until the seven-mile point. After that, it would be pure guts. Twenty-five thousand dollars for winning, and an extra five thousand for breaking the course record of 46:04. That's what he needed. Placing second would be almost as good, because it came with fifteen thousand.

Mile 2. 9:13. He could hear Deeds, whose breathing was already laboured. That was a good sign. The three Kenyans ran in a tight bunch at the front. Keita still sat at the back of the pack. Hamm waited a little way past the mile 2 marker. Keita noticed that he had a huge bandage on his left hand.

"Run hard," Hamm shouted.

"Nice to have fans," one of the Zantorolander runners mumbled to Keita.

"I take all the love I can get," Keita said.

"The guy's fixated on you," the runner said, "but he tells me he is quitting."

"Quitting?"

"Getting out of the business. After this race."

Keita glanced at the name on the runner's bib: *Moses Patterson.* "You in his stable?"

"Yup," Moses said.

"Your first race for him?" Keita said.

"First and last."

Mile 3. Mitch, on the back of a police motorcycle and carrying a loudspeaker, pulled even with the runners. "Gentlemen, a reminder that at mile five, you will turn 180 degrees, keeping the orange cones to your left. There is to be no pushing or shoving. If you break the rules, you will be disqualified."

Keita knew the rules. Mitch was not allowed to single out any particular runner for encouragement or to offer advice. Keita thought about the USB stick strapped to a tiny belt at the small of his back. He barely felt it.

Moses noticed, though. "Is that thing a heart monitor?"

"No," Keita said.

"What is it, then?"

"Makes me run faster," Keita said. He accelerated, stepping it up to a 4:20-mile pace for just over a minute. Moses fell off the pace. So did two of the Kenyans. That told Keita that Kenya had not sent its best runners to the race. Not by a long shot. A good thing or he'd need to keep up this quicker pace for the whole race.

Surprisingly, Deeds stayed with him. So did the other Zantorolander. With the remaining Kenyan and Keita, that left four in the lead pack.

He had told Maxwell yesterday, by email, that he would send the money today. He had asked for a reassurance that his sister was still alive: a photo of her that showed the date. And the photo came back: a grainy shot of his sister, with a blackened eye and a cut on her forehead, holding up a sheet of paper that said *June 20, 2018.* Maxwell added, by way of a P.S., that Charity had met a certain friend of his recently.

Mile 4. 18:24. Exactly the pace that Keita would need to run the fastest ten miles of his life. Lula DiStefano stood by the side of the road near the four-mile marker, with a personal assistant and a man to hold her purse. She smiled, but her smile was not one that suggested she was proud to see him racing. It was a smile that told him he had run out of places to hide.

At mile 5, the clock read 23:01. A hundred children from AfricTown had come out and were chanting: "*Champion of AfricTown! Run those boys into the ground!*"

Many children had come up to him in the past few weeks, when he was running on AfricTown Road.

"Mr. Keita, Mr. Keita, let us watch you run."

"You are seeing me run now," he would reply.

"We want to see you run properly. In a race. Win for us, Mr. Keita. Run those other men into the ground! You are the champion of AfricTown!"

Keita grabbed a sports drink from the refreshment table and forced down a few sips, spilling most of it on his shirt. It didn't matter if his shirt got soaked: the USB stick on his back was wrapped in plastic. Children tried to run alongside the pack, sprinting to keep up with the racers. No child was able to stay with them for more than ten seconds.

Keita would have to wear down the rest of the field. One of the runners might be much stronger than he was, and he had to find out. But would there be more than one? The only way was to surge again and see who followed. A minute after the five-mile marker, Keita threw down the gauntlet. He brought the pace up to 4:25-mile speed. And then, for about an eighth of a mile, 4:20 speed. The fourth-place fellow dropped back. Deeds stayed right with him, as did the Kenyan, so Keita settled back into a 4:36-mile pace. He had to test this out. He could not afford to finish third. He imagined his sister's voice: *You could save my life if you ran a little faster!* Within a minute of easing off, he sped up again, increasing his speed to a 4:20 pace. He heard the Kenyan breathing heavily, so he decided to keep it up for a quarter-mile. The Kenyan finally cracked and fell back, and Keita continued the fast pace for yet another eighth of a mile. Deeds was still on his shoulder. Keita slowed back down to 4:36.

"Is that all you got?" Deeds said.

Keita said nothing but made sure that he kept pushing the pace.

They hit mile 6 and the clock read 27:35.

A group of police motorcycles pulled up behind the leaders, came even with them and advanced just a few metres ahead. Keita's feet almost collided with their tires. One of the uniformed men kept looking back at him. Keita heard the police radio crackle.

"Runner identified," came a voice from the radio.

"Shall I make the arrest?" the officer asked.

Another motorcycle pulled up beside the police. Keita could hear Mitch's voice.

"No! Do not interfere with the runners. They will be at the finish line in less than twenty minutes. Please. Speak to your commanding officer. Your business can wait!"

More voices crackled, and then the cop who had been staring at him sped ahead and away.

"Jail time for Roger, is it?" Deeds was mouthing off again.

Keita believed he could outrun Deeds. But he didn't want to pull away from him too soon. If he were alone in the lead, it might be easier for an overexcited police officer to jump him. Running beside Deeds gave Keita a measure of protection.

"While you give interviews to dyke reporters, I train on the track, buddy-boy. So why don't you just go back home?"

Keita had no breath for singing now, and Deeds knew it. Keita's legs were growing heavy. His thighs ached so intensely that he looked down, wondering if something was wrong with them. They hurt like the blazes, and the last three miles would be about who could tolerate the pain more.

At the eight-mile mark, the time was 36:48. Keita looked over his shoulder. The Kenyan was holding on to the pace, just thirty yards back. One could make up thirty yards quite easily in the last two miles of a road race like this.

In his pain, Keita thought again of his nightmare: being brought sweets and drinks while his father was tortured in the Pink Palace in Yagwa. He thought of what the authorities had done to his father and of hauling the naked corpse home. He thought of his sister now, and he decided that he would rather die of a heart attack than not spend every ounce of energy winning this race for her.

It was now too risky to run alongside Deeds. The Kenyan might overtake them both, and Keita did not have a strong finishing kick. Keita glanced over and saw that Deeds' head was tilting to the side. He was hurting! Keita picked up his pace again and ran as hard as he could for a quarter-mile. Finally, Deeds cracked. Keita tried with all he had to pull ahead of him. Thousands of spectators lined the side of the road, and he was faintly aware that they were shouting and pointing. He got to the nine-mile marker in 41:24. He was having trouble breathing and hearing, but Keita knew he needed more than a strong finish. He glanced back. The Kenyan was a few yards back and smiling, as if to say, *You're toast, and we both know it.* Keita knew this might be true, but he took comfort in noting that Deeds had been broken. He was more than a hundred yards back. The Kenyan caught Keita with a third of a mile to go. A fifth of a mile before the finish line, he took off in a sprint that Keita could not match. Keita didn't even try. He had second place in the bag. Second was all he needed. *Hang on, Charity. Just hang on a little longer.*

Keita crossed the finish line in 45:58, nearly knocked over a race official and kept going.

It was crowded up ahead. Two men waited by the metal gate designed to herd runners toward the recovery area. One wore a jacket with the word *Immigration* on it. Another held handcuffs.

"Keita Ali," one of them shouted. "You're under—"

Keita hurdled the barrier and kept running.

"Stop!" someone called from behind, so Keita ran faster. He had just one hope, and just one place to go, so he darted among pedestrians and raced toward the Freedom Gates. A siren wailed behind him. Keita glanced back. Two officials were chasing him on foot, and a police car was after him too. The officials wouldn't be able to keep it up for more than a hundred metres, so it was the car he had to worry about. He couldn't let them catch him.

He knew the way; John had given him directions. Keita pulled out of sight into a grassy field and then onto a street facing traffic. He ran out Freedom Gates and into the traffic circle, darting away from cars. The siren kept blaring, a reminder of everything that he had fled in Zantoroland and in Freedom State. He ran along the boardwalk by Ten-Mile Inlet on his left, passed three government buildings on his right, and then darted through a fourth office building, from front to back, emerging and doubling around on side streets until he was able to enter the Freedom Building without any police officers or cruisers in sight.

He knew the office he was looking for was one floor up. He took the stairs in threes. There, at the end of the hallway, was a door marked *The Honourable Rocco Calder, Federal Minister of Immigration.* He opened it and tore through the outer office, past a black woman sitting at a desk and into the room behind.

The minister stood up from his desk, and the black woman came in behind Keita.

"Excuse me," she said. "It's about Viola Hill. And it concerns this gentleman, too."

"Not now, June," the minister said.

"It's an emergency," June said.

"Just take care of it," the minister said.

"I'll be a few doors down," she said. "In the lunch room. Going to make some calls on your behalf."

"OK, later," Calder said.

"Congratulations," June said to Keita, "and good luck." And then she was gone.

"Keita Ali," the minister said. "You sure got here fast."

Without a word, Keita shook his hand, slid off his tiny belt, pulled out the USB stick and reached to hand it over. Then he hesitated.

"Don't you have something for me?" Keita said.

The minister brought out a form and signed it. He gave it to Keita along with the pen. "Sign this. It gives you the temporary right to be in the country. The next step will be to get you permanent refugee status."

Keita signed and released the USB stick into the minister's hand. It was hard to believe that the process was so simple. In fact, Keita did not yet believe that he was safe.

"Fine run, by the way. I was watching it on TV. I saw you ran under forty-six minutes. That is smoking, for ten miles. Pity you lost."

"About coming in second, it doesn't matter—"

"No, it doesn't," said a voice behind Keita. "Turn that stick over to me. And that's an order."

Keita spun around. He was still gasping. His hamstrings were cramping. Standing there was a young man with pimples on his forehead and a tie that needed straightening.

"Who are you?" Keita asked.

"The only one who can get anything done here. Keita Ali, you're about to be deported."

"Geoffrey, get out of my office," Calder said.

"Make me," Geoffrey said.

"I'd be glad to," Calder said.

Keita considered running. But where? And how? He was out of breath. His legs felt like tree stumps: heavy, lifeless, useless. He looked toward the door again, but it was too late. A copper-toned black man with shades and a baseball cap had stepped into the doorway. He was pointing a purple pistol with a silencer.

"You," the man with the gun said to Keita, "get in the corner and sit down."

"There is no need to harm anyone," Keita said.

"Shut the fuck up, and do what I say."

Keita lurched to the corner. Glancing out the window, he could see the finish line less than a kilometre away, and runners who had already crossed the line were walking up the street, eating doughnuts and ice cream bars. It was just one floor down. Could he pull open the window and jump?

"Keita," the minister said. "Could you humour him? We will get through this. Here." He walked over to Keita and helped him to a chair.

The man with the gun took three steps into the office.

"Careful, Saunders," Geoffrey said. "Just be careful."

"Do you mind telling me what the hell is going on?" Calder said. And then, turning to Keita, he said, "Just stay seated, and I'll work this out."

"Put down that form, Rocco, and give me the flash drive."

"Come and get it."

"Saunders," Geoffrey said. "Exert some pressure, would you?"

"Minister, hand the stick over, and stand against the wall," Saunders said.

"I shall do no such thing."

Saunders raised the gun and pointed it at Calder.

Calder took a few steps away from Keita. "Geoffrey, what the hell is this about?"

"We need this man. We need that stick. Hand it over."

"Not on your life," Calder said.

"I'm afraid it's *your* life," Geoffrey said.

"I am the federal minister of immigration, and I have given this gentleman a residency permit. I am not relinquishing anything to you."

"Saunders," Geoffrey said again.

"Last warning, Minister," Saunders said. "Hand over the stick."

"You're bluffing," Calder said.

Saunders raised the revolver, aimed at the minister of immigration and fired. A lamp exploded, a window shattered and the minister fell back.

"You shot me, asshole!" Calder said. "My shoulder!"

"The stick," Saunders said.

"Fuck," Geoffrey said. "You have to finish him off now, Saunders. Both of them."

"Wait," Calder said. "At least tell me what the hell this is all about."

"We need this man, and the USB stick," Geoffrey said.

"Why?"

"The stick shows Bossman in a . . . situation."

"In AfricTown," Calder gasped. "With Yvette Peters."

"You're not quite as stupid as you look," said Geoffrey.

Calder clamped a hand over his bloody shoulder. "So why do you want the runner?"

"Apart from the fact that he has something I want? He left his country and is wanted back. You remember the platform we ran on, don't you?"

"But he just signed Form 179. He's no longer an Illegal."

"In about one minute, nobody will know about that form—or care."

"You're paying Zantorolander officials in exchange for information about Illegals, whom you then deport. Is that right?"

"Saunders, we are short on time. The minister, please, and then this runner. But first, Rocco old boy, give me that USB stick."

Geoffrey walked to Calder, who was now slumped against a wall. But before he reached him, Hamm burst into the room.

"Minister, I'm here to tell you—"

Hamm stopped in his tracks when he saw Saunders pointing a gun at him.

"You motherfucker," Hamm said, looking at Saunders. "You stiffed me for my money, and you fucking shot me, to boot."

"This is your lucky day, because I'm about to shoot you again," Saunders said.

Hamm charged. Saunders took aim. Hamm dived. Saunders re-aimed and shot. Hamm let out a grunt and tumbled through space, holding his left arm. Blood flew everywhere. Hamm slumped on the floor, breathing raggedly and staring at his injured limb.

Keita saw Hamm staring at him. Part of him wanted to help the man who had been hunting him down. Keita looked up at the window. He could jump through it. Or he could make a run for the door. No. Not the door. It was suddenly blocked by the tallest white man Keita had ever seen. Greying hair. Fit. In a fancy grey suit. A tanned complexion.

"Geoffrey," said the tall man, "you have buggered this up royally." He walked into the room. "Saunders, a bloody good thing you use a silencer. This is going to be one tricky matter. Sorry, Rocco, but you're going to take this one for the team. Saunders, do him first. And then this fine running specimen. And then finish off that idiot mule of ours. Wait. Do we have the evidence?"

"That's what I was to you?" Hamm said to the prime minister. "You were elected to lead a nation, but you use a mule?"

"Best way to move money, if the mule is witless, and mules always are," Wellington said. "Geoffrey, get that damn stick."

Geoffrey pulled the USB stick from Calder's hand.

"You'll never get away with this," Calder said.

"Sure we will," the PM said. "This illegal refugee burst into your office and started shooting like a madman. My man here seized his gun and shot the terrorist and saved some lives. Some, but not all."

"It will never work," Calder said.

The prime minister glared at Keita. "And you, you little prick. This will teach you to run off with things that don't concern you. I was going to come get you personally in AfricTown and watch while DiStefano gave you up. But this is better. You saved me a trip. Saunders, it's time."

Saunders walked calmly over to Calder. Keita could jump out the window the minute Saunders fired. But even if they didn't shoot him on his way out, they would catch him; he knew it. There was no place left to run in this country.

But Keita wasn't afraid. He had run second, and the money was on its way. With luck, his sister would be free soon. If he died now, so be it. Keita stared the politician right in his eyes. The prime minister turned away.

"Saunders," the PM said.

Saunders raised the gun. He aimed it at the minister's head. Keita saw movement at the door.

"Saunders, wait!" Keita shouted.

Saunders trained the gun on Keita, instead. "All right, then, you first."

With his good hand, Hamm grabbed a glass paperweight and hurled it, hitting Saunders in the stomach.

Saunders gasped. "Fuck." But he regained his balance, turned back to Hamm and shot him in the stomach.

Hamm groaned and lay bleeding from the belly and the mouth.

"This time, asshole," Saunders said, "you die."

Saunders took aim again at the minister, but before he could pull the trigger, another explosion rocked the room. Saunders fell to the ground, blood splattering on the wall behind him. Candace stood in the doorway. She lowered her gun.

"Mr. Prime Minister, you are under arrest. And so are you," she said, her gun now aimed at Geoffrey.

"Please, don't point that at me."

"What is that in your hand?"

"It's nothing."

"Toss it here," she said.

"I'd rather hang on to it."

"Things will get a lot rougher for you, and very soon, if you don't cooperate. Toss it here."

He tossed the USB stick, which she caught and pocketed.

"Stand back," Candace said. "Keita, grab that phone and call 911. Nobody else touch anything or anybody. Mr. Minister, squeeze your hand over your shoulder. Hang on. Help is coming. John! John, can you hear me?"

"Right here," said a voice from the closet.

"Open the closet door now, but don't come out. We have a crime scene here."

Keita picked up the phone and made the call.

"Minister Calder," John said.

"Did you get it all on video?" Calder asked.

"Yes," John said.

"You slimy two-timer," said the prime minister.

"Who's the slimy one?" Calder said.

June rushed into the room. "Mr. Minister! Message from Viola Hill, the reporter. She's detained in Zantoroland and might be killed. She's with Keita's sister. Amnesty International is also calling, and asking you to contact the Zantoroland authorities. Urgently!"

"Not a good time, June," Calder said.

"I already called on your behalf," June said. "I told them you insisted that they release both women and that you would arrange for their safe transport to Freedom State."

"You what?"

"I'll resign if you wish," June said. "But it had to be done. Call now to confirm."

"This is hardly the time to—"

"Yes, *now*," Keita shouted. "Minister! You can save their lives."

"Do it!" Candace said. "You're the minister of immigration, and this asshole"—she pointed at the prime minister—"is going down. Make the call!"

Calder reached with his good hand for the phone. "What's the number, June?"

She dialed for him.

"Keita," Candace asked. "Did you win?"

"Second."

"Second is mighty fine in my books."

"Today," said Keita, "second was good enough."

PART THREE

Freedom State, 2019

WITH HER MA FROM HARVARD AND HER legal status in Freedom State resolved, Charity Ali chose to leave Boston and to live in Clarkson, where she could be near her brother.

Keita was living with a staff sergeant of the Clarkson Police Department, which Charity found disconcerting. Where they came from, police were only on hand to do the dirty work for the president. But Charity had to give Candace her due: she was hard-working and loved Keita. Candace had already told Charity that she wanted to be the first woman and the first black person to make captain of the Clarkson Police Department.

Financed by Ivernia, who had finally seen the charges against her dropped and had freed herself from the clutches of the Office for Independent Living, Keita had opened a bakery in Clarkson and named it Pâtisserie Chez Yoyo. He already sold lemon tarts, poires belle Hélène and six kinds of madeleines, and he was dreaming about how to expand the business when the time came that his legs finally gave out. Keita was surely the only baker in the country who, because of his diabetes, generally avoided his own creations. He and Candace were both training with the Freedom State Olympic marathon team. Keita, who had received citizenship papers, was also helping as a volunteer with the Zantorolanders Refugee Association to advocate for a general amnesty for all undocumented refugees in the country. Charity was helping with the association, too, and looking for a job as a newspaper reporter in Freedom State.

The former prime minister and his lackey would be in prison for decades, convicted of inciting murder, bribery of foreign officials, forcible confinement, unlawful deportation and breach of public trust, among other charges. The list was endless. Rocco Calder, the former immigration minister, was now prime minister, appointed by his party to serve out the rest of the government's term. The Family Party, at this point, was sitting low in the polls.

Viola Hill had filed many news stories, been proclaimed best investigative news reporter of the year, and watched John Falconer's award-winning documentary and all his raw footage. She had written a letter of reference to support John's successful application to board at the school with all fees waived. Viola had joined a party of friends to welcome John's mother back home. Afterwards, she had gone out with Charity for a lunch that lasted for hours.

A year had gone by, but Viola wasn't finished with the story. She wasn't entirely satisfied. She still did not know exactly how Yvette Peters had come to be deported. Every time Viola thought of Yvette Peters, she ached to explain her death. So she dug like a dog in sand.

Viola finally located Darlene Wood, who was now living in Buttersby and studying to be a certified general accountant, and had changed her name to Wendy Smith. Darlene was nervous about saying a single word, but Viola promised to not quote her or identify her in any way. She just needed details. Darlene told Viola about the man she had slept with, as payment for taking Yvette to the airport. Viola pressed for more. What did he look like? And could Darlene describe exactly what had happened the night she saw him come and take Yvette away? After several interviews and endless reassurances, Viola got the answers she needed.

Next, Viola found the man Darlene had described as having a

scar like a pickle running down his right cheek. He was retired, didn't seem afraid, said he hadn't broken any laws and was happy to accept Viola's offer of dinner and booze at the best steak house in town.

Men. A fuck. A steak. They could hardly tell the difference. He didn't mind talking. No, he had not received a direct order from the prime minister to take Yvette away. It had come second-hand: Lula said the PM had ordered him to come for a D-3 pickup. What was a D-3? Viola asked him. He explained: D-1 meant the Immigration and Refugee Board had declined an application and ordered the deportation. D-2 meant it had come from the Office of the Minister of Immigration. And D-3, the only route that required no paperwork, was a direct order from the Prime Minister's Office.

It took two more months and required some pull from the new prime minister, but Viola finally found the second man, who had accompanied Yvette on the plane heading to Zantoroland. Yes, he had been told by phone on the night that Yvette was deported that it was a rush order from the PM's office, on the D-3 form. And who had told him so? By then, Viola knew the answer.

Viola asked if Yvette had said anything to the man while they travelled together. Yeah, he told her; she'd said, *Tell my mother I never did anything wrong and that I always intended to see her again when I got straightened out.* Viola asked if he had passed along the message. No, he replied, what the hell was he supposed to do with that?

Viola asked how he felt about having escorted a seventeen-year-old girl to her death. He didn't think about it, the man said, jumping up and knocking beer bottles off the table, because it wasn't his responsibility, see, because he was just fucking well doing his fucking job. That pretty well ended the interview.

JUNE 15, 2019, WAS THE DATE OF THE FREEDOM STATE National Marathon Championships. The top three male and female finishers would be selected to represent the country at the 2020 Olympic Games. They would also have their training sponsored by the Freedom State Athletics Association. Thanks to a funding drive spearheaded by Mitch Hitchcock, they would receive living expenses of five thousand dollars a month, plus a housing subsidy. It was not as much as athletes in some countries made, but enough to encourage better results from the country's best marathoners.

Keita was expected to qualify, and Candace had an outside chance of nabbing the third spot in the women's marathon. They had a bet going. If Keita finished more than thirty-two minutes ahead of Candace, she would have to make him breakfast in bed for three days in a row. And vice versa, if Candace finished less than thirty-two minutes behind.

"You are going to owe me so bad," Candace said the day before the race. "And I'd like madeleines, please. Freshly baked. And then, after satisfying my every wish, you're going to do the dishes and put them away. Properly."

Keita gave out a long laugh. Candace leaned in and kissed him deeply.

CHAPTER FORTY-TWO

L ULA DISTEFANO WOULD BE VIOLA'S LAST INTERVIEW. Viola had spent three days in the National Citizenship Registration Office making absolutely sure there was no mistake. There was no record of DiStefano being born in Freedom State. And there was no record of her having obtained citizenship in the country either. Viola had hired a genealogist to review her history. If Lula had a birth certificate from Freedom State, the genealogist would have found it.

"So she came from Zantoroland when she was young," Viola said. "And she stayed, illegally."

"You're playing with fire," the genealogist said.

"I'm a journalist, and this is what we do," Viola said.

Lula was pushing sixty, but she looked fabulous. Trim and fit. Firm arms and calves. Slim face. Regal bearing. Purple sash over a red dress, wild red lipstick, hot red pumps. The woman looked like she owned the world. This did not surprise Viola, who had read in *Forbes* magazine that Lula was worth twenty million dollars.

Lula received Viola in a private lounge usually reserved for Bombay Booty customers. It was 10:30 a.m., so they had the place to themselves, apart from Lula's minions. The woman had people checking up on her every minute. Viola glanced at the TV screen. She let out a shout when she saw Keita in the pack of five runners leading the marathon. The camera switched to the leading female runners. There were two out front. A third about fifteen metres back. And a fourth, right behind her. The fourth-place runner was Candace. The lead runners were twenty-eight kilometres into the race.

"That man and his girlfriend are quite the celebrity couple," Lula said. "How come they don't visit me anymore?"

Viola let the question hang in the air. They both knew—and Viola had already written—that Lula had planned to turn Keita over to the prime minister after the Clarkson Ten-Miler.

An assistant brought in tea and shortbread cookies. Tea with the queen. Lula dismissed her assistant.

"His girlfriend grew up here," Lula said, "and she did okay for herself. Big promotion after that shooting incident last year."

"Yes," Viola said, "she's the real thing." She let a moment go by, took in a breath and spoke again. "I want to ask you something."

"Off the record?"

"Not this time," Viola said. "This time whatever you say is on the goddamn record. Just like everyone else."

Lula leapt up from the table, knocking over the tea and cookies. In a flash she had her hands around Viola's neck.

"Listen, you bitch. I could bury you right now, and your bones would never be found. No one in the world would know where you were."

Viola stared into the older woman's eyes, clawing and scratching. It wasn't getting her anywhere, so she cocked her arm and slugged Lula in the eye. Lula finally let go. Viola gasped and slumped back into her chair. Lula fell back too and had trouble catching her breath.

"First time I've been punched in forty-five years," Lula said.

"I'm pleased to have the honour," Viola said.

Lula exhaled at great length. She looked worn out. Her eyes roamed over to the TV screen. She turned up the volume. The runners had passed the thirty-kilometre mark. Keita was on the leader's shoulder. They were on pace to break the national marathon record of 2:09. In the women's race, Candace had moved up to third.

"About Yvette Peters," Viola said.

"I knew you were coming for that."

"I know the prime minister didn't send her away. I know you did it. I was glad to see the PM sent to prison. I feel no pity for him. But I can't figure out how you framed him. And didn't you know Yvette would be killed in Zantoroland?"

Lula sighed, stood and walked to the window. Viola wheeled over and joined her. Outside were dozens of shipping containers, each painted a vibrant colour, each with its own water tap.

"I did that."

"What?"

"Two hundred new taps last year alone. At times, I feared we would have a cholera outbreak in AfricTown. But no longer. In addition to the taps, we have a thousand new portable toilets, with state funding to have them cleaned weekly. I also pay for a hot lunch program. People eat lunch there, for free. Three times a week. And I hire dancers, sex workers, cooks, plumbers, electricians—where else do you see black folks working in Freedom State? I deserve the fucking Nobel Peace Prize."

"You're a powerful queen, Lula," Viola said. "But why'd you put it on the PM?"

"I was wondering when someone would get to that. You are the first person to ask. I'll say this for Graeme. He took his lumps with dignity. He didn't try to smear me."

In the articles that followed the shooting, Viola had already written that the PM and Lula were rumoured to have been lovers decades earlier. But Viola did not raise this matter now.

"I never thought it would escalate the way it did," Lula said. "The shooting and all that. Who could have known? But framing Graeme was the only way to get him to back off the raids and give me what I wanted. What the people of AfricTown needed. If he had to deal with the fallout over the deportation of a teenage prostitute, then he would have to negotiate. He had been threatening to shut me down. Can you believe it? He and his Family Party cronies were actually talking about bulldozing AfricTown. He was saying the voters demanded it and that he meant business. I invited him over so that we could try to resolve the problem amicably. I set him up with Yvette because she was our best-looking girl. I happen to know the kind of lady he likes."

Viola hoped the recording device hidden in her jacket was working. "Don't tell her I gave this to you," John had said to her as he hooked it up. He'd wanted to come with her, but he was busy with full-time classes—and boarding at the school, too.

"Framing him was easy," Lula said. "I heard about the authorization levels when the PM began deporting people aggressively. I heard that he was paying off folks in Zantoroland. Honey, I come from Zantoroland."

"And you're still undocumented, if my research is correct."

"I'm not going to dignify that comment with a response," Lula said.

"All right," Viola said, "about the deportations."

"I knew the score. I found out who the PM was using. One man would take deportees to the airport and another would take them on the planes and escort them home. All I had to do was find the men, offer them pleasures on the house and find out how they worked. For the new deportation deal, the PM just issued verbal orders. So once I knew the men and had catered to their needs, I just called them up and told them what the PM had said to do."

Viola put down her notebook. She had what she needed.

"Go ahead," Lula said. "Tell the world. But just make sure you put in about the water taps, the lunch program and the sewers. Make sure you tell the whole story."

THREE WEEKS LATER, VIOLA PUBLISHED AN ARTICLE AS A special report on the front page of the *Clarkson Evening Telegram*. The headline read, "AfricTown Queen Admits to Deporting Prostitute." And under that: "Never admitted as citizen, holding fraudulent passport, Lula DiStefano sent teen to death in Zantoroland." The article was tight and nuanced, and the whole world wanted more from journalist Viola Hill.

The Clarkson Police Department sent five cars to AfricTown to arrest Lula. But she had disappeared—and was never found.

David Steen, my first track coach, was a two-time Commonwealth Games gold medallist in the shot put, and a *Toronto Star* reporter. The first person I met who made his living as a writer, David has been a friend for more than forty years. Any commonalities between David and the fictional character Anton Hamm begin and end with two mundane points: physical size and the ability to hurl sixteen-pound balls astounding distances. David created the Victoria Park Track Club, which gave me a reason to exist, a passionate focus and sense of belonging throughout my teenage years. The other runners in that club ran faster than me. Far faster. One, the late Brian Maxwell, became one of the top marathoners in the world. Another, Paul Craig, ran in the Montreal Olympics and set the Canadian record for the 1,500 metres. Another, John Craig, worked for decades as a senior administrator at Athletics Ontario. As a teenager, another clubmate and friend, Donald Corbett, won numerous Ontario and Canadian steeplechase championships for his age class. They became friends decades ago, and remain friends, and I thought of the Victoria Park Track Club athletes—and the runs we shared and the dogs that chased us over the hilly back roads of southern Ontario—as I wrote *The Illegal*.

I have always found it comforting to write under the same roof as loved ones, so I thank the folks who read drafts and encouraged me throughout the five years I spent on this book. Among the children: Geneviève and Caroline commented on early drafts, Andrew Hill and Beatrice Freedman nudged me all along the whole way, and Evangeline Freedman commented on the last draft and permitted the use of her middle name for the creation of Viola Hill. There is much of Evangeline's spirit in Viola and vice versa, although the resemblance ends there. My sister, Karen, introduced me to the world of undocumented refugees when she invited me several times to stay with her in West Berlin in the 1980s, and she loved and encouraged me until her unexpected death in 2014. Dan—also a runner and a writer—has shared insights about everything I've written, and he came through again this time—thanks, brother. Hats off as well to my mother, Donna Hill, for inspiring—and then accepting—the creation of the character Ivernia Beech in this novel. My mother also gave me her L.C. Smith typewriter when I was seventeen. I lugged that beast around the country when I first plunged into daily writing. The L.C. Smith doesn't get much use these days, but I've been threatening to dust it off for the next novel. My wife, Miranda, has stood beside me and cheered along every page of the journey, always knowing—as only a spouse and writer can know—how essential the creative process is to a novelist's well-being. No page of mine moves into the world without the benefit of Miranda's sharp eye. Were she not busy writing her own books, she could be a phenomenal editor.

A few times a year, I escape to writing retreats—always by the generosity of people who are kind to artists. Stella Trainor and Gayle Waters let me borrow their homes, asking only that I get on with it and finish the damn book. The Writers' Trust of Canada offered the Berton House in Dawson City; the Banff Centre provided a Leighton Studio; Max Blouw, Carol Duncan and their colleagues at Wilfrid Laurier University provided the Lucinda House; Louise Cooper, Karen Smereka and Rena Upitis welcomed me to the Wintergreen Studios. The owners and staff of the Black Dog Village Pub and Bistro and the Little Inn, both in Bayfield, Ontario, offered meals and encouragement. Thanks to my friends Stephen Brunt,

Jeanie MacFarlane, Diane Martin and Dave Stromberg for cajoling Miranda and me to buy a house in Woody Point, Newfoundland—a fabulous hideout where I finished this novel.

For friendship, sympathetic ears, sharp eyes, critical readings and assistance on all fronts imaginable, thanks to Philip Adams, Kathy and Barney Bentall, Marie Carrière, Daniel Coleman, Jennifer Conkie, John Craig, Diana Davidson, Ron Davis, Elya Durisin, Cole Gately, Hope Kamin, David Kent, Joanne McKay, Desiré Mention, David Morton, Damon D'Oliveira, Michael Peterman, Marie-Madeleine Raoult, Jana Rieger, Margaret Rosling, Alicia Snell, Agnès Van't Bosch, Marilyn Verghis, Jack Veugelers, Clement Virgo and Ing Wong-Ward.

I also thank Lauren Repei for reading drafts and helping in countless ways as my assistant, and Chelsey Catterall for being a reading consultant.

After I invented the countries of Freedom State and Zantoroland, as well as the Ortiz Sea that envelops them, cartographer and friend Graham Dudley helped me figure out where to locate them in the Indian Ocean. The cartographer Dawn Huck rendered them in final form for the book.

Thanks to the physicians who read drafts or answered questions about amputation, diabetes and other medical issues: Elaine Desnoyers, Nancy Dudek, Hertzel Gerstein, David Price and Raj Waghmare.

Anton Chekov is credited with saying that if you introduce a pistol in drama, it has to go off. So I thank Fred Braley for explaining just exactly what sort of pistol to place in the hands of Saunders, who is up to no good in this novel.

Friends also advised me about matters pertaining to refugees: Sarah Hipworth, Audrey Macklin, Alyssa Manning, Noa Mendelsohn Aviv and Sukanya Pillay.

Jennifer Larson, formerly of the Canadian Paralympic Committee, led me to two athletes who shared details about life and competition in wheelchairs: Josh Cassidy and Theo Geeve. I thank them both for taking the time to meet with me.

Two friends drew upon their extensive experiences as runners to share suggestions about the world of marathoning: Reid Coolsaet and John Craig.

Thanks to the Ontario Arts Council and the Canada Council for the Arts for grants that helped me while writing this novel, and for all the ways that they support writers and publishers in this country.

Thanks to my editor, Amy Cherry, at W.W. Norton & Co, and to my agent, Ellen Levine, at Trident Media Group, both of whom waited for years for this novel—politely, encouragingly, but tapping the desk just enough so that I would never give up.

Thanks to freelance editors Allyson Latta, Helen Reeves and Sarah Wight and HarperCollins Canada editor Lorissa Sengara for their many suggestions, and to the people at HarperCollins who have been unfailingly helpful: Cory Beatty, Norma Cody, Rob Firing, Michael Guy-Haddock, Alan Jones, Jennifer Lambert, Sandra Leef, Leo MacDonald, Lauren Morocco, Colleen Simpson, Terry Toews, Kathryn Wardropper, Brad Wilson, Noelle Zitzer and all of their colleagues. A very special thanks to my friend and editor, Iris Tupholme, publisher and editor-in-chief at HarperCollins Canada, who has stood by me over many years and through several books not merely to offer praise, but to push me through draft after draft until she believed that I had done my best work. A good editor is like a running coach: always expecting more, and making you believe that you can do it. Iris is one of the greats.